INVERTED TRIANGLES

Published 2022
by Broom Bridge Books

Paperback ISBN 978-1-7397127-0-9
Ebook ISBN 978-1-7397127-1-6

Cover design by Paula Quigley

INVERTED TRIANGLES

KAREN FAGAN

BROOM
BRIDGE BOOKS

For Tracey Lyons

PART 1

October – December 2006

1

The panic attack started in the shower. Jo was combing conditioner through her hair when the dread crept up and dealt a buckling punch to her gut. She crashed out of the bathroom and collapsed on the landing. She lay there, naked, shaking, fighting a body hellbent on extinguishing itself. Her lungs had the capacity of squeezed teabags, her limbs were being incinerated from within, her heart seemed intent on cracking open her sternum.

The wallpaper had never looked so monstrous – Louise always joked that their landlord would have incurred the wrath of Wilde – but Jo forced herself to fixate on the garish print of a shocking pink *Lonicera*. She slowed her breathing to the point where she could speak, and then she began the mantra. Though it had been three months, the words returned easily.

'I am not going crazy. I am not dying. This will pass. This will pass.'

It did pass, eventually. She got up shakily and turned off the shower, not daring – despite her unrinsed hair and her sweat-sticky skin – to get back in. In any case, there was no time. She was already running late for the staff meeting, whose vague agenda had everybody worried.

Brushing her teeth, she tried not to look at the pasty face framed by split-ended brown hair. Nor at the criminally oblong torso. Yesterday, it had all seemed so different. As she'd filled the bin bags, she'd caught mirror-glimpses of a slim, interesting, twenty-eight-year-old. A girl with a cute smile and intelligent blue eyes. Someone who, after a long-overdue haircut, would be ready to take on the world again.

Today, moving on didn't seem so simple. It was ironic – clearing out Louise's stuff was supposed to liberate her, not precipitate a panic attack. Jo suddenly felt like she'd travelled back three months, into the immediate aftermath of the break-up. She could only hope that this morning had been the last hurrah, a final shudder, as both body and mind came to the realisation that yes, it really *was* over with Louise.

In the hall downstairs, she dodged around the two bulging black sacks. Their date with the bin-men wasn't until tomorrow, but there was no going back because Louise's things had already been destroyed. Through one of the bags, Jo saw the ringed outline of the dreamcatcher Louise had bought at a reservation during the Arizonan leg of their 'holiday of a lifetime'. Louise's intelligence had certainly never stymied her love of selected spiritual bunkum. Jo wondered if the dreamcatcher's supposed nightmare-preventing powers had been blunted by its overnight marination in lashings of her ex's beloved sweet chilli sauce. For the other black bag Jo had churned up a gooey concoction of blonde colour-protect shampoo, tinted moisturiser and GHD straightening serum, and had dispensed it from a height into novels, photo albums, and the cups of the Wonderbra Louise had been wearing the second time they'd ever had sex.

The thought of this sticky and ignominious end to her ex's possessions heartened Jo; by the time she got off the bus in town, all residual jitters from the panic attack had dissipated. Hurrying along Pearse Street, she even dared to feel hopeful about today's meeting. Her colleagues were worried, but bad news seemed highly unlikely, given the paper's success. Dubliners were already so attached to their city's first-ever morning freesheet that you only had to glance around to see the cyan-coloured splash of the masthead somewhere in view. The builder walking ahead of Jo had *Dublin AM* rolled up in the back pocket of his dusty jeans. A middle-aged businessman splayed the paper across his steering wheel as he waited in a traffic jam. The woman standing beside her at the pedestrian lights was perusing Jo's latest *SciFacts* from the canopy of her baby's buggy. It was no wonder the paper's kerbside merchandisers could barely keep up with the number of outstretched hands each morning.

No, Jo concluded, it *couldn't* be bad news at today's meeting. She put her head down and hurried on towards the office.

The train was approaching, so Rachel folded up her copy of *commUte* and gently angled her handbag over the huge bruise on her ribs. A moment later, she was caught up in the melee as the crowd pressed itself aggressively into the already crammed carriage.

It was three weeks since she had started as a marketing assistant in Trenpharm, and while the job was proving to be brilliant, she'd begun to accept that her commute would be a stuffy, uncomfortable affair. Her original plan hadn't even involved the train. She'd been ready to sign the lease on a minuscule studio apartment within walking distance of the office when she happened upon Alysha's classified on UKjudo.com. From there, everything had elegantly fallen into place: the second bedroom in the flat Alysha was renting in Wheldon Green had just been vacated by Alysha's best friend Nicole, who was off to go nannying in Luxembourg.

And so, in Alysha, Rachel had found both a flatmate and a friend of her own age, because with Nicole's departure, Alysha was in the market for new mates herself. Living in N11 was convenient for both work and play: Wheldon Green was the fourth-last stop on the Piccadilly Line into central London, and there was also West Wheldon overground station, where Rachel caught the train up to Hertfordshire each weekday. The best thing about the new arrangement, however, had been getting a personal introduction to Wheldon Judo, whose home was a creaking but cosy Victorian hall on the high street. Alysha was the only Black member of the club, where she was respectfully known as The Alygator – a fitting nickname, Rachel had come to agree, for someone who could so savagely roll her opponents into submission on the *tatami*.

While nowhere near as talented as Alysha, Rachel had started judo at the age of seven and was now a second-dan black belt. It was at moments like these, as the air in the carriage grew staler, that she was glad of the stamina the martial art had conferred. A woman standing nearby was coughing, and terrified of falling ill when she had so much going on, Rachel turned away.

Of course, getting to work was a more dignified affair for those higher up in Trenpharm, like the quick and brilliant Lydia Bigham, who was thirty-five and was Rachel's new boss. One rainy evening, Lydia had given Rachel a lift to the station in her company Saab; it had a walnut dashboard and cream leather seats that hugged your body. Lydia had even switched on the sat-nav to let Rachel witness the sexy baritone of the man she called 'The Suave Commander'. They had laughed as he'd ordered them to 'turn left' and 'keep straight'.

But the best thing about that day had been Lydia telling Rachel that she should start learning to drive, because in the not-too-distant future she might well be driving a company car of her own. Rachel's heart had soared at this early vote of confidence, and she'd spent the trip grinning at the little open-mouthed faces in the knotty pattern of the dashboard. She wasn't completely surprised by Lydia's hint of future success, however, because she already knew she'd been doing well. HR and IT were delighted with her induction performances, and Lydia had called Rachel a 'ruddy great godsend' when she'd sorted out a messed-up database of doctors. Lydia's PA Narelle, who had lately been on annual leave, had misaligned the postcodes. This would have been a disaster had it not been caught before the pre-launch teaser mailers went out.

Rachel was pleased to be embodying the personal qualities she'd touted during her interviews for the role. The process had been exhausting. An extensive psychometric test plus evaluation by two separate interview panels had meant spending a fortune on train tickets up and down from her home in Newcastle. Both panels had requested she expand on a specific line in her CV, namely her 'aptitude for overcoming challenges'. There were dozens of personal-life examples she could have cited. The challenge, at the age of six, of coping after her manic-depressive mother moved to Thailand with her fancy-man without so much as a postcard since. The challenge of being an only child, which had been lonely despite her dad's efforts to be a pal as well as a parent. The challenge of getting a first in her marketing finals while that same dad wasted away from metastatic lung cancer. There was even the challenge of judo, where her tallish, slim build handicapped her with a higher centre of gravity. She had eschewed such examples, however, in favour of expounding tricky client projects she handled at Gosforth Marketing, the small Newcastle consultancy where she'd worked since finishing uni.

To celebrate the end of her morning travel-torture, she went into the café outside the station. Perfectly good coffee was available at the refreshment hubs in the office, but since starting at Trenpharm, she'd developed a taste for the hand-poured lattes at this branch of The Dock. After a lifetime of frugality, she took pleasure in handing over the two pounds thirty each day; it was a reminder of her newfound ability to indulge in whatever little things she liked.

On the shuttle bus to the business park she remembered that today she'd be meeting the notorious Narelle, who was returning after visiting family in Australia. Rachel would be happy to hand back the various admin jobs and focus on her real role – assisting Lydia in the launch and marketing of Follestra, a new oral prescription for male pattern hair loss that had the edge over its competitor in both efficacy and side effects. Although Rachel was looking forward to this, she felt a territorial trepidation about Narelle's return. Until the newly formed dermatology department expanded its staff, it would only be herself and Narelle working together in the open-plan office. Lydia had said that Narelle was prone to distraction, which could be cured by 'trapping her under an avalanche of work'. She said Rachel must absolutely add to that avalanche – because Narelle was her resource too. Having her first-ever subordinate made Rachel feel empowered, but the idea of bossing around a twenty-six-year-old Australian also unnerved her. What if this Narelle took umbrage at being controlled by a newcomer, two years her junior? But then Rachel gave herself a shake. It didn't matter a jot what Narelle thought; if Lydia expected her to delegate, then delegate she would, and with bells on!

At the end of Vancouver Avenue, the Trenpharm building glinted gorgeously in the early October sun. Rachel walked under the maples, whose leaves were turning slowly gold, then ascended onto the concourse, where her reflection jigged in the purple-reeded pond. She only wished her dad could see her now, at large, at *ease* in such salubrious surroundings. It would take him a moment to recognise the smart-suited girl with the sleek brown hair. 'Sheesh, Rachey,' he'd say, pinching lorry grease from his eyes. 'You look like a right proper businesswoman, you do!'

The high, bright foyer of Trenpharm's UK headquarters always gave Rachel a rush. It could pass as a swanky hotel. Today, as she looked across the marble, she was jarred by a flashback of herself and Kim checking in to The Newcastle Crimson at the start of a weekend that would bankrupt them both, not just financially. She blinked away the vision as though it were an irritating speck of grit. She'd already decided not to dwell on that strange time of her life. The events of the past six months felt neither real nor relevant; it was as if an impostor, someone with whom she had nothing in common, had temporarily assumed the role of Rachel. Forgetting all that nonsense was sensible for a far more pressing reason too: with so much of an impression to make at both Trenpharm and Wheldon Judo, her focus had to be kept on the present, because it was the present that would secure her future. There could be no going back to Newcastle – she simply had to make a success of her new life.

She waited for the lift under a giant illuminated Trenpharm logo. (During her training, she'd learned that the damson-coloured Pantone signified Trenpharm's innovation in healthcare, while the anthracite denoted the clinical experience amassed since the company's foundation in Canada in 1971.) A female colleague scrambled into the lift as the doors were closing; when she saw they were headed to the same floor, she cried out to Rachel in an Australian accent, 'Oh my god, are you the new one?'

'That's me all right!' Rachel offered her hand to the birdlike girl with the still-damp black ponytail, whose wide grin was dominated by a twisted upper incisor. Despite the power of Narelle's smile and voice, her handshake was limp, a social flaw so easily remedied that Rachel never understood its prevalence in others.

'So how's the tyrannical taskmaster been treating you?' asked Narelle with an ominous laugh as they got out of the lift and went down the corridor.

'Who?'

8

'Lyd, you idiot!'

Rachel was cross at being called an idiot and even crosser at being invited to criticise her manager. 'Actually,' she said, 'I've been getting on really well with Lydia so far.'

'Just you wait,' said Narelle. 'Once your training's over, that ginge witch will have you run off your tits with this Follestria launch.'

'But the *Follestra* launch is why I'm here, surely?' Rachel couldn't help correcting Narelle's mispronunciation. With such inattention to detail, it was no wonder she'd messed up that mail merge. 'Anyway,' she continued, 'with the big day coming up, I suppose we'll *all* be incredibly busy.'

Narelle poked her right on the judo-bruise. 'Well, us two suckers will anyway. Meanwhile Lyd'll be sorting out her wedding next year. That's the only *big day* she cares about. Mind you, with a sparkler that size, the wedding would wanna be shit-hot.'

Rachel didn't dignify this rubbish with a response. The concept of delegation was clearly beyond Narelle's understanding. It beggared belief that Trenpharm would hire someone like her – the interview standards for PAs must be far less rigorous than for marketing assistants.

Narelle stopped at a refreshment hub to make herself a triple espresso. 'Bloody killer getting up this morning,' she said.

Rachel's annoyance was mounting, but it was imperative she hide any outward signs – it was a subordinate she needed, not an enemy. She was already coming to the realisation that she would have to win Narelle's support with careful sleight of hand, rather than mimicking Lydia's iron fist. Rachel cocked her head sympathetically. 'The furthest I've ever flown was Spain, but I've heard that jet lag is awful.'

Narelle laughed as she stirred in a fourth sachet of sugar. 'Jet lag's piss easy. Nah, me and the housemates had a wild one to celebrate me getting back.' As she stretched out in a yawn, Rachel noticed how her blouse had been carelessly ironed, the multiple arm-creases like railway points at a busy junction.

'Oh, I see,' said Rachel, who had done her full week's ironing at nine so she could be in bed by ten, despite Alysha's protests that they should watch *Lost* together. She forced a smile. 'Sounds like fun.'

The corridor ended in a large open-plan office with *Dermatology* sandblasted into the glass door.

'I'm back, suckers,' yelled Narelle. 'Now don't all run together!'

Rachel did find this funny. 'It's quite the ghost town, isn't it?'

'I was stoked when they finally hired someone to keep me company. The interviews went on forever.'

'Oh, did they see many people?'

'Heaps. Some reps from other brands went for it. Though why anyone would give up the freedom of the open road to sit under *her* beady eyes is beyond me.'

'Each to their own, I suppose,' said Rachel. She headed for her own desk, smiling to learn that the competition she'd beaten had included actual company insiders.

Her triumphant thoughts were interrupted by an angry shout. 'Whoa, don't tell me the bastards've put you all the way down there?'

'I'm afraid so,' called Rachel, wincing behind her partition. In fact, the nice man from facilities had given her free choice on the seven available work pods. She'd sat in each seat twice, before deciding she would be most productive at the far end of the room, away from Narelle. She always liked to take her time making important decisions, so the speed at which she'd taken this job so far from home, had surprised even herself.

She was reviewing her to-do list when Narelle appeared, clapping her hands over Rachel's desk like a workman surveying a job. 'Right, kiddo. You grab those Follestria folders and I'll take the rest. We'll show that bunch of dicks!' She reached over and began picking things up.

Rachel pushed back her chair. 'Sorry?'

'You're moving up beside me. Can't have you down here on your lonesome while I'm up there on mine.'

Rachel raised her hands in a gesture of powerlessness. 'Look, I'd love to, but my phone's set up on this point here.' She opened her drawer and took out her computer. 'And my laptop connector. I can't ask facilities to connect everything all over again.'

Narelle dropped the pen holder onto the desk. 'Didn't think they gave

10

laptops to us drones! Though you've probably copped you can't get onto things like Myspace or MSN because of that gay TreNetwork.'

Rachel gave a quick laugh to hide her discomfort on so many fronts. 'I've been too busy to even try.' She respected such restrictions, especially from a firm with two thousand employees worldwide; during the interviews she'd also taken the professional precaution of deleting her Myspace. Not that there was anything incriminating on it.

They were interrupted by the arrival of the company postman, who handed Rachel a small box and got her to sign his touchscreen.

'What's that?' asked Narelle. By now she was actually sitting on Rachel's desk, her scuffed pumps dangling precariously from the toes of her lint-balled tights.

'Must be my stapler,' said Rachel. 'I did the training module on stationery requisition so thought I'd try it out!'

'I'm surprised they don't make you do a module on how to wipe your arse with company bog roll. And that dumb medical too. I was shit scared of the drug test, but thank god I was too broke to buy blow that month!'

Rachel decided not to mention how the doctor at the company medical had proclaimed her 'the epitome of fitness and health', nor how satisfying it had been to truthfully tick NEVER on the questionnaire item about lifetime illicit drug use. All the times she'd nerdily excused herself from spliffs and pills at college parties had finally come back to thank her.

Narelle seemed perfectly content to continue chatting. She was now telling a story about how her boyfriend Stevo had switched his urine sample with a female colleague's. Rachel, however, was watching the clock on her laptop screen. She was concerned that Lydia, due to arrive any second after a breakfast meeting, might discover the PA dawdling at Rachel's desk, acting like a giddy peer rather than Rachel's subordinate, her resource. After all Lydia's praise thus far, it would be awful to get caught offside.

'So, next thing, poor Stevo gets told by the doc he's bloody up the duff! But you know what the worst part about it was—?'

Rachel took a breath and tried not to sound too bossy. 'Listen, Narelle, your story's hilarious, but I need to hand back the tasks I've been covering for you. You get settled in, and we'll all sit down when Lydia's back from her meeting, yeah?'

'You mean wedding dress fitting,' said Narelle, tipping Rachel's chair playfully with her toe.

Rachel didn't respond. She pushed back her chair so Narelle couldn't reach it. 'I also want to give you a couple of new jobs for the week,' she said. 'We need to compile a list so the hotel staff know how many sales reps and senior managers will be coming to the launch.'

Narelle curled the tip of her tongue around the snaggletooth. She seemed amused by this show of superiority. But Rachel braced her gaze, like she would her core muscles when about to throw a judo opponent, and held firm until Narelle's legs slowed their swinging, and eventually stopped.

With a sigh, the PA shifted herself off the desk and began to trudge back to her own pod. 'Holler when you wanna meet,' she called. 'And it'll have to be holler at this rate.'

Rachel exhaled and leaned back as far as her ergonomic chair would allow. Her opening managerial salvo had been daunting, but she had held her nerve. She began printing out today's paperwork. When she went to open her new stapler to fasten the sheets, she got a surprise – because she'd incorrectly guessed the contents of the box.

The thick paper of the cards was embossed in damson and anthracite, and beside the Trenpharm logo in a smart black font was printed: *Rachel Driffield, BSc, Marketing Assistant, Dermatology*. She quickly slit through the cellophane with her nail. Then, ensuring that Narelle couldn't see her, she handed the first of her business cards over, as though introducing herself to an important new contact, and as she did so, a smile spread wide across her face – she had officially arrived in her new life.

As Bart O'Neill entered the boardroom, Jo worried that her assumptions about the meeting had been wrong. The managing editor seemed both jumpy *and* shocked, his face as grey as his sideburns. As he walked silently to the top of the table, the speculative chatter faded away.

'Is ... is everybody here?' he asked, his cloth tongue at odds with his usual commanding boom.

Jo added her own voice to the nervously deferential 'Y ... es'.

Bart looked grimly at the dozen or so staff. He was about to speak when the door opened again.

It was CeeBee, aka Ciara Behan, the paper's social columnist. 'Apols,' she said, teetering on heels to a seat at the front. 'Didn't get home from the *El Magnate* launch until all hours.'

Bart stared at her with irritation. 'El mag-whatty?'

Ciara laughed. 'Oh, only the new nightclub owned by our bestest advertiser and sponsor.' She winked at the others. 'Thought I better cover it, even with this mysterious meeting on today!'

'And cover it you patently did,' said Bart, curling his nostrils, as though hit by a whiff of stale champagne. 'Right then. Since we last met there's been a major development in the Dublin free-newspaper arena.'

'I thought we *were* the Dublin free-newspaper arena,' said Declan Leahy who, as Decnophile, compiled the technology column, and whose fascinatingly small mobile phone sat proudly on the table.

'Not for much longer,' said Bart. 'You've heard of *commUte*?'

'I know it from London,' said Marie O'Toole, who wrote the restaurant reviews and, under the name Marie-Celestial, also made up the horoscopes. 'Their slogan is *commUte – the capital, for U.*' She traced the letter in the air. 'You can't move outside tube stations for someone jamming one into your hand.'

Bart listened to this with thinned lips before continuing: 'When we set up here, I suppose we emulated *commUte*'s business model more than we cared to admit. We wanted to be a successful freesheet in our own capital city, and it's gone spectacularly well so far. But life's about to get complicated. I've learned from a credible source that our overseas friend is planning on *commuting* over here to produce a Dublin edition.'

Amid the ensuing gasps, Bart shook off his inertia and began to pace around the table. 'Our unchallenged days are numbered, my friends. Pretty soon there'll be a big British snout in our little trough.'

'But it'll be ages before this new crowd's up and running,' said Eoin Keohane, the Corkman who single-handedly manned the sports desk. 'We'll have time to prepare.'

'I'd naively hoped the same,' said Bart. 'However, plans are already advanced. They're launching mid-November.'

'Jesus that's only six weeks away!' said Ciara, obviously already on party-season countdown.

Bart said, 'I'm well aware of that,' then looked dismally around the faces in the room. 'You'd think that with our collective finger on the carotid of the city, we'd have sussed this a lot sooner.'

'It's you two I feel for the most, actually,' said Marie, nodding at Ursula, the Advertising Sales Manager and her flashy young assistant, Gavin. Jo couldn't have cared less about the plight of that pair, however – they cultivated an impression of sweating it out under a commercial cosh, but in reality theirs was a charmed life of expense accounts, boozy steak dinners in Shanahan's, and hefty commission cheques from ads that sold themselves.

Ursula snorted. 'Appreciate the sympathy, Marie, but it's not all down to us. Without decent content from editorial, we won't get the same readership when we have a competitor. Fewer readers equals less ad and sponsorship revenue, which means we can't sustain staff levels.' She looked round as though deciding who'd be the first victim of a cull.

'Hang on a sec, Ursula!' Now everyone focused on Jo, whose heart had begun to thump as hard as it had that morning, only this time with anger. 'I trust by "decent content" you mean *continued* decent content? All of us writers do our best, you know. Sometimes I'm so busy composing news articles that I've to work on *SciFacts* at home in the evenings, which is fairly arduous as I'm sure you can – or rather you *can't* – imagine, given that the advertising department closes at about half three every day.'

Jo sat back, hardly daring to observe the aftermath of her outburst. Part of her speech was not strictly true, or at least not anymore. While she had been with Louise, compiling *SciFacts* had indeed been a chore, but now that her weekends and evenings were empty, her weekly digest of interesting science stories from around the world had become a welcome distraction from the *SadFacts* of her own life.

Ursula banged her platinum pen on the table. 'Please don't forget, Jo and Co, that we detestable lowlifes in ad sales pay *your* wages as well as our own.'

'Oh, we'd never forget that with you two constantly reminding us!' said Declan.

'And remember,' continued Ursula, 'it was me who secured the sponsorship for your column from Emerald Pharmacies, Jo.'

'And that it's me,' said Gavin, waving a finger at Declan, 'who gets Muldoon Electronics on board every month to cover your offering, Decno-*phile*.' He uttered the last syllable with disgust, as though talking about a far less savoury kind of -phile.

'So Muldoon's continued sponsorship has absolutely *nothing* to do with how professionally my column is written?' said Declan.

Gavin raised his hands in surrender. 'Look, there'll be sod-all myself and Ursula can do if Muldoons decide to switch their sponsorship to the tech section in this new *commUte*.' He gestured at Declan's mobile phone. 'You can wave goodbye to all your freebie gadgets then.'

'Children, please,' called Bart, clapping his cupped hands. 'There's no point infighting just when need to be more unified than ever. We've no choice but to start breaking our collective advertising *and* editorial arses to make sure we don't lose readership, don't lose advertising, and don't lose sponsorship. Let's meet later this week to discuss our action plan. And I want everyone to bring at least five suggestions!'

They had been paid the previous Friday, and so, with a tuna bap bought from a café frequented by thrifty Trinity students, Jo sat at her desk and logged into her online banking. Looking forward to seeing her account somewhat resuscitated by this month's salary, she was dismayed to find her wages already decimated by direct debits for the cable TV and the electricity. Louise had previously paid both, but with the full litany of bills now in Jo's name, she couldn't keep up. Of course, the real killer each month was servicing the rent single-handedly. It was due next week, and on top of that she must find a further two hundred to pay her monthly SSIA dues. She couldn't understand how people in her situation could afford to go out drowning their sorrows and rebounding – she barely had enough money to survive even as the teetotal hermit she'd lately become.

Aware of Jo's money worries, her elder sister and only sibling, Sarah, had suggested that Jo give up the expense of renting Blackstairs Terrace and move back with their empty-nester parents in Knocklyon. But it was Jo's name alone on the lease, and it didn't expire until January. Nor, after so many years of independence, could she imagine living under her parents' prying eyes. Of Jo's three exes, her mother had loved Louise the most: Louise's Foxrock pedigree, good job and girly grooming had inspired a simpering crush in Mrs Kavanagh, who now tempered her sympathy for Jo with frustration that her careless daughter had allowed the split to happen in the first place. Jo hadn't told her family the details, let alone revealed that Louise had made off with someone off the telly. No, to avoid deeper inquisition, and out of a bizarre respect for Tamara Nic an tSionnaigh's need to remain in the closet, Jo had let on that the relationship had simply fizzled out.

If Jo wouldn't move back with their parents, then Sarah had another not-so-helpful suggestion: taking in a lodger to split the rent. The house was small, but Louise's clothes were no longer clogging up the second bedroom. Yet the only person on earth Jo could imagine living with was her friend Cillian. They had rented together years before, and when Jo had finished journalism and finally got a job, she and Cillian had even discussed buying a place together. But then Louise had arrived into her life with an all-consuming bang, and within a year Jo had insidiously repositioned Cillian – who had never really taken to Louise nor understood Jo's attraction to her – from best friend and potential home co-owner into someone she barely bothered with at all. A while later, Jo had learned – with a mix of jealousy and alleviated guilt – that Cillian had cobbled together the deposit to buy a place in Grangegorman. He was therefore ruled out forever as a potential housemate for Blackstairs Terrace. Neither could Jo rent a room from him, because he'd bought a tiny one-bedroom cottage. Of course, there were plenty of other people in Dublin looking to rent, but the thought of taking in a stranger filled her with dread. She couldn't imagine sharing her house with a straight person and could all too easily imagine living with a gay one. Whatever kind of individual, they would surely pry after a while, want to know how she'd wound up alone. She could fill a hundred rooms with the mess inside her head; it seemed insane to sacrifice half of her small home!

Before she logged out of her online bank, she treated herself to a look at the smug but untouchable balance of her SSIA: six thousand euro so far – the product of almost five years of regular deposits plus of course 'the incentive' – interest at the insanely high rate of twenty-five per cent, paid by the Irish government in an attempt to tackle the dearth of savers earlier in the decade. There were stringent conditions, of course, and so the balance was appended by a footnote: *Your Special Savings Incentive Account will mature on 9th January 2007, whereupon the full amount can be withdrawn. You must continue monthly deposits until this time.*

Only last year, Jo and Louise had worked out that their combined SSIAs would just about cover the deposit for a modest home in the bloated Dublin property market. With all hopes foreclosed on that front, the matured SSIA would prove nothing more than a financial crash mat – something to pay bills and the debts Jo would amass by January. She had no need to buy clothes, nor anyone to accompany her on holidays or nights out. She didn't believe in karma but felt that by dashing their dreams of buying a home together, Louise had done to her exactly what Jo had previously done to Cillian. In the end, it was the other two who'd won out: Cillian actually *owned* his house and Louise was shacked up in the luxury of Tamara Nic an tSionnaigh's Ballsbridge condo. Jo was the loser in the middle.

She logged out, then wrapped the remainder of her bap in stringy cling-film. Until January, scraps like that would have to suffice for her tea.

Rob took the last roll from the basket and buttered it even more liberally than the two he'd already eaten. Taking his first bite, he noticed Michael was watching him from across the table. 'And what's so funny?' he asked through a mouthful of deliciously greasy dough.

Michael's smiled widened. 'Just sweet to see you this hungry.' He raised his eyebrows above his glasses.

Rob lowered his voice so the middle-aged straight couple at the next table didn't hear. 'It's from all the … *action* this morning,' he said with a wink. 'Followed by running around a billion shirt shops, of course.'

Michael squeezed Rob's knee beneath the tablecloth and leaned in to whisper: 'Ravenous in the bedroom this morning and now ravenous for dinner. Whatever shall we do with the young man!' They laughed and sat back happily, while Rob demolished the roll and Michael sipped on his beer.

In the comfortable silence, Rob reflected on what had been a wonderfully eventful weekend. And how nice it was now, on Sunday evening, to be in love, while relaxing in this candlelit bistro in Covent Garden, bringing it all to an equally enjoyable close.

Things had kicked off with relief and excitement at the clinic on Friday evening with the news that they'd both passed their follow-up HIV tests. In celebratory spirits on Saturday, Rob had taken the train to Reading for his inaugural visit to the home his boyfriend shared with his widowed mother Joan, who was away at a bridge tournament. Although Rob was dying to meet Mrs Wyles for the first time, they agreed it was just as well she was away because they couldn't wait to try out condom-free sex. Ironically, however, after waiting five months for the moment, they hadn't done it on Saturday night, involving themselves instead with Michael's box set of *Brideshead* (which Michael was 'revisiting' for the umpteenth time but which was brand new to Rob) until they were dozing in each other's arms, way too sleepy to even contemplate anything. It had been a different story

19

this morning. Refreshed and randy, they had unleashed hot, unprotected havoc in Michael's bedroom. Rob had noticed with delight, during less frantic moments of the action, that it was a true engineer's bedroom: every surface free of clutter, the furniture lining up exactly with the pattern on the geometric carpet.

As they waited for their dinner, Rob re-imagined the morning's events through the eyes of someone watching from the end of Michael's bed. He could see it quite clearly: the twenty-seven-year-old dark-haired lad, the *tiniest* bit unfit around the middle, but with a symmetrical jaw and eyelashes whose length and density drew unending female envy, panting in ecstasy as he was taken crazily by his fairer, taller, wirier – both of hair and body – older boyfriend, whose eyes, without his glasses, were sexily squinted.

'So, was I right then?' asked Michael, guessing from Rob's expression what he was thinking about.

'You certainly weren't lying when you described it as liberating.' Rob, unlike Michael, had never been 'fluid-bonded' – as the sexual-health nurse had cleverly called it – to any of his previous boyfriends. His only unprotected sexual experiences had been a couple of drunken slip-ups with strangers, each followed by a hand-wringing trip to the clinic. 'I actually can't wait to do it again.'

'So maybe you'll give me another whirl after the theatre on Wednesday?'

Rob crossed his arms with pretend prudishness. 'Absolutely not. One birthday present is quite enough. God knows it was hard enough to find that!'

Getting the gift had indeed been difficult. Over the past few weeks there had been much deliberation about what Rob might buy Michael for his thirty-seventh birthday; it was only in the inspiring afterglow that morning that they'd decided it should be a shirt. Rob was relieved that it had been settled at last. But what hadn't been settled was the *kind* of shirt, and he'd been taken aback when, upon arriving by tube in Piccadilly earlier, Michael had suggested they head straight for Jermyn Street. Rob, whose own finances were more aligned with the high street, certainly hadn't envisaged shopping in the kind of gentlemen's shirt-makers that might kit out Prince Charles. He prayed that Michael wasn't angling for a bespoke garment, which despite costing a fortune wouldn't even be ready in time for the birthday on Wednesday. The problem was that Michael often seemed to forget that his salary as a senior structural engineer was substantially higher than what Rob got as an account manager. (It didn't help that during their online courtship Rob had inflated his own salary by five grand and painted HarropAds as a 'très-cool' place to work.) But that afternoon, as they'd walked through shirt-land, Michael had squeezed Rob's hand as a silent reminder of what they'd been doing that morning; buoyed up on love, Rob had realised that there were moments in your life when money didn't matter – within an instant his moth-eaten wallet had swollen to the size of his heart.

Luckily, the widened wallet didn't seem necessary at first because Michael was happy to check out ready-to-wear styles in more accessible Jermyn Street stores. But it was difficult to find something that both fit Michael's long arms and didn't wash out his delicate complexion. There was nothing quite right in Lewins or Tyrwhitt's. Or Hawes & Curtis. Nor three others. Starting to feel disheartened, they suddenly spotted a beautiful teal and taupe check in Thomas Pink, only to be told by the camp Asian assistant that they didn't have it in Michael's size. On the way out, Michael had apologised for being 'so wan and lanky'. This made Rob's heart swell all over again, and he'd led them to Turnbull & Asser, ready to spend a week's wages if necessary. But even James Bond's outfitter had nothing suitable. With ties out of the question – none of the engineers wore them at Stedman Sheppard Structural – and the clocks racing towards closing time, Rob racked his brain for inspiration. He spied an elegant wooden shaving set in the window of a gentlemen's groomers and was bolting in to buy it, when he remembered that Michael's face flared up if he used anything except Wilkinson Sword Sensitive. No, it seemed Rob would be arriving empty-handed on the first birthday they'd ever be spending together. It was a huge disappointment.

The restaurant was filling up, and for the third time since they'd come in, Rob felt under his seat for the matte-laminated bag with its silky rope handle.

Michael chuckled. 'You better guard that thing with your life until Wednesday.'

'With *more* than my life. Talk about serendipity.' They'd been passing by

Thomas Pink again on their empty-handed meander back up the street when the Asian assistant, who was adjusting a mannequin's cravat, had rapped frantically on the glass.

'He fancied the pants off you,' said Rob. 'That's why he rummaged round the stockroom after we left. He was determined to please the tall, sexy man.'

'Stop before you give me a big head!' Michael gestured to two steaming dishes in the hatch. 'Anyway, in other good news, our food is imminent.'

'How do you know they're ours?'

'Well, the couple beside us ordered slightly ahead of us, and they got their food literally ninety seconds ago. The guy in the corner was before them, and he got his *four* minutes ago. Ergo, my dear, we are next.'

'You're such an engineer,' said Rob. 'I love it!'

Their waiter was blond and foreign. 'Now then, gents. The steak?'

Rob nodded.

'The steak for *yourself*, sir. And the spaghetti?'

'Hmm.' Michael looked back and forth across the table as though doing a tough trigonometric equation. 'I guess that must be for … oh look, it's for me!'

Rob sniggered, but the waiter didn't seem to notice the joke. 'So, the pasta for *yourself*, sir,' he said. 'Now, can I bring some black pepper for yourselves?'

Michael smirked. 'No, I think that *myself* and *himself* are fine for pepper, thank you.' He waggled his empty glass. 'But could we get two more of these quality lager beers from *your good self*, please?'

'Ooh, you're terribly mean,' said Rob with a laugh as the boy went off. He'd been slightly taken aback at Michael's blanket refusal of the pepper, however, because he quite fancied some tonight. But when he did a recap of all the restaurants they'd visited together, he realised that Michael was actually being thoughtful rather than thoughtless, because Rob had always declined pepper before. (Michael's mind was so quick that it was only afterwards you realised how a seemingly offhand comment was actually the result of a longitudinal observation.)

'Your pasta looks good,' he said, watching Michael suck a piece of spaghetti through pursed lips. Since their first meeting Rob had been entranced by that sexy mouth; the cupid's bow cut so deep that it practically bisected Michael's top lip. Together with his dark sandy hair, it gave him a regal, lion-like appearance. 'I hate it when they don't cook pasta right,' Rob continued. 'Once in an Italian restaurant I had to complain about raw penne. I had quite a row with the waiter. He kept shaking his head, saying *is al dente*. Until I shoved a hard piece of pasta in his face and said, *no, not al dente … it's al cemente!*'

Michael laughed so hard that a strand of spaghetti slapped sauce onto his chin. 'Genius!'

Rob shrugged bashfully and took a quick swig of beer to mask his guilt over borrowing the story from his work colleague, Vicky – she'd spontaneously come up with the quip during lunch in Luigi's the other day when the usual chef had been out sick. Vicky had a wicked ability with words and a never-ending bank of hilarious anecdotes. Michael adored a comical story. He lived for trips to the theatre, especially plays by his hero Wilde (he'd described himself on MaleDate.com as an 'Engineer who's Wilde about theatre'). Rob only wished he had more funny tales of his own to relay. But for now, he accepted the praise, making a mental note that if he ever introduced Michael to Vicky, it had better not be in an Italian restaurant.

Michael was still chuckling to himself when a green light began to pulsate in his chest pocket. Rob looked away, suddenly fascinated by the middle-aged couple, now sipping on Baileys. When he eventually looked back, he was relieved to find that the critical moment had passed without detection. But thirty seconds later, the flashing started up again, and he worried Michael would find it disingenuous that he didn't alert him.

'Your mobile's ringing,' he said, pointing with his knife.

Michael clattered down his cutlery and pulled out the phone. 'Christ, it's Mum.' He looked around as though holding a screaming baby rather than a silently flashing gadget. 'Maybe she can't get back into the house or something. I better take this outside.'

'Stay,' said Rob. 'She won't even know I'm here.' But Michael was already gone, leaving Rob to retrieve his napkin, which lay on the floor like a flag of surrender to Mrs Wyles's latest demands. By the time Rob sat back up, his face, along with his mood, had drained. He could see Michael talking outside; his movements seemed overly pronounced without an accompanying soundtrack. Despite being tall, Michael usually walked with what Rob had fondly named his *engineer's tiptoe* – every footstep a little precision measurement – but right now Michael's gait, as he wandered distractedly up and down, was as random and relaxed as his hand gestures. It certainly didn't appear that Joan was caught up in any kind of crisis either – no, it looked like they were having a grand old chat about all kinds of things, which was ridiculous when she'd have Michael all to herself in a couple of hours' time.

Rob speared a slice of steak and ploughed an infinity symbol in the jus. Joan was ringing more frequently than ever, and her timing was getting worse, too. And Michael never let a call go unanswered, no matter how inappropriate the moment. It was ironic that, despite Michael being nine years older than Rob, he was more under his mother's thumb than a little boy. Joan had even rung on Friday evening, just as they'd arrived at the clinic. Despite the sensitivity of the occasion, Michael had insisted on darting outside to take it, leaving Rob to explain the delay to the nurse. It had been a miracle that Joan hadn't called while they were at it that morning, though Rob did notice Michael glancing over at his phone a couple of times during the heat of the moment.

Eventually, the call appeared to be winding up. But not before Michael gave a guffaw so loud Rob could hear it through the window, over the noise of the restaurant.

Back inside, Michael sat down and popped a congealed mushroom into his mouth, chewing as though it were the most succulent thing he'd ever eaten. He looked round just as heartily. 'It's getting busier in here, eh?'

'S'pose,' said Rob. It was always the same – despite the fuss surrounding Joan's calls, Michael never spontaneously alluded to their content afterwards. 'So,' Rob heard himself ask reluctantly. 'What was up with her, then?'

'With … whom … sweets?' Suddenly Michael's sexy mouth was annoying, smacking on strands of cold pasta between the words.

'Your mum, of course. Is everything OK?'

Michael barely looked up. 'Mum? Oh, everything's absolutely hunky dory with Mum. Hunky *dunky* dory.' He set down his cutlery and peered at the desserts blackboard. 'I sincerely hope they do banoffee here?'

'So, she wasn't locked out then?'

'Mum? God, no. She just wanted to let me know she'd got home.'

'Seemed you were on the call a long time, though?'

Michael sighed happily. 'Only because she wouldn't stop talking about the lovely taxi driver she'd had from the station. His daughter is an extra in *Casualty*, if you don't mind.'

'Right,' said Rob.

'Mum was star-struck by proxy. So star-struck that I couldn't get her off the phone. She does go on, but hey, you know our Joan!'

Rob forced a watery smile, sickened by this lack of tact. Seeing somebody's photo while secretly staying in their house and incessantly hearing about them hardly constituted *knowing* them. Neither did he appreciate the use of 'our Joan'; how could Rob claim ownership of a woman he was repeatedly denied the opportunity of meeting? It didn't seem fair – Rob's parents and two sisters had spent a whole evening getting to know Michael the last time they were down from Leicester. Meanwhile, Joan, who lived only a few miles away in Reading, might as well be living on the moon for all the contact Rob was allowed with her. He took a breath. 'I know you can't say for definite yet, but do you think it'll be much longer before I get to meet your mum?'

Michael touched his wrist. 'As soon as the time is right, we'll all go out for a nice convivial dinner, like I did with your family.'

'Really?' asked Rob, unable to picture such an event.

'Absolutely.' Michael made sad eyes. 'Come on, tell me what's wrong.'

'It annoys me how your mum is quite happy to hear the life story of some random taxi-driver's daughter but still doesn't know a single thing about the person her own son is seriously involved with. She doesn't even know I exist!' His head sank to his chest. 'Sometimes I can't help thinking you're ashamed of me.'

Michael groaned. 'I'd actually planned to tell her all about you last week. She'd been doing so well lately that I thought she'd be fine with me moving along with my life. But then Dad's eighteen-month anniversary came up. I hadn't realised the date until I got home from work to find her sobbing at the kitchen table. I knew it was still too soon to announce that I've got a new love in my life. She'd worry herself sick that she's about to lose me too. It'd be like another bereavement.'

'But can't you explain I won't steal you away?'

'She's so fragile right now, Rob.' Michael sighed and looked round, clenching his fists on the table. 'Of course, if my bloody brother wasn't swanning about in Silicon Valley, it wouldn't fall solely to me to look after her ...'

The middle-aged couple got up to leave, full of smiles and thanks for the waiter. At the door, the wife took her husband's arm. As Rob watched them strolling contentedly away, he couldn't help but feel sad for Joan, who would never again enjoy the simple intimacy of going for dinner or walking beside her soul-mate. Michael, who was the elder son, was only trying his best to ease that loneliness by always being available at the other end of the phone. Michael was so stoic about it all too – he never complained about the calls nor about his current living situation – he'd even given up his beloved flat in Hammersmith so he could look after Joan in the family home.

'Look,' Rob said. 'I promise to stop pestering you about meeting your mum. But I hope it won't be too long before I do.'

'Trust me, it will be as soon as humanly possible.'

They were deciding about desserts when the phone, now on the table, rang again. Rob, believing that Michael wouldn't answer it this time, giggled at the farcical flashing of 'Mum' on the screen.

Michael whipped up the phone. 'Maybe something's happened since she got in.'

This time, Rob didn't bother to retrieve the fallen napkin. He watched the call taking the same shape as before. When the waiter came for their dessert order, Rob told him sharply that they didn't want anything after all.

His newfound sympathy for the widow had dissipated in an instant; he was furious with her for ringing again so soon. But the longer he watched Michael (now twirling his glasses in his hand like a football rattle), the more he realised it was unfair to blame Joan herself. How was *she* to know that her calls were interrupting Michael's time with his boyfriend when she didn't even know he had one? It was Michael, not her, who was at fault. Even if he wasn't yet able to reveal he was with Rob, then why didn't he at least attempt to shorten their conversations using a cover story? Rob traced his nails along the tablecloth and came to the realisation that Michael was making a mug of him. It was time to play a little game of his own.

Michael sat back down, smiling. 'Hope you told him I wanted the cream on the side?'

Rob gave a tight shrug. 'Told him we didn't want anything, actually.'

'What?'

'Michael, is everything OK with your mum? Only I thought she was ringing again because we'd left the lube out on the bedside table. I've checked my bag twice and it's not in there.'

Michael's face drained to a pallor that the tones of the new shirt could never hope to offset. 'Oh please, no.'

'Look, I'm sure it's OK.' Rob might not know as much about the theatre as Michael, but he was certainly capable of a putting on a performance. 'We closed the bedroom door, didn't we?'

Michael gritted his teeth. 'No, I left it open to air the room after all the ...'

Rob sat back casually. 'Look, if she does see it, she'll probably think it's hand lotion.'

'It's called *Probe*, for Christ's sake. I told you not to leave any trace of us.' He stood up and waved for the bill, revealing sweaty crescents under his arms. 'If I get home now, I might be able to stop this.' He sounded like a telly detective with two minutes to save someone from impending murder. He threw a fifty onto the table and grabbed his coat. 'That's my half.'

'Wait a sec,' said Rob, touching Michael's arm. 'Actually, there's one other thing I forgot to do too.' By now, his annoyance over the phone calls had been well and truly defused – he was even feeling slightly sorry for his boyfriend.

'Tell me. This can't get any fucking worse.'

Rob beckoned him close. 'The other thing I forgot to do,' he whispered, 'was tell you that … I'm joking. The lube's been right here in my bag all along!'

Michael shuddered at first, then shook his head in happy exasperation. 'You little bitch!' he said, making a throttling motion over Rob's neck. The waiter arrived with the bill, but Michael said they'd changed their minds and would not only be staying for banoffee but also a bottle of their best champagne.

'Champagne?' said Rob. 'It's half nine on a Sunday night, Michael.'

'Oh, come on, nothing succeeds like excess, as Oscar would say. My treat anyway.'

'You're seriously buying champagne because we didn't leave the lube out?'

Michael grabbed Rob's hand, not caring who saw. 'Don't you think we should finish our perfect weekend with a celebration?' he said.

'You shouldn't be spending all your money like this,' said Rob, though the cost was far less concerning than Michael's delight that Joan hadn't found out about the two of them. Michael clapped his hands as the Taittinger was brought over with silver-bucketed aplomb, but to Rob it seemed like nothing more than an exorbitantly priced symbol of his own invisibility.

It was after eleven by the time they stumbled happily from the restaurant, Rob's initial discontent about the champagne long since dissolved. He had realised after the first glass that he'd been overthinking it; he should just appreciate his boyfriend's spontaneity. Who else had ever treated him to vintage bubbles on a Sunday night? The champagne hadn't been the last of it either – afterwards Michael had ordered snifters of brandy, and they'd laughed themselves silly with comedy poshness as they 'quaffed'.

'Thanks for a truly brilliant evening,' Rob said, now that it was their turn to walk, arm-in-arm, up the street. Everything in his life felt right and complete for once – he wanted for nothing. But it was only when they reached the corner that he realised that something important was, in fact, missing.

He thrust his overnight bag into Michael's arms and told him to wait, then ran as best he could, given the booze and his current lack of fitness. He was conscious of Michael's eyes on his back and only slowed to a jog when he was out of view. At the restaurant he panted thanks to the waiter – still glowing after Michael's extravagant tip – for having stashed the Thomas Pink bag safely under the counter. Back outside, he squinted up the street: although he had told Michael to wait where they'd parted, he was disappointed not to find him approaching so they could meet halfway. Nevertheless, Rob might as well impress him with the speed of his return. He was even wheezier on the way back and stopped to catch his breath a few yards shy of the corner; he wanted his dash to seem youthfully effortless. As he bent over with his hands on his knees, he noticed the shadow splashed diagonally across the ground up ahead.

He smiled at this simplified rendition of his lover painted out on the pavement. Like the profile he'd read on MaleDate, it only gave an outline gist of the person within, but an interesting gist at that. Breathing normally again, he arranged his expression into an earnest smile. Before he got to the corner, he heard Michael saying, 'I'm quite sure … look, I better hang up.'

Rob stopped. Bloody Joan again. Well, at least this call hadn't interrupted their togetherness. Maybe, bored waiting, Michael had called her rather than the other way around. And at least he'd had the good manners to keep it short for once, so perhaps he was learning after all. Rob came around to find his boyfriend staring into the oversized eyes of Judi Dench. Michael touched the billboard. 'Wednesday's going to be quite something.'

'I know!' said Rob. 'I mean, seeing her right there … on the stage … in front of us.' Rob liked Judi Dench but had needed to consult Wikipedia to remind him what he'd seen her in. 'I must reimburse you for my ticket, by the way. You shouldn't be paying for me on your birthday!'

Going out with a guy who was into the theatre was proving expensive. So far, they'd been to eight plays together, more than Rob had seen in the rest of his life. And while his interest in the West End was only recent, its productions were turning out to be a welcome respite from the tacky real-life gay drama he'd grown disillusioned with over the past year. His desire to escape the Soho scene had sent him down the online path towards Michael in the first place. Over the past five months he'd gradually turned his face away from the air-kisses and the bars teeming with one-dimensional twinks, to mature, multifaceted Michael, who didn't need to sniff lines off the back of a filthy cistern to enjoy himself or be quick-witted.

At first Rob's immediate circle had berated him for going out less, subjecting him to pipe-and-slippers and sugar-daddy jibes. Craig, who had first introduced coke into their previously clean, cocktail-loving gang, had been the worst – thanks to his newly drug-sharpened tongue. At first Rob had refuted the sugar-daddy accusations. ('He's only nine years older. And he hardly ever pays for me – I wish he would, because he has expensive tastes!') But as the months passed, he started not to care what their coked-up little minds thought. He started taking perverse pleasure in using Michael not as an excuse but as a *reason* for dropping out of whatever silly event they were planning next. Anyway, a ticket for *The Importance of Being Earnest* on Wednesday cost less than a gramme of coke, and the sex he was having was infinitely more enriching than the forthcoming Kylie concert, followed by afterparty at Hellraiserz, which his old clique were already wetting their knickers over.

Holding hands whenever it felt safe, they dawdled through the streets until they reached the mouth of the tube station. Rob's happy mood began to drain away.

Michael touched his cheek. 'Oh, sweets, you look so sad!'

'You know I hate saying goodbye on Sundays. And it was so nice being at yours for a change, not having that numpty staring over all the time. Say a prayer he's in bed and not up watching Italian news with a snotty look on his face because I've forgotten to wash a teaspoon or I've left my trainers out in the hall.'

Michael looked at him tenderly and shook his head. 'Robbie, I want you to do something for me.'

'What?'

'Do not let that … *curly-headed castrato* spoil our perfect weekend. Just because he's a sexless clean-freak doesn't mean he can upset you in your own home. Anyway, he can hardly blame you for making a mess when you haven't been there to make one!' He grabbed Rob in a hard hug and held him there for a full minute.

'How come,' said Rob, raising his face eventually from the soft leather of Michael's jacket, 'you always know how to make me feel better?'

'I'm not sure,' said Michael, with a frown of mock modesty. 'Maybe I'm just a natural.' He patted Rob away. 'Now go on before you miss your train! See you on Wednesday. Oh, and don't forget that shirt.'

Rob raised the Thomas Pink bag and gave it a little shake as he started down the steps. 'Would I ever!' he called, turning back with a parting smile for the love of his life.

A few minutes into the journey, Rob was already berating himself for not going to the loo before leaving the restaurant. He'd only realised he needed to pee when he'd sat down, and now, two stops later, the need had become a pain, made more acute by every sway of the train. He crossed his legs and tried to distract himself with the showbiz section in a discarded *commUte*, but the sight of Jordan's bazongas straining against a bikini top only heightened his bladder-agony. By Holland Park, an embarrassing dam-burst felt so imminent that he had to forget that this was the last tube; he ran out through the closing doors and up the steps to the street.

He gave thanks to the council as the hot torrent flowed into the open throat of a mobile urinal, still out after a recent street festival. He was zipping himself up when someone slapped him hard on the bum. He spun around, expecting to see a drunken passer-by.

'Well, little Robbie Rippin!' The man in the blazer had his hands on his hips and was tapping the long point of a winklepicker on the pavement. Even under the dim streetlights, there was no mistaking the tan, which set off the whites of his eternally protruding eyeballs.

'Hoggsy,' said Rob. 'How'd you know it was me?'

'Five years sitting behind you in geography, I'd know that arse anywhere.' Iain Hogg spoke the words without sauciness or fondness, as if to say he found Rob's bum weirdly remarkable. Rob forced a smile, hoping he could make his escape quickly. It was always the same when he bumped into Iain – his old schoolmate's efforts to undermine and out-queer were Iain's way of punishing Rob for successfully coming out two full years before Iain had. This unnecessarily competitive relationship made Rob think of a quote he'd seen in Michael's *Pocket Book of Oscar* – how right Wilde had been about there being nothing so bitter as an old friend.

'So, what's got good little Ripp-your-pants out so late of a school night?' said Iain, tucking in his weak chin. (At school the girls had joked that his eyeballs stuck out further than his lower jaw.)

'I was having dinner with my boyfriend, actually,' said Rob, determined to show that he was now spoken for. 'Yeah, we had a skin-full of champers and brandy, so I got caught short.' The best thing about the story was that it was absolutely true – there was no need to resort to the lies and embellishments that conversations with Iain usually required. Rob only wished Michael was still with him; he could show him off, and Michael could provide witty retorts to Iain's comments.

'Right, right,' Iain said. Despite his distracted look, Rob knew he was taking it all in. A tax officer who pretended to relish being eternally single, Iain always glazed over anything that threatened his supremacy. As predicted, rather than ask about Rob's new boyfriend, he was already turning the chat back to himself, ramping it up massively in response to Rob's disclosure.

'Well, I've had an excellent night myself … so far! There's this fab new bar on Archer Street—'

'You mean Brash?' said Rob, who'd been there once. 'Hardly new, is it? I'm sick of that place by now.'

'Troupe of go-go dancers up on the stage,' said Iain, pretending not to listen again. 'Total riot!'

'I'm sure it was.' Rob couldn't imagine anything he'd enjoy less nowadays than seeing a bunch of brain-dead bodybuilders pushing their pelvises over a caterwauling crowd. Iain was already off again, however, and for the next few minutes Rob endured tales of his impending promotion at work (thanks to the encouragement of his new life-coach), the new car he had his eye on, the apartment he was planning to buy next year, the salsa classes at which he was excelling … every aspect of Iain's charmed existence was being mentioned except – Rob happily noted – his love life, where Iain's lack of a man was reassuringly terminal.

Rob waited for a break in the boastful monologue, then nodded towards the taxi rank. 'Lovely talking to you, Iain, but I better head on. I'm leading a big team meeting first thing.'

'You're not still in that little agency up in King's Cross?'

Rob folded his arms; he'd managed this far without enhancements, but now he couldn't avoid them. 'We're not so little anymore,' he said with a laugh. 'We've set up a new pharma division with yours truly at the helm. In fact, I've just headhunted a fantastic account manager from one of the big agencies to work in my team.' Poor Vicky – he'd already stolen her pasta anecdote, and now he was relegating her position. She was actually the more senior person in the pharma division – a division that amounted to the two of them, sitting in what had previously been the stationery storeroom.

'I suppose pharmaceuticals sounds slightly better than working on adverts for … now what was it you used to do? … oh yes, a donkey sanctuary on the Isle of Wight!'

'That was years ago,' Rob snapped, wishing that he hadn't blabbed so enthusiastically about his new job when he'd first started. Despite Iain's air of never condescending to listen, he always stashed any fact that he could later use as a weapon. 'Anyway,' Rob continued, 'we've got much bigger clients on our books since then.'

'Isle of *Man*, perhaps?' said Iain, with a cackle at his own joke. 'Anyway, tell me, which way are you travelling?'

'I'm over in Ealing nowadays,' said Rob. 'Yeah, myself and this really cool Italian guy are sharing a lovely flat. But it won't be for much longer because my boyfriend wants us to move in together.'

'In that case, we'll share the cab with you,' said Iain. 'Sally fancies a bop at Tearaways, of all places.' He peered across the street at the illuminated doorway of a corner-shop. 'If she ever returns from buying her filthy cigs, that is.' After an expensive weekend, Rob was broke enough to travel with Iain and whichever member of his awful gaggle of fag-hags was with him tonight.

Iain waved across the street. 'Over here, Sally, you daft bint!' Rob watched in confusion as the shortish but striking male figure looked around for a moment, before his angular Hispanic face reacted with a flash of dark eyebrows.

'Sally's not his real name, is it?' Rob heard himself ask quietly, as the man, who had a black quiff and a stringy rip in the knee of his jeans, approached.

'It's Salvador,' said Iain. 'As in Dali. Funnily enough, the sex *is* rather like a Dali painting – *surreal*!'

Rob had even more shock to absorb when Iain detonated the 'boyfriend' bomb during the introductions. Rob shook Salvador's hand and returned the Spaniard's warm smile. He couldn't understand how this polite and sexily stubbled man was going out with Iain. Well, whatever the situation, Salvador certainly seemed glad of Rob's intrusion now: as they chatted, he kept nodding and smiling at him.

'Rob and I go back years,' Iain said as he led them to the taxi rank. 'We used to terrorise all the straight boys at school together, didn't we?' Rob was tempted to mention how Iain had actually been too chicken to come out until the second-last day of sixth form, but there was no point in being nasty, especially now that Salvador was sidling up beside him as they walked.

'You come the Tearaway too, Rob?'

The dark, discreet murmur made Rob melt a little. He shook his head slowly. 'I'm afraid I can't,' he said. 'Up early for work tomorrow.'

The deep brown eyes collapsed. 'Even for just a half a hour?'

Rob thought about Michael; he would nearly be in Reading by now. He'd be thinking about Rob, believing him to be getting into his bed at the flat, which Rob wasn't anywhere near right now. Though his circuitous route home was completely innocent, he already felt like a kind of traitor for having deviated. 'I'm sorry, Salvador. Maybe some other night?'

34

Iain spun around on his heel. 'What are you ladies whispering about?'

'I just ask Rob to come the Tearaway too.'

Iain patted his boyfriend possessively on the bum as they got into the black cab. 'Don't waste your sexy breath, Sally. Master Rip-your-pants here's too much of a sensible little boy to go out on a school night.'

Rob clambered in and took the seat facing Iain. 'You know what?' he said with a shrug to cover his malicious grin. 'I think I *will* come along for a bit.'

'Suit yourself,' said Iain. He rolled his eyes at Salvador, but his boyfriend was too busy smiling at this news to notice.

For a moment, Rob felt brilliantly defiant, but as the cab pulled off, he was struck by another pang of guilt about Michael. But it was all right for Michael – he had gone back to his dear mum, whereas if Rob went home right now, he risked encountering Orlando. He'd drunk so much earlier that a quick nightcap wouldn't make any difference, and it was worth it just to spite Iain by flirting harmlessly with his hot boyfriend for an hour. The detour would be so brief and banal that he needn't bother even mentioning it to Michael tomorrow.

The cab driver wasn't sure of the best route, and while Iain twisted round to give directions, Salvador leaned forward and squeezed Rob on the knee. 'Glad you come, Rob,' he whispered. 'I promise, we have good time. *Really* good time!'

5

It was Rachel's first time inside Trenpharm's spectacular, blonde-wooded boardroom. With the webcast imminent, the small group faced the giant screen, which was flanked by the flags of the Union Jack and the Canadian Maple Leaf. An uplifting electronic track began to play, and the screen flashed with a damson and anthracite pattern, whose pixels ultimately coalesced into the Trenpharm logo. This gave way to a smart, middle-aged man sitting at a presidential desk, behind which the Vancouver dawn was twinkling. Before his caption had even appeared, Rachel knew him to be Trenpharm's Global CEO, Ray Hallander Snr.

'Good day to you all, my Trenpharm colleagues,' said Ray. 'No matter who you are, where you're watching, or when your territory plans to launch Follestra to market, let me tell you, the future is already well and truly *hair!*'

The pun elicited a giggle from the group. Rachel tittered along politely, ensuring her laugh was no louder or longer than anyone else's. Surrounded by the cream of Trenpharm UK, she'd been conscious of her every move since arriving. She strove to appear both humble and intelligent in front of the group, which included the tall, uncompromising Country Manager, Anthony P. Watson, the brightly bow-tied Medical Director, Dr Roger Moss, as well as the dynamic Tim Greenacre, who was Lydia's boss. Rachel felt privileged to meet this collection of colleagues, especially having read their biographies on the TreNetwork yesterday. The most awe-inspiring CV had been Tim's – at thirty-three he was the youngest head of marketing in all of Trenpharm's territories; despite this huge responsibility and his ever-growing catalogue of business accolades, he still found time to be a father to three young children and a prize-winning skipper on a forty-four-foot catamaran. It was Tim who was sitting beside Rachel now. 'Yikes, here comes the science bit,' he whispered, making Rachel like him even more, for being funny as well as successful. 'Better take some notes!'

'I know,' said Rachel, who already had her Cardiophex ballpoint at the ready. Erik Geddes, captioned as *Emeritus Professor of Dermatology & Trichology, University of Vancouver*, was now on screen, his name embroidered on his surgical coat. As he spoke, the background became a scrolling montage of famous shiny pates, including Julius Caesar, Napoleon, Anthony Hopkins, even the port-splashed forehead of Mikhail Gorbachev, which had fascinated Rachel as a child, even on their tiny black and white TV. 'Contrary to popular belief,' said Professor Geddes, 'male pattern hair loss is not the result of high circulating levels of testosterone but rather a genetic inheritance of hair follicles that are susceptible to the deleterious effects of this hormone over time.'

'Hang on,' said Tim, who pointed at the sizeable bald patch in his short-shaven hair. 'You mean I'm not turning into a slaphead because of my sizzling virility?'

Lydia was sitting to Rachel's left. 'Apparently not, Tim,' she said, with a laugh and a teasing toss of her own bob, which was resplendently red and shiny today.

Anthony P. Watson looked slowly around from his place at the top of the table, like a stern grey owl. Rachel prayed he didn't think she'd been involved in the disruption. 'You'll find, Rachel,' he said, with a look right at her. 'That we don't call Tim the *Head* of Marketing for nothing.'

Rachel laughed graciously, while on screen the Canadian continued: 'Follestra, generic name stalaseride, represents a major advance in treating male pattern hair loss. We can now offer sufferers of this debilitating condition a treatment that is seventeen per cent more effective in regrowing hair than existing treatment options. Follestra also offers a superior adverse-event profile with fewer reports of erectile dysfunction, low libido, and gynaecomastia.'

Next up came Veronique Parratt from the Global Communications Team to tell them about the advertising campaign targeted at healthcare professionals. 'The concept you are about to see is the culmination of a full year's work between Trenpharm and our global creative agency,' she said.

'Fingers crossed they've done a decent job,' whispered Lydia. 'God knows we'll be looking at it long enough.'

'And so,' said Veronique, as she wound up her preamble, and the image appeared, 'I give you … Troy!'

Troy was in his early twenties, wearing a polo shirt and jeans. He stood against a background that, from the paraphernalia behind, appeared to be a sports shop. He was athletic and fresh-faced, or as Alysha would have less delicately put it, 'a right bit of beefcake'. The image was cropped strangely, however, with the crown of his head falling beyond the top of the screen. Rachel half-expected to see a sticker saying, 'Mind your framing' like those that had adorned her dad's photos when they came back from Boots, after he'd been snapping her judo competitions on his battered little Agfamatic.

While Troy's folded-arm pose, age and build suggested the confidence of a healthy young man – possibly even a graduate about to embark on adult life – his sad eyes were directed upwards, suggesting the source of his disillusionment was his hair, or rather the lack thereof.

Veronique continued: 'As you can see, the strap-line – *At 24, Troy deserves more* – not only rhymes but is also placed level with Troy's eyes. This will enable the viewer to make an empathic connection with Troy and feel the impact that hair loss has on patients …'

Rachel loved everything about the new campaign – it was clever and eye-catching. By the end of the webcast, she had a stiff wrist from taking so many notes.

'So then, what do we all think?' asked Anthony P. Watson, turning around squarely as the screen faded to black. It was clear he had his own opinions but wanted firstly to test the astuteness of his staff.

'I think it's pretty good,' Tim said. 'Not actually showing Troy's hair loss is a clever way of co-opting the physician's imagination, which will make them engage with the image.'

'Agreed,' said Dr Moss, with a quick nod down the table. 'Nice-looking chap, succinct but memorable line, judicious use of colour. Pop the UK prescribing information on the bottom and off we go.'

'Sorry to spoil the party.' Lydia's engagement ring clattered as she tapped her hand on the table. 'But it's way too North American for my liking. For starters, those baseball bats and lacrosse sticks in the background … well,

I assume we have free rein to photoshop in some tennis racquets and cricket bats instead. Then there's his name – Troy won't wash with a UK audience. We need something homegrown, like Ben or Scott.'

'Good calls, Lydia,' said Tim. He gave a wink. 'Anyway, Troy *is* a bit of a gay name.'

'Indeed,' said Dr Moss with a chuckle. 'No doc will want to prescribe the stuff if they think our cover boy's a poofter!'

Everyone, including Anthony P. Watson, found this highly amusing. Rachel laughed along too, but inside her mouth she was biting down on her cheeks. Biting so hard that she tasted blood.

'And finally,' said Lydia, as the room came to order. 'Let's tone back his California tan and those ridiculously white gnashers while we're at it, eh?'

'All those localisations will be well within Command-eye's remit,' said Tim.

'Exactly,' said Anthony. 'They did a terrific job on the Cardiophex launch last year.'

Lydia leaned forward. 'Cardiophex was a blue-sky campaign,' she said. 'Why pay a big creative agency when we're simply localising from global this time around? A guy from my MBA class, Ed Harrop, runs a small agency that's recently set up a pharma division. Competitive hourly rates *and* he's poached Vicky Plimpton from Command-eye. Vicky's the brightest account manager around, so we'll get the service we need but without the bloated big-agency costs.'

'Not that money is an object here,' said Anthony, a bit crossly, as though accused of being a cheapskate. 'But Lydia, whomever you think is most appropriate. And on a related note, how is the launch to the new sales team coming together?'

Lydia nodded in encouragement at Rachel, who cleared her throat and said, 'I'm liaising with Ascendant Events about booking the Byatt Bucknore for the two days. And I'm currently in negotiations with a couple of well-known UK dermatologists about being keynote speakers.'

Anthony frowned and gestured at the now blank screen. 'But surely Geddes himself would cut more mustard?'

Rachel hadn't been expecting a grilling but recovered quickly. 'I completely concur that having the world's pre-eminent hair-loss expert would be an amazing motivator for the reps,' she said, looking Anthony right in the eye, 'but unfortunately the professor's fees for a transatlantic appearance were prohibitive.'

'Rachel's right,' said Lydia. 'Geddes would gobble up most of our budget for the whole event.'

Anthony half-closed his eyes, but only for a moment, as though debating over a minor trifle like which pure-silk tie to wear. He clicked his gold pen a couple of times and looked down the table. 'I think we can just about stretch to Geddes. As Rachel says, he will be an *amazing motivator*. Tell finance that I've authorised whatever extra budget you need. Oh, and get yourselves a better venue than that blah-blah Byatt while you're at it. Somewhere like Gravenden maybe. The estate up there's pretty decent in the springtime.'

Lydia gave a low whistle. 'Geddes and Gravenden – are you sure, Anthony?'

'First impressions are everything, Lydia. Far better to wow our team from the get-go, don't you think?' He gave a knowing nod at Rachel, who shivered with delight to think he'd also been alluding to *her* successful first impression.

'Marvellous, thanks, Anthony,' said Lydia, making a thumbs-up sign at Rachel under the table. 'We'll make sure it's a worthwhile investment, won't we, Rachel?'

'Absolutely,' said Rachel, smiling confidently at Lydia and then at Anthony himself. 'We most certainly will.'

6

Chemotherapy regimens that included Deltraxin increased the overall ... the overall survival ... the overall survival rate ... of children with Stage IV ... Stage IV rhabdomyosarcoma ... by a median of 6.6 months.

It was no good. Despite renewed efforts today, Rob still couldn't concentrate. The sales aid he was supposed to be re-referencing for his favourite client, Hettie King at Mennchem-Gorelle, was already late, and thanks to his desperate state for the past three days, the booklet was in more of a jumble than when he'd first laid his dehydrated eyes on it on Monday.

Hettie was the brand manager for Deltraxin and although she was an upbeat, jolly-hockey-sticks type, working on her material was always a sobering task. A few times recently, Rob had welled up as he thought about the kids who made up the statistics on the pages he was checking. Behind the bar charts, p-values and percentages were actual lives being annihilated by childhood cancer, lives that could be extended by a few measly months by a drug, but one whose 'very common' side effects included facial oedema, rectal haemorrhage and intractable bone pain – all of which sounded almost worse than the symptoms of the cancer itself.

Today, however, Rob felt even sorrier for himself than he did for the sick kids; at least *they* didn't have to blame themselves for the terrible situation they found themselves in. The kids had the support of everyone around them, whereas he must bear the horror of his guilt and confusion alone, unable to confide in, or seek counsel from, a single soul.

He bit down on his pen until the plastic began to crack. He had never messed up like this at work before, where his personal motto was 'I put in effort, not excuses'. He always got the job done, no matter how late he had to work. He helped his clients look good in front of their bosses, their sales reps and ultimately their customers – the doctors who wrote the prescriptions. He was pretty good at it too. Hettie had called him a 'little diamond' only last week; now he was letting her down, along with several other important clients. No doubt they would soon start ringing to query the atypical delays, but any possible excuses were lost in the brain-fog brought on by three nights of writhing insomnia, studded with short but violent dreams, including one where Rob had kicked Michael's beautiful mouth into bloodied mush.

Vicky sat opposite in the small fourth-floor room they shared, her plump hands dancing daintily across the keyboard, unaware of his torture. He'd explained his wan appearance, lack of appetite and his frequent trips to the loo by telling her that Sunday night's restaurant had given him food poisoning.

The clock on the filing cabinet appeared to be at a standstill; Rob willed it to advance to twelve, though every passing minute was another minute Hettie was left waiting. Worse still, it was another minute closer to Michael's birthday trip to the theatre tonight, an event which had changed from a source of excitement to one of intense dread. The two hands of the clock were finally aligning. He slipped his mobile into his pocket and went upstairs to the men's toilet, praying he would finally get the answer he desperately needed.

He had developed a format for these calls over the past three days and, as always, stood with his fingers crossed as the call connected. Through the little window above the sink, he saw the builders working on the site opposite. He envied them their simple manual tasks – nailing this to that, slopping mortar onto bricks and then smoothing out the edges. If he could lay a plank from the windowsill to the scaffold he would gladly risk the trip to leave his own life behind. The phone rang on. He crossed his fingers even tighter and mouthed 'please' into the mirror. He did a little leap when, for once, a male rather than a female voice answered, and then snuffled, 'Tearaways, what can I do *you* for?'

'Is that Tigs, by any chance?' Rob had found the name ridiculous at first, but right now it was the most beautiful sound in the world.

'Depends who's asking.'

'I don't know if your colleagues have told you,' said Rob, 'but I've been on about a shirt—'

'Been on?' Tigs snorted. 'Heard you've never been bloody off, mate! Hanging round here like a pissy pong every night. Never mind the gazillion phone calls.'

Rob winced. 'Sorry, it was just on the off-chance you might pop in.'

'To this dump on me days off, mate? Don't bloody think so. Anyway, it's in me locker if you still want it.'

Rob collapsed against the sink in gratitude. 'Fantastic. I'll collect it straight after work, around six?'

Tigs clicked his tongue. 'No can do, mate. I'm on an early today.'

In the mirror, Rob watched his face grow ashen.

Tigs said, 'You better come over now. If I leave it behind the bar it'll probably have gone walkies by tonight. Your choice, though.'

Rob began calculating – the round trip might well take longer than his lunch-hour. After Monday he couldn't risk being spotted arriving back late. But then he remembered with relief that Edmond and Vicky were meeting a new client at two so wouldn't see him returning.

'I'll be over at lunchtime,' he said. 'You'll definitely be there?'

'Yeah,' came the sighed reply. 'I'll definitely be here.'

Vicky eyed him as he slid back behind his desk. 'Guts playing up again?' she asked.

He nodded and rubbed his belly, which was paradoxically distended despite how little he'd eaten the past three days. 'Think it's finally settling down a bit, though.'

'Please tell me you've told the restaurant.'

'I rang last night like you said to,' he said, adding yet another lie to the pile that Sunday night had unleashed and then quickly thinking up another one: 'They're sending me a voucher to apologise while they investigate. Not that we'll be rushing back there, of course.'

He redoubled his efforts on the Deltraxin mark-ups, then emailed them to Daryl in the design studio. At ten to one, he was throwing on his coat in the hope of getting a head start to Tearaways, when Edmond came into the room. The boss gave Rob a withering look on his way to Vicky's desk, leaving Rob no choice but to sit back down in his coat and pretend to work.

He cringed to remember Monday, when Edmond caught him skulking up the back stairs, late, unshaven, mumbling unconvincingly about a stomach bug. 'Not like you, Rob,' Edmond had said, his nose twitching at the compound stink of liquor and lies. 'Not like you at all.' The boss had walked off then with a dismayed shake of his floppy hair, leaving Rob to feel far worse than if he'd actually been shouted at.

'There's been some good news, Vicky,' said Edmond with a beaming smile solely for her. 'I've just had a call from Adrian in Salutio Health. Thanks to your *outstanding* presentation to him on Monday morning, he's awarded us the Envinel account.'

'Fantastic,' said Vicky, her cheeks dimpling.

'Nice one, Vicky!' said Rob, who had been grateful for her absence on Monday morning as he'd collapsed into his chair.

Edmond glowered as though to say Rob's opinion was no longer welcome or relevant. He lowered his voice. 'Envinel's going to take up a huge amount of your time, Vicky, so I've no option but to let Rob handle that Follestra campaign we're being briefed on later. I know you had a good relationship with Lydia in your previous job, but I can't have you overstretched.'

Vicky paused for a moment. 'That's fine with me,' she said quietly. 'But Lydia's quite the stickler and poor Rob's already so busy—'

'Sorry Vicky, I actually don't give a crap how busy *poor* Rob is,' said Edmond. 'I'll spare you the sordid details, but he's lucky I'm letting him within fifty yards of any client right now. And with only two of you in the pharma department for the foreseeable, he'll just have to cope with whatever he's given.'

Edmond turned, then stopped halfway to Rob's desk as though he couldn't bear to approach any further. 'Change of plan, Rob,' he snapped. 'You and I are meeting Lydia Bigham and her new marketing assistant here. Two o'clock *sharp*.'

'Perfect,' said Rob in his most positive voice. He was already late leaving for Tearaways, and the thought of handling a new account on top of his other work made him want to curl up in the filing cabinet and pull the drawer closed behind him.

Edmond glanced suspiciously at Rob's coat. 'And don't even think about being late this time.'

'Of course not, Edmond.' Rob waited for the boss to leave, then, before a perplexed Vicky had a chance to ask what was going on, he rushed out to the stairs.

'So, this Vicky Plimpton's a good account manager?' asked Rachel as the Saab made its way between the autumnal maples on Vancouver Avenue.

'Ruddy great,' said Lydia. 'Poor girl went for promotion at Command-eye only to be outdone by some hot-to-trot chick, half her size and one-tenth of her ability.'

'That's so unfair,' said Rachel.

'Command-eye's a bitch-eat-bitch agency. Apparently they used to call her Vicky *Blimpton* behind her back. No wonder she jumped when Edmond headhunted her. Anyway, it'll suit her better at HarropAds. Less fashion, more function.'

'Really?' said Rachel, suddenly concerned that her new multicoloured Paul Smith silk scarf (her most expensive ever accessory, bought out of her first month's pay cheque) must look ridiculous with her sober grey suit.

Lydia glanced to her right and surged the car onto the main road. 'Don't expect Philippe Starck sofas or chai lattes. They've got a couple of floors in this brutalist monstrosity in King's Cross that could do with a spruce. But I'd rather spend our budget on our Follestra materials, not subsidising soya milk and iguana tanks. I've known Edmond years anyway, he's a good guy, takes it all so personally.' They were interrupted by a call on the hands-free. 'Speak of the devil,' said Lydia with a laugh. 'Hi Ed, what's up?'

'Lydia, I just wanted to apprise you of a slight change of plan for today. Vicky's had to go home because she's quite poorly, I'm afraid—'

'For Christ's sake, Edmond, we're already on the way.' Despite knowing this *good guy* for years, Lydia certainly wasn't afraid to berate him.

'I do appreciate that, Lydia,' came the quivering reply. 'Rest assured

Vicky's devastated to have let you down. However, the good news is that another member of our pharmaceutical team, Rob Rippin – who's just as able, if not *better* placed in fact – will attend the briefing in her stead.'

'But there's sod-all point briefing him when we'll be dealing with Vicky,' said Lydia. 'I'd rather turn back and postpone until tomorrow, inconvenient as it is.' She glanced over her shoulder as though contemplating a risky U-turn.

'The thing is that Vicky's likely to be absent for a while,' Edmond said. 'I can't divulge medical details, but it's probably best if Rob manages the Follestra account altogether.'

Lydia said nothing, only rapped the steering wheel slowly with the band of her engagement ring. Rachel blinked at the grain-faces in the walnut dashboard – they looked like they were feeling the awkwardness too.

Eventually there was a gulp on the line. 'Lydia, is this all OK with you?'

'Hardly ideal, Edmond. I only awarded Follestra to Harrop's because of Vicky. But with the launch in February, I don't have the luxury of waiting for her to recover. So this Rob person will have to do, I suppose.'

'You'll be delighted with Rob, he's worked for me for years and really knows his stuff.'

'Sure,' said Lydia tartly, as though she'd decide for herself.

After hanging up, Lydia's face hardened even further. 'You're going to have to watch this Rob like a hawk,' she said, shooting Rachel a hawkish glance of her own. 'If anything goes wrong it's our heads on the block, especially as we insisted on using Harrop's over Command-eye.'

Rachel straightened in her seat and gave a serious nod.

'I told you to be tough on Narelle, and you've acted on that admirably,' continued Lydia. 'But with this chap I want you to be a *tyrant*. Show your teeth, accept nothing less than perfection, keep him on his toes from the get-go.'

'Don't worry,' said Rachel. She straightened her silk scarf – on second thoughts, it did look the part after all. The dashboard faces looked back at her with pop-eyed encouragement. 'I certainly will.'

Tearaways' only customers were two anoraked lesbian tourists sitting in the window. They looked up in concern as Rob rushed in, wheezing and sweating. His new friend with the hot-pink hair was on a stepladder cleaning the mirror behind the bar, and Rob coughed to get her attention. She was about to descend but stopped when she saw it was him.

'I believe Tigs is finally around?' he said.

She turned back to her wiping and caught his eye in the mirror. 'Afraid you've just missed him.'

His hot forehead collapsed onto the steel counter. 'Please tell me you're joking. I've got to be back at work by two.'

'No need to get your dick in a twist. He's just popped out to get more limes. We keep running out, all thanks to those things.' Rob could barely stomach looking at the poster she was gesturing at – it said *LimeLights, 3 for the price of 2*. Those same lethal green cocktails had soured his stomach as well as his whole life on Sunday night, and now were causing him further pain by despatching Tigs to the shop. He waited at the bar, drumming his sweaty toes inside his shoes and keeping a sniper's eye trained on the door. The lesbians were planning out the rest of their day on a city map. He hated their laughter and their relaxed, open way with each other and wondered how the hell he would keep it together tonight. He kept having visions of standing up in the theatre and confessing to everyone – including an open-mouthed Judi Dench – about what he had done.

When Tigs finally came in, Rob accosted him before he'd even delivered his bag of limes to the bar. Mid-forties, with a greying pompadour and a tattooed neck, he seemed both too old and too straight to work in a place like this.

'I've come about the shirt,' Rob gasped.

Tigs cocked his twice-pierced eyebrow and looked at Rob as though he were an awkward Mormon in a suit trying to recruit him. 'Oh yeah,' he said eventually. 'The shirt.'

'I'm in a little bit of a rush, you see,' said Rob. 'I have an important meeting at two.'

Tigs sighed and swung the bag across the bar. 'Jules, quick, take these limes urgently. We cannot have this gentleman getting his nuts crushed by big brother!' He led Rob through a *Staff Only* door and down steps into a long cellar that reeked of urinal cakes and stale lager. Despite their excruciatingly slow progress, Rob still managed to bash his shin on a broken barstool in the gloom. He imagined what Edmond would say if he could see him now, limping through the beery bowels of a gay bar, twenty-eight minutes before their meeting with Lydia.

Tigs kicked open the door to a harshly lit room whose back wall was a spaghetti-mess of tubing, gas cylinders and pressure gauges. To the left were the mythical lockers Rob had been fantasising about since Monday. It took Tigs an age to shuffle the few short steps to his own one, sending Rob's internal pressure gauge soaring into the red, but he knew that trying to hurry proceedings would only have the opposite effect.

Tigs patted down his pockets for the key. 'You musta been pretty upset when you'd copped you'd left it here.'

'Upset doesn't cover it,' said Rob. 'It's a birthday present for my boyfriend.'

'Ah right, your boyfriend,' said Tigs, finally finding the key in a pocket he'd already tried. 'Looked expensive. You two must be serious?' He tried to turn the key, but the lock seemed to be stuck.

'Very,' said Rob, now almost dancing with frustration. 'We're together five months.'

'Long time … well, in *gay* years anyway,' said Tigs, frowning at the key but then laughing to realise he'd been turning it the wrong way. The locker swung slowly open, and a moment later Rob was grabbing the bag from Tigs and wrapping the corded handle round his fingers, like a glorious tourniquet.

'Receipt's in the bag, mate,' called Tigs, as Rob said his thanks and made for the door. 'In case you need to return it.'

'I won't, believe me. This thing's the perfect fit!'

'Really?' said Tigs. 'Thought the arms looked a bit too long for your bloke.'

Rob turned in the doorway. 'But you've never seen my boyfriend.'

Tigs furrowed his brow. 'Upstairs toilets on Sunday night. Oh, I get it … so that wasn't … ?'

Rob thought he was going to vomit. Tigs cackled and tapped the side of his nose. 'Don't worry, mate, a good barman never tells! But do us a favour – next time you're getting a hand job, use one of the shitters, eh? Tearaways ain't the fanciest place, but we do have *some* standards!'

7

Jo and Declan were the last to leave the office. Earlier, Bart had annihilated the latest draft of 'FutureBodies' – a collaborative illustrated spread, one of the many special features planned for *Dublin AM*'s spoiler edition on the day of *commUte*'s launch. That was still a month away, but an antsy Bart had arranged the illustrator's briefing for the following morning, meaning Jo and Declan had no choice but to stay late yet again to finalise the content for handover.

At half eight Declan switched off his desk-lamp and handed some sheets to Jo. 'I've overhauled the bionic arm section, so if you can check for anatomical inaccuracies.'

Jo added the sheets to her own pile. 'Let's keep our titanium fingers crossed that Bart prefers this new version.'

'As soon as this one's finished, he'll have us working up the next feature. This spoiler's going to be some behemoth.'

Jo rolled her eyes. 'A behemoth that nobody's going to read because they'll all have their novelty-loving noses stuck in *commUte*.'

Declan sighed. 'Right, Bróna says if I'm not home before nine tonight my dinner's going in the bin instead of the microwave.' He looked at her with avuncular concern. 'You OK to lock up by yourself?'

'Sure,' said Jo, wishing she had someone at home who'd throw her dinners in the bin, someone who'd raise the alarm if she tripped on her way down the deserted office stairs and never arrived home.

After Declan left, Jo put the sheets aside and took another piece of paper from her bag. She looked at the two names printed on the motor insurance certificate, the only document that linked herself and Louise in any legal capacity. She had delayed this moment in some vague hope of a reunion, but the break-up had survived the tricky first trimester and could certainly be deemed viable. She dialled the number in the header.

'Hello, Sigmar Ireland Insurance, you're speaking with Regina.' Jo usually had sympathy with call centre staff, having spent an interminable college summer in one, but not for this woman, who sounded as royally officious as her name. She pictured a back-to-work Cavan mother, a minister of the eucharist who meddled in the affairs of the local school. When Jo confirmed her name and address, Regina – who could obviously also see Jo's marital status – asked, 'What can I do for you today, *Miss* Kavanagh?'

Jo was annoyed by the emphatic phrasing, but to a holy joe like Regina, 'Married' and 'Miss' must be collectively exhaustive as well as mutually exclusive. 'I'd like to remove a named driver from my insurance, please.'

Regina did some clicking. 'So your named driver is a ... *Miss* Louise Kelly, of ... oh, the same address as yourself?' She seemed doubly perturbed by two women sharing a house as well as a car.

'That's right,' said Jo. 'And how much will I save without her on my policy?'

'Hold while I check that for you.'

Jo endured the shrill panpipes in the knowledge that this was a positive step, both personally and financially. In her deteriorating money situation, every cent counted.

Regina came back on the line. 'Miss Kavanagh, there won't actually be any discount for removing Miss Kelly.'

'But it cost me extra to put her on,' said Jo, 'so surely I should be entitled to a discount now I'm taking her off?'

'Since Miss Kelly turned twenty-five, you weren't paying anything extra for her.'

Jo sighed. 'Please just take her off anyway. I never want to see her name on my documents again.'

'Certainly, Miss Kavanagh. However, I must advise there's a thirty-euro charge for amendments between renewals.'

'What?' Jo's voice filled the empty office. 'Thirty quid just to press delete?'

Regina gave a thin, border-county chuckle. 'I'm afraid it's not quite as simple as that. But if payment is an issue, I suggest you leave Miss Kelly as the named driver until your policy expires.'

Jo spoke through gritted teeth. 'Well, to borrow one of your own phrases, Regina, leaving her on my policy *is not quite as simple as that* because

Miss Kelly was actually my girlfriend. And no, I don't mean the way the *Sex and the City* women have girlfriends. No, we were *lesbian* girlfriends. For three and a quarter years, before she suddenly fecked off with a younger, prettier, richer model – famous too, but I won't name names. As a result of all this, Miss Kelly will not have the need, nor the opportunity to drive my shitty little car now that she's swanning round in her fancy-woman's Mini Cooper. Not to mention saddling me with so many bills that I can't afford the thirty quid to take her off the policy!'

There was silence on the line, Regina clearly so appalled by dealing with a crazy lesbian that she'd either pressed mute or even hung up. Or maybe she'd put Jo on speakerphone and the whole call centre was racking with silent laughter.

'Regina?' said Jo eventually.

There was some furious keyboard clicking. Regina came back on the line. 'Miss Kavanagh. I've put that amendment through for you now. There won't be any charge on this occasion.'

'Oh?'

'We have discretion to waive fees in extenuating circumstances. Now, do you need anything else from me today, Miss Kavanagh?'

'That's everything. Thank you so much, Regina.' With a disbelieving smile and a shake of the head, Jo let the receiver fall from her burning ear.

It was after ten and bitterly cold when Jo got off the bus in Stoneybatter. She turned onto Arbour Hill and walked past dozens of windows – intermittently lit oblongs in the old red-bricked street. She didn't encounter anyone until she reached the prison at the top of the hill – two jovial officers came out of the gate, obviously glad to be free of sex offenders for another day.

Turning onto Blackstairs Terrace she was relieved to see the hyperactive O'Harridan boys weren't around. Last night Wayne had cycled silently up behind her, only to skid the tyres of his oversized mountain bike within a millimetre of her shins. Her fright had given great hilarity to Wayne's little brother Brandon, and the pair had shouted 'ya sap' at her as they had wheelied away.

With delight, Jo remembered that for once she wasn't arriving home to an icebox. She could almost feel the toasty glow from here, because she had finally mastered the heating timer. Setting it had always fallen to Louise who, unlike Jo, had no problems understanding the arcane control panel under the stairs for which the landlord had lost the manual. Earlier that morning, armed with a torch and a notepad, Jo had spent fifteen minutes pressing buttons and taking notes. The resulting eureka moment had put an end to two years of misunderstanding, all caused, she knew now, by Louise's unnecessarily convoluted explanations.

She cursed as she stepped into the hall. The house was freezing. As she leaned under the stairs to quickly press BOOST she heard Louise. *Enough points to get into medicine in Trinity and you still can't work out how to set the heating? What are you like, babe!*

Jo had never lived alone until Louise's departure, and since then she'd discovered the ability of RGB pixels to cheer up an empty room. The thirty-two-inch flatscreen that she switched on now, was one of many co-owned appliances that she had inherited. The inheritance had happened by default rather than design, however, because Louise had simply abandoned everything – from the smoothie maker to this fancy TV to the stereo that could play MP3 CDs. Initially Jo believed Louise had sacrificed her share in these expensive items as compensation for the hurt she had caused. But as time wore on, Jo began to see it as an indictment of how dispensable everything at Blackstairs Terrace, including Jo herself, had ultimately been to Louise. What would Louise want with such pedestrian old gear anyway, now she had seamlessly slotted in at Tamara's 'smart-tech' apartment with its remote-controlled curtains, underfloor heating and a sound system that piped music into every room?

She was taking a Lidl beer from the fridge when there was a knock at the front door. She nearly dropped the bottle. She wasn't expecting anyone – she never was these days – and her mind raced ahead like it did whenever her inbox pinged or her mobile rang in her bag. It was a hope against hope, but still. She tidied her hair on the way to the door, wishing she'd had the chance to finally get it cut, then threw on the expression of someone who was managing just fine.

'Cillian!' she gasped.

'Yes, only me,' he said, scrutinising her from the step. 'No need to look quite so disappointed.' He took a final drag before grazing his cigarette off the brickwork. 'Don't tell me you wanted it to be *her*?'

'Who?'

'Louise, you plank! Her standing here with a tear-stained face begging you to take her back. Go on, admit it.'

'God, no.' Jo led him inside. 'I just didn't know who it was. You never said you were calling over.'

Jo had no brothers, but people often mistook Cillian – who also had pale skin, dull brown hair and a skinny build – to be her sibling. In the sitting room he sank into the opposite chair. 'I was passing by with somebody so thought I'd check in on the well of loneliness.'

'And is that glint in your eye anything to do with said somebody?'

'Remember I told you about the divine new guy in my book club in the library, the one I suspect of being an invert although he's straight acting?'

'Kind of.' With her own love life in tatters, Jo had little interest in his lustful ramblings.

'Well tonight he – Liam – was there again, and I found out he lives on Buggery's Treat of all places.'

'Boggerah Street? I've probably seen him around so …'

'I pretended I had to drop in here so I could walk his way.'

Jo laughed. 'I knew you'd an ulterior motive. Anyway, why do you suspect inversion?'

'No girlfriend. Lives alone. And then the most *incontrovertible* clincher tonight when he suggested *The Line of Beauty* for next month. Looked right at me as he said it too. God, the other teachers will explode when I tell them tomorrow. I've been banging on about finding an intelligay for ages and now I've finally got one!'

'You haven't exactly *got* him yet,' said Jo, who'd always been jealous of how out Cillian was at work (at *Dublin AM*, she'd only ever told Declan). 'Anyway, intelligays aren't the be-all and end-all. Look what happened to me.'

Cillian laughed so hard that it brought on a rolling spasm of his smoker's cough.

Jo looked at him crossly. 'You don't think Louise was intelligent?'

'I suppose,' said Cillian, recovering his breath, 'that successfully conducting a double life for months right under your partner's nose does require a certain type of intelligence.' He slapped the armrest in delight at his own joke; Jo bit her lip and looked away. Cillian had lately become a master at double-edged digs which condemned both Louise's infidelity *and* Jo's inability to notice it. But despite her hurt at this latest jibe, she couldn't ask him to desist – or at least not just yet. Cillian had earned this period of righteousness: he'd been the one to warn Jo from the start that there was 'something a bit underhand' about Louise, an observation Jo had thought so ludicrous that she'd relayed it back to Louise in bed that same night. The new couple had laughed it off as jealousy – which was understandable, when Jo had found her soul-mate while Cillian was trapped in a soulless spiral of promiscuity. Despite the unpopularity of Cillian's concerns, he had persisted, until one day Jo had asked him, rather impolitely, to keep his misguided observations about her new girlfriend to himself. A row had ensued, and soon afterwards Jo had moved out of their shared flat and into Blackstairs Terrace with Louise.

Obviously sensing that he'd gone too far this time, Cillian shifted in his seat. 'Oh,' he said brightly. 'I've been meaning to show you something I found online.'

Glad to change the subject, Jo passed the laptop and perched beside him as he typed into the browser. 'LesbiansInDublin.com?' she said, recoiling with a laugh from the two lip-locked girls in vests superimposed on the night-lit Liffey. 'Wow, catchy name. And you're showing me this why exactly?'

'Last time I looked you appeared to be a lesbian in Dublin,' he said, making a face at her. 'And it's the sister site of GaysInDublin, which is actually quite good.'

'Good for what?'

'It's about time you got some online presence, Jo, especially now that … well, you're on your own.'

'You want me to set up a profile? Ok, let's see … boring twenty-eight-year-old, recently dumped but with extensive collection of Onitsuka Tigers seeks trustworthy, Superdry-wearing, athletic blonde with high IQ for rebound-sex, maybe more. Yeah, I'll be *swamped* with responses, Cillian.'

'It's not a dating site, Jo. It's for making some online friends. I've had some fascinating discussions on the guys' forum.'

'But the lesbian scene is so much more incestuous and competitive.' She crossed her arms. 'And I've already got plenty of friends.'

He snatched her mobile up and held it out of her reach. 'So, let's see. Last dialled numbers … Sigmar Insurance, Mum, Dad, your sister, oh look … *moi*!'

She grabbed the phone. 'I thought you'd like having me all to yourself again?'

'Jo, I can't be your only friend. Couldn't you do with some female company too? Whatever happened to that couple you two used to go clubbing with?'

'I haven't seen Sinéad and Sinéad in aeons. They were more Louise's friends anyway, and just like us, they went off the scene.'

'Then what about your journalism college crew?'

'I can guess what response I'd get there,' Jo said. 'Well deserved too, seeing as I dropped them like a hot rock when I met Louise.' She closed the laptop. 'Cill, I appreciate your concern, but I'm not ready to make new friends, let alone lez-be-friends. However, I solemnly promise to make that website my first port of call should the need ever arise. Now can we please talk about the gig instead? Have Helium confirmed your slot?'

'They've said it'll be within the next month.'

'Exciting! It'll be like the old days seeing the techno superstar DJing again.'

Cillian snorted. 'Playing in a scuzzy club to underage druggists just so I can repay my stamp-duty loan is hardly Richie Hawtin. Anyway, the club scene's practically dead these days. But we should still definitely procure a nice gramme of *Charleroi* for the DJ booth!' He gave a wild sniff as though half-crazed already.

Jo smacked his arm. 'Thought you were getting back into gigging to make cash, not spend it!'

'I know, I know. But look, it's a special occasion. And I'll need a little bit of Columbian courage just to get me started behind the decks again.'

Before Cillian left, they looked at the heating timer, worked out what Jo had been doing wrong and correctly set it for the following morning.

'Thanks,' said Jo, seeing him to the door. 'And thanks for calling in. Gets a bit lonely when you're on your own.'

He looked at her. 'I know.'

She cringed at her own tactlessness. 'Cillian, if you're still pissed off that we never got to buy a place together, then think about how I feel – at least you *own* a house now.'

'And to that same overpriced shoe-box I must now retire,' he said with a frank flash of the eyebrows. 'Especially as I'm starting *Romeo and Juliet* with those unromantic little second-year scuts first thing tomorrow!'

Unable to sleep, Jo felt for her phone in the darkness. Although its light would disturb no bedfellow, she pulled the duvet over her head before switching it on. Inside her little illuminated cave, she was like a sly child reading after lights out, the duvet shrouding her actions from the world and, more importantly, from her rational self. She scrolled through the contacts until she reached Louise – a point she'd been loitering at so much lately there must be a digital divot worn into the listing. She stared at the number she had used thousands of times (oh how nervous she'd been even texting Louise at the beginning!) but which she must never use again – even once – in all the years of the rest of her life.

She clicked into the accompanying photo and Louise's face illuminated the cotton grotto – a saintly apparition. Louise hadn't even known she was being photographed by Jo as she'd stood among the Pride crowd that sunny afternoon, being roused by Panti Bliss's marriage-rights speech. And so the photo had candidly captured everything from the summery quiff pinned into her hair (Jo had loved how it always became a sexy falling-down mess during sex) to the sunglasses dragging down the neck of her t-shirt just enough to reveal the callus on her clavicle – the result of a childhood fracture when she'd crashed her yellow bike in order to avoid hitting The O'Rahilly, the cat belonging to her elderly neighbour Delia Deegan, who wore a Cumann na mBan brooch and had never married.

It struck Jo just how many intricate and intimate Louise-details she'd absorbed – knowledge that no longer rightly belonged to her, yet was impossible to delete. She stared at the photo until her eyes began to blink and flicker.

She woke up with a bolt from the appalling dream. Lost in the Sonoran desert with the sun crimping her skin, she had spotted Louise standing on a nearby crag and had tried to scream for help. Like the turkey vultures circling overhead, however, she was only able to emit a low hiss. Louise was oblivious to her entreaties, but the birds above certainly heard her: their divebomb descent revealed puce scrotal faces, ravenous eyes.

Waking just as their beaks had begun to gouge, Jo had instantly regretted having desecrated Louise's dreamcatcher: even as it languished in a faraway landfill, it was capable of wreaking a feathery revenge of its own – one far hotter than sweet chilli sauce.

More horrifying than the nightmare itself was the phone, still in Jo's hand since falling asleep. With a pounding heart, she confirmed she hadn't accidentally rung Louise, imagining the shame of having vulture-hissed down the line or, worse still, giving her the silent psycho treatment.

The air in the bedroom was inexplicably stifling, her pyjamas drenched in sweat. No wonder she'd been dreaming of the heat. She stumbled out to the stagnant landing and heard the pipes pinging under the floorboards like the veins of someone trapped in a sauna. In the bathroom, the radiator boiled under her touch. She went downstairs in the darkness, ready to smash that blasted timer to pieces; as she ducked under the stairs, she was sure she heard Louise, sniggering in the shadows.

8

Rob groaned at his ringing phone.

'Surely not Fussbudget again?' said Vicky, using the nickname she'd come up with that morning.

Rob gave a roll-eyed nod and took a deep breath. He'd only been dealing with Rachel Driffield for one measly week and was already dreading her calls, which were now more frequent than Mrs Wyles's calls to Michael. He picked up. 'Hi Rach—'

'Hello Ro*bert*.' She cut him off, giving him no time to utter the last syllable of *her* name, but as always, she insisted on using the formal version of *his* name – even though he'd used 'Rob' at the meeting and as the sign-off on his emails. 'I've got some feedback about the sales aid,' she announced.

'Great.' He wedged the phone under his ear and began a panicked scramble through the pages on his desk.

'No, *not* great.' She gave a huffy little laugh. 'We're extremely disappointed with the draft sent last night.'

She'd been stern and demanding with him all week, but this was something different. His trembling hand retrieved the printout from the pile. 'What … What was the problem?'

'*Problems*, Robert. Two amendments from our call yesterday haven't been implemented.'

'Oh?' Already knowing how fussy she was, he'd checked over every amend three times before sending the draft.

'I asked you to put in a statement on page four about the prevalence of androgenic alopecia,' she said.

'Oh, I'm pretty sure we did that one.' He raced to the page and smiled in smug relief. 'If you look to the right of the graph—'

'What you added was a line about something called *andregenic alepecia*. It's spelled with o's Robert, not e's.'

He looked again at the words – admittedly his spelling did look a bit odd. The problem with being a bad speller was not knowing which words you didn't know – he assumed he'd written them up correctly.

'Apologies,' he said. 'Daryl the designer must have misread my handwriting and then I somehow missed his mistake when I was proofing it.'

'Well, if that's the case,' she said, 'Daryl misread it twice, and you missed his mistake twice. The same error's on page seven!'

His elbows melted through the desk. 'Apologies, we'll get those fixed up immediately.'

'And we've finally decided on our patient's name,' she said.

Rob flicked back to the photo of gorgeous Troy, the only perk of working on this new account. 'So did Scott or Ben win out in the end?' he asked, keen to show he'd been paying attention at the briefing.

'We're going to use Rob,' she said flatly. 'So you can amend that on everything.'

He pressed his ear to the receiver. 'Sorry, did you say *Rob*?'

'Yes,' she said. 'R-O-B.'

He couldn't believe it. Not only was she was telling him how to spell his own name – or rather the shortened version that she refused to use – but she was too much of a robot to even acknowledge the funny coincidence. She moved on, dictating further text changes at a furious pace. Her lack of humanity baffled him. As the call wound up, he threw her one last chance to engage over the joke – an opportunity for humour might never arise between them again. 'I just hope I don't lose my hair as early as our new Rob,' he said, 'but then again, I wouldn't mind looking like him in other ways!'

The silence she returned was so intolerably long that he checked the screen on his phone to see if he'd been cut off. He imagined her querying her Trenpharm employee handbook to see whether humour with suppliers was ever permitted.

'What time will the new drafts be ready?' she said eventually.

'Could we say tomorrow morning?' Rob was already dreading the hours he'd have to spend with Daryl, who was likely to throw one of his metrosexual strops over the tight deadline.

'Too late,' she said. 'I'm meeting with Lydia at five to review them.'

'Five today it is, then,' he said, wondering how they'd complete even half of the changes by then.

'*Excellente!*' she said, but this was merely self-praise for securing yet another ridiculous deadline.

Rob hung up and shook out his cramped hand. 'No matter what I try, she refuses to treat me as a fellow human being. Even though I'm the same bloody age as her.'

Vicky tutted sympathetically. 'Some of the younger, up-and-coming ones can be tricky all right. Happy to trample on the agency if it means looking good in front of their boss.' She got up and grabbed their coats. 'Right, let's go eat before you have a meltdown.'

'No, I need to write up a tonne of amends for Daryl. And then check through every last word – she's just murdered me over misspellings.'

'*I'll* check over the spellings for you afterwards,' said Vicky, shoving his coat at him. 'Now come on, we haven't had lunch together in aeons.'

Rob's old colleagues from the FMCG division were already in Luigi's as they arrived, but after a brisk hello, Vicky led him to a table tucked behind an ivy-painted pillar.

'So,' she said after Luigi had taken their order, 'care to tell me what's going on?'

Rob suddenly realised her motive for the secluded spot. Last week's acute guilt about Salvador had since distilled into a kind of generalised anxiety. He thought he'd been hiding it quite well from her, though. 'What do you mean?' he asked.

'You've been jumpy, you look like shit, and you're practically anorexic.'

'It's just Fussbudget,' he said. 'She's getting to me.'

Vicky cocked an eyebrow. 'Then why did all this start two full days before you first met her? And how come Edmond's suddenly got it in for his golden boy?'

He folded his arms. 'It's nothing.'

'We're not leaving here until you tell me.'

He stared at the framed poster beside them. It showed different types of pasta captioned in a curly font. He tried desperately to conjure something up.

'*Penne* for your thoughts,' she said, giving him a pointed glance of her own.

He squirmed in his chair. 'I've … *done* something with someone else … if you know what I mean.' Telling another person brought relief as well as renewed horror.

She slapped the table. 'Rob!'

'In the toilets of a trashy gay bar in Acton. It only happened because I was pissed on these lethal cocktails. The guy was an outrageous foreign flirt, and he's seeing this old schoolmate who's a complete bitch whenever we meet. Edmond caught me sneaking in hungover the next day, hence his mood with me.'

'Never mind Edmond,' she said. 'What about the gorgeous boyfriend that you're so sickeningly in love with?'

Rob stared at the table. 'I've been using all this Follestra work as an excuse to avoid him since his birthday. Oh, Vicky, that was the worst night of my life, especially the moment when Michael said it was the *best* night of his. I wanted to walk into Shaftesbury Avenue and let the traffic plough through me. I cried all that night with guilt while he slept. At four in the morning my hand was a millimetre from waking him up and confessing, but I was too gutless in the end. I'm going to tell him this weekend, though, because it's just not fair to hide it any longer.'

She looked at him sternly. 'And it'll be even less fair if Michael gets his heart broken. Why ruin a great relationship because of a drunken slip-up that's completely out of character and will never happen again?'

'So … I just get away with it then?'

'But can't you see, Rob? Your penance *is* your silence. Do your guilty writhing in private and then make it up to Michael by being the most amazing boyfriend ever. Your mistake will eventually fade to an insignificant blip in the grand scheme of your relationship. You'll be so grateful you didn't throw something brilliant away for nothing.'

Rob sat back and exhaled heavily. The vile tagliatelle nest in his brain was finally beginning to soften and unravel. There was a huge amount of mental work to be done, but at least he had a plan. Luigi was approaching with their food. 'Thanks, Vicky,' he said. 'And thanks for not judging me.'

'Who says I'm not?' said Vicky, as Luigi laid a garlic bread and a large pizza in front of her. 'I think you're a total arsehole for what you've done, but you'll be a bigger one if you let it destroy things.' She pulled some crust off the pizza and held it sensually to her lips. 'What I wouldn't give to be dating a man like Michael, my god, the things I'd do …'

'I can only imagine,' he said with a laugh. Then he tucked into his lasagne – the first proper thing he'd eaten in ten whole days.

9

'Sorry for disturbing you, Jo. You're not in the middle of your dinner, are ya?'

Jo pulled open the front door, trying to hide her disappointment that, yet again, it wasn't Louise. 'No, Elaine, you're grand. It was just a sandwich anyway.' She smiled at her next-door neighbour, whose pencil-thin frame was kinked by the sturdy toddler on her hip. Although Elaine was only twenty-five, to Jo she always seemed to be from a different generation altogether, because she already had two kids. Today she looked even older again, and a bit frantic. Her tracksuit top had a giant saliva patch at the shoulder, and the pile of the velour had been clawed into furrows. The cause of these defacements – red-faced Jayden – stared menacingly at Jo as he teethed on his mother's Creole-gold earring.

'Just wondering would you be free to help Kayleigh later, Jo? She's crying her eyes out over her homework.'

Jo's face fell. 'What's up?'

'She has to write an *essay*. Carl says it's the same thing as a *story*, but I think it's something else altogether. We're after killing each other in there. Then I remembered you know about that kind of thing from your work. If you could sit with her, even for a few minutes—'

'I'd be delighted to.'

Elaine's body went limp with relief. 'You're a star, Jo. Sure you didn't have anything planned?'

'I never do these nights, Elaine. See you in five.'

Jo smiled as she put her runners back on. Not only would the visit break up the ennui of the evening, but she was highly flattered at being invited to help a child she barely knew. She wished Louise could witness this show of unconditional acceptance. Louise, who hailed from Foxrock, had always been wary of their neighbours here, especially city-council tenants like Elaine and Carl; she'd even issued diktat to Jo that, for their own safety, they must conceal their sexuality from the locals. Jo had found this overcautious and snobbish, and one day, during a neighbourly chat, she'd told Elaine of their relationship. Louise had been furious, warning that, despite Elaine's ostensible acceptance, they must prepare to be branded perverts and paedos by the whole terrace. Jo didn't know whether Elaine ever did blab to other neighbours, but in any case, they'd never received an iota of homophobic hassle. And now, as Jo knocked confidently on the peeling varnish, she concluded that the most prejudiced person on the terrace had been Louise herself.

Carl was in his usual uniform of Celtic jersey and grout-flecked Snickers trousers. 'C'mon in, Jo,' he said. 'You're a bleedin' lifesaver so you are.'

Smiling, Jo entered the miasma of stale smoke, tinned spaghetti and sickly sweet baby powder. Carl's buzz-cut head nodded at the kitchen door. 'The teacher does be giving her impossible homework for a nine-year-old. And then fucks them from a height if they get anything wrong.'

'Ah,' said Jo, 'that's not fair.'

From upstairs, came a series of screams and splashes that sounded more ferocious than fun. 'I'm just bathin' Jayden,' Elaine called down. 'Carl, I hope you gave the place a wipe, I don't want Jo going in to filth.'

Carl rolled his eyes at Jo as they entered the kitchen. 'Now, Kayleigh,' he said, 'you can tell your Miss Moriarty that a proper writer done your homework with you. Maybe that'll shut the fussy cu— *cow* up, eh?'

Still in her maroon school uniform, Kayleigh looked up warily, her dainty freckled face still blotchy from crying.

'I'll just …' said Carl, already backing out to the front room where a commentator's voice was intensifying by the second. 'Sorry, I've a tenner on Celtic to annihilate those foreign fucks.'

'Hey, Kayleigh,' said Jo in her kindest voice as she cleared the spare chair of the Barbie schoolbag. 'Mind if I sit down?' With her hair pulled into what must be an uncomfortably high ponytail and gold sleepers piercing her tiny earlobes, Kayleigh looked no different from the other girls in the area who, as Louise had always observed, wanted to pass for women of childbearing age before they were even fully grown children. Jo had never felt the girlish need to experiment with her mother's clothes or makeup and so found all forms of premature femininity rather discomfiting. Kayleigh was displaying a more accurate approximation of womanhood than Jo was herself, as she now sat, knees apart, in her boyfit jeans, loose hoodie and Onitsukas. The other depressing thing was the lack of a dedicated space for Kayleigh to do her homework. On the small kitchen table were today's *Irish Star*, a landslide of nappies, a carton of John Player blue and a blackened tumbler that functioned as an ashtray. It was a far cry from Jo's childhood bedroom with its capacious desk, and shelves long and strong enough to hold the full adult set of the *Encyclopaedia Britannica*, a birthday gift she'd received around Kayleigh's age.

Jo cleared space for her elbows. 'So what class are you in now?'

'Fourth.'

'Wow. Yeah that would be right because you're nine now.'

'Ten,' she corrected. 'Don't mind Carl saying I'm nine, he doesn't remember anything.'

'Dads are a bit silly sometimes, eh?' Jo said with a confidential nod. 'I'm twenty-eight but guess what age my dad still thinks I am?'

'Dunno.' Kayleigh looked away with a disheartened shrug. 'Anyway, Carl's not me Da.'

Reddening at her gaffe, Jo said, 'Sorry. I must be more forgetful than dads myself! Anyway, let's have a look at this essay.'

Kayleigh inched the copybook across the sticky vinyl tablecloth. 'We only done *stories* with our last teacher so I dunno how to do an essay.' She fiddled with one of her earrings as Jo read what she'd written.

My Favourite Hobby is dancing. The disgoes are in the Church hall on satuday. They give you oringe and coke and crips. They play Beyonce and we do the rooteens we made up ourselves. Me and Shannon and Nikita love dancing. We're sad when the music stops. We want to dance all night.

Jo blinked away a tear. Although doing routines at a kids' disco would have been her worst childhood nightmare, she was touched at this insight. And who could blame the poor thing for wanting a little bit of escapism.

'Told you it was stupid.'

'It's a really good effort, Kayleigh. There are a few spelling mistakes, but we'll soon sort those out.'

'But Miss Moriarty says we've to write one of them full pages. I dunno what else to put in.'

Jo looked around. 'Let's find a blank sheet so I can show you a special trick.' After a fruitless hunt, Kayleigh conceded to co-opting the inside page of her Barbie colouring book. Using a tiny Ladbrokes biro, Jo drew a large inverted triangle on the grainy grey card. Perhaps believing that Jo had confused arts and crafts with English, Kayleigh gazed on with worried wonder. 'This upside-down triangle is going to help you do your essays,' said Jo.

'How?' said Kayleigh, shifting forward.

'The big important bit of this triangle is at the top, so we need the big important things right at the top of our essay. So, what's the most important thing about your favourite hobby? Well, I think that it's telling people what your favourite hobby is, so you write *dancing* up here.'

'Ok,' said Kayleigh, taking the biro.

'Now, the next most important thing is the *kind* of dancing that you do? I'm sure it's not that awful posh stuff from *Strictly Come Dancing*, is it?'

Kayleigh giggled. 'It's hip-hop.'

'Ok, so write that into our triangle. Great! And how long have you liked dancing?'

'Since I done Streetsteps classes ages ago.'

'Ok, write down Streetsteps. Now, what was your teacher called?'

'Michelle T.'

'Michelle is hard to spell because it's actually French. So get ready and I'll spell it out.' Jo began to call the letters, but Kayleigh's hand remained static.

'Nah, she spells her name another way,' said Kayleigh who, without the slightest difficulty, wrote *M'Shell Tee*.

Jo laughed. 'So this M'Shell Tee sounds like the real hip-hop deal. Is she from New York or something?'

'She lives in Ballymun.'

Jo cringed at her own corniness and moved quickly on. 'So, when do you do the classes?'

'I don't do them anymore.'

'Aha! So you're probably too good for classes now, are you?'

'Me Mam can't afford it since it went up to a fiver. Shannon still goes. She teaches us the routines at her house afterwards.'

Jo, who had done a multitude of after-school activities, kicked herself for yet another presumptuous blunder. 'That's a pity,' she said. 'How come M'Shell put up the prices?'

'She's saving up for extensions that are made of *real* hair.'

Jo stifled a laugh. 'Oh, right. Anyway, let's keep going with our triangle.'

They continued their work until 'Christmas disco' had been squished into the apex. Twenty minutes later, and under Jo's spellchecking supervision, a delighted Kayleigh had filled almost two copybook pages.

A doorbell sound chimed under Jo's chair. 'That's me phone,' said Kayleigh, retrieving it from her schoolbag.

'You've got your own phone?' said Jo.

'Me Da sent it to me from England. Sorry, I just have to read this text.' Kayleigh's pink nails worked over the buttons of the latest Nokia.

'Now, let me guess,' Jo said, feeling quite in the know about Kayleigh's life now. 'Is it Shannon or is it … Nikita?'

With a boastful kind of blush Kayleigh looked up. 'It's me boyfriend.'

'Oh,' said Jo, threatened by this revelation far more than she should be. But it was hard not to feel like a gay loser when a little girl could boast about a boyfriend and she – a grown lesbian – didn't have so much as an admirer. Kayleigh kept the message out of view as she read. Jo told herself then it was absurd to deny the child a bit of sweet and harmless fun. She pressed her generosity into a smile. 'So, who's this boyfriend of yours then?'

'Wayne from up the terrace.'

'O'Halloran?' asked Jo, her heart sinking to discover this was far from sweet and harmless after all. 'His mum's Teresa?'

'D'you know her?'

'Not that well,' said Jo, though she already knew way too much of the foul-mouthed, dog-kicking chain-smoker who'd inspired Louise to dub the household the O'Harridans in the first place.

Kayleigh narrowed her eyes. 'Do *you* have a fella?'

Jo couldn't tell if the child's coyness was because she suspected (or perhaps even knew) that Jo was gay, or whether it was because boyfriends was a naughty topic. She crossed her arms, amazed at how squirmy this child had made her. 'Not right now,' she said. Technically it was the truth. And it wasn't her place to explain the intricacies of sexuality to other people's children.

'And what about your friend, does she have a fella?'

'Oh, Louise?' said Jo with a quick laugh. 'Well, she doesn't live there any more so I don't actually know!'

Kayleigh gave her a strange look; perhaps she was puzzled about them not staying in touch, or maybe she already knew the truth and thought Jo pathetic for not admitting their gayness. Slipping the phone back into her schoolbag, she announced, 'Well, I'm not replying to him now.'

'Fair play,' said Jo. 'Homework and education are way more important than boys, aren't they?' It was easy for Jo to spout the aphorism since it had been girls that had driven her to distraction until the start of fifth year, at which point she had sublimated her pent-up sexuality into her studies.

Kayleigh gave a coquettish shrug. 'Shannon says you shouldn't reply to boys straight away. You need to leave them hangin' on.'

Jo laughed. 'I must remember that one!'

A little later, Jo was on the doorstep accepting Elaine's vociferous thanks as Jayden devoured her shoulder. (After his bath – during which he'd pissed into Elaine's eye – Jayden had finally settled, only to be woken by Carl's cursing when the foreign fuckers were awarded a penalty.)

'Any time, Elaine,' said Jo. 'I'm here every evening now herself has gone.'

Elaine bit her lip. 'If you're every lonely in the evening, Jo, just pop in here and have a chat and a cup of tea, or even a beer with Carl!'

'Thanks, that's really sweet,' said Jo, touched by an offer she would likely never take up.

Back at home, she sank onto the couch, appreciating the peace and clean air. It wasn't long before the loneliness began to creep back in, however – tonight she was feeling it even more keenly. She had never realised just how much life was breathed into a house by the random, mundane sounds made by another person. She missed Louise's murdering of Róisín Murphy songs in the shower before they went out for the night, the ceramic snap of GHD paddles interleaved with long hisses of hairspray. She missed Sneezy Louise's 'photic sternutation' (how turned on Louise had been by Jo's medical jargon) when they opened the bedroom blinds on a dazzling summer's day. She even missed the irritating keypad tones on Louise's mobile that, despite Jo's pleas, she doggedly refused to mute.

Jo stared at the empty mantelpiece. Everybody else's lives were moving along nicely – even Kayleigh had a boyfriend as well as her two confidantes. Jo did have Cillian, but his escalating obsession with book-club Liam, whose gayness still hadn't been confirmed, was beginning to wear thin. The laptop was on the coffee table. After a minute of indecision, she opened it up.

Despite her lack of interest at the time, she still remembered the name. She knew LesbiansInDublin probably wouldn't be her kind of thing, but it couldn't hurt to have a peek. And she'd always thought that *Deltoideus*, the Latin for one of her favourite muscles, would make a really good username.

10

Rachel finalised her makeup with a bold touch of blusher, then checked herself out in the mirror. Although her seventh week at work had been the most hectic so far, she looked and felt pretty good right now. Beneath the dressing table, her knee bounced to the beat from Alysha's massive stereo, which they'd dragged onto the landing after dinner. Alysha couldn't wait for tonight either – she'd had a tough week of her own at Sunray House, where she was a care assistant for kids with physical disabilities. She was incredibly excited about bringing Rachel on her inaugural night out in Wheldon Green. Rachel had insisted that socialising must wait until she'd settled in properly at work, and although tonight's timing wasn't *quite* ideal, it was high time she let her hair down, while making some new friends too.

There was a flash of movement as Alysha danced into the bedroom in a towel, shaking two tops like cheerleader's pom-poms. 'Need your help, babe,' she said over the radio. 'Which of these with my new skirt?'

Rachel looked from one top to the other, quickly skimming past the body between them. Alysha's towel was skimpy and only tenuously tucked in at the bust. Rachel was finding herself a bit unnerved by other women's nakedness nowadays and, in turn, had ramped up her own modesty levels. In both the flat and the judo changing rooms, she avoided showing anything that she wouldn't show in public. 'The blue,' she said, glad to safely fix her gaze on it.

Alysha pulled the top to her chest and perched on tiptoe to check out her reflection. 'Just about long enough to hide my booty anyway,' she said as she clenched her bum up and down. 'Too damn muscly, that's my problem. Then there's all the cakes the mums of the Sunray House kids keep dropping in to thank us staff.' She lifted the towel to show Rachel her bum-cheek. 'Look Rach, I'm putting on a layer of fat on top!'

'Don't be ridiculous, you have a fabulous figure,' said Rachel. She turned back quickly to the dressing table and began tidying away her makeup.

'Well, at least one of us will look hot tonight,' said Alysha, coming up behind. She ran her fingers down the feathers on Rachel's new earrings. 'I should have borrowed these for my date last week. Though I still doubt Mr Cop-a-Feel would've called me back.'

Rachel laughed and pulled free. 'Stop being a negative numpty and get ready, would you? I'm not planning to stay out *that* late, so the sooner we get to this infamous pub the better.' She blotted her already perfect lipstick with the tip of a tissue.

Alysha gave Rachel's shoulders a playful shake. 'Please don't go all boring because of the tournament. A few measly drinks won't push either of us into a higher weight class, we've got all day tomorrow to recover, and The Mill is totally *fierce* on a Friday night.'

Rachel stood up on the pretence of choosing a scarf from the rack hanging on the door. Alysha's increasing tactility was starting to rattle her. She was running out of ways to extricate herself from all the friendly touches, let alone Alysha's penchant for warming her feet under Rachel's bum on the sofa. The other night it had got so bad that Rachel had feigned a judo-induced back spasm so she could divert to the straight-backed armchair. She laid a scarf down on the bed, not sure if it was even the right one. 'Of course I won't be a bore,' she said, 'but Kev's excused us from training tomorrow so we're well rested for Sunday, not so we can get stupid drunk tonight. I'm not letting him down when he's been good enough to put me on a team so soon.'

'Ooh, get you, Sensei's little pet!' Alysha ran her hands over Rachel's blow-dried hair (Rachel had recently spent a fortune on highlights at a salon Lydia frequented). 'I shall personally ensure that your first night at The Mill is kicking! I can't wait for you to meet Mel and Ollie and the rest.'

'Well go and flipping get ready then!' The brand-new Girls Aloud song was just kicking off on the radio. Alysha bopped her head in acknowledgement, then danced out of the room, waving her tops in time to the *oohs*, *toot-toots* and *boom-booms*.

Alysha hadn't been wrong about the popularity of their local on a Friday night: even before they arrived at the corner of Wheldon High Street, Rachel could hear the distant roar of voices; as they drew nearer, she saw tall Victorian windows framed with condensation.

They paused inside the door to survey the craziness. Rachel had to shout. 'Now I know why they call it The Mill.'

'Told you,' said Alysha. 'Ok, let's do this!'

They pushed their way through a clique of trendy types, including a statuesque Black boy wearing lip-gloss and an eighties-style leather jacket, and a heavily pierced girl whose cowled houndstooth scarf was the same fluorescent orange as the 'lunch specials' cards that hung in constellation behind the bar. Rachel was glad to discover, as they went further inside, that there were also plenty of people who'd made a similar effort to herself and Alysha to dress smartly. This included a fresh-faced guy in a polo shirt, who politely surrendered his personal space so they could squeeze up to the big mahogany counter.

While Alysha bought the drinks, Rachel got a better look at her new local: unlike its Friday night clientele, The Mill was neither smart nor arty, but its claret-coloured walls, high cream ceilings and sepia images of windmills formed a nice traditional backdrop to offset the grunge and glam of the customers.

It was eventually determined via text that Mel and her boyfriend Ollie were in the back lounge. Rachel and Alysha pressed themselves through the little archway until they reached the couple, who had secured a table in the corner. Rachel smiled warmly, determined to make a good impression.

'What hour do you call this, ladies?' said Ollie, standing up and, thanks to his lankiness, banging his frizzy, ponytailed head off the TV screen above.

'Yeah,' said Mel, a round-faced girl with a button nose and white-blonde hair. She gestured at the cluster of empty Stellas on their table. 'We're half, no sorry *three-quarters* pissed already.'

'It's all Rachel's fault,' said Alysha, pushing her forward for introductions. 'She's a total *mentalist* when it comes to deciding what to wear.'

'Don't listen to a word,' said Rachel, shaking their hands. She was slightly

74

disappointed that Mel and Ollie weren't sitting with anyone else, especially after Alysha's earlier claims that they knew 'hundreds' of people at The Mill. But she saw how this foursome could be useful too – having their undivided attention at first would allow her to get two friends firmly in the bag before spreading herself around later. Even better was that the couple had no links to judo, so they represented a totally separate social branch to the friends she was making at the club.

Mel thrust the empties at Ollie. 'Right, bring these back and get another round in.'

'You've got him well trained,' Rachel said, watching his head dipping under the arch.

Mel nodded. 'Has to be done, eh Alysha?'

'Totally. Treat 'em mean,' said Alysha, who then collapsed against Rachel with a sad laugh. 'Not that I'd know, being desperately single and all that.'

'Don't tell me the sexy Welshman's come a cropper already?' said Mel.

Alysha sighed. 'I texted to say thanks for the meal. When I heard nothing back, I resent the message.'

Mel smacked her on the leg. 'What did I say about double-texting, Aly?'

'That's exactly what I said, Mel,' said Rachel, keen to get involved.

'It was just that I really liked him,' said Alysha. 'So much that I let him feel me up in the cab home. Mind you, I'm so sexually frustrated at this stage I'd have let him do it out on the street. Or even under the table in Nagano with one of his chopsticks!'

When the laughter and table-slapping had eventually died down, Mel turned to Rachel. 'So, have you left some hot bloke behind up north?'

Rachel ran her finger around the rim of the ashtray, skimming over the cigarette-notches. It was time for the same carefully worded story – all of it true – that she'd already used on Alysha, Narelle and even, in the last week, Lydia who, now that they knew each other better, had made friendly enquiries into Rachel's love life. She looked Mel right in the eyes and said, 'I've been so focused on getting a new job that I've not had time to go on a date the past year.'

'At least you've got a good excuse,' said Alysha. 'What've I got?'

'Don't fear, either of you,' said Mel, her eyes flickering with vicarious excitement as she snatched her drink from the returning Ollie. 'There were at least six hotties in here last Friday. And I'm not talking about the emo-boys in sperm-reducing jeans either.' She banged her bottle on the table like a gavel. 'I am talking proper beefcake!'

After three bottles of Coors Light, Rachel thought about the tournament and decided to switch to lemonade. She was having such a good time that she didn't mind, and her internal reservoir of tipsiness would easily stretch to the end of the night. Lots of friends of Mel and Ollie's had turned up; half of the back room was made up of their extended group, which was now by proxy Rachel's too. She must have met over a dozen people; while waiting to be served, she gave herself a mental test of the names she'd been committing to memory. Everyone had been incredibly friendly, wanting to know her story. Most had been surprised to hear she was from Newcastle because she didn't have the accent, or, as Ollie's cousin Penny had hilariously put it, 'You don't sound a tad like Cheryl Cole!'

Equally pleasing to Rachel had been people's reaction to the details of her new job – all agreed that the role at Trenpharm was well worth uprooting for. Buoyed by the beer and the lovely chatty atmosphere, she now felt comfortable enough to go into that back room and strike up conversation with any of them.

As the barmaid set down the drinks, she said something that Rachel couldn't make out over the noise. Then, before Rachel could pay her, she rushed off to serve someone else. Rachel stood up on the rail and waved her tenner. Though they'd never had much themselves, her dad had always insisted they were honest with other people's money. They had once walked the full mile back to BargainBuys in a hailstorm, the grocery bags biting into their blue fingers, when he'd discovered the cashier had given him back a pound too much. Just like the supermarket, the pub wouldn't miss the price of two drinks, but it was their money, and Rachel didn't want to get barred from her new local should the barmaid later realise her mistake.

The barmaid eventually spotted her. 'I better spell it out for you, love,' she said as she shovelled ice into highballs. 'You've not paid. But someone else has.'

'Who?' said Rachel. 'Like ... a man?'

The exasperated woman almost shot her with the lemonade gun. 'No, the queen bloody mother! Give you a clue. Grey shirt, smiley, sitting with a bald bloke by the window.' A surreptitious glance confirmed he was one of several men who'd already been remotely appraised by Alysha and the hilarious Mel. Alysha had thought this guy's smile sexy and deemed his teeth to be perfect; Mel had liked his grey shirt but said she'd like him even better without it. As with all their male prey that night, Rachel's opinion had been polled too. She'd declared that his hair – dark brown with the subtlest little upturn at the front – had been 'subjected to a far more judicious use of styling products' than some of the other guys there. Like all her other verdicts that night, Alysha and Mel had found it riotously funny.

Aware he might be watching, Rachel picked up the drinks with a confident nonchalance and nipped back through crowd; she was acting as though this kind of thing – which she'd only ever seen in movies – was a regular occurrence.

Although Alysha was wrapped in animated conversation with Mel and Penny, she noticed Rachel's glass immediately.

'Thought I'd switch to vodka and lemonade,' said Rachel.

'Phew,' said Alysha. 'Don't want you going soft on us now.'

'Would I ever!' said Rachel. She sat down, feeling as fizzy as the drink in her hand. Of course, the vodka cover-up was insignificant compared to not mentioning who'd bought the drinks. But if she did say anything, then Alysha – especially in her high-spirited state – would bolt out to the bar with the girls to investigate. The guy would think them a gang of silly gigglers and Rachel's chances would be ruined. She sat for a while, only half-listening to the conversation – which was still all about men – and contemplating her next move. At the next bout of laughter (Penny was telling how she'd accidentally spat on a man's dinner during a date), she picked up her handbag, hid her drink behind it and said she was off to the loo.

'Don't talk to any strange men,' Mel called after her; this was followed by Alysha's even louder, 'But bring 'em back here if you do!'

He was alone and looking at his phone as she approached, and Rachel saw then that the shirt wasn't grey at all, but rather a woven matrix of black and white. On the shelf beside him sat a pristine pint of Guinness and an impressive bunch of keys with coloured plastic tags. 'Hi there,' Rachel said, projecting her voice into the space between his downturned face and his phone. Her free hand reached for the security of the mahogany divider, but she didn't need any support and so diverted it to rest on her equally confident hip.

He looked up, surprised, and awarded Rachel with an exclusive edition of his already infamous smile. 'Wow … hi. I'm Stuart,' he said, jumping off his barstool.

'Rachel.' As well as being an introduction, the handshake served as a physical clincher; even if it all ended here, Rachel would have some impressive trophies to bring back to Alysha – the tale of the free drinks, the smile especially for her, his first name, his actual touch. She wouldn't bother disabusing Alysha either, of the notion that he had perfect teeth: up close they were neither brilliantly white nor perfectly straight, but this just made his smile even more genuine. As Rachel smiled back, she was struck by the mortifying thought that his true target might actually have been Alysha and that, having observed their round-buying behaviour, Stuart had merely been using Rachel as a mule. Alysha had claimed to have caught his eye a couple of times earlier, though she'd said the same thing about at least three other men. Any doubt was dispelled, however, when Stuart quickly moved his pint and keys and offered Rachel the free seat.

She slid fluidly onto the stool and tilted her glass. 'Thanks for the drink, by the way.'

'Just thought it would be a nice way to say, well … hello.' He nodded at her hopefully for a moment, but then his face collapsed to a wince. 'God, sorry, it's a such a cheesy move, I can't believe I actually did it!'

She laughed. 'It was sweet of you. I'm glad to hear it's not a regular tactic, though.'

'I wanted to come and say hi, but I didn't have the guts to push through all your mates in the unknown territory of that back room. Unlike you regulars, I've never actually been in here before.'

'You're not going to believe this,' she said, looking at him with widened eyes, 'but it's my first night in here too!'

He seemed almost cross at the coincidence. 'And now you've just killed off my next question,' he said sharply.

She worked it out after a moment. '*Do you come here often?*' She shook her head. 'And I thought the free drink was cheesy.'

Laughing, they clinked glasses. He asked what had brought her here. Although it was her tenth time that night to talk about moving to London, she approached it with more effort and enthusiasm than ever. Stuart listened intently, taking polite sips of Guinness between smiles and nods. A couple of times, the drink left a feather of cream foam on his top lip – an image that Rachel committed to memory – before the tip of his tongue neatly licked it away. Even minor moments like that would prove fascinating to Alysha later.

'My business partner Al definitely needs some of your Follestra stuff,' he said when she'd finished her story. 'I mean, we're both only thirty, but he's already thinning out.'

'I'll let you know once it's on the market then,' said Rachel, pleased by both his age – the perfect balance between youth and maturity – and the fact he had a business – wow, when Alysha heard all this! 'So … what do you and Al do?' she asked.

'Nothing as glamorous as Trenpharm, anyway. We run a property maintenance company. We've just moved our little office to the area, hence we're checking out our new local tonight.'

'It must be nice being your own boss.'

'It is,' he said. 'Well, until you're called at three in the morning because a forgetful old lady's left the bath running and it's inundated the flat beneath.'

'Oh no.'

'Or when some tanked-up idiot's evacuated a whole block by falling asleep with a twelve-inch ham and pineapple in the oven. True stories both, by the way.'

She laughed and drained her drink. He took out his wallet, as though ready to get her another.

She was about to say it was her round but decided to allow him the simple masculine pleasure of spending money on a girl. 'I'll have another vodka and lemonade, thanks.'

She watched his shirt turn grey again as he went off. She'd only said it was vodka to save face, but another lemonade would have been fine; despite boldly approaching a nice-looking stranger and then holding her own with him, she wasn't in the slightest bit nervous. It seemed that the move to London, winning the job as well as a place on Sunday's judo team, had given her self-confidence a major uplift. She was enjoying all this and enjoying being so good at it too. And why wouldn't she be? This was exactly what any attractive, upwardly mobile young woman was designed to do. It was a return to her original ways; it had been far too long.

She realised she hadn't even told him about judo yet. That had always been a major turn-on for her two college boyfriends, Neil and Josh. In recent months, she'd been concerned that some inherent flaw in herself might have caused those break-ups, but tonight brought the clarity of knowing it had been mere personality differences and life circumstances that had caused things to fail.

At the bar, Stuart turned and made a face of embarrassment at how long it was taking him to get served. She liked how he wasn't afraid of his shortcomings – that was a strength in itself. She smiled back sweetly, knowing that it didn't matter who saw her: flirtation between a girl and a boy was not just accepted, but *expected*.

She had an overwhelming sense of being part of something bigger. Right now, on this Friday night, in pubs, bars, clubs, all over the country, the same thing was happening over and over. A million different iterations, yes, but all underpinned by the same essential force: *boy meets girl*. She had been the girl in that natural order before, and now she would be again. Tonight was surely proof of her natural aptitude for attracting the opposite sex – she hadn't even been trying and look what had happened! Stuart was turning back, grasping his stocky black Guinness and the clear, ladylike cylinder of her own drink. Above the bar, the clock showed a full hour to go before closing – plenty of time to glean even more details about him. She sat up straight in readiness for his return, shaking out her hair so that it fell elegantly over her shoulder.

11

Driving to Mulbrook gym, Jo realised she had no idea where her membership card was – it had been months since she'd used it. At the next red light, she rummaged through the Carhartt messenger bag, which currently served as her 'handbag'. By the time she'd located the card in a triple-zipped annex she swore she'd never seen before, the lights had changed, and the car behind was honking.

'Hold onto your knickers, you impatient asshole.' She moved off too quickly to check the identity of the honker, so it could just as easily have been 'your Y-fronts' or 'your boxers' or 'your thong'. It was a point that Louise would certainly have clarified: she'd always insisted on getting a long, hard look at anyone who dared to criticise Jo's driving, even when Jo, who wasn't a natural behind the wheel, was at fault. At the slightest beep or flash, Louise would declare the other driver *a flatulent old codger who thinks his Padre Pio sticker confers god-given rights* or *a loboto-mom in a breeder-mobile full of bawling sprogs*, or even shout out of the window at someone who had dangerously cut into their lane, *it's an indicator, not a vindicator, you Mercedes micropenis!*

Jo had always taken these passenger-seat ejaculations as a sweet sign of Louise's loyalty; it was only during the ugly episode in Edgeworthstown that Jo herself had finally become the victim of such vicious epithets. Turning off the engine in the gym carpark, her head now echoed with the cruellest and catchiest insult from that evening – *narcissistic nerd.*

She stared dismally at the windowless gym-wall for a minute, and then, with a sudden rush of resolve that today wasn't going to be about Louise, she jumped out and slammed the door, trapping the negative memories inside. Boldly grabbing her gym bag, she walked towards the entrance.

It was hard to feel down on this autumnal morning, anyway. In the limpid blue chill, the sun shone like a bright, beneficent ulcer, setting off the copper in Louis Muldoon's beech hedging. She was suddenly lifted by a sense that tonight would work out well: her wallflower-worries yielded to a glimpse of herself as the centre of attention, of others vying to chat to this cute, witty girl, furious they'd never met her before. But then the fantasy faded and her anxiety returned.

The fancy glass door at Mulbrook was ridiculously heavy; not wanting to appear weak to the person coming in behind her Jo gave it a shove with the flat of her hand.

'Like a workout in itself, isn't it?' the girl remarked as she accepted the glassy weight with comparative ease. Jo twisted around in the lobby, her legs colliding with her own gym bag. She must have looked puzzled, because the girl added, 'The door, I mean. Heavier than most of the weights in there.'

'Oh yeah, mad, isn't it?' said Jo, taking in the attractive early-thirties face and the tanned athletic tallness, the hoodie and tracksuit bottoms. Before Jo could think of something slightly less inane to add, the girl had already bounded towards the reception; a moment later the penduluming ponytail was disappearing through the dressing-room doors.

Jo continued to the desk. The boyish sportiness had pinged her gaydar, but the 'gym-look' had caused false positives in the past, when she'd mistakenly assumed vests, runners, baseball caps and bare ring-fingers were lesbian-signifiers, rather than merely the prerequisites for exercise. She'd seen enough cute tomboys transmogrifying into frilly feminine creatures in front of gym mirrors to know one couldn't assume. Besides, in school it had always been the most boy-hungry girls who'd looked the best in their sports gear.

As she scanned her card, she heard the second impertinent beep of the morning. The receptionist, who obviously made the most of the gym's sunbeds, consulted her computer. 'I'm afraid your membership expired two weeks ago.'

Jo caught sight of her own morose mugshot, which had the word EXPIRED – quite apposite, she thought – flashing in red above it. She might as well cut her losses, give up and head home. She should probably forget about tonight too; both the return to the gym and her plans for later had been based on a deranged faith that she could propel herself out of her current rut. Anyway, she didn't have the cash for annual memberships or nights out with strangers.

The receptionist blinked sympathetically. 'If money's an issue, we've started letting people pay by the month. A lot of students do it that way.'

'OK, stick me down for a month,' said Jo, passing her credit card. She could be in there ogling the fit girl while getting fit herself, or slouching around at home, enduring another empty weekend. And at least this meant that Louise's membership had expired too, so she would probably never bump into her here. Louise had been addicted to Mulbrook all summer, claiming she couldn't function without her five stepper sessions a week. Of course, Jo knew now that Louise's real impetus had been working up the perfect bedroom-body for her trysts with Tamara. Nowadays Louise probably frequented some fancy Ballsbridge gym. (Jo felt queasy at the thought of her and Tamara jumping out of the Mini in matching tracksuits and trading saucy winks between adjacent steppers.) Even still, it was prudent to find out for certain. As her credit card was being processed, she said casually, 'I must tell the friend who joined with me that her membership's up too. She mightn't have realised.'

'I can check if she's already renewed if you like.'

'Only if it's no trouble,' said Jo with a nonplussed shrug. 'Her name is Kelly. Louise Kelly.'

'Kelly ...' said the receptionist as she typed it in. Jo remembered how Louise had hated her own surname, thinking it banal and Oirish, saying that if Ireland ever did allow gay marriage, she would happily jettison Kelly in order to assume, what she called, the 'poetic gravitas' of Kavanagh.

The receptionist looked up. 'So, you'd better remind your friend she needs to renew too.'

'Oh, I certainly will,' said Jo, her toes uncurling in gratitude.

'Mind you,' said the girl peering at Louise's record. 'She hasn't been here since March so probably no point in her renewing!'

'M ... March?' said Jo, feeling the blood drain from her face. 'Oh really, are you sure?'

Still in her coat, Jo sat in the changing room, processing the shock like a winded Olympian who'd just come last. Her fingers flitted over her phone, wishing it weren't too early to tell Cillian what she'd just discovered. She was grateful that the fit girl wasn't here to witness this meltdown. Eventually she grew calm enough to put on her black Nike vest and capri pants (relics of her almost fetishistic addiction to buying gym gear back when she had money). Having accessorised with her MP3-player armband, weightlifting gloves and baseball cap, she left the changing room, catching her reflection in the mirror as she went. The Holiday Skin she'd applied last night made a nice change from her recent wanness and although only her arms and neck would be visible this evening, she'd gone to the trouble of applying it everywhere, just in case. She snorted at her own presumptuousness and went out into the gym.

The main hall of Mulbrook was a massive amphibious panopticon, the weights and cardio equipment encircling a twenty-metre swimming pool. Only a tiled, waist-high wall delineated the wet and dry areas, allowing exercisers to observe the swimmers, and the chlorine whiff to circulate to all. In the absence of windows, the lights were always kept low, perhaps to tactfully dull the skin of the reddening exerciser. It certainly wasn't to save on electricity bills; Louis 'The Tycoon' Muldoon never scrimped on anything. The radio playing on the PA system was loud and perpetually tuned to *DublinBeat FM* – a station recently bought by Louis, and whose family-friendly chatter, mainstream music and incessant adverts for various Muldoon businesses provided little by way of athletic inspiration. Jo pushed her headphones in, turned on one of Cillian's mixes, and began pedalling lightly on one the upright bikes; she was determined not to overdo it on her first day back. As her legs began to circulate, so did her eyes. She soon spotted the hot girl working hard on a stairclimber on the far side of the pool. Instantly, Jo's own legs redoubled their efforts on the pedals.

Voluntarily taking exercise was a relatively new thing for Jo, who had been terrible at all forms of sport at school. During PE, she would teeter in the corners of pitch, court or gymnasium, terrified of making a holy show of herself in front of attractive sporty classmates as they wove nimbly to the basketball net or made plucky runs down the wing of the hockey pitch, ponytails suspended horizontally behind. She found herself bonding with the other sports-defectors, all cool, disaffected rebels who made no effort at anything in school. But for Jo PE was the *only* class where she didn't excel, and the teachers certainly knew it. In sixth year, Sister Brigid had granted her an unprecedented dispensation to cease PE altogether, because the school's great white skinny hope needed every available minute to study and make the Sacred Faith Convent just as proud as when the first XI had won the Senior Hockey Cup.

The school did indeed have its day of glory: soon, their six-hundred-point student was walking across the four-hundred-year-old cobblestones of Trinity, gulping at the blackened granite, the statue-studded lawns, the fabled campanile, and making her way, vibrating with anxiety and excitement, down to the School of Medicine.

If she'd been under pressure to perform at school, then this escalated tenfold at college, where she faced a completely different calibre of classmate. The opportunity for distraction unfortunately escalated too, because the whole campus was teeming with gorgeous, intelligent, interesting young women. Whenever Jo caught herself daydreaming of an attractive classmate in her lab coat, or a grungy girl she'd seen reading Nietzsche in The Buttery, or a sexily sweaty tennis player darting around Botany Bay, she had no option but to reach for her heaviest medical textbook and use it to bash her futile fantasies on the head.

It was only the following summer that she found the headspace to admit to herself what her feelings about girls over the years actually *meant*; she whispered *I am gay* repeatedly into her pillow, until one sleepless September night she realised she must find a way to say the same three little words to somebody else. Up until then her lack of interest in the opposite sex had always been indemnified by her dedication to her studies; nobody ever suspected. By the time that summer had ended, and before she had worked out exactly what she might *do* about being gay, the academic pressure of second year had already piled up. With so many new modules, the last thing she needed was to take on an additional voluntary subject – that of her own sexuality – with its terrifying, potentially volatile, experiments, and worse still its practical exams, which she would abysmally flunk due to her lack of experience. It was a ludicrous notion anyway – she had never witnessed a gay male, much less a lesbian, doctor in real life; even on *ER*, Kerry Weaver, with her internalised homophobia and bigoted colleagues was hardly an uplifting role model.

Jo had also started to worry that there was something terribly disingenuous about being a lesbian doctor – it didn't seem fair that someday she would palpate the bodies of female patients who didn't know she was gay, and even more underhand to examine a woman who had specifically requested a female doctor. She eventually came to the distressing but practical realisation that being gay and being a doctor must, by necessity, be mutually exclusive vocations. It was then that she decided to focus on being a doctor, a decision that had seemed to work brilliantly, until everything unravelled – quite spectacularly – bang in the middle of the second-year exams.

Jo finished on the bike and moved to the weights area, which despite her slim body's inability to build muscle, was her favourite bit of the gym. She loved the butch, pumped-up mood there and enjoyed feeding off the energy of the men as they clanked and cursed and blew out their cheeks. Today she started at the shoulder press, selecting the lightest plate, relieved that the fit girl was too far away to see.

Pushing the paltry weight with all her strength, she noticed that the young guy on the pec deck opposite shared none of her obstacles to athletic progression. With every rep, his well-defined chest and deltoids contracted so divinely that she found herself staring. It was a pity that he had spoiled nature's beauty with such crap tattoos – Tupac in his badly drawn bandana looked like a comical lop-eared rabbit across his shoulder, clashing in both style and theme with the bold ogham strokes that ran the length of his arm. At one stage she caught him staring back; she gave a little smile and looked away. Louise often claimed to have been chatted up by men in the gym, and although, like her ex, Jo had no interest in them, it was nice to be considered for once. If she could be admired in her gym gear, then surely there was hope for tonight, when she'd be dressed up and have a fresh haircut. As she finished her third set, he got up from his machine and approached her. She felt sorry for his wasted errand. If he asked for her number she would say she was seeing someone else, but tell him that his muscles were fabulous all the same. She pulled out her headphones.

'Howaya,' he said in a Dublin accent as broad as his chest. 'C'mere, I see you done three sets of the same. But if you switch grips you can work different bits of your shoulder.'

'Right,' she said, crossing her arms across her boobs. Well, if he was going to patronise … She blinked up at him and said, 'So you're saying I should use this machine to work *all three heads of the deltoid*, then?' She stopped short of telling him that she'd once meticulously dissected all three heads on an actual cadaver named Seamus and that her chosen online moniker was in fact *Deltoideus*.

She presumed he would cut his losses, but he stayed and shook his head. 'This machine can only work the lateral and the anterior heads,' he said. 'To work the posterior head, you want a rear-delt fly.' He bent over, then raised his arms up and down, scrunching up the Tupac-rabbit. 'Now with this one,' he said, looking at her through his armpit, 'you gotta keep your upper arms perpendicular to your torso, otherwise you involve the lats and rhomboids, which means less contraction in the posterior delt.'

She could hardly argue when he had a body like that, and to her further irritation, everything he said sounded correct. 'Thanks,' she muttered. 'I'll try all those next time.' She needed to get away from him immediately anyway, because the fit girl was now approaching the weights area. Fearing a further dressing-down from himself (and how embarrassing if the girl were to witness!) Jo reluctantly went to a row of empty treadmills, where she started one up and began a sensibly paced run. The girl passed right in front of her on her way to the weights, not particularly noticing Jo, but looking even hotter (in both senses) than before, cedillas of damp hair on her nape and a patch of breakthrough sweat on her chest. But she had only gone past to refill her water bottle, and a moment later Jo gulped to see her coming back and taking the treadmill directly beside her one, despite the four other free machines.

Jo pretended not to notice her arrival, but she was baffled by the crowding behaviour. The girl had seemed eager to talk at the door, so could it be a blatant come-on? Or was she someone who performed better with company, or worse still, competition? Whichever reason, there was now an onus on Jo to run well. And not just well but *better* than she'd run before. It didn't matter that she hadn't been on a treadmill in three months. It didn't matter that the furthest she had ever run was 1.81 kilometres or that her legs already felt heavy from the exercise bike. No, right now she must simply obey the imperative printed on her Nike vest and *JUST DO IT*.

She watched surreptitiously as the girl input her age (31), weight (53 kg) and pace (8.5 km per hour – reassuringly the same as Jo's), and started to run. At first their footfall on their respective conveyor belts was out of phase, like a learner-DJ trying to beat-match. But as time wore on, their respective rhythms gradually fell into step, until eventually Jo noticed, with a little smile to herself, that their movements had completely synchronised. From that moment on, every twin stride sounded as a unified rubbery thud, while their respective elbows pistoned in stereo, like the wheel-rods on either side of a steam train.

Locked in this sexily tacit tandem, they ran on for a while. Jo had never felt this good on a treadmill and couldn't believe it when the screen showed completion of her first kilometre. Each machine was fitted with a TV branded with the Muldoon Electronics logo. Neither Jo nor her travelling companion had switched on theirs, but Jo did have her music. After the tricky insertion of headphones into her ears while keeping pace, she was soon listening to another of Cillian's techno mixes. The first track had a gorgeously portentous beat that sent a shiver up Jo's spine – she only wished her neighbour could hear it too, so that its stimulating kick would add yet another dimension to their shared experience.

Before long, the screen was showing two kilometres, further than Jo had ever run. By now her body was starting to feel the pressure, but she distracted herself by wondering about her companion – what her name might be, where she lived, what her job was. She had a flash of the two of them kissing in the changing rooms afterwards, banging against lockers in a wordless mess of heavy breaths and Lycra. She would run her fingers up the girl's top and arrest the rivulets of sweat that – if she were as hot as Jo right now – must be streaming down her back. They would peel off each other's gym gear under cascading water in the showers.

Jo's capacity for fantasy might be limitless but her lung capacity was not; as she reached the three-kilometre mark, her breathing had become so laboured that she could hear it over the techno. She dreaded to think how it must sound to her headphone-less friend. Her legs were stinging and heavy; she had to will her swollen feet consciously into every step, afraid that at any moment they might mulishly give up. Even a half-missed stride would have dire consequences. For two full minutes she eyed the red STOP button, knowing that pressing it would shatter their silent contract. It would also betray the fact that, despite Jo's good runners, gym gloves and technical clothing, she wasn't particularly fit at all. Still, it was less ignominious to stop this madness now than to falter and be summarily dumped off the belt. As her hand finally reached for the button, the girl looked – briefly, but definitely – over, as though to say *don't you dare.* Jo diverted her hand to her water bottle, took a glug and ran on, her legs and lungs instantly invigorated by that stern, sexy look.

She'd never dreamed of running four kilometres in one day, let alone in one go, but here it was, incontrovertibly illuminated on the screen, and fast increasing too … 4.01 … 4.02. As she tore along the belt, the ensuing endorphin rush responded in spades, causing her to give more again – it was an infinite win-win cycle! She had felt mild exercise-induced wellbeing before, but never the euphoria that was mounting now, erasing all pain, making her weightless, delegating every effort, even her breathing, to some force far beyond herself. Despite the heat, she was shivering deliciously, the hairs erect on her hot skin. The sweat that trickled into her eyes was soon rinsed away by tears of joy, joy that after months of feeling awful, she could now feel like this.

As her efforts grew progressively easier, the music was doing just the opposite; the track coming through was the hardest and heaviest so far – sinister synths lurked on the outskirts of a bassline so huge she was surprised the swimming pool wasn't rippling in sympathy. This music, oh this music. It was a primeval call to arms, and more importantly – Jo smiled at her own clever joke – to legs! She would have to tell Cillian that one. She would have to tell *everyone*. She would write a column on runner's high so that others could experience this. She cranked up the volume, grabbed her bottle and shot more water into her mouth.

When her new friend upped her speed in a series of increments to nine, ten, and then eleven kilometres per hour, Jo lunged for the button and mirrored each increase. Somewhere in the blur beneath, her legs duly answered these unprecedented questions. Now she was running faster *and* further than she ever had before. The thrill inspired her to go one more: she threw down the twelve-kilometres-per-hour gauntlet with a grimacing smile.

4.89 … 4.90 … 4.91. The display dissolved before her eyes.

She was on a long, empty road with a distant white horizon. She looked around for Louise, only to remember passing her out miles ago, on a hill littered with the sticky detritus of their life together. It had been so hard to get up that killer hill. Jo had thought at times she would surely never make it, but she had dug deep and she had succeeded. She had pushed through the pain, pushed on from Louise and was now where she deserved to be – striding effortlessly across this ecstatic plateau.

The tune was rising to a climax now, the electronic elements melding together in beautiful confusion.

The white horizon sizzled in the distance. She eyed it defiantly and strode on.

Step after step after step. She was strong. She was unstoppable. She was finally free of Louise.

And this … well, this was just the beginning.

Sitting in the car, she rang Cillian, whose nasality suggested he was still in bed. 'Wake up, you slattern,' she said. 'I've major news from the gym, where I've just been killing myself, incidentally.'

'Don't tell me,' he said. 'You walked in on two sweat-drenched muscle-studs barebacking in the sauna?'

Jo snorted. 'This is Mulbrook, not *The Swimming-Pool Library*. Not that you'd know what a real-life gym is like. Anyway, I've just discovered that Louise hasn't been here since March.'

She could hear him sitting up against the pillows. 'Well, so much for her beloved stepper. I think we can all guess where she was raising her heart rate instead.'

'I know. Can you believe it?'

'Course I can,' he said with a snappy laugh. 'The bitch was hoodwinking you so adeptly on everything else, so why not throw in the gym too?' Jo heard the self-congratulatory click of his cigarette lighter, followed by an even smugger inhalation.

She rolled her eyes in the rear-view mirror, which was steamed up from her body heat. She'd been doing so much tongue-biting at all these glib *told-you-so's* lately, but after her heroics on the treadmill she was finally ready to confront him. 'Are you ever going to stop loving this, Cillian?' she asked.

'Loving what?'

'Reminding me what an awful person Louise is and what a naive eejit I was not to realise. Message duly received, thank you.'

He went quiet for a moment, then let out a sigh. 'You're no eejit, Jo. But it's hard *not* to feel vindicated when all my inconvenient truths have turned out to be true and I've got my best friend back.'

'I won't be your best friend for long if this keeps up.'

'OK, I admit I've spent a bit too long in the gloat-zone. But henceforward I shall remain resolutely mute on the subject of Loucifer.'

'Thank you,' Jo said. 'I just want to forget about her now.'

'Which is precisely why tonight's so important,' he said with a fresh burst of energy. 'You better still be going?'

'Can't say I'm relishing the thought of socialising with a bunch of saddos who have to resort to meeting friends on the internet instead of in real life.'

'The internet *is* real life, Jo.'

'What if someone I know sees me at it? The shame!'

'Going to a meet is actually cool nowadays. Look, it'll be good to put a face to the people you've been chatting with, like that interesting girl … Polly?'

'Pollymath. With two L's.'

'See. She even has an intelligent username.'

'She hasn't put up a profile picture, though, so she's potentially hideous. But at least I can talk to her while the others continue their *Angelina vs. Aniston* debate. Oh, and there's another girl, Ericaceous, coming too. Dry and wry. Knows a lot about indie music.'

'See, you've nothing to lose by going.'

'OK, I'll go, but only if you promise you'll rescue me if it all goes pear-shaped? You could just pretend to bump in to me in the bar and—'

'You've got to do this by yourself, Jo. Anyway, I'm busy tonight.'

'Oh? Ordered something in from Gaydar?'

'No chance. I've precisely two weeks to get my records sorted for Helium. Anyway, the only man I can think about right now is Liam. I've decided to just come out and ask him if he's gay at the next book club and—'

'Shush a sec,' said Jo, staring out the windscreen. 'This hot sporty girl's just come out into the carpark. We ran for miles beside each other in this sexily competitive silence.'

'Sounds like *Personal Best!*'

'Every time I increased my speed, she did too. But I drifted into oblivion, and when I opened my eyes, she'd gone. I suppose she wanted to concede before I went any faster.' Jo watched the girl bending over her car boot. 'Jesus, that arse in those tracksuit bottoms … she's taking out shopping bags, she must be heading across to the supermarket.'

'So now's your chance, then.'

'Eh, I look like a radish and I don't even know if she's gay.'

'Just leave a note with your name and number on her windscreen. If she likes you, she'll text. If not, then nothing to worry about.'

'Until the next time I see her here.'

'Grow some *cojones*, Jo. I'd never get laid if I didn't put my pride on the line. You need to get your girl-loins stirring again. And this one sounds so much more your type than Louise who was hardly … oops, sorry, I've forgotten my promise already.'

But Jo didn't mind. She was staring after the girl's flared back as she jogged (how did she still have energy?) out of the carpark. 'You're so fucking right for once, Cillian,' she said. 'I need to start making starts.'

'Now's your chance to be with that athletic hottie you've always dreamed about.'

She caught her own eye in the mirror. 'OK, I'm gonna do it,' she said. 'But quickly, I've the hairdressers at eleven and the beautician at twelve … ' Cillian was laughing. 'What's so funny?' she asked.

'Strange to make so much effort for a *bunch of saddos*,' he said.

'I needed it all done anyway.'

'Yeah, yeah. Right, enjoy your meet and don't dare be texting me. Your new lez-be-friends need your full attention.'

'I promise, teacher. Ring you tomorrow for the post-mortem. Enjoy your night in with the vinyl.'

'I'd rather it was latex with Liam than vinyl on my lonesome, but what can you do?'

12

At the first whoosh of the hoover, Rob sprang from the sofa, splashing pomegranate juice onto his pyjama top. He wondered where to hide. It was already too late to sneak back to his bedroom or even the bathroom, so instead he went out to the balcony, sliding the door behind him to trap the racket of the vacuuming inside. It was a freezing afternoon; the air pricked his bare arms and ankles, but far better to shiver out here than endure another of Orlando's Saturday-afternoon cleaning sprees. Today's spree was likely to be particularly vicious too, because it was obvious from Orlando's mood that he'd lost his volleyball match that morning.

Rob sipped his juice and gazed at the block of identical flats opposite, which spoiled what would otherwise have been a moderately good view from here on the fourth floor, over Ealing and beyond. He was always on the lookout for eye-candy on the balconies. He never saw any, especially not the flat directly opposite – it was inhabited by a short, rotund Eastern European, who now staggered out wearing only underpants and the Bluetooth headset whose mouthpiece was forever buried in his jowl. His moobs drooped and quivered as he bent to light a cigarette. One of the bedrooms in his flat always had its curtains closed, and Rob liked to imagine that something illicit was going on in there, especially as the man was constantly shouting into his headset, but in reality he knew the unopened curtains were more likely a symptom of his neighbour's general slovenliness.

Despite the double-glazed door, Rob could still hear the hoover as Orlando manoeuvred it around. Rob hated the sound almost as much as he hated Orlando's voice nowadays. He couldn't believe he'd once been able to hear that voice without wanting to punch its owner. But things had been so very different at the start, when the pair of polite and respectful strangers (Orlando worked in the same language school as one of Rob's exes, who had introduced them) had moved in to the flat together, each keen to make a good impression and make the arrangement a success.

Orlando, with his loud voice, mop of quivering brown ringlets and love of purple, had also displayed his quieter, thoughtful side to Rob soon after moving in. By the third week he was listening, his plucked brow creasing with empathy, to Rob's complaints about having to work so hard and for such long hours. Even if it was ten at night, Orlando would throw on his mauve apron and lovingly cook up some of his *deliziosa* tarragon pasta for Rob, who hadn't had a minute to eat all day. After supper, he would give Rob one of his famous shoulder massages (beloved of the boys on the volleyball team) to melt away the workday stress. In return for such kindnesses, Rob began to develop a genuine interest in Orlando's hobby, especially the results of the weekly matches. He would wait nervously in the flat on Saturdays for Orlando's return, ready to assume the appropriate mood at a moment's notice. On the days when Orlando strolled in chest-first, belting out verses of some triumphal Italian tune, Rob would high-five him and want to know all about the match. Orlando's stories of the serves and the settings, the crucial digs, kills and spikes, were enacted so emphatically that Rob often felt like he'd actually been on the winning team himself. He would go about the rest of his day basking in reflected sporting glory.

But although the Lambda Wings were a talented team, they didn't win every Saturday. There had been other days when the front door slammed and Orlando's sports bag was sent skidding on its studs across the hall. Rob would rush to make a cup of English breakfast tea with three sugars and a soothing dash of Rescue Remedy. He would sit with Orlando in the kitchen, listening sympathetically to his rants about a teammate who was a *testa di cazzo* for turning up hungover, or a homophobic *stronzo* of a referee who'd been biased in favour of the straight opponents.

It was hard to pinpoint exactly when their friendship had begun to turn sour, but it had mainly been over housework, or rather Orlando's ridiculous obsession with it. Nowadays their only conversation involved Orlando complaining about Rob's mess; in return, Rob took tremendous pleasure in neglecting to make any volleyball-related enquires on a Saturday. He couldn't stomach the sight of post-match Orlando anyway – the zip of his purple team tracksuit pulled down to reveal all three hairs on his chest – a chest which, despite all the exercise, was as puny as a boy's and certainly nothing to show off.

Orlando came into the sitting room, yanking the hoover behind him like a disobedient dog. He began jabbing at imaginary patches of dust in every conceivable place, even behind the TV, where no one ever went. Still unaware of being watched, he attached the pointed nozzle and knelt down to run it through every last furrow in the rug.

As Orlando stood up again. he spotted Rob through the window and gave a scoffing laugh, as if to say only the lowest of the low would sit outside in pyjamas instead of helping. Rob looked away with narrowed eyes, reminding himself that he and Michael would have the flat to themselves tonight; he'd overheard Orlando on the phone yesterday, arranging a trip to the cinema with one of his nerdy friends. Michael was looking forward to their night in too. He had texted Rob to tell him two things – firstly that he was bringing over the DVD of *An Ideal Husband,* and secondly that he was incredibly horny, as due to their respective work and Joan commitments, they hadn't seen each other in over a week. Rob replied saying he liked both bits of news, then rushed to read the film's IMDb reviews so he could appear 'quite the incisive critic', as Michael would say. It was great to be able to worry about normal stuff again, like what clever things to say after a film or play, rather than being strangled by guilt over a silly drunken fumble. He couldn't wait to have his own *Ideal Husband* beside him on the candlelit sofa tonight.

By the time he dared to glance back inside, Orlando had gone. He always attacked the tasks in the same order – next would be the bleach-smell and squeaking from the bathroom, followed by the mopping, when Rob would be confined to his bedroom for an hour lest he make a footprint anywhere. He decided to slink back to his room now, while Orlando's head was down the loo, but as soon as he came in from the balcony he could tell, from the very distant drone of the hoover, that something was wrong.

He ran through the flat and flung open the door to his own bedroom.

For a moment he said nothing, just watched the tracksuited arse bobbing up and down behind his bed.

'Orlando,' he yelled above the noise, which had suddenly become high pitched because something (Rob dreaded to think what) must be choking up the hose. 'Orlando!' He stamped on the cord, popping the plug from the socket. Orlando jumped up. Poking like a flag from the nozzle of the hoover-pole were Rob's long-lost red aussieBums. The fact that Rob's favourite underpants had finally been found did nothing to lessen his fury. 'What the fuck are you doing?'

Orlando gulped. 'I thought you were out on balcony.'

'So you decided to sneak into my room … ?'

'But it's so full with dust.' Orlando's hand closed around his throat. 'My asthma. I can't breathe.'

'Asthma?' said Rob, wheezing with disbelief. 'Since when do you have asthma?'

'Since the dust comes out of this room and infect the whole apartment!'

'Oh please, what's this, *Revenge of the killer dust?*'

Orlando turned to the window and paused, his still-damp ringlets vibrating with irritation. 'You know, when first I moved in, I thought he OK, this Rob, he is overworked, he is stressed, he has no energy for cleaning. But now …' He spun around and hurled the hoover pole onto the bed. 'Now I know the real story. Rob is filthy. Rob is lazy. Rob is not tired, he just like to sit in his pyjamas all day!'

'I actually came in to get dressed, but then I found a *trespasser* in my room.'

Orlando looked scoffingly at his watch. 'Dressed so early? Are you going out? Out of this filthy home?'

'I'm not going out, as a matter of fact. Michael's coming over, we're having a nice night in – *just the two of us.*'

'So you wanna spend time make yourself look good, smell nice, style your hair,' said Orlando, with a nod to the crowded shelf of gels and aftershaves. (Admittedly some of the lesser-used bottles did suddenly look rather dusty.) 'Meanwhile the apartment is a *peeg-*sty!'

Rob had a vision of ramming the wide-shouldered Dior Homme bottle right into Orlando's left nostril. 'There's nothing wrong with looking nice for my boyfriend,' he said through gritted teeth. 'Then again, you wouldn't know about that. Maybe if you had a shag now and again you wouldn't be so sexually frustrated and want to clean all the time.'

Orlando folded his arms with an exasperated sigh. 'I don't know how this polite, lovely guy Michael put up with someone like you.'

Rob had to laugh. Orlando always fawned over Michael when he came over – it was all *hello Michael, I agree Michael, would you like a glass of this Pinot Grigio Michael?* Little did Orlando know how much Michael loved to mock the curly-headed castrato. Rob nodded towards the door. 'Just get out of here.'

'With pleasure.'

Rob stood shaking beside the bed for a couple of minutes, listening to Italian profanities coming from the kitchen, as the dishwasher was violently emptied. They'd had arguments before but never like this. He pulled his underpants from the pipe and used them to dust off some cologne bottles. A few minutes later, he rushed to listen at the door, because Orlando had stopped his clattering and was now on the phone.

'I don't feel well … just a *viroos* … let's see the movie another night.'

Rob nearly crushed the glass Gaultier bust in his grip. 'You lying, *sabotaging* little bastard,' he muttered. 'Bet you'll make an ultra-nuisance of yourself tonight too, just to spite me.' He ground his forehead into the doorframe, while all his sexy candlelit plans for the evening were snuffed out in an instant.

'Effing madness again tonight,' said the driver, with a shake of his grey head, as the taxi crawled along Parliament Street.

'It's busy all right,' said Jo in a small voice. She was sitting rigidly in the back, observing the night-crowds with agitated detachment. She couldn't see one person who was on their own like she was. No, everybody was paired with a lover or a friend, or part of a bigger gang, bursting with banter and laughter and cajolery. She had felt exactly like this before: a few months after dropping out of medicine, she'd forced herself to venture alone to Denny's. It had been her first time ever in a gay bar and it had terrified her. The clientele was mostly men, except for a handful of women at the pool table, all of whom looked like men and all of whom very much liked the look of Jo. She'd left without even finishing her drink.

The driver was sighing. 'Where's all this Celtic Tiger shenanigans going to end, I wonder? I had an economist chap in the car yesterday who said all our spending and borrowing is hurtling us towards a crash.' He gestured out the window where a group of lads were whooping and taking swigs from a Grey Goose bottle. 'But no one wants to know, especially not the youngfellas and youngwans – sure they're all off their faces on cocaine anyway.'

'Terrible, isn't it?' said Jo half-heartedly, as she jealously watched two girls greet one another with makeup-sparing air-kisses outside The Oak. The driver's incessant moaning was beginning to grate, but she still wished she could stay in the car all night while he drove around town: listening to him would be a breeze in comparison to the ordeal she was letting herself in for – an ordeal that, she reminded herself with renewed anxiety, was due to start in a matter of minutes.

His talk of coke had reminded her that there was half a wrap, a relic of her and Louise's last big night out, hidden somewhere in the medicine drawer back home. She hadn't thought of it in months but regretted not bringing it; a little line in the loos of The Medusa would have provided a confidence boost before the meet. As the driver counted her change she checked her hair in the mirror. She loved what the stylist had done – the side-fringe swept an attractive line just above her freshly shaped eyebrows.

The October night was clear and sharp, but her trembling was independent of the cold. As she turned onto George's Street, a pair of kind, distinguished eyes met her own. She looked back at the never-for-sale tapestry portrait of Mary Robinson in the window of the Persian rug shop. The piece, so at odds with the Middle Eastern exotica surrounding it, had been a source of hilarity on many nights out, but tonight Jo was grateful for Mary's mollifying eyes – they seemed to say, *Be brave, everything will be OK.*

The little rush of courage only lasted a moment, however. Turning onto George's Street, Jo had a sickening premonition of Louise turning up to The Medusa. While Louise had always disliked the place as much as Jo, her current love-buzz might predispose her to its bouncy, upbeat ambience. Jo imagined the double-ignominy of being seen at a meet, wearing one of Louise's left-behind Desigual t-shirts. But it was highly unlikely that Tamara would risk being spotted out in a gay bar, even if she and Louise were there under the pretence of fag-hagdom.

'Evening,' muttered the bouncer from beneath the turned-up collar of a black coat that seemed as heavy and long as the hours ahead. Jo paused in the dim antechamber between the two sets of doors and willed her limbs to stop quivering. The slanting bristles in the coir mat urged her feet forward, but she dreaded the cringeworthy first contact: *excuse me, is this the meet?* Even worse if she made an erroneous approach to a naturally occurring girl-gang, whose polite titters would explode into guffaws as she retreated, having realised her mistake.

Setting her expression to neutral nonchalance, she pushed open the door, ready to survey and be surveyed. But there wasn't a soul at any of the front tables – she was a terrified actress braving the stage only to find the auditorium deserted. There were people sitting further back, but as she walked down the cathedralesque length of the place, she saw they were all male and mixed gatherings. She shuddered with the relief of postponement.

A pint of Smithwicks in hand, she contemplated her next move under the cobalt-LED eyes of the bronze Medusa bust upon the bar. *A gaze to petrify the gays*, as Cillian had quipped the first time he and Jo had wandered agog around Dublin's newest gay bar. Now, four years later, the place retained the same gaudy gestalt, purple flock wallpaper forming the backdrop to everything from elegant gilt mirrors to gurning gargoyles to a massive screen-printed array of Medusas, all Warholised in different colour-clashes. Every available nook was filled with some form of curio, too. A suit of Arthurian armour guarded the stairs, its lance poised to disembowel drunken punters who got too close. Elsewhere were Turkish vases big enough to contain whole families of faggots and from whose necks belched flamingo-pink pampas grass. Even the entrance to the toilets was embellished – by a 1960s curly-wigged mannequin in an Irish dancing outfit, her shin raised and slanted, as though performing a particularly vigorous *haon-dó-trí*.

But despite its kooky, nonconformist décor, The Medusa had descended into a den of the generic soon after opening. The mediocrity of its clientele, music policy and mood meant that Jo and Cillian – and later, Jo and Louise – had learned to avoid it except when it was a necessary evil in an evening's plans.

Jo perched on a barbed-wire effect barstool picking at the logo on her glass. Ten interminable minutes went by in which there was no arrival of any potential meet-attendees. Just as she was concluding that she must be the only LesbianInDublin stupid enough to honour her online promise, she heard a burst of female laughter from the mezzanine above, an area she'd presumed empty because no one went up there until at least midnight. She set down her glass and listened. The laughter came again.

It could only mean one thing. She turned to Medusa, allowing herself to be held in the piercing blue gaze for a long moment. Then, shaking off her petrification, she got up and made her way towards the stairs.

14

As the credits rolled on *The Bourne Identity*, Rachel took a sip from the bottle and rested it back on Alysha's thigh, which was draped over her own. 'I think the poor dehydrated Alygator needs more water,' she said.

Alysha contemplated the Volvic. 'Do I have to?'

'You know what Sensei Kev always says about pee being pale and plentiful!'

'Mine's definitely plentiful anyway,' said Alysha. 'I missed all Jason Bourne's best bits thanks to trips to the flipping loo.'

'Then again,' said Rachel with a laugh, 'no amount of Matt Damon's *ever* enough, is it?'

It was amazing: it had been less than twenty-four hours since she had met Stuart, or rather *Stuart Adam Gaskell*, and already so much had changed for the better. Not only did she feel qualified to talk about men again, but here she was, calmly curled up under the legs of a hungover Alysha, without a shred of guilt or deceit. She couldn't have known or hoped that her first night in The Mill would prove such a watershed, but she'd woken up that morning feeling that a wet sponge had wiped clean the slate of past mistakes, including the stubbornly dusty edges that had been niggling her lately. She would never dwell on any of that nonsense again; she was completely back to normal.

As Alysha sat up to drink, her legs bore down even more heavily on Rachel's. Despite being trapped, Rachel had never felt as free inside the flat. She smiled at Alysha's teal toenails. The lovely moment would be repeated again and again: the innocuous innocence of two girls sprawling in front of a romcom, chatting about men like Matt Damon, and of course Stuart, who thanks to his performance last night was the *real* star of the moment.

A perfume ad inspired Alysha's next enquiry. 'I bet sexy Stu smelled nice?'

'So many questions!' Rachel said, giving her friend's toes a squeeze. In truth, she was delighted by the inquisition; it was helping her recall details she'd forgotten in her original report, delivered to a drunk, disbelieving Alysha as they'd ambled home arm-in-arm last night. 'His aftershave was spicy, like cinnamon … but still quite masculine,' said Rachel. 'Mind you, I didn't even notice it until we were …' She turned away with a sheepish smirk.

'Until you were rolling around outside on that picnic table?'

'We were merely leaning.'

'It was like the piano scene from *Pretty Woman*! So much for me worrying the new girl had gotten herself locked in the loos.'

'I apologise unreservedly for my behaviour,' said Rachel. 'Kissing men outside pubs isn't something I'd normally do.'

'Whatever,' said Alysha. 'Bet you can't wait to tell your girlfriends back home you've pulled a London hottie.'

'I know,' said Rachel. She had let Alysha believe she was still in regular contact with several old friends, though in truth her only link with Newcastle was a perfunctory weekly call with her fretful aunt Cassie, who wanted reassurance that Rachel hadn't fallen under the wheels of a London bus or been knifed by a passing gang.

Alysha nodded at Rachel's phone. 'Do you think he'll text tonight or tomorrow?'

'Who knows, Alysha? He might not contact me at all!' Rachel did have a distinct feeling that he *would* be in touch, and soon too. As they'd parted outside the pub, Stuart had recited her number three times to ensure he'd saved it correctly.

Alysha shook her head. 'I can tell he's not one of those bastards who never calls.' She balanced her chin dreamily on the remote control. 'Still cannot *believe* he bought us those drinks. I've been going to that Mill for nearly two years and never got so much as a glass of tap-water from a man.'

'I have a little confession,' said Rachel, wincing. 'The first drink he bought me was lemonade. I was going easy because of the tournament.'

'Lemon-bloody-ade for Sensei's little pet? You are so lame, girl. Thank god sexy Stu didn't find out.' She reached beneath the mess of their legs and began to tickle Rachel. 'I might just have to tell him ...'

'Oh, don't you dare girl,' said Rachel, who was now laughing and squirming but making no real effort to escape because it was such good fun. 'Don't you bloody dare!'

15

'It's amazing how your tastes can change with your circumstances, too,' Jo was saying. 'I used to adore *Stories from the City*, but since splitting from my ex I can't bear the happy jangliness of "Good Fortune".'

Heather drained her Beamish and set her glass down on the cocktail table they'd been standing at for the past half hour. 'Jangly's an understatement!' she said with a low laugh. '*Stories* was always my least favourite PJ Harvey album, anyway. I maintain she was possessed by an insane love-high when she wrote it. Then again, as soon as something wins the Mercury I go off it, so it never stood a snowball's with me.'

'Ooh, harsh!' said Jo with a humorous grimace. 'The Mercury's hardly the Brits.'

Heather shook her head beneath the severe black stripe of her ultra-short fringe. 'Awards are all the same to me, Jo. People call me a music snob, but I'd rather be discerning than a member of the sheeple.' She gave a patronising nod to their left, where the dozen other members of the meet sat around a banana-shaped table.

Jo glanced over at the slanted backs, interested eyes and moving mouths – the group now reassuringly indistinguishable from any regular gathering in the busy bar. 'Ah, the girls aren't so bad,' she said. 'Mind you, it *was* funny when BánDearg got all indignant when you said that about Pink.'

'Indignant? I thought the little scut was going to attack me. Glassed to death by a baby dyke with a side-shave and a skinny tie. All because I said she was mad to pay two hundred for a concert ticket.' She rocked her glass. 'Anyway, time for another tipple methinks.'

'My round!' said Jo, who'd just finished her fourth.

'I'd recommend you go downstairs,' said Heather. 'The mezz bar's teeming with identikit twinks ordering cosmos. Oh, how I hate this horrible lair!'

Jo strode down the steps, her confidence so at odds with her initial wary ascent. The night was turning out so well that she was high on excited relief. Her gym-primed cheeks were rosy from the alcohol and the happy drama of it all. There'd been nothing to be scared about — despite their demographic differences, every single person in the group had a certain thing in common — they were all absolutely *lovely*.

At the start of the night Jo had been grateful to SilkenSorcha, a well-groomed brunette of thirty, who'd been mature enough to take on the role of facilitator. It was she who'd clocked Jo's arrival — she'd shot out to welcome the nervous newcomer with a comforting double-handshake, and then introduced Deltoideus, aka Jo, to the fold.

Jo had soon realised that *everyone* seemed anxious, with a couple of girls utterly at sea. It was hard to believe, given her peppy online incarnation as CraziJen, that Jennifer would be so terrified, but her voice had quivered when she spoke, and Jo had felt her feet worrying the floorboards under the table.

Then there was Slamantha. Online, the shaggy blonde sprinkled her posts liberally with smileys, but at first her face was like the nausea emoticon, the poor girl as green with fear as the pints of Fat Frog she was downing in a dipsomaniacal effort to buoy her confidence. The effort had patently paid off too, because now, two hours later, Slamantha was the liveliest of them all, holding the rapt attention of the graceful, red-tressed Rapunzel and the mid-forties, masculine ElderLemon.

But Jo soon discovered that the person she probably had most in common with was Heather. The sociology master's student had caused confusion after plodding up to the table in her vintage black dress and biker boots, because people had assumed from her online moniker Ericaceous that her name must be Erica. But Jo had got it, and loved the clever coded twist, explaining, 'Erica's the Latin for heather!'

Heather, taking off her coat, had registered the remark with an impressed little nod. Later, when the group discussion turned to the bar itself — which divided opinion greatly — Jo had borrowed Cillian's joke about Medusa's gays. Heather had cackled so heartily that her tongue piercing flashed and her boobs nearly heaved themselves free of her dress. The

Tintin-quiffed Dublinette and Pink's biggest fan, BánDearg, had giggled along politely, obviously not getting the joke.

As the night had worn on, Jo and the ebullient student had become detached from the main gang. At this adjacent table, they'd got stuck into a witty chinwag about all kinds of things – Jo couldn't even remember half the subjects they'd touched on. And best of all, although Heather was fascinating, and single – recently dumped by a bisexual ex who'd fallen for a man – Jo didn't fancy her and was therefore in full social freeflow without a smidge of attraction-anxiety.

Coming back with the drinks, Jo was surprised and flattered to see that Heather hadn't re-engaged with the others. She wiped the base of Heather's Beamish on a beermat and shook off her thumb. 'Sorry, that meniscus wasn't as resilient as I thought!'

Heather laughed. 'Obviously compromised by the vibrations of the music, if you could even call it music.' She glowered above, to where a speaker spewed out yet another Kylie dance-remix.

'It's getting louder *and* cheesier,' said Jo. The increased volume brought their heads closer together as the conversation turned to authors. As Heather extolled the virtues of Margaret Atwood (whose Booker Prize she was 'just about' able to overlook), Jo noticed Sorcha glancing over from the head of the main table. Jo caught her eye and grinned to show that, despite her physical distance, she still very much felt part of the meet. Sorcha's return smile was clipped, however, and was followed directly by a quick but critical flash of her immaculate eyebrows, as if to say that Jo and Heather's extended absence was being duly, and rather disappointedly, noted.

'Suppose we better head back to the others,' said Jo after a minute.

Heather snorted. 'You reckon?'

'I feel a bit bad, especially when they were so nice to me earlier.'

'But that's exactly the problem, Jo. They're all so bloody *nice*. And none more sickeningly so than that do-gooder SilkenSorcha. Oh look, now she's off on her rounds again. Who appointed her Head Girl for the evening anyway?'

They watched as Sorcha began a smiling trot round the table, handing a flyer to each girl. 'Wonder what those are?' said Jo.

'Probably invitations to a grooming class where you learn the secrets of hair as *glisteningly* healthy as hers. Oh, and the best way to starch your Ralph Lauren collars and steam-press your jeans. She's so perfect I bet she GHD's her pubes and all!'

'She is a bit preppy,' Jo conceded. 'But some of the others were nervous at first, she made them feel welcome.'

'And in so doing became an even more puketastically wholesome person,' said Heather with a laugh. When she saw that Jo wasn't laughing, however, she tucked in her chin. 'Be honest, Jo, I can tell that Sorcha and that lot aren't your kind of people. Am I right or am I right?'

Jo shrugged in a non-committal way and took a long swig of her beer, refreshed at her newfound reluctance to join in on the criticism. In the past she'd been quick to deem others as too boring to bother with, but recently she'd been more drawn to kindness and honesty. She couldn't imagine any of the meet-girls ever being as cruel as Louise; her ex had become a dirty yardstick against which even the most mundane person – as long as they were decent – could measure up well. 'Well, they mightn't be my usual kind of friends,' she said. 'But I don't want to insult them either. It's called a *meet*, not an *ignore*, after all.'

Heather leaned across the table and touched Jo on the arm. 'Look, I'm only here tonight because you, and to a lesser extent, Pollymath, were coming. The others were never of interest.'

'Right,' said Jo, aware of Heather's fingers, outstaying their welcome on her bare skin. She released herself with a questioning gesture. 'God, yeah, I wonder why Pollymath never showed up?'

'Who cares about that no-show?' said Heather. She gave Jo a slow, loaded look, that took in both of them and seemed to refer to some supposed intimacy. 'I'm glad she didn't come, if you know what I mean?'

'I wouldn't have minded meeting her in the flesh,' Jo piped brightly, unnerved by the suggestion that this was anything more than a friendly chat. She rushed on nervously. 'Do you remember that thread Pollymath started about the girls' scene being more of a scorority than a sorority, I thought that was brilliant.'

'Pollymath's certainly got a better command of the English language compared to that lot, but I have my suspicions about her. I can't put my finger on it – there's just *something* not right there …'

'Really?' said Jo, who was starting to feel that Heather, rather than just having exacting social tastes, was actually a bitter misanthrope, ready to find fault with everyone. Except Jo herself, of course. And it was clear that Heather, now swallowing her pint in a series of worrying Dutch-couragey gulps, had misinterpreted Jo's dam-burst of chat after so many lonely nights at home to be a come-on. Jo feared a drunken lunge any moment now, but as soon as Heather had drained the glass, her expression was draining as well. 'Oh great,' she said. 'Here comes the saccharine shepherdess.'

'Hello ladies!' Sorcha said, slipping a hand around each of their waists so that Jo could feel the hard nub of her cufflink in her side. 'How are we doing all the way over here?'

'Great thanks, Sorcha,' said Jo, as Heather stiffened and pushed her tongue stud out through the side of her clamped mouth, like a foreclosing full stop. Jo wanted to show that their separation from the group had been merely been happenstance, but it was hard when Heather seemed determined to portray the opposite.

'And are you getting on OK, Erica?' Sorcha asked.

The tongue stud was rapidly retracted, like a fly-catching toad. 'It's *Heather.*' Behind the cold correction, Jo could sense Heather's delight in causing Sorcha's sole social *faux pas* in an otherwise perfect performance.

Sorcha drew her hand to the neck of her blouse. 'My sincere apologies. I've so much going on that I got mixed up!'

'You have been busy,' said Jo, with a grateful smile.

'It's been a super-duper night so far though, hasn't it?' said Sorcha. 'And now we're all vamooskying to the girls' night in *El Magnate*, that sexy new club on Dame Street.' She took two flyers from the pocket of her pristine jeans. 'And if that's not temptation enough, this gets you two euro off admission.'

Before Jo had even read through the flyer, Heather was returning hers, like a restaurant customer handing back a disgustingly overpriced dessert menu. 'We'll pass, thanks,' she said. 'I mean, The Medusa's appalling, but it's a hell of a lot better than this ... *Miss*.'

'You've already been?' asked Jo, annoyed by Heather's inclusive refusal, and worried about being left with her here, unchaperoned.

'I don't need to, Jo. You can just tell by the stupid name it's going to be full of efforty trendykes trying to outdo each other. And if you thought the music here was bad ...'

'You're very critical for someone who's never actually been there,' said Sorcha, a bit crossly. 'And what's wrong with the name *Miss*?'

Heather gave a condescending chuckle. 'Well, there's the small matter of how feminists have been fighting for centuries to get the neutral *Mizz* accepted, only to have this shower come along and undo all their good work. Something *A-Miss* there methinks!'

Jo shrugged. 'Well, I'm willing to risk my feminist reputation.' She turned to Sorcha. 'Yeah, I'll come along thanks.'

Heather shook her head slowly. 'You'll hate it.'

'Can't hurt to try,' said Jo. No matter what *Miss* was like, it couldn't be as irritating or risky as remaining here. Anyway, the drinks part of the meet had gone so well that she was ready to push the social envelope a notch further.

'Fandabidozi!' said Sorcha, giving Jo a pat on the side. 'I'll tell the ladies to get their coats.' She turned to Heather. 'And thanks for coming tonight, *Erica*,' she said. 'It was marvellous to meet you.' Then, with a lustrous shake of her hair she left them, leaving Jo to smirkingly suspect that this time the misnomer hadn't been an accident, but rather a final, censuring goad.

'Did Heather not wanna come with us?' enquired Dublinette, as the gang meandered down the dark, bustling street.

'Yeah,' shouted Slamantha, giddy and gamine after a veritable colony of Fat Frogs. 'What happened to Horrible Heather?'

Dublinette reached across and slapped her on the arm. 'Don't tell everyone what we were calling her!'

Jo, who was walking confidently among the merry mob, laughed at the antics of the two youngest, blondest members of the group. Eager to avoid a Heather-style put down – even when the object of derision was the deserving Heather herself – she said diplomatically, '*Miss* isn't her bag, she only likes indie music.'

'I'll tell you what she likes,' said Slamantha, so loudly that the others, including Sorcha, turned back to look. 'She likes you, Jo.'

Jo shook her head. 'Nah …'

'Ah Jo, she totally wanted to lob the gob at ya,' said Dublinette, puckering out her lips comically. 'Amn't I right girls?' There was a chorus of 'yeahs' from everyone, except Sorcha, who kept her gaze firmly ahead, as though slightly upset. Jo remembered Sorcha's arm around her waist earlier, her glances from the other table, her kind attention. She couldn't help but wonder. 'But now,' continued Dublinette, 'we've saved you, dude!' She flung her brave little gay arms around Jo, who succumbed to the hug and laughed; it was crazy how much she was being touched by other people in a single night, especially when no one had come near her in months.

'Whoa, kids,' said ElderLemon, turning and tottering backwards on her the heels of her Doc Martens so that Jo felt even more the celebrity. (Jo's isolating stint at the other table had certainly bestowed a prodigal-son kind of advantage.) 'Maybe Jo liked Heather? Did you, Jo?'

'She's an intelligent girl, but not my type.'

'Told you!' said Slamantha, in a triumph of youthful savviness over elder wisdom.

BánDearg gave a sighing yawn. 'Enough already with the Heather talk, everyone.'

'Exactly,' said Jo. 'I haven't been to a lesbian club in two years. I'm actually quite excited.'

'Wait until you see all the dykecandy in here, Jo,' said Slamantha. 'You'll be so over your ex once you get the ride from some hot piece of puss-ay!' The others cheered and whooped, but it was unclear to Jo whether Sorcha's pained reaction was due to the crass language or the thought that Jo might hook up with someone other than her.

El Magnate on Dame Street had only opened recently, but the *Miss* collective had already wangled itself a monthly residence to host – as the flyer-concession Jo handed in at the desk proclaimed – *Dublin's hawtest night for gay girls & their male friends*. As the bouncer branded her hand with an inky MISS, Jo smiled to realise it was the second of Louis Muldoon's properties she had been in that day. There was something subversive about getting to work out, and then later play, in his rich, hetero-playboy world. As her group headed down the strip-lit walkway, towards the boom of the music, Jo could only hope that this Muldoon venue might facilitate a more successful lesbian adventure than the one in the gym carpark earlier.

Though Sorcha was right about *El Magnate* being sexy, it was not the suave interior that struck Jo the most but rather the sheer number of girls. It seemed that every young, trendy lesbian in the land and at least a hundred more besides, must be in here. Jo ground to a happy standstill. While her companions went to the bar or cloakroom, she sheltered by the cigarette machine to take it all in. How things had changed since she and Louise had last gone out with Sinéad and Sinéad to a night called *She-Bangers*, which resembled a community-hall disco: the beer sold in lukewarm cans, the lights too bright, the older clientele throwing off their fleeces to chug to the dreary disaster of the music. One night the DJ had seen fit to finish off with *Riverdance*, which had led to a rather unedifying dance floor invasion.

Tonight at *Miss*, however, it was not about wimmin, but very much about *girls*. They were everywhere – stuffed into candlelit rows on the minimalist couches, clinking shot glasses at the bar, standing in loose, chatty groups with drinks held against t-shirted torsos; there were even a few trailblazers swaying tastefully on the dance floor. As well as girls who were patently out on the pull, there were lots of lovers too: a pair of anaemic emos played handsie across a table, gazing into each other's blackened eyes. And posturing in heels and sheer dresses against one of the suede-covered pillars, a couple of Celtic tigresses regarded the scene coolly between straw-sips on their snipes of champagne, and lip-glossed kisses with each other.

Without a drink herself, Jo was content to continue drinking in the giddy vista for now. In any case, there was no hope of getting near the bar where a measly duo of barmen (the management must have wrongly predicted that women didn't drink as much as men), struggled to keep up with constantly renewing rows of customers. If the barmen had been looking forward to an easy night of observing girl-on-girl action, then they must be sorely disappointed – they wouldn't get a second to raise their heads!

A trio of girls in zingy-coloured t-shirts pushed past Jo on their way towards the smoking terrace. Though they didn't apologise, Jo couldn't help following them with her eyes. The one with the blonde spikes and boyish smile was cute, but Jo could tell by the silly slagging as they went up the stairs that she was one of those empty trendykes Heather had mentioned, the kind of girl who always found Jo's conversation too scientifically obscure or, when Jo attempted general chit-chat instead, too boringly obvious.

It was strange that, of all the girls present, Jo seemed to be the only one who was in any way fazed and amazed by the place: everyone else was too busy thoughtlessly enjoying themselves. The composite clamour of so many female voices drowned out the higher registers of the music, which to Jo's further astonishment, was cool vocal house being spun by an even cooler Black DJ, grooving fluidly round her booth in a backwards cap and oversized basketball vest.

'Well, things have certainly evolved on the lesbian scene since we were last out on it,' said Jo with an incredulous shake of the head. Mortified to realise her mistake, she checked to see if anyone had noticed her acting as though Louise was still by her side, like she always had been on nights out. Luckily everybody was too wrapped up in their own excitement to have noticed the wallflower in the borrowed top, talking tipsily to an invisible ex-girlfriend. She scanned the room but the meet crew had disappeared – in a matter of minutes, she'd been relegated from the centre of attention to an anonymous, ring-rusty gawker. She and Louise had always been each other's social saviours, but now she looked wearily into a future of having to make an unrelenting effort just to remain involved and relevant on nights out. She picked at a little rip in the neck of Louise's t-shirt (probably the result of tearaway sex with Tamara) and felt a sudden respect for all those single gay girls who managed to navigate nightlife without the safety-net of a partner.

'Glad you came, then?' This time the person beside Jo was real and holding a glass of white wine and a pint of Smithwicks.

Jo nodded. 'Even the music's great!'

'*I'm* glad you came too,' Sorcha said with a slow-burning smile that was far more personal and direct than the nerve-settling grins she'd been indiscriminately doling out earlier. She handed Jo the pint.

'Wow, thanks. How'd you know I drink Smithwicks?'

Sorcha tapped herself coyly on the nose. The preferred brand of alcohol was exactly the kind of thing Jo herself would notice in someone she fancied, but interestingly Jo hadn't noticed what Sorcha herself had been drinking. Sorcha was attractive yes, but her image, especially the heart-shaped Tiffany pendant, which she kept touching, and the high-heeled boots, was way too ladylike for Jo to find fanciable. Jo, who had her wallet and lip gloss in her jeans pockets, wasn't a fan either of the elegant leather handbag looped over Sorcha's shoulder. The prejudice appeared to be unilateral, however – Sorcha seemed fine with fancying someone less girly than she was.

Jo saw the others nab a free table near the dance floor. She was about to suggest they go and join them, when Sorcha said, 'I hear you're a journalist?'

'Yeah, but not for one of the big papers though.' Earlier Jo had bigged up both her job and her column to a star-struck Dublinette and BánDearg, but now she must downplay, lest it prove a further turn-on to Sorcha.

'*Dublin AM* not big?' said Sorcha, betraying that she'd been mining the finer details of Jo's job from the others. 'But it's absolutely everywhere. In the stockbrokers where I work there's more people reading it than the *Financial Times!*'

'Well, when something's free and new ...'

'It must be so exciting to have to rush out and capture an unfolding story,' said Sorcha, as though picturing Jo holding her own amid a mob of microphones.

'We don't actually do any investigative stuff. I'm stuck in the office all day rewriting soft news into a digestible format.'

Sorcha rubbed her thumb slowly against a button on the cigarette machine. 'But what about your science column?'

'Again, mostly just rewriting.' Jo smiled back weakly, then turned to glance around. Slamantha was desperately trying to get the others up for a dance.

Sorcha was undeterred; she raised a lust-loaded eyebrow. 'Now that I know who writes it, I'll be reading it every day!' Jo needed to get out of this risky situation. She was grateful to feel a little dig at her side, and spun round, ready to accept Slamantha's request to dance.

The tongue piercing glinted. 'Hello, Jo.'

'Heather!'

Sorcha stepped forward in disbelieving disgust. 'Thought you'd gone home.'

'Missed the last bus so might as well hang here until the first Nitelink at half twelve,' said Heather, looking at Jo and then archly back at Sorcha. 'Or maybe even a *later* one ...'

There was a silence, during which both girls turned, almost entreatingly, to Jo, who took a long swig of Smithwicks and stared down at where their feet were forming a triangle made up of two very different pairs of boots – one battered, the other immaculate – along with Jo's yellow and grey Onitsukas. She wasn't sure whether to feel empowered or entrapped, but it was clear she must apply this new pulling-power to someone more suitable. She'd already spotted a ponytailed brunette in a turquoise t-shirt and jeans with sliding-down pockets – until she could engineer an approach she might as well enjoy the hilarity of the stand-off; she took relaxed sips of her free drink and nodded to the music.

She waited until the current song had fully segued into the next one before she broke the silence. 'So ...' she said, looking at each girl in turn. Heather and Sorcha leaned in, a pair of opposing barristers, desperate for the judgement. But Jo said, 'I see the others have got themselves a table. Let's all go and sit down, shall we?'

16

'I think he's coming round, nurse. He keeps groaning.'

'Noel, can you hear me? *Noel.*'

Noel opened his eyes to find his boss, Richard Good, peering down at him. A female face hovered nearby. The ceiling was bright white. Something was beeping away to his left, but he didn't have the energy to turn his pounding head. He felt like his right temple had been hit with a chisel. His eye stung with every blink.

Richard touched him lightly on the forearm and spoke very clearly and slowly, as though to a child. 'You're in A&E in North Middlesex Hospital, Noel. It's nearly midnight on Saturday. You had a diabetic hypo in the Goodstep warehouse at lunchtime. Keeled over and hit your head.'

The nurse joined in. 'We've given you a CT scan, Noel,' she said. 'Your brain's OK, but you needed three stitches.' She fiddled with the drip-bag that fed into his left arm and adjusted the blood pressure cuff that was tightening around his right bicep. She looked in his eyes with a torch, then wrote onto her clipboard. 'I'm going to inform the doctor that you're awake,' she said. 'But we need to find out why this happened in the first place. We've retrieved your records from the diabetes clinic upstairs.' As she pulled back the curtain she paused to regard him almost crossly. 'You shouldn't be getting hypos if you're following your insulin and diet regime. This is serious, Noel. Really, really serious.'

After she had left, Noel turned to Richard. 'You don't need to stay here any longer,' he said, his voice weak and raspy. 'Go home to Esmé. Weren't your grandchildren coming over this evening?'

Richard sat down on the plastic chair and rested his hands on the bed frame. At five years older than Noel, he was the fittest, trimmest sixty-two-year-old imaginable. 'Noel, you've worked for me for over thirty years, I'm hardly going to abandon you here. Can you even remember what happened?'

'Em …' It felt like an age had passed. As Noel inched himself up in the bed he realised that he was wearing a hospital gown. He prayed that Richard hadn't witnessed the nurses stripping and then manoeuvring his hefty body into it, or sticking all these wires to his flabby chest. 'No, I can't recall …'

Richard said, 'So, the two of us were counting out the oak multi-ply planks for that new restaurant in West Wheldon. You came over all sweaty and pale. Said some very strange things to me. I got you sitting down, but by the time I rushed back to the warehouse with your emergency glucose tablets, you'd collapsed and whacked your head off the stack of planks. I had to shout to the girls in the office to call an ambulance. Everyone was incredibly upset to see you like that.'

'Oh lord.' It was disconcerting to have been mentally absent for such a dramatic show in which he'd played the starring role. He was also terrified that he'd let something slip. 'Did I say anything … *particular* when I was confused?' he heard himself ask, though he didn't want to know the answer.

'Oh, something about microfibre cloths and having to set up appointments. Total and utter gibberish.'

Noel's body went weak. He had come so close. He made a laughing sound. 'Absolute nonsense all right!'

'I've informed the Sutherlands about all this,' said Richard. 'They're obviously very concerned too.'

'But why on earth did you contact them?' said Noel, moving quickly on to his next worry. 'Where did you even get their number?'

Richard sighed. 'They're listed as your next-of-kin in the company files, Noel. We had to call *someone*. Anyway, Hazel's your sister.'

'She's technically just my cousin,' he said. 'I only see her and Martin once a month and they're already a bundle of nerves because Chloe's off to Burundi this weekend. They don't need to worry about *me* too.'

'Well, as soon as they've dropped Chloe to the airport tomorrow morning, they're coming in here.' Richard went over to where Noel's coat was hanging. 'In the meantime,' he said, patting down the coat as though looking for something, 'I'll pop round to Wheldon, fetch your pyjamas and toothbrush. All I need's your keys. Oh, and your address, of course, seeing as I've never been invited there!'

The thought of anyone, let alone his boss, rummaging through the upper cupboard in the bedroom made Noel's pulse spike to 119 on the screen. 'There's really no need,' he said, hoisting himself fully upright. 'Hazel will get those tomorrow. Besides,' he said, concocting a massive lie, 'the flat's in a bit of a mess. I'd be mortified …'

17

Heather grabbed a beermat and fanned air into her gaping mouth. 'So, Tamara Nic an tSionnaigh's become a dirty skirt-lifter,' she said. 'Well, ho-lee fuck!'

'Seems like she's always been one, actually,' said Jo.

'My brother will be devastated when I tell him,' continued Heather. 'But turned on too. Poor lad spaffs his pants whenever she's on *The Funky Forum*, or *The Spunky Forum* as I call it!'

'Less of the grossness please,' said Sorcha, sitting the other side of Jo. She gave a mature shake of her head. 'I don't see what the big excitement is anyway. Attractive women who look after their appearance *can* be gay too.' She gave a sweep of her hand that seemed deliberately limited to just herself and Jo.

'Oh, whatever,' said Heather. 'Some of us don't actually believe in GHD-ing our … never mind.'

Jo smiled and settled back. She was drunker and having more fun than ever, thanks to the glut of complimentary Smithwicks that kept coming her way from both sides of this cosy three-seater.

'How did your ex meet Tamara in the first place?' Sorcha asked.

'Louise works at Celtic Smoothies and they booked Tamara for the launch of their tropical range. I was excited by proxy because I've always thought Tamara was gorgeous. Then Louise was given the job of glad-handing her at the photoshoot down in Brittas Bay.'

'And glad-hand she did,' said Heather with a ribald laugh. 'Quick fingerbang in the marram grass afterwards, was it?'

Sorcha hooded her eyes in disgust. 'Do go on,' she said, rubbing Jo on the thigh. Since they'd sat down, Jo's legs had been the recipient of a dozen touches from both sides. In the toilets, BánDearg had hilariously remarked to Jo that Sorcha and Heather might end up splitting her in two.

Jo continued. 'After the shoot Louise and Tamara became friendly, which always puzzled me: why would an up-and-coming kids' TV presenter want to hang out with a lesbian? I nearly died when Louise eventually told me in strict confidence that Tamara was a closet case. Their illicit fling probably started soon after that.'

'Did you ever meet her?' asked Heather.

'We were introduced briefly one night, but I doubt she'd even remember. Even so I probably shouldn't be telling you any of this. Tamara's not even out to her own family for fear of it getting out and ruining her career. And I haven't even told *my* own family what happened.'

'The whole thing must have been awful for you, Jo,' said Sorcha, her face tilted like a solicitous counsellor. 'But it's great you've been able to offload this tonight. You can take it as gospel that none of this will go any further.'

Heather snorted. 'If Tamara had broken up *my* relationship I'd be telling all her doting little devotees what she really gets up to. She must have about thirty-thousand friends on Myspace.'

'Thirty-three thousand, two hundred and sixteen at last count,' said Jo, who'd checked the figure only yesterday.

Heather wiggled her fingers over an imaginary keyboard. 'And not a single one of these friends knows about Tamara's one *special* friend, aka your ex … imagine the damage!'

Sorcha's nostrils curled. 'You'd actually commit treachery against one of your own?'

Heather gave a sharp laugh. 'And Tamara wasn't being treacherous to the sisterhood when she stole Jo's girlfriend?'

'Enough!' said Jo with a wave of her hands. 'You're both right. Heather, yes, I'd love to punish Tamara for stealing my girlfriend, but I'm with Sorcha when it comes to outing people.' As she spoke she spotted the passing profile of the turquoise t-shirted girl.

'Anyway,' she added, with a rush of hope, 'I think justice has prevailed. I'm free to be myself but how's Louise going to cope with being perennially labelled in the press as a *close friend* of Tamara's?' She placed a hand on each girl's knee and pushed herself up, ready to catch her quarry before it disappeared again. 'Thanks to all the drinks you've been buying me, I need a trip to the ladies,' she said.

It was taking a while to find the girl. As Jo passed the dance floor for the second time, Slamantha rushed out and gave her a sweaty hug. 'Come dance, Jo. You've been wedged between that pair all night.'

'I'm actually trying to find this hot girl I saw earlier.'

'Told you you'd fancy someone. Now you just need to go and get her!' She gestured drunkenly around. 'Sure I've shifted four girls since I came in. Including Dublinette. I must be ovulating or something. And this real-posh couple bought me a little bottle of champagne because I promised to go back to their gaff in Ranelagh for a threesome after this. Mind you, all I'll want at that stage will be taco fries with garlic sauce.'

'You're brilliant, you know!' Jo patted her back to the dance floor and plunged into the crowd with a smile that masked her own apprehension. Slam had been right – Jo must go and get this girl, but that was exactly the problem. Once located, how would Jo go about *getting* her? As she wove through hot bodies, she realised soberly that she'd never even attempted to chat up a stranger in a club before. There was only one thing for it.

Several minutes and stifled grimaces later, the double sambuca was already working. She set the glass down on the bar with a much steadier hand. As she turned, she spotted the pretty profile above a shoulder embellished with the orange Superdry label. The girl was leaning against a pillar talking to a bony guy in a lamé tank top. His presence brought both frustration and relief, but Jo's moratorium on approaching proved short-lived: suddenly the urgent bassy intro of 'Standing in the Way of Control' was effecting a stampede to the dance floor, one that included the lamé-man, but – as luck would have it – not his sexy friend.

Under cover of the charging bodies Jo moved to the opposite side of the pillar. A quick, brave glance to the right revealed that herself was even more gorgeous up close. Jo loved the jeans resting slouchily on the brown runners, the loose loop of the silicone charity bangle dangling from the wrist, the slim fingers twitching lightly to the music as their owner stared ahead.

A few deep, aniseedy exhalations later, Jo found herself leaning round the curve of the pillar and saying into the girl's warm ear: 'I *do* like this song, but I wouldn't want to risk the dance floor right now!'

She turned and looked at Jo, but there seemed no surprise at having been approached by a stranger: her handsome mouth remained closed and the dense circumflexes of her eyebrows didn't lift a millimetre. Nonchalance was to be expected, however, in someone who probably got hit on all the time. Maybe she already had a girlfriend. Or maybe she didn't but simply wasn't interested. Maybe she had her eye on someone else. The two of them stared silently at the leaping crowd until the girl finally broke the silence. 'Ditto,' she said.

Jo beamed, seeing now that her apparent detachment was just part of her humour; it was all about comic timing. To come up with such a great wordplay, at this hour of the night, was quite something. 'She's just so original, isn't she?' gushed Jo, with an acknowledging nod to the soulful, deep-throated *whooa-ohh* now taking the roof off the room. 'To think that an out lesbian managed to win NME's Coolest Person in Music!'

One of the circumflexes collapsed. 'Sorry, who are you talking about?'

'Beth,' said Jo eagerly. 'You know, from The Gossip? Or should I say just, *Gossip*.'

'Gossip?' The girl stared at her with a suspicious derision that made Jo want to kick herself hard on the shins.

'The band that's on now,' said Jo. 'Sorry, I thought when you said *ditto* you meant … oh, never mind …' Jo pressed her mortified body against the pillar, wishing it would vacuum her away like the pneumatic money chutes they used in supermarkets. Her back was firmly against the wall, and there was certainly no one home to call: her effort to appear clever had made her appear quite the maladroit moron. As soon as the dancers dispersed, she would sneak back to the table, where Sorcha was probably murdering Heather or vice versa.

The touch on her shoulder was so unexpected that she jumped. 'Anyway, never mind this Beth chick, what's *your* name?'

'Oh, it's Jo, yeah, Jo.' She told herself sharply not to fluff it, especially now that her self-made mess had miraculously turned around. She smiled. 'And you are ... ?'

'Clíona.'

'Hi!' Jo extended her hand, but instead of shaking it with her right, Clíona grabbed it with her left. 'Come with me,' she said. Jo gulped and nodded and duly allowed herself to be pulled along. As they moved through the club, Clíona didn't speak, but Jo knew that this was because she didn't need to – if the electricity running through her fingers was anything to go by, then this was heading towards something really sexy, really fast! Her heart galloped arrhythmically, adding its own ectopic beats to the hollow snare in 'Yr Mangled Heart', which had come on next. Jo returned Clíona's grip, realising that she should never have doubted her own ability to pull this sexy girl. In fact, she could claim the double triumph of having done so *despite* the chat-up line fiasco. She had woken up that morning hanging on to sad memories of Louise, but in the gym earlier and now tonight, well, she was letting go of everything she used to be.

At first Jo thought that Clíona was bringing them to the dance floor, despite their mutual desire to previously avoid it; she did a quick mental rehearsal of some moves that wouldn't make her look like a tool. But dancing was not in the plan because, having circumnavigated the floor twice (during which, the lamé-man had given Clíona a thumbs-up as though he approved of Jo) they were now headed towards a chillout area beyond the bar. There were two candlelit tables there, the further of which, Jo noted with delight, was unoccupied. It seemed that Clíona had been looking for somewhere suitable for them to get down to getting down! Jo sucked in her own breath in an effort to taste it, praying the sambuca had freshened away the Smithwicks-malt. She was so focused on nabbing the right-hand seat (to display her best side) that she was yanked back by Clíona, who had instead come to an abrupt halt at the other table, behind which sat three girls. Jo staggered into line as Clíona raised their joined hands and announced, 'Right, everyone, this is Jo.' Jo smiled and nodded at each of them, baffled by this pitstop on the way to a snog, but wasn't it great that Clíona wanted to show her off to her friends? She must already be thinking of this as a long-term thing!

The three stared at Jo, their faces flickering incredulously the candlelight. The most agog of all was the one in the centre – a pretty girl with textured red hair and silver rings on both thumbs. She looked at Clíona and said, 'Well, *you* didn't waste any time, did you?'

'Yeah,' said the long-chinned one on her left, who stared at Jo with a kind of snide sympathy. 'Bit of a premature rebound, eh, Clí?'

Clíona leaned in, almost threateningly. 'Well, I just wanted you to meet her now that we're together, OK? I hope you all have a brilliant night huddled in your little corner here, you bunch of bitch-brained losers!' She spun round and tugged Jo away, but as soon as they were out of sight, she threw off Jo's hand as if it were filthy.

'What the hell was that about?'

Clíona laughed. 'That was my ex in the middle. She did the dirt last week with a girl from work, so I just wanted to make her jealous. Hope you don't mind. She's a total psycho.'

'So this was all … ?' Jo stood back. 'Sorry, I think it might be you who's the psy—'

'Thanks a mill for your help,' said Clíona, giving Jo a brotherly nod – as though Jo were a stranger who'd helped push Clíona's broken-down car to safety. 'Right, I'm off for a boogie.'

In a daze, Jo headed back to the table, where at least the attentions of Sorcha and Heather might help salve her tattered ego. She was rooted to the spot when ElderLemon came up behind. 'I'd a feeling that might happen in the end.'

Jo tore her eyes from the snogging couple. 'Is this for real?'

ElderLemon nodded. 'They've been at it for the past fifteen minutes.' She gave Jo a nudge. 'I knew all that bickering could only mean one thing …'

'I suppose,' said Jo, gulping with disgusted fascination as Sorcha's manicured hand began to circulate on Heather's breasts.

'It'll be *get-a-room* level within the next minute, mark my words,' said ElderLemon. And she was right. 'Oh yep, there she goes!' Heather's fingers were inching up the inside thigh of the pristine jeans. 'You look like you need a stiff one, Jo' said ElderLemon with a laugh. 'Come to the bar, I'll stand you a Smithwicks.'

Jo took a last glance at the rummaging couple; she knew it wouldn't be much longer before Heather could confirm whether Sorcha actually *did* straighten her pubic hair.

She strode down greasy cobbles on Sycamore Street with no intention of even trying for a taxi. No, she was going to walk all the way home, maybe even break into a drunken run on the quays; she must blow off every molecule of that icky lesbian den from her body. She wasn't sure what had been the worst – Clíona's cruel trick, Sorcha and Heather's clinch, or the *coup de grâce*, ElderLemon's attempt to kiss her at the bar.

She took out her phone and deleted the numbers that Heather and Sorcha had so eagerly given her earlier. The minute she got home she'd delete her whole profile too, as though the vile night had never happened. She should have trusted her initial instincts, stayed clear of all this.

Outside the tacky facade of Lapsang she spotted Carl from next door queueing with a gang of jacketless lads in thin shirts. His was the first truly friendly face she'd seen all night so she stopped to say hello. They chatted for a few minutes (Kayleigh was doing 'deadly' at her essays since Jo's intervention), while Carl's friends looked on, obviously unused to girls who didn't wear heels and dresses on nights out. The queue lurched forward. 'You won't tell Elaine you seen me going in here?' said Carl. 'Only it's me mate Squishy's birthday and he hasn't been with a young wan in ages …'

'Course I won't.' Jo grinned encouragingly at the bejowled birthday-boy and the rest of Carl's pals. 'Enjoy the crotch and knockers, lads!' They looked at her incredulously, but she felt no regret for her demeaning words

… because women, well, they were all just headwrecks and psychos.

Further on, she passed the industrialised black and yellow entrance of Helium. Muffled techno thumped from within. She looked forward to next week when she'd be partying in the DJ booth, with not a lesbian present. She smiled to see 'DJ Cill Switch' on the listings poster beside the door. She walked on, then turned back on the cobbles to check something. She thought it might have been an error of parallax, but closer inspection revealed that she'd seen it right.

'Who's playing tonight?'

'Some new fella,' said the bouncer. 'Anxious-looking chap.'

Though she wanted to rush straight over, Jo waited in the shadows beside the packed dance floor. When the incoming track had finally been let loose on its own, she climbed up into the dingy little pulpit, lifted up one side of Cillian's headphones and shouted, 'Surprise!'

He turned down his monitor. 'What on earth are you doing here, Jo?' She had expected delight, but he seemed almost annoyed. She put it down to first-night nerves.

'I might ask you the same,' she said. 'Thought you were on *next* week?'

He shrugged. 'I wanted you to go to the meet so I lied.'

'Sly bastard!' She gestured to the crowd. 'Anyway, they seem to like you here.'

'They're so off their student noggins that they'd dance to a fart,' he said dourly. 'And I'd forgotten how much hard work this is. I preferred it before the ban – at least I could have a few smokes while I worked.'

'You'll find your feet again soon,' she said, giving him a rub on the arm. 'So, the meet was a disaster, in case you're wondering …'

'Right,' he said. He fished something from his pocket and pressed it into her palm. 'I need to get the next track sorted. Make mine a mousetail, OK?'

'I've actually got some at home too,' she said. 'I was kicking myself for not bringing it earlier.' Crouching down, she chopped out two thick lines on the lid of his record box. There was a nudge from above, and Cillian passed down a chrome coke snorter. Though more convenient than rolling up cash, his possession of this was worrying – it suggested heavy use, hardly appropriate for a teacher who was always moaning about being broke. But her concern dissolved as the coke melted into her nasal mucosa. Cillian crouched and hoovered up his line, not even bothering to swap nostrils halfway.

By the time they resurfaced, his mood had improved. 'Wooh, that's better,' he said. Now wait'll you hear this cocky little blockbuster of a tune. It's got the most *crenulating* bassline coming in right about … now!' The kids loved it too – a volley of whoops came up from the floor and a wide-eyed guy in an Atari t-shirt stood on tiptoes to give Cillian a high-five.

Jo, soaring herself now, felt a strange but unplaceable bond to the song. It came to her. 'That's the one that sent me into oblivion in the gym earlier. What's it called?'

But Cillian had already turned away and was twisting the filters on the mixer.

She decided to leave him to his work; anyway, for the first time all night, she actually fancied a dance.

18

At half past two in the morning, the doctor, who was tied up with a critical patient, still hadn't arrived, so the nurse sent Richard home. Noel lay alone in the cubicle, staring at the ceiling. So the blasted diabetes had finally caught up with him; he hadn't managed to outsmart its incessant demands after all.

The whole debacle had started two years earlier, when a protracted period of fatigue and an unquenchable thirst had sent him to the GP in Wheldon Green for the first time in a decade. To his shock, a diagnosis of type 2 diabetes had followed. In his innocence of all things health-related, Noel hadn't even known there were different types, let alone understand how someone who'd never taken a sick day in his life could wind up with such a condition.

He took it all so seriously at first. His endocrinologist was a small but stern lady, Dr Ling, who said that unless Noel agreed to fully comply with the medication and lifestyle plans, he might as well go home without them. He left the clinic that day with a bagful of NHS informational bumf, prescriptions for 'pens' – injections in a slyly benign disguise – and, most important of all, a resolute new mindset. Before long, the fridge in his rented flat was emptied of sausage rolls and scotch eggs, and its doors adorned with healthy-eating fact sheets. As advised in chapter four of *So you've just been Diagnosed with Diabetes*, he cut down severely on beer, nursing only a single pint whenever he visited the local. An attractive Irish nurse called Martina taught him how to inject; within a matter of weeks he became a dab hand at stabbing himself in the belly or thigh, and recording everything in the grids of *My Diabetes Diary*. He had another diary for exercise, where he logged his prescribed walks, partnered by his first-ever pair of trainers. His whole life began to revolve around his diabetes, but he didn't mind – it was right to spend some time on his health, having blissfully ignored it for so long. Moreover, he enjoyed having a new focus and relished the attention of the sweet nurses at the clinic who praised his weight loss (a stone after only six months!) and the progress of their new 'model patient'.

But over time, his interest in this new hobby began to wane. His skin was increasingly tender from the injections, and he was bored of being the only sober one, especially when Wheldon won the rugby and the regulars celebrated in The Arms. The commandment to eat six small meals a day was proving a nuisance too: it was ridiculous to leave a perfectly good afternoon in the pub just to have tomato and mackerel on Ryvita at home which, due to his lack of booze, he wasn't even hungry for. He wondered if all the fuss was necessary and whether the doctors and nurses were just overly cautious. He started to test this suspicion by skipping the odd scheduled snack and missing the occasional injection. He waited for something terrible to happen, but nothing ever did, and so he allowed things to slacken a little bit more. Nothing happened then either, except that he started to get his life back to normal. He began to inject and eat only when it suited *him*, rather than the diabetes diaries. He ditched the unsatisfying salads and went back on the beer, much to the relief of the barmen and the regulars in The Arms, who admitted he hadn't been himself lately. He sometimes did feel a bit weak and dizzy, but these spells passed off without incident. Until today, of course.

He decided he must discharge himself from A&E before Hazel and Martin arrived tomorrow and caused *real* trouble for him. He would get back to his flat, resume his insulin and diet with renewed vigour, and everything would be fine. He must find that nurse immediately and explain he was leaving. He peeled the sticky pads off his chest, which made the EEG-screen whine, swung his legs out of the bed and grabbed hold of the wheeled drip-stand. But as soon as his bare feet took their first shaky step, he knew he wouldn't be able to make it to the curtain, let alone down the corridor. Everything was turning brown. His legs couldn't support him. Worse still, the flatlining EEG had set off some kind of alarm and now the nurse burst in, furious with him for even standing up.

There was nothing for it but to get back into bed and spend the night dreading the Sutherlands' arrival tomorrow.

19

The cold tap was working, thank god; Jo ran water over her wrists, hoping it might convey some coolness round her body.

'Boiling out there, isn't it?' said the girl beside her; she was using loo roll to blot sweat off her freckled face.

'Oppressive,' said Jo, glad of the chat. 'They could do with air conditioning.'

'Aircon in this kip?' She was young, not more than eighteen. As a rule, Jo didn't like dresses, but hers was fun – rows of cartoon owls, big eyed, beaky and sweet. 'You on anything yourself?' the girl asked.

'Just a couple of lines,' said Jo. 'Big ones admittedly.'

'Lucky for some. I took one of those cheap-ass herbal yokes about an hour ago and it's only kicking in now.' She examined her pupils in the mirror. 'Well, I *think* it is anyway.'

'Did you know they're not actually herbal at all?' said Jo, turning around to lean on the sinks. 'They're legal, yes, but not herbal. You won't actually believe what they're made from.'

'Please don't say rat poison or something?'

Jo shook her head. 'They're a chemical cousin of that worm medicine you probably had as a kid.'

'Fuck off!'

'BZP is an anthelminthic compound that kills internal parasites like worms.' Jo smiled at the irony of how taking drugs, the most un-nerdy thing she ever did, always brought out a nerdy verboseness in her.

'Ugh.' Owl-girl extended her tongue as though she half-expected a tapeworm to swim up her gullet.

'Well, at least you know you *don't* have worms now!' said Jo.

'You're gas craic, you a doctor or something?' she said as they walked to the door.

'Quarter of one. Don't ask.'

Outside the toilets she grabbed Jo's arm. 'Hey, come sit with my friends for a minute and tell them about the worms, will you? I can't wait to see the look on their faces.'

'It's not all it's cracked up to be, you know,' Jo said to the young barman who'd come to clear away the tableful of tequila glasses, the empty relics of Jo's coming-up generosity towards the skint schoolgirls. He looked back at her blankly. 'Your t-shirt,' she said. *'Dip me in honey and feed me to the lesbians.* Been there, done that. Don't think I'd bother buying the t-shirt!'

The girls screamed with laughter as he edged away. They were all up now, including Jo who had taken a real, illegal E that owl-dress-Amy had procured for her from a dreadlocked guy working behind the bar. The coke had carved a coming-up conduit through which the pill had been fast-tracked into action; now she was having the best time, sitting with these beautiful and bubbly sixth-year schoolgirls.

'So glad I've met you all tonight,' Jo announced, smiling into three sets of dilated pupils. She couldn't be sure if she'd already told them that. It didn't matter, because they all smiled back and returned the sentiment. 'When I was your age,' she told them, 'I had my head stuck in my books, but it was all sublimation for my sexuality, y'know? You're dead right to be out enjoying yourselves!'

They hadn't flinched earlier when Jo had told them she was gay. In fact Danielle, the prettiest of them with her languid glossy lips and her pools-for-eyes, had kept her arm protectively around Jo's waist ever since learning about the Louise fiasco – a gesture so sweet and sensitive, especially when felt against the backdrop of Cillian's techno, which was becoming more vicious by the minute; Jo had always loved the clubland juxtaposition of brutish music with soft words, solicitous touches, the sharing among strangers of water, chewing gum, even useful information – about the music, the toilets, the whereabouts of the dealers.

Now scenes, moments, words, thoughts were happening in an unpredictable mixture of fast- and slow-motion, of time lunging forward, then deliciously dragging. Jo's motor-jaw was uncontrollable, but the jutting and teeth grinding were manifestations of pure happiness rather than being uncomfortable. Her eyes zigzagged; she let them fall shut and blissfully half-listened to the conversation, while delighting in the sexy pressure of Danielle's arm as it melted into her lower back.

She hadn't even noticed that another of the girls, Niamh, had left the table until she returned a little while later. 'It's deffo him,' Niamh champed through a wad of chewing gum. 'I snuck right up to the booth.'

'Hope he didn't see you?' said Amy. 'I don't want the school ringing my mam on Monday.'

'No,' said Niamh. 'Anyway, Gavigan's too sound to snitch. And he hardly wants Sister Carmel knowing he does DJ nixers.'

'What's all this?' Jo asked, trying to seem casual. With all this talk of her own life, she'd never asked which school they attended.

'Our English teacher's DJing,' said Amy. 'There's a rumour he used to do it years ago.'

'Just surprised it's not in a gay club, seeing as it's Gay-vigan!' said Niamh. Jo tried her best not to smile. Poor Cillian, although he was fully out to the other staff at the school, and forever regaling them with gay tales, he was never quite sure whether the pupils knew. And now Jo had found out the answer before him. She resisted the impulse to say anything; it would be more valuable to listen.

Danielle ran her hand up Jo's back. 'This poor guy's not like you, Jo. He's completely closeted.'

'Oh?'

'We all wish he'd just come out,' said Amy. 'He must be a nervous wreck at work. I feel bad for him.'

'I obviously can't speak for the guy when I don't know him,' said Jo, 'but he's probably afraid other students wouldn't be as open-minded as yourselves. I'm sure all the teachers know anyway.'

Niamh shook her head. 'My cousin did teacher-training last year and said he was always banging on in the staffroom about his *girlfriend*, some doctor called Joanna. It's nuts because the whole school already knows about him, even the nuns!'

'Oh really? That's mad,' said Jo. Rather than anaesthetise her upset at having been lied to for so long, the E refracted her feelings into a hyperreal unease, causing a double emotional exposure: a low experienced from inside a high. Joanna the doctor needed something to obliterate all this.

'Right,' she said, getting up unsteadily, 'who's for a shot of Aftershock?'

After the schoolgirls had left to catch a lift home from Amy's brother (despite Jo's insistence that she'd pay for a taxi later on), Jo bought a double Jameson, then went to observe the dance floor chaos that a coked-up Cillian was wreaking.

'Excuse me?' said a voice to her right. She turned to see an earnest goateed face, whose dilated eyes swam behind steel-rimmed glasses. 'Hey,' he said. 'I'm Paul.'

She shook his sweaty, gentle hand. 'Jo. Hi.'

'Sorry to bother, only I saw you in the DJ booth earlier.'

'He's a friend of mine.' She hoped this wasn't a chat-up.

Paul pointed smilingly at the sweat on his t-shirt. 'He's brilliant, I can't stop dancing. Look, do you think he might play a track I brought?' He rummaged in an old-school Adidas bag.

'Doubt it,' Jo said, but as kindly as she could, because he seemed a sensitive soul – and observant too for remembering her face from hours earlier. 'He's particular about his setlist, plus he's in a weird mood tonight.'

'Oh, but if you heard this …' Paul handed over the home-burned CD which had 'Loved Every Minute – Demo' handwritten in marker. 'I mean it's nothing as hard as what he's playing, but it'd make a fantastic last song. My friend in London got it as a bootleg. The singer, Lynette Lost, has the most haunting voice.'

'Well, you've sold it to *me* anyway,' said Jo. 'I'll ask the vinyl-queen if he'll condescend to play a *CD*. But only because you seem like a lovely person, OK?'

'So do you,' he said, eyes glistening behind his glasses. He pulled her in and gave her a sweet, bristly kiss on the cheek. 'In fact, you *definitely* are!'

A couple of minutes later, she was joining Paul on the dance floor. 'Cillian's in much better form,' she shouted in his ear. 'Fingers crossed!'

'The lyrics remind me of my ex, Cara,' said Paul, as they danced. 'We split up over the summer.' He put his hand on his chest. 'Still heartbroken.'

'I know the feeling,' said Jo, pulling him into a hard hug. 'My girlfriend Louise dumped me for someone else.'

'Sucks, doesn't it?' he said, moving back to hold her gently by the shoulders. 'I doubt I'll meet anyone quite like Cara ever again.'

Jo said, 'The first time Louise came over to my place was at half nine on a Sunday morning.'

'Paul laughed. 'Unorthodox!'

'We'd met each other at a housewarming the week before,' said Jo, her eyes narrowing in a renewed rush of ecstasy at this treasured memory. 'I overheard her joking that if they use kittens to advertise loo roll, why aren't there human baby pictures on bags of cat litter?'

'Hilarious *and* clever.'

'She was such a ride, even the way she was sipping on her can of Franziskaner was gorgeous. I plucked up the courage to introduce myself and we ended up swapping numbers because we got on so well. We both assumed the other was straight during our first week of relentless texting. That Saturday, she was dropping her grandad to a funeral in the church near my house, so I told her to pop in afterwards for a coffee.'

'And?'

Jo gave a gurning grin. 'I never even got to put on the kettle!'

Paul's face bloomed into a smile. 'Smooth.'

'We were still at it when the Angelus rang at six. We called it our *day of holy fuck*!'

Paul looked a bit perturbed.

'Sorry, I've gone overboard,' said Jo, annoyed by her E-motormouth. 'I'm sure you don't want to hear all this.'

Paul shrugged. 'Nah, I was just worried about the grandad there. I hope he's not *still* waiting outside the church for his lift home?'

'Jesus,' said Jo, putting her hand over her mouth with mock shock. 'I bet he is too, you know!'

A few minutes later there was a boo from the crowd as Cillian was finishing – the final track decelerating on the turntable into a low, satanic drawl. As the music died away, Paul turned towards the booth, holding Jo's hand, the fingers of his other crossed and aloft, praying for the encore. She felt his grip tighten at the emergent pulse of a melancholy synth. He closed his eyes and began to dance in a languid rhythm. By the time Lynette Lost had started singing, Jo was doing the same.

> *There's not a minute of the day*
> *I haven't seen your face*
> *And not a minute of the night.*

The song presented a beautiful but mind-boggling concept: being with someone during each and every numbered minute of the twenty-four hour clock. As Jo danced, she wondered if she could claim the same with Louise. Middle-of-the-night minutes would be well covered by that first summer together – the many times they'd talked animatedly until dawn (yet still had a million more things they wanted to say). The day-minutes could be ticked off in hundreds of ways: hangovers together in bed, feeding each other cold pizza while watching *Antiques Roadshow*. Louise, detaching a disc of mozzarella and announcing, 'This cheesy fob-watch was bequeathed by my Uncle Randalph before his death from yellow-pepper fever'. Evening minutes were well covered too – like on their first 'proper' date in town: walking home from *Salome* in The Abbey, Louise dragging Jo into a dingy shop doorway and whispering, 'May I kiss thy mouth, JoKav'nagh?'

> *I've loved you every minute*
> *And with every minute that goes by*
> *I'm starting to believe*
> *That I can put things right.*

Whatever it may take
Gonna get you back tonight.
I've loved you every minute
Now's the time to get love right

Jo's hands clasped around her own neck, feeling the damp heat of Louise's top. And suddenly it was not her own body but Louise's shoulders, Louise's back, Louise's abs that she was touching through the fabric. Ruby disco lights penetrated her closed eyelids, hexagonal warning signs that she'd played it all wrong during the endgame: she had appeared angry, desperate, pathetic, when she should have taken a masterful stand to keep Louise from leaving. She could have saved everything.

It was very late at night to ring, but if not now, then when? And the weird timing would be testament to her newfound bravery, to the urgency of her need. She opened her eyes. Paul had disappeared. She took out her phone and scrolled to the number she'd hovered over a thousand times these past few months. She'd been wrong to applaud her avoidance. She focused on the photo above the magical string of digits – Louise at Pride, her beautiful eyes, her wry smile, the adorable callus on her clavicle. With her brains and her beauty, she knocked the socks off any girl – straight or gay – Jo had met, not just tonight, but in her whole life. She felt a rush of sexual repossession as her thumb reached for the CALL button. She imagined Louise in a darkened bedroom pushing the sleepy forelock from her phone-illuminated face. She would be annoyed, confused by the call at first, but then overjoyed to hear Jo saying what she should have said months ago. In half an hour they would meet on the apex of the Ha'penny Bridge. They would smile silently at each other and then come together in a kiss. A kiss so long and so hot that the Liffey beneath them would come to a rolling boil, then burst its granite banks and flow out, drowning the whole city in liquid love.

Jo waited until they'd crossed the bridge before asking for her phone back.

Cillian tapped the top of his record case. 'Not until I know you won't do anything stupid.'

'Still can't believe you killed the music like that,' she said. 'How'd you know who I was about to ring anyway?'

'Who else would you be ringing at four in the morning when you're off your mammaries, dancing to a love song?'

Jo grimaced guiltily at the river: it would not boil over tonight, or any other night. 'I don't think the manager was too happy with the abrupt ending. Did he say anything about you playing there again?'

Cillian shook his head. 'It had to be done, Jo. Imagine your lifelong embarrassment if she'd answered.'

Empty taxis went past, but they decided it would be nice (especially now they'd been freshly energised by the last of Cillian's stash before leaving Helium) to walk down the north quays – a homage to their flat-sharing days, when they'd so often stumbled home this way together.

As Cillian lit a fag, Jo gazed across the glinting Liffey. So much had changed since those good old days. Three years of her life had flowed irretrievably away, like water lost to the Irish Sea. The fact of youth passing was sad enough in itself, but Jo's loss was compounded by the wasting of one-third of her precious twenties. Like her love-starved schooldays and her two fruitless years doing medicine, the Louise years marked yet another lacuna in her life history.

Cillian shifted his heavy record box to his other hand. Jo felt a renewed fondness for him tonight, her only true friend in the world, loyal to the last despite everything she'd done. She told him about the meet and watched his alternately amazed and amused expressions. She had decided to defer confronting him about being in the closet at work to a more sober setting: there was no point souring the mood when they were about to hammer into that long-forgotten gramme back at hers. Anyway, she knew he hadn't lied out of a desire to deceive her, but rather to save face.

A couple of streets shy of Smithfield, they were laughing. 'Dear old Manly Butches,' said Jo, looking at the sign above the tiled shop, whose logo bore the head of a pensive brown heifer. 'Shame on Mr Manly for not fixing his missing letter R after all this time.'

'Obviously *still* easier to buy an E than an R around here!'

'Are we the only people who get a kick out of things like this?' said Jo, as they passed the dyed sheepskins and empty meat-trays rimmed by fake grass.

'Definitely the only gay ones. Oh, speaking of butches, what about your gym woman from earlier?'

'I got all psyched up and went over with the note. But when I saw the rosary beads hanging from the rear-view, and a double baby seat in the back, my hard-on swiftly wilted.'

'A god-bothering breeder? Your gaydar needs recalibrating, Jo.'

'Must have been rendered ineffective by my runner's high, which by the way, you should try sometime. It was almost as good as real drugs.'

He laughed so hard that his smoker's cough began its throaty roll. 'Exercise? Eh, no thanks. That stuff can kill you, y'know.'

'I saw a poster in the gym for this 10K run before Christmas in the new Port Tunnel,' she said. 'It's the week before it opens to actual traffic. Imagine it … ten thousand people pouring into the underground for this weird one-off event. It'd be like being at a rave.'

'One with no music and full of fit tits,' he said.

'I might well put my name down for it,' she said. 'I've never done a race and I'll need a new challenge now that my gay-scene forays are already over.'

'Whatever you're into,' he said with a tart kind of laugh that betrayed his jealousy at her willingness to do something he'd never have the nerve to try himself. Halfway up the hill, he dragged his hand wistfully against the padlocked gate of the library. 'Only nine days until I see book-club Liam in there again.'

'And still no proof on the fag-status?'

'Nothing definitive. Anyway, I've been temporarily distracting myself with rabid sex with this carpenter from Leitrim. Not a brain cell in his head, god love him, but he's got a terribly big drill-bit.'

'I don't want to know!'

He twisted his index finger into her kidney. 'Don't worry, I won't bore you. Well, not the way *he* bores me anyway.'

They stopped at Cillian's so he could drop off the records and change his sweaty clothes. Alone in his tiny kitchen, Jo filled a glass of tap water and leafed through the pile of sixth-year essays on the counter. The topic was 'The Rights of Minorities'. That same chestnut had come up in her actual Leaving Certificate; she'd played a well-prepared blinder – writing feverishly about racial rights, women's rights, the rights of animals, the rights of third-world children. But nowhere in her ridiculous number of foolscap pages had she gone within ten yards of homosexuality. Halfway through the pile she found the bubbly handwriting of Amy O'Keeffe, her owl-dress friend from earlier. Directly underneath was Danielle's essay, with writing as pretty as she was. Jo imagined the burble of irony around the class as they were handed an assignment by a teacher too scared to admit his own minority status.

She heard Cillian coming back; as she stepped away from the essays, she noticed a scrap of paper under the ashtray.

'Right,' he said. 'Let's get this flight to *Charleroi* airport off the ground!' He stopped and looked at her. 'You OK?'

She stuck out her tongue and set down the glass. 'Why do they have to ruin D7 tap-water with so much chlorine?'

Leaving the kitchen, she hung back briefly to take a second glance at the note. But no, despite the drink and the drugs and the dramas of tonight, she'd been right.

User: Pollymath

Password: help_jo

Jo=Deltoideus

The moment they arrived at Jo's, Cillian despatched her upstairs to grab the coke while he put on the kettle. She felt around at the back of the overstuffed medicines drawer, then pulled out the boxes and blister packs, and peered in. She lifted the drawer off its metal runners and tipped everything out on the bed. Then did the same with the two drawers beneath in case it had somehow slipped down.

A spoon clinked downstairs. 'Coffee's going tepid, darling. And so am I!'

'Slight problem, Cillian.' She went down to the sitting room.

'You can tell me after a nice *line bán*.' He spun his snorter around on the coffee table. 'Y'know, I've always thought *Lena Bawn* would make a great drag queen name.'

'Louise obviously took the coke with her. I can't believe she remembered *that* when she was happy to leave so much of her stuff …'

Cillian's face flickered as though Jo had promised him a lifesaving drug, an antidote to a fatal snakebite, only to retract the offer at the crucial moment. He stood up. 'Jesus, Jo, what the fuck?'

'Chill, would you? I've got some whiskey for our coffee. And as a special consolation treat …' She went to the kitchen and returned with an ashtray. 'I'll even let you *smoke* in here.'

He took the ashtray without expression and tapped it hard against his knuckles a few times. When he eventually looked up, she saw how the insides of his nostrils were as salted as margarita glasses. 'I asked you three times if you were sure about that coke, and each time you lied.'

'Not bloody intentionally, Cillian. And, by the way, it's not the end of the world.' She fixated on his reddened septum. 'Well, not of *my* world anyway.'

'What's that supposed to mean?' he said, surreptitiously pinching away a powdery sniffle.

'I saw how your mood changed earlier,' she said. 'You were in foul form when I arrived, then you do a huge line and suddenly everything's wonderful. Like, how much money are you wasting on it these days? It's no wonder you're broke.'

His cheeks were turning as red as his nose. 'Well, seeing as you've decided to diagnose me as some kind of cokehead … the reason I was off with you earlier was because I bumped into Louise before the gig. And she told me something that made me really fucking angry, Jo.'

Jo was sure she must have misheard. Or maybe she was so wrecked after tonight that she was in the throes of a nightmarish microsleep. She blinked at him. 'Sorry, what … ?'

'Before the gig I went into The Sycamore for a quick pint to settle my nerves. The next thing Louise had sat down beside me at the bar. She was pretty tipsy after some work thing in the function room upstairs.'

Jo felt behind for the wall. The room, the world, inverted. It was a sickening vision, Louise whispering in his willing ear. She couldn't stomach to ask if Tamara had been there too.

His stared ahead and continued. 'When Louise started telling me about what you did to her on the way back from your trip to Edgeworthstown, I thought she was lying because surely, *surely* my oldest friend Jo would have mentioned something like that, especially when she's been boring the absolute hole off me with the minutiae of her awful break-up. But as Louise went on, I started to believe *her* because you could not make that shit up!'

Jo pushed herself off the safety of the wall and stepped forward, her voice slow and cracking. 'I had just found out for definite that my girlfriend was having an affair, Cillian. I snapped. What would *you* have done?'

'It was two miles to the nearest house, Jo! Louise had no phone or coat or anything. She could've been knocked down or dragged into a field and raped. What she did to you wasn't nice, but at least no one's *life* was actually put in danger.'

'No one's life?' screamed Jo, as her fingers became fists. 'What about mine? I've been practically suicidal over this break-up. But I don't expect you to understand because you've never been with anyone for more than fifteen minutes!'

He set down the ashtray slowly and studied it for a moment, then looked up at her quite suddenly. 'That's an awfully low blow, love,' he said. 'And if you think that being dumped gives you a monopoly on loneliness, then you're mistaken.' He grabbed his jacket and strode into the hallway.

She followed him, her toe clipping his heel. 'You're supposed to be my best friend, Cillian. I can't believe that you've just sided with *her*. '

'Best friends are honest with each other, Jo. At least I was honest enough to tell you about meeting Louise.'

'Only because you got in a rage. You managed to keep your little rendezvous secret while it suited, right up until you couldn't get your ikkle bit of coke. No doubt if I'd served it up here, then the rest of the night would have been just marvellous! You think you're oh so decadent Cillian with your coke and your casual sex and your chain-smoking, but all I'm seeing is a pathetic, directionless mess. You join book clubs and dabble in DJing and pretend to be a lesbian called Pollymath to help your poor loser friend, but it's all just half-assed attempts to distract from the fact that your life has no meaning.'

The margarita rims curled. 'I can see why Louise left you. You're a judgmental cunt.'

'Well, now you share a common hatred, why don't you go hang out with her? She might even still have that wrap of coke!' She slammed her palm against the radiator. 'All that shit about saving my ass earlier by stopping me ringing her. You just didn't want her to mention your little coven earlier in the evening.' She pushed him down the hall. 'Get out. And don't ever come near me again.'

'Come near you again? Well you needn't worry about that!'

The whole terrace shook as she slammed the door. A moment later, she heard baby Jayden's howls coming through the wall.

She was on her third whiskey before her fingers were in a fit state to text:

Btw Mr Honesty, you forgot to tell me about your girlfriend Dr Joanna. Your sixth years spilled about your pathetic efforts at pretending to be straight. But don't worry, no one has fallen for it. They all know you're a fake.

20

'Aw, bless, look!' said Dave, glancing in the rear-view mirror.

Aaron turned around from the passenger seat to grin at them. 'Hard to believe we've got a couple of badass black belts back there,' he said. Rachel smiled back but Alysha, without opening her eyes from where she dozed on Rachel's lap, raised her middle finger at him. 'Too bloody early,' she said, her voice muffled by Rachel's fleece. 'Who agreed to this dumb tournament anyway?'

Rachel stroked Alysha's hair. 'Boys, for our own safety we better let sleeping alligators lie.'

'Especially when they're as snappy as that one,' said Dave. 'Our Alygator isn't a morning person, as you've probably realised by now, Rachel.'

'I couldn't possibly comment,' said Rachel, in a mock-politician voice. 'What I *will* say, is that it's helpful to bring Mademoiselle Niles a *toxically* strong cup of tea before she gets out of bed. It helps ease her into the day.'

Aaron had brought some CDs, and as the laughter died away, and the car filled with the grungy punch of Kasabian, the sense of today's occasion washed afresh over Rachel. She'd only been in Wheldon a short while and here she was, on a team with Alysha and two other new friends – Dave, who was a late judo-starter, married and in his mid-thirties, and the sweet and eager Aaron who had just started uni. She would do everything she could to repay Sensei Kev for taking a chance on the new girl.

Dave's Avensis, while nowhere nearly as classy as Lydia's Saab, was still a comfortable ride. 'Thanks so much for driving,' Rachel said. 'It's such a luxury to get door-to-door transport.'

'My pleasure!'

'When I was young me and my dad would spend hours trekking to competitions on buses and trains,' Rachel continued. 'He'd give me pep talks on the way, of course. *Nerves means that it matters, Rachey. I wanna see some good* ippons *today, not just borin' old* kokas.'

'He understood the scoring!' said Aaron. 'Was he a judoka himself?'

'No, actually,' said Rachel. Last week, she'd told the others the basic facts of her family, or rather lack thereof, when they'd gone for coffee after training; now she felt comfortable to elaborate. 'A while after my mum left, a local judo class started up. My dad thought it might distract me from moping around at home. I think *he* wanted the distraction more than me, though. He devoured every judo book in the library and would check my form against the pictures. I always had the whitest, most perfectly ironed *gi* in the club. No mean feat for a man whose hands were constantly covered in lorry grease.'

'He sounded amazing, Rachel,' said Aaron, turning around to squint sadly at her.

'A cool dude, indeed,' said Dave. 'My old man just thinks a *koka*'s some kind of pot-noodle!'

Rachel laughed but then turned wistful. 'I'm sure my dad chose judo because he wanted me to fight my corner in life, unlike him. He didn't even put up an argument on the day my mum left us, just sat in a daze on the stairs, while she rushed around filling suitcases.'

'God, the poor bloke,' said Dave. 'Don't know what I'd do if my Jacqui announced she was upping and—'

Alysha bolted upright, suddenly alert. 'Your phone just buzzed, Rachel. Quick, check if it's him!'

Rachel sighed as she took the phone from her fleece. 'It's probably just Auntie Cassie checking I've not drowned in the Thames or become a prostitute in Soho.'

Hi Rachel. Good luck today in you're judo competition, I am sure you will do well. Listen, if your free Wednesday would you maybe fancy dinner in Nagano on the High Street perhaps? Hope to hear from you soon, Stuart (from Friday in The Mill)

'Result!' said Alysha, who'd been reading it aloud over Rachel's shoulder, which she now squeezed with delight. 'He even remembered the competition, how keen is he, boys?'

'Sounds well interested,' said Aaron. 'Nice one, Rachel.'

Rachel put on a modest smile as she read through the message again; Alysha hadn't even noticed how he'd mixed up *you're* and *your,* and had used *maybe* and *perhaps* in the same sentence. But tautologies and grammatical inaccuracies didn't matter; she had a date on Wednesday!

She sat back and smiled while Alysha apprised the boys of the full Stuart story. She could hardly believe how well everything was going. She was forging ahead at Trenpharm, she had clinched Stuart, and now there was every chance that she and her lovely new friends could win the tournament today. As she gazed out the window, she got a sense of herself, standing in the centre of a triangle of self-made triumphs – job, judo and now her love life too.

But there remained one quite concerning aspect to the good news. 'I've never been to a Japanese restaurant before,' she confessed to her friends. 'I won't have a clue what to order, never mind using the chopsticks!'

Alysha grabbed her hand. 'Let's pick up some sticks and a menu on our way home tonight. Sexy Stu will think you've been noshing down noodles all your life!'

By ten o'clock the weigh-ins were finished and the hall was a hive of white activity as competitors from a multitude of clubs geared up for the long day ahead. In the middle of the floor, blazered male officials inspected the *tatami* and set up the timing clocks and scoreboards. Meanwhile, the sole female official was fitting slit tennis balls onto chair-legs so they wouldn't damage the mats once the corner judges sat down.

Sensei Kev looked cross as he arrived in. 'I see three of you've already broken your promise about post-weigh-in hydration anyway,' he said. 'Rachel's the only one drinking water!'

'Sensei's pet,' whispered Alysha, prodding her on the bum.

'I've got some bottles in the car,' said Kev. 'One of you can nip out after the draw sheets go up. But first I want to discuss tactics …'

Suddenly everything went dark. Rachel couldn't tell which was more raspy – the sandpapery fingers covering her eyelids or the Geordie voice demanding, 'Rachey Driffield, guess who!'

Kev's voice came to a stop, and she sensed the group staring at her. She pulled the hands from her eyes and spun around. 'Tiny!' she gasped. His short, strong arms clamped her in a hug. He was just five foot three, so the nickname wasn't ironic; as Rachel's chin was tickled by the greying stubble on his head, she said, 'Sorry, everyone, this is Tiny, from my old club.'

Tiny extended a hearty hand and said, 'Nice to meet ya,' to everyone individually. Alysha looked especially enamoured of this flirty fifty-year-old, who told her through a cheeky, gold-incisored smile that he was sure he recognised her from somewhere.

'You've come all the way down from Newcastle?' said Kev. 'Now *that's* dedication, folks.'

'Stayed with me kid brother in Clapham last night,' said Tiny. 'About time I seen the lad, to be honest. Then they let us have a late entry in this competition, so I thought, might as well.'

'That's brilliant, Tiny!' said Rachel. She felt a pang of guilt for not having stayed in touch with him, but the silly thing with Kim meant it was simpler to cut ties with *everyone* in the club, harsh as that was. Anyway, now word would get back to Newcastle that Rachel was doing great in London; this would hopefully inspire Kim to put those strange times behind her, and get back to normal too. For all Rachel knew, she might already have done so.

After Kevin's pep-talk, Rachel went to find Tiny again. She sat down beside him on the practice mats. 'Sorry I haven't been in touch, Tiny. It's just been crazy with the new job, which is going great by the way.'

'Not at all, pet. We all knew you'd text soon as you'd caught your breath. Your new mates seem cool, too. Though I can't wait to throw that older gadgie flat on his back later on!'

'Dave's lovely, but watch out for his *deashi harai.*'

Tiny laughed. 'Ya shouldn't be giving away secrets about your new clubmates!'

'Only for an old friend,' she said.

'I've actually got a little secret of me own for you.'

Rachel grabbed his arm. 'Oh my god, is Caitlyn finally expecting?' Tiny and his younger wife had been trying for a baby for ages.

'Nothing like that, I'm afraid. The thing is, it's not just *us* that's here from the club. Wasn't even my idea to come to London at all in fact …'

'Right,' said Rachel in a small voice, as her embarrassment about the non-existent pregnancy transformed into a dawning horror about something entirely different.

'So gan on then,' said Tiny. 'Guess who's here with us?'

'Eh … ?' Rachel couldn't breathe as the pieces of the story clicked sickeningly into place. She couldn't even bring herself to say 'Who?' lest the awful answer came any sooner.

Tiny shook his head in comedic exasperation, but then something caught his eye in the corner of the hall. 'Too late for guesses now, anyway!' he said as the door of the ladies' changing room opened and a familiar figure, wearing a *gi*, came out. He called and waved, while his other hand pointed at Rachel. 'Hey, Kim, over here. Look who I've found!'

Noel couldn't remember what time he had eventually fallen asleep, but he woke to find Hazel and Martin standing on either side of the hospital trolley.

'Thank heavens you're OK,' said Hazel, leaning in to kiss his cheek gently. She made a face. 'But your poor head …'

Martin gave him a manly nod. 'You gave us quite the fright, old chap.'

Noel sat up and tried to look as normal as possible, though he still felt desperately woozy. 'I'm absolutely fine,' he said. 'They merely kept me in as a precaution. And the cut on my head only happened because I was in the blasted Goodstep warehouse at the time.'

'But it's a blessing that this *did* happen at Goodstep,' said Hazel. 'What if you'd been alone in your flat? You could have …' She shuddered as though imagining him lying for days on the floor of his little kitchen.

'Don't even go there, love,' said Martin with a shivering wince of his own. He turned to Noel. 'Anyway, no need to worry about any of that now, Moody.'

'Exactly,' said Noel. 'Look, I confess I've not been great with injections and meals lately. But all that changes from today. As soon as they discharge me, I'll get a cab home. And I'll be following the clinic's orders to the letter this time!'

But Hazel was shaking her head. 'You'll be staying with us for a while, Noel. We need to keep an eye on you while you recover.'

'God, no,' he cried. 'I couldn't impose …'

'But you've timed it all magnificently,' said Martin with a chuckle. 'Chloe's room is all yours for the foreseeable.' He looked at his watch. 'In fact her plane's taking off in exactly seven minutes.'

Hazel nodded. 'I've put fresh sheets on already. It'll be nice to have you stay while we're empty-nesters.'

Noel stared at the holes in the woven hospital blanket. He was trapped:

yesterday's events had transformed him from being an independent relative whom the Sutherlands invited to Sunday dinner once a month, and into a worrisome liability. A liability that they, as his default next-of-kin, must now monitor. Manage. *Control.*

Mustering his last shred of strength, he hardened his voice and looked at them in turn. 'Hazel, Martin. I don't mean to be rude, but I really *cannot* stay. I will be absolutely fine at the flat.'

'It's too late, Noel,' said Hazel. 'We've already spoken to Dr Ling, the nurses, even Richard Good. Everyone agrees this arrangement's the only way. In fact, Dr Ling won't even entertain discharging you otherwise.'

He gave a shuddering sigh. So they'd all been conspiring while he slept, this cabal who hadn't the faintest idea of the impact this would have on his life. He would lose the one thing that kept him sane. Or, worse still, get found out if he tried to continue doing it.

'I'm tired,' he said. 'I need to sleep.' He sank into the pillows and closed his tearful eyes. This was going to be awful. Truly awful.

22

Jo hoped Cillian's coke habit would escalate until his septum dissolved, leaving a grotesque cyclops of a nostril. She hoped that his smoking would, in time, bear him the gift of alveolar carcinoma, that he would spend his last days hacking up throatloads of putrid sputum in some dingy, understaffed hospital. She hoped too that before the illnesses kicked in, Cillian would finally pluck up the courage to ask his beloved book-club Liam out, only to be universally ridiculed because everybody knew that Liam was straight.

She lay back on the couch and felt the anger slice through the muzziness of her comedown. After she'd texted Cillian last night (still no reply, and nor did she ever want to hear from the deceptive, Louise-sympathising prick again) she'd knocked back a few more whiskeys – the last of which had been salted by her own tears – before crawling into bed.

She'd been woken a few hours later by an intense wave of nausea. Her legs had seized up in her sleep, too – delayed payback for her temerity on the treadmill. Her agonised stagger to the loo had been undertaken with vomit-filled jowls.

She turned on the telly, hoping it might distract. Discovery Channel was having a Death & Diseases Day and a show documenting *The World's Biggest Tumor* was starting. She sat up; within seconds of seeing the patient's swollen torso she'd diagnosed a plexiform neurofibroma. She was proved right a moment later by the pioneering surgeon who outlined the planned fourteen-hour, life-changing operation. She watched with jealous respect as he and his team examined scans, discussed tactics and scrubbed up to a soundtrack of emotive music. Of course, Jo had had her own chance to radically improve people's lives too, but instead here she was, sitting in the failed filth of last night, cheated on by her girlfriend and her best friend, and made a fool of by bitches at *Miss*. She felt as powerless and unsexy as the poor woman being anaesthetised on the reinforced operating table. As the surgeon's scalpel made the first cut, she changed the channel, unable to stomach his expertise nor the inevitable success to come.

RTÉ2 was showing a body with the opposite problem to the patient, in that it was far too skinny. The piebald pony had been abandoned on debris-strewn waste ground. Her eyes stared out sadly from beneath a brittle, bleached fringe.

'You can see the malnourishment in her ribs,' the uniformed ISPCA man was saying. 'And her hooves are so overgrown they're curling back.' He patted the animal gently on the rump and untied the too-short cord that bound her to a contorted palisade fence. 'Let's get her to the shelter, then try to find out who's responsible.'

'It's hard to believe,' said a lilting Kerry accent that made Jo's skin bristle, 'how cruel people can be.'

'*Very* hard to believe, Tamara,' he said. They led the horse away, Tamara's light brown ponytail swishing and shimmering in obscene contrast to the animal's limp and ragged tassel.

'You'd certainly know all about cruelty, Tamara,' muttered Jo. With nothing left to lose she might as well torture herself by observing 'the other woman' through the one-way window of television. Tamara was easy on her exhausted eyes, and unlike Louise, and now Cillian, had never actually defaulted on any loyalty to Jo, having never known her.

Jo was not the only one staring at Tamara – even the poor beast was enamoured as they reached the carpark, nuzzling the breast of her Fanta-coloured Helly Hansen jacket and enjoying caresses from her sallow hands. Jo had always found that olive complexion and those brown eyes to be preposterously at odds with her having a surname *as Gaeilge*. Right beside the equine rescue van was parked the key piece of evidence in Jo's uncovering of the affair – Tamara's ice blue Mini Cooper. The roof decal – a geometric image of a fox's head – had been created uniquely for Tamara, by Dublin's coolest street-artist, Murphio.

Back in a bright studio that Jo recognised as the set for *The Funky Forum*, the fresh-faced male presenter said, 'So that was just a taster of my multitalented co-star Tamara's new show, *Animals Matter*, kicking off this

Tuesday.' He stood on his tiptoes, shielding his eyes with his cue cards. 'And speaking of animals, where are you, Mizz Fox? You need to tell everyone about our text-in!'

A camera swooped up to Tamara, who was laughing graciously at being called the English version of her surname. (If her Irish surname was at odds with her appearance, then its English equivalent was certainly more fitting.) She'd stuffed herself into the top row of the audience, and the teenage boys on either side didn't seem to know whether to look at her, at the camera, or down at their incipient erections. The cerise foam of the mic was the only jot of colour in her dark outfit, which comprised tight jeans, black feather earrings and the latest fashion affectation, a skinny-fit Ramones t-shirt, with the central HN of JOHNNY hidden in the gully between her irksomely pert boobs. Her face had a freshly fucked glow. 'Annie-ways ...' she said, adopting a favourite phrase of the person who'd been doing the fucking (it galled Jo that Louise's language was insinuating itself into the presenter's professional life). 'Today's text-in is about the sorry topic of break-ups.' She turned down the corners of her mouth and rallied a boo from the audience. 'Ultan, our resident agony uncle, will give advice on recovering from heartache, so get messaging! But first, some live rap music ...'

During Seanie K's Dublinese dirge, the text-in number remained at the bottom of the screen. Jo was struck by a devilish idea.

My g/f of 3yrs left me for sum1 else. Was doing the dirt for months and I found out. Feel so depressed, how can I get over her? Help pls! Joe

As the message went off, she imagined an unwitting Tamara reading it out on air, presuming it from some lovelorn little schoolboy. Jo laughed aloud and went to call Cillian, the only person on earth who'd fully appreciate the subterfuge.

It was only when she had scrolled to his name that her exhausted brain suddenly and sadly remembered that she would never be ringing him again.

23

'I'm off to do me stretches,' said Tiny, patting each girl on the back. 'No doubt *The Inseparables* need a proper girly catch-up anyway!'

The moment he left, the smile Rachel had been faking during their three-way chat collapsed. 'What the fuck are you playing at, Kim?' she whispered, acutely aware of the people milling around, and also her teammates who might well be watching from the corner.

Kim's face fell too. 'I just thought it'd be nice to come visit you …'

'Stalk me more like. Making poor Tiny drive you all the way down. God, if he knew what you were really up to …'

Kim threw up her hands. Even her wrists seemed skinnier than before. She'd lost so much weight her jacket was almost billowing out over her belt. 'What else could I do?' she said. 'You never answered my texts and you've deleted your Myspace.'

'Can you blame me when I'm being hunted down? How'd you even know I'd be here today?'

Kim brightened up immediately, like a child ready to show its mastery of a self-taught subject. 'Well, get this, right – I bumped into your auntie Cassie a while back, and she told me you'd been picked for the judo team in a place called Wheldon Green. So, I looked up tournaments in the general area and rang around to see which competition your team was registered in. Clever, eh?'

'That's not clever. That's creepy.'

'But I only wanted …' Kim's chin dimpled.

Rachel wondered how she'd explain to Alysha and the others why she'd made another competitor cry. She softened her voice. 'Sorry if I sound hard, Kim, but we already agreed that our little … *experiment* was finished. That it was destined to end anyway, because that kind of thing just isn't us. No big deal, let's move on for once and for all, shall we?'

Kim dried a lone tear with the sleeve of her *gi*. 'After we split and you left, I

155

kept telling meself I was fine. Being with a lass was just one of them strange experiences you have in your life. I went to work and to judo and all the usual, until one night the club went out to The Otter. I was drinking and chatting away when suddenly it hit us – I felt completely empty inside. I was just going through the motions, because I was missing you *really* badly, Rachel. I'd been denying me true feelings, but the more I drank, the clearer everything became ...'

Rachel sighed. 'Look, you got trolleyed and it made you emotional. Happens to everyone. Things always seem bigger when—'

'D'you think I'd come all the way here because of some false drunken emotion? That night I locked meself in the pub toilets and couldn't stop sobbing. I wrote you a million different texts that I never sent; I was afraid of making a fool of meself and turning you off forever. I was gone so long that Lauren came in to look for us. I had to invent a story that a lad I was crazy about didn't want to know me.'

Rachel shuddered. So Kim was *crazy* about her? This was getting more preposterous by the second! The only crazy thing was Kim herself. 'Imagine if Lauren had copped what was actually going on, Kim. Christ, you'd be annihilated. You need to stop this before you get caught out and labelled as something you're not.'

'But I must be a lesbian if I can't forget about us.'

'There is no *us*! We're just good friends who got a little bit carried away.'

Kim paused, fixing her with a strange, calm gaze. 'I wouldn't class two people fucking each other senseless every chance they got, including in a bath, a shower and every corner of a hotel room, as *getting a little bit carried away*, Rachel.'

'Keep your fucking voice down.'

'None of this fits in with your fancy new life. You've dumped your mates from back home, people you've known since you were a kid. You've got a new job, new club, new mates. Even a new bloody accent.'

'Now that's ruddy ridiculous, Kim!'

'Rudd-*ay* ri-*dic*-ulous,' Kim mocked with overblown poshness. 'You think you can just paper over this major aspect of your life by running away to London?'

Rachel could taste blood in her cheek. 'There is no major aspect,' she said coldly. 'It was a one-off.'

'And what about that Georgina lass in school you were in love with for three years?'

Rachel was furious for having bigged it up like that. 'All girls get crushes. It's a normal part of growing up.'

'Well, I hope you don't get a crush on your new friend who, incidentally,' said Kim, with a threatening flash of her eyebrows, 'is coming over right now.'

'Mention any of this and you're dead,' Rachel just had time to say, before she felt Alysha grabbing her from behind and singing into her ear, 'I know who you're fighting!'

Rachel turned around to face her friend, hoping that Kim would just leave. 'So tell me.'

'You've got Veronica McAdam first – which should be OK – but then Natasha Coates, who's pretty sick at groundwork.'

'And my third?'

'Kim Arrowhead or some such weirdness.' Rachel froze but then realised that Alysha must have mixed up the lists.

'I think you mean *Arrowsmith*,' said Kim, as she pushed her way around Rachel.

'What am I like!' Rachel said with a laugh. 'Totally forgot to do the introductions. Alysha, this is Kim from my old club. Kim, this is Alysha.'

'Sorry about buggering up your name there,' said Alysha as they shook hands.

'Don't worry, everybody gets it wrong,' said Kim with a glowing smile. 'So, you must be one of Rachel's new clubmates, then?'

'Yeah, myself and Rach live together.'

Rachel winced inwardly at Alysha's unfortunate choice of words. Kim had looked uneasy when Alysha had grabbed Rachel; now her eyes flicked suspiciously between the two of them, as though trying to divine the true nature of their relationship.

'You must have it wrong though, Alysha,' said Rachel, rushing in before

Kim could make further stalkerish enquiries masked as small talk. 'Kim's in the next class up.'

Kim patted her flat stomach. 'Not anymore.'

'You've gone *down* a class?' said Alysha. 'Nice work, girl.'

'It only happened because I've not been eating properly.'

'Wish I could *not eat properly* for a while!' said Alysha with a laugh. 'I've tried loads of times to cut weight for competitions – diets, dehydration, cardio, even a sauna once! Nothing ever worked so I've just given up.'

Kim gave a sad shrug. 'Oh, it's easy to lose weight when you've got a broken heart.' She looked levelly at Rachel, whose molars had just removed a large chunk of her inner cheek.

'Oh no, honey!' said Alysha, obviously touched by this revelation from someone she'd only just met. 'I've got the exact same problem. The blokes, they always let you down.'

'They certainly do,' said Kim, with an empathetic chuckle, but with a burning eye still trained on Rachel. 'As they say, *true love hurts.*'

Alysha slapped Rachel on the shoulder. 'No bad luck with the boys for this one, though!'

'Oh?' said Kim, her eyes widening and her lips thinning.

'She hasn't told you about sexy Stu yet, then?' asked Alysha.

'No,' said Kim, staring coldly at Rachel. 'She hasn't told me a thing about *sexy Stu.*'

'So, I bring this one down to my local for the very first time on Friday. And there's this gorgeous guy sitting near the bar and then …'

Rachel imploded invisibly with every syllable in Alysha's delivery. It was horrible for Kim to have to hear it like this, but if nothing else it might inspire her to finally surrender her misguided struggle.

'Wow,' said Kim, when Alysha's tale, complete with '*Pretty-Woman*-style snog on the picnic table', had concluded. She blinked slowly at Rachel. 'This all sounds very exciting …'

'Nothing concrete's been arranged yet,' said Rachel, looking away.

'Nonsense,' said Alysha. 'He's already booked a Japanese restaurant.'

To Rachel's relief, Kev was calling them from across the hall. She began to pull Alysha away.

'Catch you later, Kim,' said Alysha.

'Not if I catch you first!' said Kim, her levity dripping in threat. She turned to Rachel with a chilling smile. 'And as for *you* ... well, I'll see you on the mats!'

Jo couldn't help but feel flattered. A handwritten invitation from Louise to visit herself and Tamara in Ballsbridge! In a mature, reconciliatory spirit she decided to accept: seeing Louise's new life would end all torturous speculation about them reuniting.

Bizarrely, however, it had been *Cillian* – wearing Louise's Desigual t-shirt – who had answered the door, as though he lived there too. Jo hugged him and Louise, then shook the sallow hand of Tamara, who beamed with a welcoming smile.

The duplex apartment was far smaller than she'd imagined, but the three residents insisted on giving her 'the grand tour'. The sitting room featured well-worn velvet sofas and – strangely, given Tamara's occupation – a tiny black and white television with a clothes-hanger aerial. On the mantelpiece was a frame with four sections, three of which were filled with passport photos – Cillian, Louise and Tamara. The fourth section lay empty.

Cillian's room was plastered with pictures of Tamara, torn from the social pages of magazines. He whispered to Jo, 'You didn't want to buy a house with me, but I'm fine here so no worries.'

At the door of the master bedroom Jo resolved not to show any sexual jealousy when she saw the conjugal bed. As the door opened, she laughed with relief, because the room might belong to a couple of chaste bachelor brothers. She walked gaily between the two single beds (a lube bottle on the locker caused momentary concern until she copped that it was sweet chilli sauce). Her heart swelled with joy – Louise and Tamara were no more than friends!

Back on the landing, Jo noticed an extra door – a third bedroom? Halfway back down the stairs, she turned to the others. 'Annie-ways, how'd you fancy me as your new housemate?' She could already picture lively dinners in the kitchen, followed by Scrabble marathons, where she would wow Tamara with her lexical prowess, and Louise would shout, 'I told you my Jo was clever!' There would be Sunday drives to Dun Laoghaire and summer picnics where Jo, having joined Tamara's gym, could reveal her tanned, toned arms. Wild nights out would culminate at home, lines of coke raked out on the mantelpiece. As dawn approached Jo would invite Louise and Tamara to her new bedroom for drug-fucked fun and games.

She waited for the response that would make this happy mirage a reality. Louise and Tamara blinked slowly at each other and then angled their heads back towards Cillian. Then the same satisfied smile appeared simultaneously on all three faces, as if to say they'd been waiting for her to ask.

Suddenly they were in the kitchen, making freshly brewed coffee. Although no one had answered her question, Jo knew words were superfluous between friends. She was already noticing some of her own things around the place, including the set of mugs they were all about to use. It wouldn't be long before the frame on the mantelpiece was completed with the fourth photo.

She held her mug aloft. 'Here's to squaring this triangle!'

The others gathered round, but their expressions had turned sour. 'Cheers, Jo,' they cried, in deafening, unfriendly voices as their indestructible mugs smashed her one apart, sending coffee and crockery shards everywhere.

'Look what you've done, Jo,' roared Louise, her face as hot as the coffee now scalding Jo's chest and arms.

Tamara said, 'For fuck's sake,' and rubbed disgustedly at a droplet that had sullied the thigh of her white jeans. Cillian's brow was contorted with disappointment.

Jo gasped. 'I'm so sorry.' She fell to her knees in the coffee-puddle and began picking up the pieces. The others remained static, smirking. So this was her punishment for being presumptuous about moving in. She pulled over the bin to deposit the broken crocks, but every time she turned back more crocks had appeared on the floor. She picked and dropped, picked and dropped, her mortification turning to despair. A shard pierced her knee and soon her own blood had seeped into the spillage.

There was movement by the sink – Louise and Tamara coming together in a kiss. Jo tried to turn away, but her neck was locked. Louise fell against the sink and pulled Tamara between her thighs. Their kissing and caresses soon became sighs and pelvic grinding.

'My girls,' said Cillian, his arms folded as he observed them like a filthy pimp. 'Oh yeah, I love my two girls.'

The first mug Jo grabbed was the one Tamara had been using, and it was Tamara that she took aim for too. It made a gorgeous clunk as it hit her skull. The multitalented presenter shrieked and writhed out of her coffee-soaked top. Louise roared for someone to call an ambulance and the police – she was going to have Jo locked up. Sensing he was next, Cillian sprang behind the table, but Jo was too quick, and the next mug struck him elegantly on the temple. He stumbled around before collapsing into the vertical blinds at the patio door, which enveloped him like malevolent tagliatelle.

Jo set her sights on Louise now. The mugs weren't particularly aerodynamic, but this last one soared so very gracefully – rotating on its axis, maintaining a perfect trajectory. Any second now it was going to reach Louise's screaming face. And Jo could not wait.

She sat up sharply, her heart thudding. The dream had been so vivid that the reality of the darkened sitting room seemed surreal in comparison. The evening news cast a cyan glow on the walls. It must be after six! She didn't remember falling asleep; she was furious for missing the text-in. Despite the low probability her problem had been selected, there was a discernible charge in the air – was it the aural afterimage of *Joe's* message, read to the nation by Tamara herself? Jo would never know what advice the agony uncle had given.

Her leg muscles had grown even stiffer and sorer in sleep; she hobbled over to close the curtains. At the window she froze. A pale yellow mess, gloopy rivulets dripping down the glass. Three broken shells on the windowsill – one for each mug-impact in her dream. Afraid she was being watched by the culprits, she yanked the curtains closed. They were only eggs, she told herself, through quickening breaths as she began to pace the room – comic-book missiles, silly and schoolboyish. With Hallowe'en next week the local kids were in ballistic spirits. She must not allow the comedown-paranoia and the alco-fear to paint this as something personal. The same thing had probably been done to everyone on the terrace: tomorrow she would laugh it off with her neighbours, when everyone came out with their buckets and sponges.

A hand banged against the window. 'Lezzie, lezzie!' A boy's voice. A thrum of knuckles on the glass. 'Did I wake ya up in there, ya big dyke?' Even though the curtains were closed, she was grounded to the spot, as though he could see through them, as though he might reach in and grab her. A guffaw and a scuffle. A bike being ridden away.

She knew who it was. She knew too the feeling that was approaching – that looming doom. As the familiar symptoms of a panic attack began, she had never before felt so exposed or alone.

25

'Come on Alygator, you almost got her there.'

'Get in, Alysha!'

Dave and Aaron were shouting from the edge of the mats, where Alysha appeared to have a good chance of beating her final opponent of the day. She'd been outstanding in her previous bouts too, and was now poised to take the trophy for her division.

'Gan on, lass!' Even Tiny had come over to support his new pal; to Alysha's delight, he'd been flirting with her all day.

'*Morote gari*,' roared Sensei Kev.

'*Morote gari*,' Rachel echoed, trying to sound like she meant it, but as with all her encouragement today, she was simply parroting someone else's words. Apart from her dad's funeral, the last eight hours had been the most fraught and exhausting of her life, and there was at least another hour to go – an eternity in which Kim, whom Rachel was going to fight next (a prospect that filled her with more dread than any previous competitor ever) might still execute her threat of telling Alysha. Rachel had been monitoring the unhinged little bitch's whereabouts all day, but for all Kim's talk she'd spent her free time in the corner with her head buried in a novel. Tiny had reported 'lady pains' and said Kim wasn't up to socialising after all. Whenever Kim did raise her head, Rachel met her eye with a *don't you dare* stare, so that Kim knew she was under surveillance.

There were whoops and claps as Alysha dumped her puffing opponent onto the tatami at the last second.

'Flawless!' said Kev.

Rachel said, 'Flawless, Alysha,' though she hardly had the right to pass judo-judgements after her own performance today. Kim had made her so anxious and distracted that she'd managed to clock up two losses in as many bouts. To make matters worse, Sensei Kev had been so kind; he'd patted Rachel on the back, saying she was having 'one of those pear-shaped days'.

But behind the sympathy, Rachel sensed his bewilderment at her sudden lack of ability. It galled her to have let him and the others down like this. Still, the temporary blemish of underperforming was far less heinous than the indelible reputational stain that would ensue if she took her eye off Kim for even a minute. In that event it wouldn't matter what Sensei, Alysha nor the boys thought of Rachel's competitive prowess, because her relationship with all of them would be over, her new life ruined.

She kicked off her trainers and did some jumps and stretches. Her face was hard with competitive readiness, but in truth she'd decided, after a massive internal wrangle, to do something she'd never done in her life. Her dad would have been flabbergasted and furious: *Let the other lass win, Rachey? What the hell!* But it must be done, and with today's scoresheet already decimated, a further failure hardly mattered. She knew that thrashing Kim (which she could easily do) would only provoke her – this was especially dangerous because directly after the fight Kim would be free to mingle with the Wheldon crew who'd be supporting from the sidelines. But Rachel must not lose *too* obviously either. If Kim copped her plan it would infuriate her even more, and if Sensei noticed, he'd kick her off the team, maybe even out of the club. The worst part would be having to actually *touch* that weirdo, a weirdo who had finally put down her beloved book and was now approaching.

A couple of minutes later, the middle-aged referee, blissfully ignorant of the backstory between his two presenting competitors, was ready to start. As Kim arose from her bow, Rachel saw that her expression had curdled into something far harder than her standard game-face. The fight began. Kim rushed immediately at Rachel, trying to grab at the cuffs of her sleeves. Rachel skipped lithely to the side but offered no counterattack; faced with the physical proximity of Kim, she couldn't stomach her touch … not just yet. Kim, however, was tracking Rachel's every move; she lunged in again, angling for a grip. Rachel's crabwise dance across the mat evaded her, and physical contact was deferred again. Sensei Kev yelled at her to 'stop mucking about and get in there'. After another few seconds the referee was annoyed too – he pointed at Rachel, exclaiming, '*Shido* for passivity!'

She could no longer avoid contact. She let Kim take hold of her lapels and then reciprocated with a perfunctory grasp of her own. Kim yanked her inwards until their temples were butted together. Rachel's skull recoiled from Kim's sweating head. She began to fight back – their limbs in a push-pull, pistoning motion. Kim's lips came close to her ear. 'Not like you to be so passive,' came the grunted whisper. 'Not with *me* anyway!'

Rachel momentarily lost her grip. There was blood in her jowls – she wanted to spit it full-force into Kim's face. But there was no need to resort to catfight tactics when she could annihilate the bitch by legal means, right here in front of everybody, and in so doing save her reputation as a judoka. With a flashing blast of energy, she surged forward, letting out an involuntary battle cry. She didn't just want to beat Kim, but to *kill* her.

'That's more like it, Rachel,' someone shouted.

Kim, however, didn't seem particularly surprised by the onrush; she was matching Rachel's tugs and shoves with equally brutal moves of her own. The mangled dance for supremacy now began in earnest. They manoeuvred each other across the mats, then back again, their jackets growing baggier, their hair wisping out of their ponytails, their faces growing hotter and sweatier and more intent by the second.

'Watch your ankle, Rach!'

Rachel pulled her foot back from the attempted reap just in time, but this left her other side vulnerable. Kim took advantage with a nasty two-handed yank on her jacket; it broke Rachel's balance, and sent her into a flat-footed stumble, landing on her side, just within the perimeter of the contest area. She clambered back onto all fours, expecting Kim, whose groundwork was nothing special, to allow her time to get up again, but suddenly here was Kim, skidding onto the floor. This time she grabbed Rachel's collar from above and lifted her up, like a mother cat scruffing a naughty kitten.

Rachel told herself not to panic. She must take her time. If the little bitch wanted some groundwork, well, she would get it – with bells on! She extricated her neck and they entered a grunting scuffle on the mats. The referee's stockinged feet paced around, leaving damp prints on the floor.

His face appeared at odd angles as he crouched to peer into the knot of their bodies. All Rachel needed was to apply a decent strangle or armlock; Kim would submit and the match would be hers. It was simply a matter of picking the right moment. Kim would soon tire out; she just had to be patient.

She was right. After a further minute of attrition on the floor, she sensed a little more give in Kim's limbs; it wouldn't be long … it *couldn't* be long: there were only two minutes left on the clock! Rachel slyly freed her hand from the tussle and then slapped it suddenly, like a manacle, onto Kim's wrist. She tried to put on an armlock, but before she could exert the necessary pressure, Kim had already pulled free. As the tumble of cotton, sweat and hair continued, Rachel was comforted by the knowledge that all this would be sapping Kim's energy even further.

'Sixty seconds. Gan on both of yiz!'

There was no time left to wait for the perfect moment. *Do it now, Driffield,* she told herself. In a final push that called on every single one of her well-hydrated muscles, she shoved Kim flat onto her back and then pinned her at a perpendicular angle with her own chest. She fed her arm around Kim's disgustingly sweaty neck and took a firm hold of her collar, then hooked her other arm through Kim's legs (vile, but it *had* to be done), until she caught hold of Kim's belt. With both grips in position she exhaled and then pulled her arms tighter than she ever had in her life.

The referee pointed and shouted, '*Osaekomi*'; the hold was officially on. As Kim tried to wriggle, Rachel solidified her grip, arching her spine to keep her chest wedged tight. She gripped and pulled, pressed and held. Though holds seemed static, they demanded so much concentrated action in different directions – you had to renew the messages to the various muscles over and over: do not give up, do not *dare* give up. How pleased Sensei and her friends would be, seeing her win like this – they'd only been practising *yoko shiho gatame* last week. Over Kim's writhing body, Rachel watched the clock. Ten seconds in, fifteen to go. *Come on, Driffield, you can do this.* And how good it felt to get revenge on Kim for trying to ruin this important day.

'Last few secs, Rach, keep it locked!'

By now, Kim's attempts to escape lacked any real power. It struck Rachel that, despite the look on Kim's empurpled face, she might be *enjoying* being pinned down by another lass. The little perv. Maybe that was the reason she'd taken up judo in the first place, so she could roll around with all manner of girls! It wasn't fair on the other compet—

An elbow rammed into Rachel's abdomen. There was a savage tug on her belt. She was momentarily deafened, blinded as she was flipped over, right onto the flat of her back. She had lost concentration for a millisecond and now Kim had not only escaped but was wrapping her legs into a vice-tight triangle around Rachel's neck and right arm. 'Nice *sankaku jime*!' someone yelled, but there was nothing nice about the triangle choke, about having your head caught in the crotch of a creep like Kim.

As Rachel felt her face growing purple, her brain screaming for oxygen, she warned herself not to submit. This was just another challenge. She had an aptitude for overcoming challenges, didn't she? She pulled at Kim's knees, then tried to twist her own head to give her carotid artery some space. But Kim was now arching her hips, constricting her even more. The referee looked down into Rachel's eyes, which felt like they might pop from their sockets like champagne corks. The hem was coming down on his left trouser leg and a thin grey thread fluttered out horizontally, like a bird riding a thermal. She would rather black out, she would rather die of asphyxiation than to tap in submission. She stared at the tennis balls on the legs of the corner judge's chair. Tennis, now that was an idea. A nice, dignified, non-contact sport. Smiling sun-kissed faces, lemon barley and a ladylike handshake afterwards. Not this. Not this. Not even with her aptitude for challenges.

The vice-grip ratcheted up another notch, and she heard Kim whisper between breaths. 'Glad ... to have been part of ... your little experiment, Rachel.'

The tennis ball began to slowly roll away. Far, far away. Until all she could see was a pinpoint, fading into nothing, at the end of a darkening distance.

26

'Lunch specials for Rob and his friend,' Luigi set down the plates with a smile, then hurried on to serve the next table. Between smart suits and ravenous builders from the high-rise, the place was hopping today.

Michael beamed at his lasagne and side salad. 'Well, this looks *deliziosa* anyway.'

'Yeah, myself and Vicky come here a lot,' said Rob. As he took his first bite of lasagne he realised that they were sitting at the table where he'd told Vicky about his silly little dalliance with Salvador. That already seemed a lifetime ago. 'Actually, one day Vicky was really down in the dumps,' he continued, his mouth running ahead of his brain as usual. 'Wouldn't tell me why so I dragged her in here.' He pointed up at the framed poster. 'I said, "*Penne* for your thoughts!" She found it so funny she cheered up right away.'

Rob knew he'd claimed yet another of Vicky's pasta witticisms for his own, but he was so happy to see Michael in this new weekday context that he was eager to impress.

Michael peered up at the poster. 'Ah, I see, yes, *penne*, very good. And what's even better is that I can actually *read* something like that, now I've got these new lenses. Dr Littlejohn said that my eyesight had deteriorated by a full dioptre since my last visit. At this rate I'll be half-blind by the time I'm forty.'

'Well, if the silver lining's your sexy new glasses then that's OK with me. Littlejohn has good taste. They suit you.'

'When Dad was alive he used to swear by Littlejohn. He's a meticulous optometrist, he even does all Patrick Moore's monocles. Old-school as hell though. Refuses to open on weekends or evenings so I have to take a day off work every year.' He winked across the table. 'But at least I get to meet my beautiful Robbie this time.'

'It's nice to have you visit my work stomping ground. Not that it's particularly fancy round here, mind you.'

'I must return the favour and have you to lunch in Wheldon Green some weekday.'

'Are there any decent restaurants near your office?'

Michael used his finger to trace a map on the checked tablecloth. 'So, Wheldon high street's fairly long, say from here to here,' he said. 'My office is a big building down this end. But further up here are shops, pubs and cafés, plus a fantastic Japanese called Nagano. We should totally go there.'

Rob frowned and nodded at the invisible map as though trying to imagine the local topography. But he didn't need his imagination: he had already been to Wheldon Green. He would never admit it, but he'd gone there one night during the heady days of his online courtship with Michael, before they'd ever met in person. Tired of his friends' coked-up jeers to 'stop being a bore and do a little line', he'd escaped from Craig's twenty-sixth birthday at Brash Bar and had taken a midnight cab to the deserted workplace of a man he'd never met, but who already meant more to him than the 'friends' who probably hadn't even noticed his departure.

That night, Rob had sat on the shadowy steps of the office, thumbing the concrete and smiling at the sign bearing the three interlocking metal S's of Stedman Sheppard Structural. It was a thrill to know that Michael's eyes saw that sign daily, that his soles touched these steps, that his hand slid along this same steel banister as he went out to lunch with the other engineers. Rob had closed his eyes and allowed the deep connecting presence to overwhelm him for a while. Upon leaving, he'd blown a kiss towards the topmost windows (Michael had mentioned that he worked 'at elevation'). That night, Rob had promised himself that it wouldn't be much longer before he met this wonderful man in real life.

That same wonderful man, now sitting opposite him, was talking animatedly. 'But Robbie, if we do go to Nagano, there's one dish we should avoid.'

'Oh?'

'Once I had their chicken ramen directly before a meeting where I had to fire one of the trainee engineers. He was a little brat, always taking sick days and making mistakes. The meeting became fractious and when I had to raise my voice at him he pulled back and called me "garlic breath".'

Rob laughed. 'It must be quite the power trip getting to fire someone. As long as they deserve it, of course.'

'The two directors do most of the hiring and firing, thankfully. But on that front there may be some good news.' Michael leaned in. 'Word on the grapevine is that I'm being considered for a directorship very soon. Kenny Stedman keeps dropping little hints.'

Rob's fork fell from his mouth. 'But Michael, that's fantastic. Why didn't you tell me before?'

Michael shrugged. 'Oh, it's been a long time coming. It's actually a bit embarrassing they haven't given it to me yet.'

They finished their meal in high spirits. After a quick espresso, it was time to go. It had been one of the nicest lunch hours of Rob's life. And, for once, Joan hadn't rung to interrupt proceedings.

As they waited to pay at the till, Rob gave Michael's thigh a sneaky little rub. 'It's a shame I have to go back to work. Otherwise we could head to mine for some …' He imagined snogging Michael in his new glasses; and even better, carefully removing them in the bedroom later on.

Michael leaned to whisper in his ear. '*Afternoon delight?* Ooh, yes!'

Rob threw down a generous tip. Still giggling, they turned to leave. Just inside the door, however, waiting to be seated, were two people whom he would never expect to be here. And certainly not keen to encounter, especially when he was with his boyfriend.

'Lydia, Rachel. Great to see you both,' he said, stepping ahead of Michael to shake their hands. 'What brings you to Luigi's?' He needed to keep this as brief as possible. He could already sense Rachel's eyes flicking behind, a bit suspiciously, at his anonymous companion. While Hettie King and a couple of other clients knew he was gay (Hettie was always enquiring after Michael), he definitely didn't want these two finding out.

'We're meeting Corinne, actually,' said Lydia. 'Ascendant Events did a recce up at Gravenden this morning. She needs to fill us in.'

'That's right,' said Rachel coldly. 'Corinne suggested this place because she has another appointment around here afterwards.' She kept glancing at Michael as though waiting on an introduction.

'Wonderful,' said Rob, sick to think she might have seen their flirtation at the till. 'Your launch is shaping up to be something special.'

'It will need to be,' said Lydia with a curt laugh. 'The money we're spending.'

Rob clapped his hands. '*We* better get back to the office,' he said, hoping to paint Michael as one of his co-workers. 'Anyway,' he added with a jovial nod, 'I know you're expecting the first draft of the patient information booklet by close of business, so we better get cracking!'

'Indeed,' said Rachel, but then a thought seemed to strike her. 'Actually, if you send it over by *four* we can get our own changes back to you today.'

Lydia nodded in agreement. 'Good thinking, Rach. We'll be back in the office in a couple of hours anyway.'

'Perfect,' said Rob, already dreading relaying this deadline to Daryl.

Lydia caught Michael's eye. 'So you're the designer who works on our materials?' she asked.

Michael chuckled and stepped out of Rob's shadow. 'Well I *do* design things, but it's more about bridges than booklets,' he said. 'No, I'm Rob's other half. Michael Wyles. Lovely to meet you.' He extended his hand to a slightly amused-looking Lydia, then to Rachel, who afforded it a limp, fingertip shake as though it were contaminated. Rob felt as horrified as Rachel looked. He wanted to kill Michael for outing him but then realised his boyfriend was just being super-polite to his clients. Michael wasn't to know that this was the Fussbudget that Rob continually complained about.

As he said goodbye and quickly steered Michael out of Luigi's, Rob had a feeling that things on the Follestra account were about to get a whole lot worse.

27

Jo eased her house key into the microscopic pocket of her new Nike capris and secured it with the exquisite little zip. If Finbarr in Planet Run hadn't brought the pocket to her attention earlier, she might never have noticed it! The evening terrace was dark and deserted, but she still felt incredibly self-conscious as she turned on the doorstep to start her first-ever outdoor run. It was one thing to wear running gear in a gym where many members' abilities were as dubious as her own but quite another to sport it outdoors, where the look became a public declaration that she could indeed *RUN* – as touted by the reflective text emblazoned on her new top. She was fearful of encountering any real runners – they might deem her an impostor, a huffing embarrassment to the clan.

She was toying with the idea of changing into unremarkable tracksuit bottoms, when a door opened further down the terrace. She knew, from the shouting, exactly whose door it was too. Suddenly, she found herself racing in the opposite direction, the houses and their Hallowe'en adornments a ghost-train blur in her peripheral vision. During their long chat at the till, Finbarr had said novices must always warm up with a five-minute walk. But Finbarr hadn't had his front window egged last Sunday by Wayne O'Harridan.

She hadn't told a soul about what Wayne had done, and wondered if helping his young 'girlfriend' with her homework had made her a target. None of the neighbours had found out either – her hands still trembling after the panic attack, she'd snuck out with a cloth and a freshly boiled kettle while they slept: the thing was awful enough without them copping why her house alone had been singled out.

She couldn't believe how quickly she reached North Circular Road, especially given her suboptimal footwear. Finbarr had booked her in for gait analysis on Saturday so he could fit her with her first pair of proper running shoes. He was also printing her out the *10K-OK!* programme, to prepare for the Port Tunnel Run, only seven weeks away. In a fit of defiance against Cillian, Louise, Tamara and Wayne O'Harridan, she had, with disbelieving fingertips, registered her details on the race website yesterday.

She hopped briefly into the gutter to bypass two older powerwalking women, then felt their jealous eyes on her young back as she raced on ahead. The thrill quickened her even more, and it wasn't long before the her new gear was subjected to its first-ever sweat-test.

She ran on towards Phibsborough, then made a snap decision to turn in to Great Western Square. Halfway around the green, she heard a massive bang from the far side, followed by teenage shrieks and the whiff of gunpowder. The kids would surely deem a lone female runner a hilarious target for one of their pre-Hallowe'en incendiaries. Yet a meek retreat from the square didn't fit with Jo's newfound empowerment. She spotted the entrance to a back lane up ahead on the left. Before the kids had time to register her presence, she had powered through the middle of their group, and was disappearing into the dark mouth of the passageway.

28

'Ta da!' Alysha released the final curl from the grip of the GHD. Rachel had been anxious about the new style but now, as Alysha arranged the final hairstyle into shape in the mirror, she saw it had been worth the risk.

'It looks amazing, Alysha!'

'Not bad for someone who only saw them doing it yesterday on *This Morning*, eh?' She clapped Rachel up from the bed. 'Right, give us a three-sixty before I release you to the man.'

Rachel turned around a couple of times. They'd decided against her wearing a dress – Nagano was so authentic you had to sit on cushions on the floor – but still, she looked pretty good in her new black bootcuts and purple top.

Alysha wolf-whistled. 'I'd actually do you myself!' she said.

Rachel gave a nervous laugh and grabbed the chopsticks from the dressing table. 'One last go?'

Alysha handed her the bowl of potpourri they'd been using to practise with all week. 'Now remember, don't let that bottom stick move, not even a millimetre!'

29

If Jo had known how dark and long this lane was, she would have thought twice. Running at pace for a full minute, there was still no end in sight (and, glancing over her shoulder, no sign of the beginning either). Just unending ten-foot walls on either side. She hadn't encountered a single person, which was both comforting *and* concerning. A cloud slid across the moon, cutting the already poor visibility to a couple of metres ahead. She wasn't sure whether it was safer to decelerate or accelerate in such circumstances but decided on the latter. A moment later, something brushed against her ankle. She jumped, her petrified yelp ping-ponging off the walls. But it was just a vodka bottle. It spun away – as rattled as she was – before coming to rest with a glassy clank.

The fright was an adrenaline-pen to the heart. Gathering speed again, she came to the conclusion – amid the quickening rhythms of steps, breaths and the throb in her carotid – that she must be crazy. An anonymous neophyte in a deserted laneway, without a phone. No one aware of her whereabouts. No one expecting her home. It would take the forensics ages to determine the identity of the waxen athlete with the ligature marks on her neck. A five-foot-seven female, pale, mid-brown hair. Her body discovered by an insomniac pensioner who always walked his dog at first light, and now, would never sleep again. It would only be when the state pathologist discovered the microscopic pocket, and the Gardaí tried the key in the door of 26 Blackstairs Terrace that they would contact Jo's bewildered parents, who had never known their daughter to go running, especially not alone, especially not at night. She had allowed the streamlined shorts to fool her into thinking that phones and ID cards were superfluous encumbrances. But the shorts were meant for joggers on the sunny safety of Californian boardwalks, not fools running rape-lanes in darkest Dublin 7.

Suddenly the end – but of the lane, not her life – was nigh. She burst into the safety of an illuminated residential street, panting with the exhilaration of someone who'd just drawn on their own grit to survive a life-threatening event. She certainly wasn't taking breather after her ordeal either; if she thought she'd experienced the ultimate runners' high on the treadmill then it was nothing compared to this! Grinning wildly, she ran through the streets faster than ever before, and then bounded up Arbour Hill towards home.

30

Rachel cringed, recognising the kimonoed Japanese lady at the front desk. As they'd popped in on Sunday night to get the practice chopsticks, Alysha had blabbed whole Stuart story to her. Thankfully, the waitress was the epitome of discretion this evening. She gave Rachel the tiniest nod of acknowledgement, then led the way past several floor-sitters to where she'd already installed Stuart, so thoughtfully, at one of the upright tables.

Stuart set down his Blackberry and gave Rachel a neat, fresh peck on the cheek, quite at odds with the full-on Guinnessy snog they'd had outside The Mill on Friday. 'Wow, your hair!' he said, curling his finger in the air.

'Thanks, I often wear it like this when I'm going out.' Smiling, she made a pretence of looking at the menu, but Alysha had already told her what to order. *Chahan* was the safest bet because it wouldn't splash onto her top (like noodles or teriyaki), nor fall apart mid-lift (like sushi), yet would still showcase her new chopstick skills.

As Stuart perused his menu, Rachel got to take a second look at him. *His* hair was different too; the raw edges and his reddened neck betrayed a recent barber visit, obviously in preparation for tonight. His Jack & Jones shirt with the skinny epaulettes was nice, but what adjectives would best describe the colour? Baby blue sounded lame so she decided on pale azure. Alysha would love that!

After a minute he looked over his menu, wincing. 'I have a confession, Rachel. I've never eaten Japanese before.'

She fought the urge to reciprocate the admission. 'And I thought everyone living in London was into exotic food!'

'I'm more of a cheese and pickle man myself. It was my business partner Al who suggested I bring you here. I'm sure you know all about this kind of food because of judo. That's Japanese too, isn't it?'

'It certainly is.' So the haircut hadn't been his only preparation. She snapped her menu closed. 'Think I'll have my favourite old *chahan* tonight.'

'At risk of being a pathetic copycat, I'll take the same,' he said.

She gave him a teasing look and nodded at the drinks list. 'Well, if you're going to copy, then at least you can make the decision about the wine!'

Rachel was regaling him with her latest efforts to tame Narelle's waywardness when the waitress arrived with their matching meals.

'Do either of you need a knife and fork?' she asked, giving Rachel a brief but loaded look.

'I'm fine with these, thanks,' Rachel said. She slid the chopsticks from their paper sleeve and splayed the webbed base apart. Stuart let go of his wine glass and touched his own pair with unease. 'Would you mind … ?' He gave the waitress an embarrassed grin.

Rachel felt even more pressure to perform now, but as he gratefully gripped his cutlery, she slipped the sticks around the c-bend of a king prawn, and popped it elegantly into her mouth.

'So, your judo competition,' he said, stealing an impressed glance at her dexterity. 'Your text said it went fine?'

'Yeah, I did some really good throws so Sensei was delighted. Oh, and remember my friend Alysha? She won her whole category.'

'Victory to The Alygator!'

She smiled. He had really been paying attention on Friday. 'And a guy from my old club in Newcastle turned up out the blue too, so that was a nice surprise.'

Stuart's fork stalled halfway to his mouth. 'An ex of yours … ?'

'God, no,' she said, pleased at his concern. 'Tiny's happily married, a foot smaller than me, with a gold tooth and the broadest Geordie accent *you've eva heard, man!*'

'Sounds like a cool guy,' Stuart said, gushing with the generosity of relief. 'I'm sure you had lots to catch up on. Telling him about your swanky new Lahndahn life, innit?'

'Absolutely.' She took a large gulp of wine. All this talk of Sunday was bringing up silly thoughts of Kim again. It had taken a lot more than a gulp after the tournament to ease the day's tensions. Her teammates had jeered as she'd ordered herself a large bottle of rosé at The Wheldon Arms, but she'd explained that she was both toasting Alysha's win and drowning her own sorrows at her poor performance. She'd spent the next day a sickly pink spin, but coping with the hangover and hiding it from Narelle and Lydia had been welcome distractions from thinking about Kim and the competition.

Twenty minutes later she was precision-picking the last grains of rice from her bowl; the chopstick-challenge had been an unmitigated success. Stuart had no problems understanding the dessert menu and they had a funny argument when Rachel claimed she *would* rather die than eat Stuart's favourite, 'Death by Chocolate'. He polished off a portion of that dessert, while she ate her lychee mousse (another of Alysha's diktats – suitably ethnic yet not bloaty). Then they agreed that a drink at The Mill was in order. Rachel was pleased at Stuart's desire to prolong the evening as well as his insistence on paying the bill, but really she wasn't surprised because it had been going so well. It was wonderful how confident she had felt all night – she hadn't allowed first-date nerves to spoil a single second. She hoped Mel and Ollie would be in the pub to witness their entrance – if they were, then Mel would surely text a favourable progress report back to Alysha.

As they walked up the high street, Rachel nodded at Dry-Klean King. 'That's where I get all my suits for work done.'

'Ooh, I bet you look quite the powerful businesswoman when you're laying down the law to Narelle or that ad agency guy who can't spell.'

She swished the end of her scarf playfully. 'Maybe you'll see me in one of my suits sometime. If you're lucky!'

'I really hope I ... god, sorry hang on ...' He scowled at the screen of his buzzing Blackberry. 'It's Al, what the hell does he want?'

As he took the call, Rachel wandered to a respectful distance and looked into the harshly lit WWWheldon, where an array of slaves to keyboard and screen sat in facing rows, typing, clicking and staring. A small, skinny man with a greasy combover and a flushed face rose from a booth at the back that was hidden by a vending machine. Pulling his shabby anorak down over his crotch, he came up and threw the cashier a couple more coins before scuttling back into his furtive corner.

'I'll get over there now,' Stuart was saying. 'Which neighbour has the key?'

Rachel didn't like the sound of this. Wasn't it a first-date tactic to arrange an escape-plan with a friend? She might be out of practice with men and their often contrary ways, but surely she hadn't misread tonight's signs that badly?

'Everything OK?' she asked when he had hung up.

'There's an alarm going off on the far side of Wheldon and the neighbours are losing the will to live. Al was supposed to be on call tonight because I was meeting you, but now his little girl's got a roaring fever and they're waiting in casualty.'

'The poor mite.' She inspected his face for signs of lying but found none.

'I'm so sorry, Rachel. I'll ring you tomorrow to arrange another night.'

'Don't worry about it.' She already dreaded Alysha's disappointment as she arrived home so prematurely, without any sexual swag – not even a smooch. Alysha would find his exodus suspicious, and there would be the anxious wait tomorrow to discover if the alarm and the fever had been fabrications. Rachel would rather know now if he didn't like her – at least then she could say to Alysha that *she* had been the one to end the date. She would say that he wasn't her type after all.

Stuart flagged down a cab and took out his wallet. 'Let me pay your fare home since I've messed up our night.'

'No,' she heard herself announce. 'Why don't I come with you?' She readied herself for the telling refusal.

His hand froze on the cab door. 'To Wheldon Court? Surely not the fanciest place for the end of our date.'

It was hardly the resolute refusal of a cornered man, but could his oblique demurral be another tactic? 'I don't mind,' she said. 'The more I get to know my new neighbourhood, the better.'

He shook his head. 'You really are …' His gaze slipped shyly to the footpath.

'I'm really … ?' She tried to draw his eyes back to hers. 'Stuart, what?'

'Sorry,' he said, giving himself a little shake. 'Let's just say I'd be most honoured for you to be my beautiful assistant in this exhilarating alarm crisis.' He admitted her to the cab with a chauffeur's flourish, then slid tightly in beside her with a delighted smile.

'*This premises is managed by Alart Property Management,*' said Rachel, reading from the little placard inside the Formica-panelled lift. 'I'm impressed. Though Al *did* get the better deal with his full name at the front, while you only get the last three letters of yours!'

'Story of my life,' said Stuart. He gave her hand, which he'd been holding since they'd left the cab, a quick squeeze. The doors opened. 'Brace yourself for the noise,' he said. 'These old alarms are literally hell's bells.'

In the shadowy corridor they passed a tall man with his fingers in his ears, a couple of Sainsbury's bags swinging across his face as he walked. Rachel thought she knew him from somewhere, but he hurried quickly by, clearly just as desperate as them to escape the ringing. She was finding a certain comfort in the racket, however: the alarm, just like the sign in the lift, was yet more evidence that Stuart wasn't a liar.

The key was in the next flat, answered by a late fifties woman, square-jawed and stout, in a cleavage-revealing dressing gown. Her eyes widened as she clocked the dashing gentleman who'd come to save her from the noise, then contracted crossly when she spotted his beautiful assistant. She brought them into her hallway. 'Thanks so much for coming,' she said breathily to Stuart. 'The girls are away for a month. I was afraid there was a burglar in there.'

'Don't you worry, madam,' said Stuart, in a calm, masterful tone. 'We'll check the place and silence the alarm. I'll leave a note telling them to get it serviced because alarms are supposed to turn off after twenty minutes. At least they were sensible enough to leave you a key and the code. There's plenty who don't.'

'Oh, Stephanie and Althea are quite responsible,' she said. 'Though to look at them you wouldn't think it. They're good neighbours too, despite being … well, *y'know*.' She turned on the heel of her velvet slipper and went to find the key, while Rachel and Stuart stared at each other in puzzlement and tried desperately not to giggle.

The siren came to a halt. 'Sitting room window,' said Stuart, bending to consult the little screen. 'Probably a gust of wind.'

Rachel had been waiting by the open door, but at Stuart's beckoning came in and closed it behind her. 'Your lady-friend will be ever so grateful,' she said.

He gave a squirming shiver. 'Myself and Al are always getting hit on by sexually frustrated older women. He just flashes his wedding ring and shows them pictures of his daughter, but it's harder for me to escape.'

'Just as well I came along, then,' she said. 'But what did the neighbour mean about the girls who live here?'

Stuart looked around the hallway, his mouth twisted in thought. 'I reckon they're mass murderers. See those red trainers there? Perfect for hiding blood.'

'I bet they're androids from the future,' said Rachel. 'Check out that strange metallic vase – a portal to another dimension, perhaps?'

Stuart laughed. 'I'll check that window sensor while you look for any further clues. Though I'm *fairly* confident you won't find anything android-related.'

'I wouldn't be so sure,' called Rachel. She checked the bathroom first, which revealed nothing except a tonne of cosmetics left messily around the shelves, and a bone-dry shower and sink. Then she entered the one and only bedroom.

She must have subconsciously been expecting twin beds, because she was taken aback to find a double. Her surprise was mild, however, compared to the shock she got when she switched on the light and saw the painting above the headboard. Her reflex was to turn off the light and leave, before Stuart came in and saw it too. She would say she'd found no evidence of murderers nor androids, they would lock up and get out of there, with Stuart none the wiser. But before she could stop herself, she had gone across the room, and her eyes were roaming over the strange watercolour painting – rather in the same way the hands of the passenger-girl on the Vespa were roaming all over the bare breasts of the driver. As well as wearing nothing on top, neither girl wore a helmet – in fact their outfits comprised only of sawn-off denims and brightly coloured, laceless trainers. Their trendy mullet-esque hairstyles, one blonde, one copper, were flowing in the wind. Between these girls and bumping into Rob and his weird boyfriend yesterday (which had been so icky she'd found it hard to concentrate during the meeting with Corinne afterwards), it felt like she was being creepily stalked by gay people this week.

'So, murderer or android, then?'

'God, Stuart,' she said with a jump and a guilty kind of gasp. She spun round to face him in the hope of blocking the view behind. 'Don't sneak up on me like that.'

'Sorry,' he said, but then he peered over her shoulder. 'Oh my word, what's going on with that painting?'

She turned around and gave it the briefest of glances, unable to look at it properly in his presence. 'I didn't even see that thing, I was too busy admiring the lovely duvet cover.' She cringed at how ridiculous this was because the painting stood out a mile – both in content and colour – compared to the bland beige bedclothes.

But Stuart wasn't listening; he leaned across the headboard to check the handwriting curved around the front wheel. '*Hooters on a Scooter*,' he read. 'To Steph and Thea, my fave couple, love from X.' He turned back to Rachel, grinning. 'So much for androids and mass murderers. Shock horror, our girls are merely … *lesbians*!'

'Oh, is that all!' said Rachel with an airy little laugh, though right now it felt as though an alarm, far louder than the one they'd just switched off, was blaring out from her body.

Stuart said, 'Pretty cool painting, isn't it?' He came and stood behind her, wrapping his arms round her neck, as though they were honeymooners in a foreign art gallery. She had no choice but to look at the picture again and hope he couldn't sense the stiffness in her shoulders nor, as he rested his cheek against hers, the heat rising through her skin. She berated herself for the ridiculous reaction – if she hadn't pretended she hadn't seen the picture, nor made that stupid comment about the duvet, then she wouldn't have unnerved herself about it in the first place. In trying too hard to convey how cool she was about it – and why *wouldn't* she be cool about a picture that had nothing to do with her? – she'd wound herself into a silly, self-conscious mess.

Still transfixed by it, Stuart rocked her in his arms. 'I wonder which one's Steph and which one's The— *oh*!'

She had spun round and was gripping him hard, kissing him even harder: he struggled at first to match her furious rhythm. He did catch up, though, and before long the bedroom was filled with sighs, and the sound of their coats sliding to the floor.

She could feel the piped edge of the mattress against her thigh now and, as soon as his hands were busy with her boobs and bum, she made her move. Hooking his calf with her own, and grasping an epaulette on his shirt, she pulled backwards, taking him with her.

'Smooth move,' he whispered, as they bounce-landed, still face to face, on the previously unremarkable duvet.

She shrugged humbly against his body. 'Just some basic *ashi-waza*. Nothing special.'

The Japanese had an effect on him. 'Say that again.'

'You should see my *sode tsuri komi goshi*,' she said.

'Mmm, I'd love to ...'

Horizontal for the first time together, the intensity began its inevitable increase, but after he'd slid his hands up to undo her bra, he stopped and pulled his head back. 'I don't usually make a habit of doing this in clients' homes,' he said, 'let alone their *beds*.' He nodded ominously at the painting. 'What if they were to suddenly come home?'

She pulled his face back to hers. 'Forget about them … they're away … for a *month*,' she said, between a set of smothering snogs. Before he could respond she reached down and ran her hand across the front of his jeans; there it was, the same erection that had pressed her thigh outside The Mill. She'd been unable to acknowledge it then because they'd been in public, but now …

She pulled the point of his belt out of its loop, then stopped to look at him. 'I do hope you came prepared?'

Propped up on a tremulous elbow, he worked his wallet out of his jeans, and placed the foil square into Rachel's hand, which was flapping like Lydia's when she needed a delayed document back from Narelle. It had been a while since she'd put a condom onto a man, but that didn't matter because right now she was possessed with a spiralling confidence and knew, as she popped the metal prong out of his belt and undid the zip to free the curving bulge beneath, that she would manage it all perfectly. She wasn't shocked or scared by her spurt of sexual spontaneity nor where it was taking her – these actions were only natural for a woman who'd spent too long without a man. And the man to end this drought was Stuart, and here he was pressed up against her, sighing and writhing, his fingers dipping beneath the lacy waistband of her knickers. He let out a sound as she tugged down his jeans and boxers. A *manly gasp* … yes, that was how she would describe it later. With a final defiant glance up at the two weird Vespa-girls, she got down to work.

She could already imagine the look on Alysha's face when she heard about all this!

31

As soon as Hazel and Martin had left for work, Noel sat up in Chloe's bed. It was only half past eight. Back at the flat, Noel had always slept late on a Thursday – his regular day off from Goodstep – often snoozing until after eleven. But such lie-ins were history now; this was his only time alone in the house, *their* house, a semi-detached three-bed, at the blind end of a Croydon *cul de sac*.

Earlier, he'd pretended to sleep while they rushed about getting ready for another day at the local council office, where they both worked. He'd even let out few false snores as they passed the door. Now, he sprang out of the bed – insofar as this was possible for a six-foot-two, heavy-set man with partially numb, diabetic feet.

As he dragged his dressing gown around his belly and scratched his jaw, he felt judged by the skinny, callow lads who watched from the bedroom wall. The pop stars in Chloe's posters had swooshy fringes, pouting mouths and innocent skin, rendered even more flawless with foundation. Still, it gave Noel a little kick that these girly chaps were considered sex symbols by girls themselves nowadays.

He was shaving when his main mobile phone pinged with a text. It was Hazel asking him to take pork chops out of the freezer for tonight's dinner because she'd forgotten to earlier. She also reminded him to have his banana and muesli, to record his blood sugar, to inject his insulin, and to rub Vaseline on the scar on his forehead. He sighed – Hazel meant well, but he'd been living here three weeks now, and her incessant imperatives were starting to wear thin.

Down in the kitchen, he pricked his finger for his blood-sugar test, then wrote the result into his resurrected diary, which Hazel checked every evening, like a schoolteacher. He pushed a syringe into a vial and injected his belly. (The type of insulin in the pens was no longer suitable for him, apparently, but he appreciated the honesty of seeing an actual needle instead of some pretend pen.)

He drenched his muesli in insipid skimmed milk and added the banana, splaying the empty skin into a starfish inside the bin, so that Hazel would see he had complied. He took three chops and squeezed them onto a plate to thaw. Three was an odd number. And how odd it felt at his age to be suddenly living with a married couple, also in their late fifties. Even though Hazel was both his cousin and his adoptive sister, no matter how she tried to subsume Noel into her own little family, he still felt like a huge intruder.

By now it was nearly ten. He hurried back upstairs to the bedroom. Hazel sometimes came home for an early lunch – that left just two and a half hours. He opened a drawer in Chloe's dressing table and took out the sock in which his other phone was hidden.

It took three attempts to switch it on; the buttons on pretty pink phones were not designed for thickset fingers. As the screen sprang to life, he held his breath. He knew already he wouldn't be hearing from Steph and Thea because they were travelling abroad; nor was he hopeful about Bethany and Christine, whose relationship was struggling. There were his old reliables Anouska and Ruby, of course, but he'd seen them only last week. He was expecting one message, however – from Xenna. On Monday he'd texted to ask about today (as an artist she was at home on weekdays), but he hadn't had a safe opportunity to see if she'd responded. The screen finally lit up … but remained blank. It seemed that nobody needed him at the moment. He sighed and slumped to the bed. What an awful pity; what a waste of his day off.

After a minute he shook off his funk: even if no one wanted an appointment, he still had plenty to do. Other girls like Taylor led such busy lives that he might get a request at a moment's notice later in the week. It always paid to be prepared.

The suitcase was deep under Chloe's bed. He knelt down to grab the handle. He brought it onto the duvet, sensing both distant history and immediacy in the name emblazoned on the brown leather. EILEEN MOODY. He ran his fingers over the letters – though she'd used a standard stencil, there was still something incredibly personal about this suitcase, especially because Eileen had used it as a young woman during the war.

Nobody knew Noel had it, nor had anyone ever questioned its whereabouts since he'd snuck it back to his own flat after her funeral. Then, three weeks ago he had smuggled it here inside a large holdall, pretending it was just another bag of his own clothes. He'd rushed it upstairs to Chloe's bedroom upon arrival, while Martin and Hazel unloaded the rest of his things from their car.

Now, as he gazed at the case he pictured it on a luggage mesh aboard a wartime train, Eileen sitting beneath, in a hat and a fitted coat, gracefully sipping her flask of rationed tea. Noel hadn't been born a Moody, of course; but now the O's in the surname, a name that he'd happily and legally assumed at the age of ten, looked back at him like eyes – they were Eileen's eyes, regarding him kindly from beyond this life, but also telling him, as his lip began to quiver, to stop being soppy and get a move on.

He opened his wallet and fished out the little key. He was just about to insert it into the rust-freckled lock when there was a sound from downstairs. He froze for a moment, but it was just today's post, flopping onto the doormat.

The next feeling he got was intoxicating: the thrill of the suitcase open on the bed, its contents exposed freely to the air of the house. It felt as though his own chest was split open – his heart in plain view, pumping wildly, as it was now. The feeling surged as he took some things from the case out onto the landing, and then carried them right into Hazel and Martin's bedroom.

He always winced as he went in – nowhere were his hosts' messy tendencies more evident. Downstairs they at least tried, but here in the privacy of their own room, they didn't bother. Having to live and sleep in proximity to such chaos upset Noel. He stepped over Hazel's inside-out skirt, then averted his eyes from the streams of flesh-coloured tights hanging from a drawer, like intestines spilling from roadkill. There was a fresh brown stain beside the vanity unit: bronzing balls walked carelessly into the carpet. He wanted to pick up the remainder of the fallen balls before they got crushed too but stopped himself lest they might notice and find it peculiar that he'd been tidying the conjugal bedroom.

He was able to look away from such horrors, but poor Eileen had no such option, observing the scene with her unswerving smile from the frame on the bedside table. Today, to add further insult, her perfect grey coiffure was obscured by the toe of a discarded popsock. Noel took up the frame and dusted it with the corner of his dressing gown. He blinked into her beautiful face. 'I know how much you'd love the two of us to get going in here. I still cannot comprehend how someone as messy as Hazel could be *your* daughter!'

He resentfully replaced the popsock and then retrieved the ironing board from Martin's side of the room, where a pile of *National Geographic* grew dustier by the week and the locker was a swamp of loose change and spent packs of Rennies.

He turned the iron up to max to deal with the badly creased fabric. He'd had to transfer things quickly into the suitcase from his bag when he arrived home from Ruby and Anouska's on Friday because Hazel was pottering around the landing, waiting for her hair dye to take. The iron hissed and slid, hissed and slid: twice he had to replenish the reservoir; thanks to his big bones, there were yards of fabric to get through. He paid attention to the smaller details too, imagining Eileen's clucks of admiration as he worked the point of the soleplate into every last dart and gather. Finally finished, he folded everything up and angled the stack of clothes towards the photo.

'Think these would be up to your high standards, eh, Aunty Ei?' Although it was of course impossible, he was sure her lipsticked smile had widened with dignified approval.

He would have loved to hang the things up in a wardrobe like he did at the flat but instead, back in Chloe's room, he tucked them neatly into the suitcase beside the floral wash bag and the photo album. There was a roll of film in there too – pictures that Xenna had taken with her vintage Leica on his last visit. He decided to go to Hackney that afternoon to get them developed in the huge, impersonal one-hour photo shop. It was an arduous three-bus trip, but he didn't dare leave the film in anywhere around here, nor near his usual home in Wheldon Green. Someone might recognise him. Anyway, with no requests on the pink phone, he had nothing else to fill the afternoon.

He locked the suitcase. It felt annoyingly light as he slid it back under the bed – a reminder that Xenna had the rest of his gear. She'd offered to do his laundry now he was living here, but it was two weeks since he'd heard from her. Despite Xenna's whimsical ways and volatile life, such a protracted silence was still odd. He didn't like to pester clients, but he felt a further text was justified. He typed carefully on the pretty pink keys.

Sorry to text again Xenna, but could I call to you Saturday? Even to just collect my things if full session does not suit. Let me know. Regards and Thanks, Noeleen.

32

'Oh god, sorry!' Jo sputtered to a halt on the toes of her new Mizunos and bent to retrieve the nappies she'd knocked down with her overzealous elbow. She handed them back to the Roma woman, hoping the dark evening would conceal the busted-open corner on the plastic. In any case, before the woman could complain, Jo had taken off again. Since starting the *10K-OK!* programme three weeks ago, she'd taken many different routes around the north inner city, but this stretch of the North Circular Road – between Hanlon's Corner and the NCR entrance to the Phoenix Park – was the most challenging yet. Firstly, there were the London planes whose swollen old boles constricted the already narrow path and whose protuberant roots, in a cunning conspiracy against runners' ankles, were hidden by swathes of slippery autumn leaves. This, coupled with the proliferation of bin bags and so many pedestrians, made it impossible to travel at any meaningful speed without inherent risk to oneself, or indeed the shopping of others.

She had no choice but to defer the tantalising arrival of tonight's runner's high (which usually kicked in after a stiff two-kilometre slog) and decelerate to a sensible jog that allowed her to dodge the various obstacles. Further ahead, however, she saw something she actually *wanted* to stand on – she took pleasure in grinding her sole onto the discarded copy of yesterday's *commUte*. The sponsored glossy outsert had caused bitten lips in *Dublin AM*, especially as all four pages had been taken by the Muldoon Group. Muldoons had never taken such a radical splash in *Dublin AM*, yet seemed happy to spend recklessly on a paper that had only been around for a mere week.

Even more fickle than the advertisers was the readership itself: it was clear that *Dublin AM*'s fiercely loyal fans had only been fiercely loyal while there was no alternative. Now they were flushed with love for the sexy newcomer, leaving *Dublin AM*'s kerbside merchandisers reporting overstocks, and Jo and her colleagues wondering why they'd expended so much effort crafting articles for an utterly distracted audience.

Soon she was racing through the gates to the Phoenix Park, which would provide exactly 4.3 kilometres of her route tonight. It was her first time venturing in there after dark. Though it was always full of runners in the daytime, she encountered no one as she headed down the footpath flanking the North Road. Eventually a couple of wire-limbed older men came running towards her, sporting the ultimate in wearable trophies – 2006 Dublin City Marathon Finisher t-shirts. Jo must be the only runner in Dublin who had to resort to shop-bought tops: she had discovered that the *real* must-have t-shirts couldn't be purchased on a maxed-out credit card from Finbarr at Planet Run. Still, it wouldn't be long before she was sporting her own Port Tunnel 10K t-shirt. She would wear it while training for her next race and hoped that Cillian might see her in it as she silently whizzed past him on the street someday.

As the marathon finishers ran by, the elder one shot Jo a look of avuncular concern – as if to signal that Europe's largest enclosed city-park was no place for a lone female runner to be entering at nine o'clock on a freezing November night. Even he – much bigger and male – was training as part of a pair, a pair that was now on its way *out* of the park. Jo took note of his concern and then ran boldly through it. Tonight's circuit was just the latest in a litany of risks she'd been taking on her evening runs. That first eerie laneway had awoken something in her, and now she planned progressively riskier routes as the nights went on. She had tramped through piss-stinking railway underpasses where teenagers dry-humped against dripping concrete; she had jogged along the towpath of the tar-black canal all the way down into Phibsborough and then turned at the lock only to run all the way back again; she had ducked into every unsavoury back lane she happened upon. She had sidestepped dozens of used hypodermics, dodged a couple of half-collapsed drunks and gatecrashed a hostile gathering of feral cats. Last Friday night, needing relief after a hellish work-week, she'd even ventured into the industrial estate at Glasnevin, where the cars of drug dealers and doggers lurked in the shadows of shuttered-up units.

Arriving home each night, she ticked the boxes on the grid Finbarr had given her, barely able to write because her arms were so tired from pistoning and her fingers so numbed with the tingling confusion of heat-cold. It was her legs, however, that bore the real brunt of the regime – the only time they didn't hurt nowadays was when she was peaking on a runner's high. Finbarr prescribed things to help the muscles adjust, and the *Dublin AM* gang were amused by her thrice-daily stretches beside her desk. Of course, she'd led her co-workers, Finbarr and her family to believe she was training for the race on the gym treadmill each evening, and only running outside on weekend mornings. Finbarr hated treadmills but deemed them a necessary evil for Jo's own personal safety if she were to be race-ready in time.

Deeper inside the park, the traffic began to thin out, and the lights of the few passing cars blinked in disbelief as they bumped over the speed ramps, incredulous at her temerity. A few minutes later the cars died away altogether. She realised that her heavy breath and the sound of sole on cold tarmac were now inaudible to everyone else on the whole planet. In the aftermath of the break-up, she had been unnerved when nobody knew of her whereabouts, freaked when no one expected her home, but now as she passed through the dim midpoint between two antique gas lamps, she experienced her new favourite feeling – the liberation of being out at night, alone, and utterly unaccounted for.

By the time she passed the Cabra gate, the endorphins had crept in from the edges, killing off the twinge in her knee, loosening the stiffness in her calf that had concerned her during desk-stretches that morning. To her right she saw the start of a trail that led deep into the deciduous darkness. She just couldn't resist.

Thirty seconds later she was at full tilt between the tree trunks, drunk on the must of fallen leaves, her heart thumping wildly. The gibbous moon jigged like a pinball in her vision, sending just enough light between the bare branches to guide her way. Although the air in the woods was still, her self-generated breeze tossed her hair back as, again and again, her feet magically adapted to every random turn, crater and undulation in the compacted clay path. She felt amazed and grateful, oh so grateful for this night! She had transformed these times of relationship let-downs, crazy lesbians and egg-bullies into something as wonderful as learning to run. She would only get better every time she went out too. And never again would she be cowed by Wayne O'Harridan either: in fact, the next time she saw the little prick she was going to—

She stuttered to a halt for the second time that night – but this time for something infinitely more entrancing than fallen nappies. She gulped and blinked and stared. And it seemed she was not alone in her surprise: the doe and the fawn, who was sidled into her dappled flank had also both come to a mesmerised standstill. They were only ten feet ahead on the path – close enough for Jo to hear their exhalations, and watch the breath from their wary nostrils rise and curlicue in the moonlight.

She stood for a full minute marvelling at their beauty: the magnificent symmetry of the mother's face, wide ears filtering down to her brown snout – the perfect inverted triangle – and then the daintiness of her baby, only a few months old, its innocent eyes big, liquid, glistening.

Jo's own eyes welled with joyful tears at this reward for her efforts, this precious prize that was hers alone on planet earth tonight. 'You're so beautiful,' she said softly to them. 'This is such an honour.'

'Yes,' came a voice to her left, so close that it made her scalp fizz with fright. 'Aren't they just gorgeous?'

She was running amid a blur of branches, whimpering between breaths, begging her legs not to give in nor the atria in her heart to pop open like bombs. Her initial reflexive scream had scattered the terrified creatures; before her mouth had even closed again, she had fled like an Olympic sprinter who'd spent a lifetime perfecting her millisecond-start.

He had sounded around fifty and had stolen up so slyly behind that even the deer hadn't registered him. Or had he been waiting behind one of the trees, watching her all along? She couldn't be sure that he wasn't following her right now, but she was afraid to look back. She ran and ran, the sprint becoming a steeplechase as she jumped a fallen trunk. Just as her lungs and legs could take no more, she saw the glorious glow of a gas lamp through the branches; the trail was curving back to rejoin the road.

She imagined flagging down the first car she saw, like someone on a *Crimecall* re-enactment. Comfortingly, it would be a people-carrier with a Padre Pio sticker, rosary beads and a baby seat. But what to say to the kindly driver? *I went running in the park alone at night and got scared when a man spoke to me about some deer. Now please drop me home.*

She left the park through the Ashtown Gate, deciding all this 'bravery' had been a grave mistake. She couldn't imagine ever running at night again, but neither could she stomach driving three miles every night just to churn out more miles on one of Louis Muldoon's boring treadmills. Her Port Tunnel dreams began to dissolve; she would never be race-ready on time.

The houses and gates on Blackhorse Avenue were locked up for the night and, apart from a lone runner far ahead, there was no one about. Her energy reserves depleted, she began a slow jog beside the high stone park wall. A sharp frost was descending fast; the hardening footpath began to twinkle white beneath her feet. Despite her poor pace, she eventually started to catch up with the other runner, but it proved nothing to be proud of because this guy hadn't a clue what he was doing. His outfit was all wrong for a start – baggy, unaerodynamic tracksuit bottoms, a cotton t-shirt heavy with sweat and, worst of all, a pair of shin-splinting plimsolls. Even his head was weighed down – with a pair of overlarge headphones, whose band looped over the crown of his baseball cap. The cans were emitting a sibilant techno-ish tssk, and every eighth beat was accented by the stertorous whoop of his breaths.

He must have no idea she was so close, and so she remained a few steps behind, sickened by each grounding of his thin-soled shoes (how sore the poor eejit's legs would be tomorrow), but also motivated by his audio slipstream.

By the time they passed the gilded gates of Grangegorman military cemetery, her companion's breathing was growing faster and more ragged, his pace decelerating. After her scare in the woods, it was comforting to run in the presence of another runner, but it was time to overtake or she would never get home. She rallied her resources, stepped off the kerb and sped up, sensing his head flick in surprise. Once past, she made a supreme effort, tricking him into thinking she'd been travelling at speed all along.

Halfway to the corner, she heard the choked shout.

'Jo, wait!'

The voice was so shockingly out of context that it took a while to process. But despite the bizarreness of the situation, she certainly wasn't going to let Cillian speak to her. She ploughed on with a hardening sense of righteousness, her eyes fixed on the corner, where she would lose him. She must act as though she had earphones in herself.

'Jo, please!' This second shout was so much sadder, more impassioned, that her sympathetic legs ground to a halt. She turned around slowly under a streetlight and crossed her arms. He lumbered up, pathetic, desperate, his DJ headphones in his hand. She didn't know why he bothered – she had nothing meaningful to say. She would keep it cold and brief and then speed off into the distance, never to see him again. Although he could barely speak, she refused to talk first.

'Hey,' he eventually gasped. He took off his cap and rubbed sweat off his forehead. 'How've you been, Jo?'

'Perfectly fine, thank you,' she replied, folding her arms even tighter and looking around to confirm she wouldn't be returning the enquiry.

He gave a nervous laugh. 'This is all a bit surreal isn't it?'

'What is?'

'Meeting like this, I mean. Imagine it, *me* of all people, out running!'

If he was expecting her to congratulate his latest pathetic effort to do something meaningful with his empty life, he was mistaken. She threw him an acid glance and said, 'I wouldn't exactly call it running. Even in the two seconds I was behind you, I could see you weren't up to much.'

Cillian looked away for a moment, wounded, then turned back and gave a sad shrug. 'I'm obviously a long way off your level. Jesus, the speed you were going at there! But even if I have to crawl, I'll get through that Port Tunnel somehow.'

She sighed. 'Please don't tell me you've signed up for that thing?'

'But aren't you doing it?'

'God, no,' she said. If she needed any further encouragement to abandon that plan, she had it now.

'The way you described it that night piqued my interest. So I got up off my arse and just started running. I've given up fags – both kinds – and no more coke either!'

'Do you want a prize or something?' she said sarcastically.

He raised his cap and headphones. 'Stop being so mean, would you? Look, we both said some terrible things that night. I know I shouldn't have spoken to Louise or been a dick over not getting a bit of pissy coke. Let's put it all behind us. God, if you knew the number of times I wanted to ring you in the last three weeks, even despite your horrible text about the school.'

'Which I wouldn't have sent had you not been lying to me, Cillian.'

'You do know the nuns have the legal right to fire me if I officially came out, Jo? And I didn't want to look pathetic to you. A man of my age having to hide who he is!'

'I can't hang round discussing this, Cillian. My muscles are getting cold and the last thing I need in my marathon training plan is an injury.'

'You're doing the *marathon*?'

'Dublin's a year away, but my friend Finbarr says I'm so far ahead I could run Cork in June. OK, I really have to go.' She flashed her eyebrows, then turned and sprinted away.

'Bye, Jo,' she heard him call sadly after her. 'Good luck with the marathon!'

She sniggered at his gullibility (although right now she was running so well maybe a marathon *was* within her reach next year). She was delighted at how she'd handled it. Of course, it suited Cillian to forget the fight because he'd been in the wrong. But she hadn't fallen for his nonsense tonight. She was strong. She was principled. And above all, she was *right*. But just as she got around the corner, back onto the North Circular, she realised she was something else too – she was crying. As she ran it only got worse. She told herself to cop on, but soon she could neither breathe nor see. She lurched for the granite steps outside one of the houses.

Even with her face buried in her arms, Cillian still recognised her.

'Jo?' She felt heat and an arm around her shoulders: 'Are you OK?'

It took a minute before she was brave enough to lift her head. She gazed at him through tears and snot. 'I'm so sorry, Cillian. The horrible things I said to you that night … and … you've still forgiven me. You put your pride on the line back there and I was a cunt to you. Everything's so fucked up.'

He shook his head and looked as though he might cry himself. 'C'mere,' he said, pulling her into his embrace. She surrendered herself to his damp t-shirt and his evaporating deodorant. She remembered him saying how she didn't have the monopoly on loneliness, and that made her cry even more.

He spoke into her hair: 'You do know all this has *her* at its core?'

'Yeah. Even now she's still coming between us.'

Cillian lifted her chin and looked sternly into her eyes. 'But no more fighting, OK? It's been vile.'

'I promise. Sorry, I've ruined your t-shirt.'

'Don't worry, Jo.'

'Anyway, you're going to need a better top than that,' she said. 'One with wicking fabric, not to mind proper shoes and clothes. Meet me after work tomorrow and we'll get you kitted out in Finbarr's running shop.'

'I don't like the sound of this Finbarr. He sounds like a bit of a drag.'

'He's actually lovely,' Jo said. 'He's been a fount of advice and he'll help you too. But yeah, I suppose he's not quite our kind of person.'

Cillian laughed. 'I think the only two examples of *our kind of person* are sitting right here …'

Jo nodded and smiled and then jumped to her feet. 'Right, easy jog to the end of the road. But once you're attired in your sexy new gear the *real* training starts. I don't want you making a show of me in that tunnel.'

'But I thought you weren't … ?'

'I was just being a dick.' She offered her hand and pulled him up. 'And wait until you hear what happened to me in the park earlier. I'll actually be glad to have someone with me when I go back there tomorrow night …'

33

As Rob's luck would have it, the building site beside the office was even more raucous than usual this morning. Rachel Driffield, who was taking off her coat, grimaced at the meeting-room window, which was rattling in its frame. 'That's awful, isn't it, Robert?' she said, giving him a sympathetic look as she sat down opposite.

'I *know*!' Rob said, jumping at the chance to finally engage his coldest and most homophobic client in something resembling a regular chat. And she *was* definitely homophobic: since the meeting in Luigi's she'd become ten times more officious on the phone. Upon arrival in reception earlier, she'd even employed her folder and handbag as protection against any possibility of a handshake. Despite all this, today would still be their first contact without Lydia present. Rob hoped that, free from the need to impress her boss (he was certain Lydia was within earshot whenever Rachel gave him a bollocking over the phone), Fussbudget might finally realise he was a human being, and one of her own age too, even if he was a filthy gay. 'If you think that noise is bad,' he said gesturing towards the window with a smile, 'you should try working here in the afternoon when they get the *angle grinders* out!'

He hoped for a laugh, but none came: only a look that said her comment about the noise had not been meant in sympathy but as a slight against the HarropAds office, a place which was patently proving to be even more of a disappointment today than it was on her first visit. He could tell by the sour way she unzipped her leather Trenpharm folder that his suggestion that she 'try working here' was laughable, because she would never work in a place with rattling windows, foot-scoured carpets and Marjorie, whose wattle-neck he could now see advancing through the wire-gridded window in the door. He curled his toes as Edmond's great-aunt – the office administrator – pushed open the door with her ample arse and came in with a tray, upon which rested two of the snot-green 'good' office cups, a huge heap of Garibaldi biscuits (Vicky always joked that Marjorie's food-presentation was 'agricultural') and, most embarrassing of all, the lower curves of Marjorie's boobs.

'Here's your coffee, my dears,' she said, breathlessly setting down the tray. 'I *do* hope there's enough biscuits, though. I know you young folk like to skip breakfast!'

'Thanks, Marjorie, there's more than enough,' said Rob. He opened his notepad to discourage her from lingering, but it didn't work.

'I heard this professor on the radio the other day,' she continued. 'From King's I think he was … or maybe it was Cambridge? … one of the colleges anyway. So, this chap maintained that even a small biscuit is better than no breakfast at all. Settles the blood sugar.' She winked at Rachel. 'Mind you, my dear, you must know all about healthy eating already – I noticed your lovely figure the last time you were here!'

Rachel gave a pinched little smile and Rob sensed her horror at being given compliments and dietary advice by someone like Marjorie. Other clients actually *liked* Marjorie's mumsiness and enjoyed these pre-meeting chats; Hettie King said Marjorie made a delightful change from the po-faced receptionists in other ad agencies. Rachel, however, seemed to be growing more clenched by the second.

'So interesting, Marjorie,' said Rob, 'but we really need to start our meet—'

'The builders are dreadful today, aren't they?' Marjorie went to the window, pulling her cardigan around, lest someone on the scaffold might catch an eyeful. 'They're saying it'll be another four months, god help us.' She turned back, shaking her head. 'Anyway, I'd love to chat except I've to nip to the shops because there isn't a sheet of loo roll in the entire office! Edmond got caught short this morning. Bye now.'

'Sorry about that,' said Rob as the door eventually swung closed. 'She's Edmond's great-aunt and, well, she's a bit …'

Rachel said, 'Don't worry about it,' but in an acidic way that made Rob worry even more. She tapped her pen on the long list in her diary. 'We've got a lot to get through. Only fourteen weeks to launch, with the ruddy big Christmas break in the middle.'

Rob wondered what kind of twenty-something used the word *ruddy* nowadays. 'Time's flying all right,' he said. Christmas was still over a month away, but he was already living for it; Michael was coming to Leicester on Boxing Day to stay over. Rob couldn't wait to show him around, and even more exciting, show him off to the neighbours.

'Can I see the latest proof of the long-term data leaflet?' Rachel asked, her fingers flapping.

'Of course.' She had only rung in the amendments at five o'clock yesterday, which had necessitated him staying in late, along with a very disgruntled Daryl. After Daryl had gone home, Rob had spent a further hour checking the piece. His OCD had been worth it: the document he now happily passed across was as immaculate as the flat after one of Orlando's cleaning sprees. Fussbudget would have no complaint today!

He sat back and watched her scrutinise the changes (of course, there was zero acknowledgement of the quick turnaround). By the time she reached page four he had slipped into smug relaxation and was gazing out at the men on the scaffold. If only Stedman Sheppard Structural had won the contract, then Michael, who had overseen the engineering on umpteen high-rise projects, might be out there in his wax jacket and hard hat, doling out instructions to the foreman.

He looked back at Rachel, whose sleek hair was tucked behind her pearl earrings as she read. She was pretty enough, he supposed, though he hated to admit anything positive about her. He wondered if she had a boyfriend. As she turned the page, her bracelet slid down her wrist to reveal a greenish bruise. It was a weird place to get a bruise, and the vision that followed nearly made him giggle out loud – Rachel tied up in an S&M dungeon, offsetting her dominatrix workdays by being a weekend sub.

The hilarious thought was cut short by a sharp intake of breath. She was glowering at the text she'd added to page nine yesterday, the sentence about *bitemporall hairline recession*.

'Is there a problem?' he ventured.

She set down her pen and stared at him. 'Robert, it's become clear to me that you cannot reliably accept amends over the phone. This leaves me no choice but to *email* you all changes going forward. I've better things to spend my time on than spoon-feeding you correctly spelled text rather than conveniently ringing it in, but I couldn't show this to Lydia let alone our medical director. Dr Moss would be furious to see bitemporal spelled with two l's, let me T-E-L-L you!'

Rob stared at the Garibaldis, untouched, just like her coffee. He wanted to ram a dozen of them sideways into her mouth. She had been horrible about mistakes before, but this was ten times worse. So much for his hope of them bonding.

'I'll mark this up and *email* any further amends to you later,' she said, returning to her list with a sigh. 'Now, regarding the stage in the Gravenden ballroom, I need your designer to size up artwork for a huge vinyl backdrop of the Follestra advertisement. This is how we'll first reveal the campaign to our team, so it needs to fill the whole wall, with a nice big tagline so it's legible from the back of a crowded room.' She gave him a clipped, insincere smile. 'Do you understand?'

'Y–es.' Under the table Rob's thigh muscles pulsed so hard they were in danger of ripping through his trousers. If the horrible homophobe was going to make him feel this awkward then he would return the favour – he knew exactly how to unnerve her too. He raised an eyebrow like a Blackpool drag queen. 'Well, it certainly sounds like a nice big one all right!'

The colour drained from her face. 'Sorry?'

'The backdrop.' He stared at her, his tongue pressing out his cheek. 'So tell me, what exactly are the … *dimensions?*'

'Um …' She scrambled through the pages of her diary like a secret agent looking for a bomb-defusal code with seconds to spare. 'I wrote all this down during our meeting with Corinne,' she muttered, her cheeks inflaming. 'Why in god's name … can't I find it?'

'Ah, your meeting in Luigi's,' he said. 'What a lovely surprise to bump into yourself and Lydia that day. Lovely too that you got to meet my boyf—'

'Fourteen by twenty!' she gasped upon finally finding the page. She drew three lines under the information, digging her pen into the paper. 'Yes, fourteen foot wide by twenty foot high.'

'OK.' Rob wrote it down carefully then looked up at her with a wink. 'You certainly weren't lying when you said it was huge!'

It was after eleven when she finished dispensing orders. As Rob brought her downstairs he took the risk of making obscene faces behind her back. But it turned out to be no risk at all, because she didn't even bother to turn around before she left. Nor deign to shake his grubby gay hand. She just snapped, 'Goodbye, Robert,' then went straight out the door.

34

Jo gazed into the popping craters, then gave the porridge a final stir and tipped it into a bowl. Her hand shook as she added sliced banana. As predicted by Finbarr, first-race nerves had gagged her appetite, but she obeyed his advice and forced down a few spoonfuls. It was hard to believe that the energy bestowed by these carbs would be expended in the actual Port Tunnel in an actual race in only a couple of hours! She pictured Cillian anxiously eating his own breakfast – if last night's phone call was anything to go by, the porridge would be exiting his body before he even left the house.

DublinBeat FM was sponsoring the race, and Jo froze mid-chew during the sports news. 'Ten thousand athletes are limbering up for a unique 10K in Dublin's new Port Tunnel, a week before it officially opens to vehicles,' said the presenter. 'Our BeatCaster will be at the finish, with our mystery reporter interviewing athletes as they cross the line.'

So, she was an *athlete* now! She ran her hand across the number she'd fastidiously pinned to her top, feeling a surge of pride. But then her stomach lurched again. She must stop being preposterous: yes, she'd done well in her training with Cillian, but there was every chance she would fall on her arse, trip up another runner, wet herself due to fluid mismanagement, or worst of all, hit 'the wall' and have to be stretchered into a siding by the Order of Malta.

Well, whatever ignominy might befall her, at least she wouldn't be alone. During their training, she and Cillian had repeatedly iterated their pact in breathless voices: no matter what happened, they would stick together. They were well matched in terms of speed now anyway – in three measly weeks, that gym-shy ex-smoker had jammily caught up on Jo. He was amazed by his evolving body and kept making Jo feel his rock-hard quads.

Like all good runs, today's was to be completed without the encumbrance of a phone, so she sent Cillian a text before she left.

On the way now, sexy legs. They called us 'athletes' on radio! Hope you put Lucozade in fridge?

She waited a couple of minutes for a response, then figured he must be in the toilet. And he was obviously still in there as she jogged up to his little cottage, because at first he didn't answer. When a second ring on the bell did nothing, she called through the letterbox and listened. Still nothing. And no means to ring him either. She went to the closed curtains of the sitting-room window and banged on the glass. If he'd fallen asleep in front of the telly, he would have missed his alarm.

After five minutes of banging and knocking she was less worried about being late for the race and more concerned for his wellbeing. He'd been so worked up on the phone last night she'd despatched him on a calming walk to buy Lucozade Sport. What if he'd never made it home, if he'd been queer-bashed by one of the gangs that loitered in the lane behind the Spar? She needed to ring him, but there was no sign of life in the other cottages. She remembered the payphone on the main road, but she had no money in her stupid streamlined capri pants. She would have to touch a passer-by for an emergency euro. She turned and began to run.

'Jo, wait!'

She ran back twice as fast to the figure standing in the doorway, grey-faced, unshaven, naked apart from white underpants. 'Jesus, Cillian, I thought you'd been attacked or something ...'

'I slept it out,' he said in a scratchy voice. 'Something went wrong with my alarm. You see, the thing—'

'Today of all days? God, you *dickhead*.'

'I'm sorry, Jo.'

'Don't just stand there in your knicks. Gimme your phone, I'll ring a taxi while you get ready.' She checked her watch. 'We should just about scrape in on time.' She pushed on his bare arms to usher him inside, but he stalled in the tiny hallway.

'Jo, you can't really come in ...' Seeing her nostrils flaring, he turned his mouth to the side.

'Why the fuck do you stink of cigarettes and drink, Cillian?'

He grabbed her by the shoulders. '*You* go on to the race, Jo, you'll be amazing. You don't need me slowing you down.'

She stared at him for a moment, then pushed her way past.

'Jo, don't go in—'

She beat him to the sitting-room door. As she reached for the light switch, she was hit with a fetid fug of alcohol, cigarettes and sex. The sandy-haired man on the couch sat up, saying, 'What the fuck?' He pulled the duvet round his chest like a girl.

Jo laughed wildly at him, then turned to the pathetic sight that was Cillian, prancing in his pants beside her. 'The new you certainly didn't last long, did it?' she shouted. There were condom wrappers and clothes on the floor. On the coffee table, the chrome snorter rested at the edge of a chalky little mirror. She took a swinging kick at a pair of jeans. They landed on an open bottle of Lucozade, whose contents splashed onto a pair of boxer shorts and an overflowing ashtray.

'Watch my stuff, bitch!' said the man. He wriggled into his boxers under the duvet, then jumped up to get the rest of his clothes. 'I don't even *want* to know what is going on here.'

'Liam, I can explain,' wailed Cillian. 'Myself and Jo were supposed to be—'

Liam came over and waved a finger in Jo's face. 'Sorry darling, but your boyfriend here likes cock. Or he certainly did last night when he was off his face on coke.'

'He's not my boyfriend, arsebreath!' said Jo, recoiling. 'Oh, hang on a minute ... you're *book-club Liam* that I'm sick to the tits of hearing about. But no, obviously not, because Cillian said Liam was good-looking and intelligent. And you seem neither.'

'Charming!' said Liam, stuffing his socks into his pockets. 'Anyway, you've got the place to yourselves now. Jesus, if I'd known you were bisexual ... ugh!'

The door slammed. Cillian slumped onto the piled-up duvet. 'Jo, I'm so sorry. I bumped into him in Spar last night, we got chatting and he came out to me. I only invited him over for a cuppa, but then he produces this bag of coke. If it's any consolation, I doubt I'll be hearing from him again.'

'I couldn't give a flying fuck,' said Jo, blinking back tears. 'Because you won't be hearing from me either.'

He jumped up. 'Please don't say that. I can't go through us not talking again.'

She shoved him back onto the couch. 'Then why did you let me down?' The thought of doing the race alone terrified her, yet her rage had unleashed enough power to complete an ultramarathon. She made her decision. 'Just give me my Lucozade and I'll be on my way,' she said. 'The race starts in twenty-five minutes.'

His head was low when he returned from the kitchen. 'We seem to have drunk it all last night.' He nodded sheepishly at the mess. 'And you spilled what was left …'

'It's no problem, Cillian,' she said calmly, as she walked to the door. 'I can do this without it.' She turned and blinked at him. 'Just like I can do it without you.'

35

'I've anchored the stand. You ready up there?'

Noel stood on the pouffe, gripping the Christmas tree with both hands. 'Ready.'

'Right,' shouted Martin, on his knees beneath the branches. 'Crouch and hold … *engage!*'

Shaking his head at this latest awful rugby reference, Noel tried to force the trunk downwards.

'Come on, Moody, don't be such a flippin' pansy,' said Martin. 'Use those big paws of yours.'

Noel rolled his eyes and spat away a faceful of fir as he pushed even harder. 'I've never … actually … played rugby, remember?'

'Such a dreadful waste of a number eight,' said Martin, too wimpy and short-sighted to have been competent at *any* sport, let alone rugby. '*Heave* … yes, that's it!' Martin jumped to his feet. 'Referee,' he announced, pointing at the base of the tree, 'you may award the try.' He slapped Noel on the back. 'Not bad for a Wheldon supporter. Actually, your lot could do with someone of your size this season, they couldn't win a scrum against the local playschool!'

Noel gave a thin smile but refused to be drawn into yet another defence of his team. This new habit of Martin's – relating everything back to rugby – was no doubt intended to make Noel feel welcome and less emasculated while living under another man's roof, but as well as making Noel cringe, the comments revealed that Martin didn't have the faintest clue about the game.

'Finished just in time for Edinburgh v Leinster too,' Martin said as he turned up the telly. 'You watching?'

'I better clean this sap off my hands…' Noel did want to watch, but not if it meant enduring Martin's moronic commentary. Martin had never supported a specific team, and this gave him freedom to criticise *all* of them. Last week's punditry during the Northampton match had been so irritating that Noel had feigned a headache and gone out walking in the drizzle.

The door of the downstairs loo was closed. Hazel might be in there and he didn't want to bother her by knocking, so he went into the kitchen, where he found her instead at a table strewn in baking tins and jars of mincemeat.

'Sorry, I didn't know you were in here.' In trying to constantly make himself scarce, he paradoxically kept getting in their way. He dreaded the thought of next week, when the three of them would be off work together. He always spent Christmas Day with the Sutherlands, but this year there would be no escaping back to his flat at eight to sleep off Hazel's dinner. He prayed some clients would get in touch over the festive season, but these days appointments were drying up at an alarming rate. Christine had texted last week to say that she and Bethany had finally separated and moved in with their respective parents. Then, as soon as Steph and Thea had returned from their travels, Steph had been put on nightshifts and needed to sleep during Noeleen's usual visiting hours.

He was grateful at least that those girls had been decent enough to explain their situations. Unlike Xenna, from whom there was still no word, leaving Noel to write off the outfit she was supposedly washing for him. For all he knew, Xenna had left to chase some girl she fancied. (Although her girlfriend was a pretty, up-and-coming pop singer, Xenna was forever having rampant one-night stands.) Still, the loss afforded him the perfect excuse to see Irene about commissioning some new outfits; he must start thinking about fabrics and styles.

Hazel was shaking her head at him. 'For god's sake, Noel, I wish you wouldn't dawdle in doorways. And stop apologising every time you come into a room. You live here now!'

For now, he silently corrected. He was looking forward to getting back to his flat in the new year. The landlady had let it out to someone on a short-term basis, but as Noel was an excellent and longstanding tenant, she would let him move back in as soon as he was ready, or rather as soon as Hazel believed he was.

'Tree's up now,' he said, going to the sink to wash his hands.

'It's wonderful to have you around,' said Hazel. 'It took Martin three hours and packet of Elastoplast to do it last year. Now, open that for me, will you?' She handed him a jar of mincemeat. Even though it was shop-bought – Aunt Eileen had always made her own – the spicy sweetness was so evocative that he couldn't take his nose away from the jar.

Hazel clicked her fingers. 'Give it here before you fall into a diabetic coma.'

'Ah, that smell brings back memories. The day I came to live with you in Cadston Crescent, your mum made mince pies. You were standing up on a chair helping.'

'*Pretending* to be helping, like the unwilling housekeeping participant I always was. The only thing I can recall from that *first Noël*, as Mum called it, is being mortified at you seeing me in that hideous Victorian pinny-thing she used to put me in.'

Noel frowned away the intense frisson. 'Can't say I remember a pinny …'

The truth was, he'd only folded it on Thursday when he'd been sorting out the suitcase. Every time he saw that pinny, it brought back the exquisite pain of it cutting into his armpits, as his neglected little body finally began to grow, thanks to Eileen's nourishing meals. By age eleven, it wouldn't fit at all and Eileen had given him a woman's apron to wear. It was lemon and navy check, with a brilliant white frill on the shoulder straps. Noel still had that in the suitcase too, and liked to wear it during the summer, albeit sparingly because it was becoming fragile with age.

He took Eileen's recipe notebook from the kitchen shelf. He'd helped her to cover it in a double-layer of brown paper, which Hazel, in the years since her mother's death, had windowed with grease-stains. He leafed through it casually but knew exactly where to find the mince-pie entry; he loved that page because Eileen had added footnotes as she'd perfected the recipe.

9/12/1964 – New oven, better at 375°

2/12/1966 – Using extra raisins, currants very dry this year

Then, in 1968, when Uncle George had surprised her with a freezer bought with his Christmas bonus, she'd written: *Freeze lard for 30 minutes in advance.*

He propped the notebook up against a mixing bowl for Hazel, but she was shaking her head. 'I know you love Mum's pies, Noel, but we're going healthy this year.' She gestured at a magazine half-hidden by a bag of porridge. 'These mince-oat squares are much lower GI.'

'Oh lord, please don't change the recipe on my account,' he said. On the day Eileen had found out she had six weeks to live, she'd come home from the hospital and made her famous mince pies. Now, thanks to his stupid diabetes, they had been sidelined. He wanted to scream.

'It's no bother,' Hazel said as she weighed out the oats. 'I only wish we could send some to Chloe.' She set down the bag and looked mistily out the window. 'God knows what kind of Christmas dinner they'll have in Burundi, but you know Chloe, she won't even mind because she's such a selfless kid!'

Noel nodded, but he could see through the twenty-three-year-old's motivations. Chloe wasn't in Burundi to help the poorest orphans on earth, as the volunteering booklet had touted; no, this spoiled only-child was there solely for her own benefit. The trip meant she could embellish her CV, mingle with an international array of male volunteers, and defer getting a graduate job that would necessitate paying back her massive student loan. Not to mention the kudos that had been ladled onto her at the farewell party: the prosecco-swilling 'saint' had swanned around in a new Stella McCartney dress, the cost of which would have fed, clothed and vaccinated a whole Burundian village for a year.

'We'll raise a glass to her, though, won't we, Noel?' said Hazel, blinking away a tear.

'Of course,' he said, hoping his annual Christmas-dinner tribute to Eileen and George wouldn't be upstaged by a toast to Chloe. Even as a young child, Chloe had displayed no integrity whatsoever. When he lived in the flat, he would have to stow his gear in the bathroom attic whenever Hazel brought her over. Chloe would disappear 'for a wee-wee' only to be found twenty minutes later, snooping through his bedroom cupboards. She would inform him that his clothes were even more 'brown and boring' than her dad's, or would mock a long-haired Polaroid she'd rooted out of a shoe-box. When Noel had politely suggested to Hazel that she shouldn't let her daughter poke around other people's property, Hazel had laughed it off as childish inquisitiveness, and wondered what on earth a boring bachelor needed to conceal anyway. But Noel did have a lot to hide, and as the years passed and the visits continued, he couldn't help but wonder if Chloe might somehow have developed an inkling about him. Nothing was ever said, but when they spoke, he would often notice a flicker of suspicion in her eyes, or see her lip twitch ever so slightly, as though on the brink of an accusation that was slowly but very surely taking shape. But then, he'd always been so meticulous about hiding every little clue; he told himself it was probably just paranoia.

He left Hazel to roll out her oat-ridden mixture. Having confirmed that Martin was ensconced in the match, he went upstairs to Chloe's bedroom and closed the door. He wished he could lock it, but a boring bachelor couldn't legitimately ask for the key. He slid the pink phone out from the sock. After the canonisation of Chloe, the tiresome rugby jibes and the bastardised mince pies, he deserved some good news. He had texted Anouska last night to arrange a date, and possibly even two – because homes got messy over Christmas – and his heart leapt to see she'd already responded. He needn't have doubted Anouska and Ruby – they were always so kind and reliable. As he sat down on the bed to savour the message, the impending Christmas claustrophobia seemed suddenly manageable.

We'd love to see Noeleen, but my mum's staying over Xmas. Definitely arrange something in January though. Thanks for everything during 2006, R&A xx

He sank back against the posters on Chloe's wall. This was terrible news. Just terrible. He completely understood the postponement, of course; clients often couldn't accommodate him because their house guests wouldn't be cool with a grown man dressed as a Victorian washerwoman doing the cleaning, even a washerwoman who asked for nothing in return except their acceptance and a safe space. He wanted to text back and check if they had any friends who might want to try Noeleen over Christmas, but there was no point. He'd already canvassed them – and all his other clients too – for new contacts, to no avail. He was approaching an unprecedented tipping point; if the situation deteriorated any further, he could lose his last threads of connection to the lesbian world; pulling himself back in would then become impossible.

He looked up eventually, and scowled at the boys on Chloe's posters. *They* were free to express their girly side to the world, but he was trapped in this stifling house without any outlet. And now Martin was calling him from the hall, 'Edinburgh are making a haggis of this match, Moody. Not that those Leinster *ladies* are capitalising, mind you. Get your big backside down before you miss it!'

With a sigh, Noel stowed away the pink phone and began to trudge down the stairs. One thing was for certain: if he wanted to preserve his last shred of sanity, he would have to come up with some kind of plan, and very soon too.

36

'Keep it up,' said the Order of Malta boy standing at the first-aid station in the recess. 'You're nearly there.'

Jo widened her grimace until it might pass as a smile. The boy was dweeby and pimple-ridden, dwarfed by the diagonal white strap of his kit-bag, but she could have snogged him. If she hadn't been in such a rush, of course. She made a mental note to put the Order on the list for thank-you letters, a list which was already quite long. It included Finbarr, the tunnel authority (who'd allowed their tunnel to be used in this amazing event), and Clonliffe Harriers (the organisers and perhaps her future running club). She was also going to write to Dublin Fire Brigade to praise their three men who had run in full uniform, carrying a recumbent colleague dressed as Santa – all in aid of Crumlin's paediatric burns unit. Most importantly, she'd somehow track down the name of the blind man who'd been tethered to his guide-runner and tell him that his brave strides had inspired her to keep going – even through the airless heat at the 7.5K mark, even through the cramping agony in her calves, even now, up this killer incline that was bringing her up, out of the mouth of the amber-lit tunnel into the white-grey cool of the outside world, where a giant digital clock two hundred metres ahead on the tarmac tantalised her with the thought that she might – if she could find one last push – cross that line in under an hour.

A few other athletes were about to finish too, including a man whose young family were waving a banner that said, *Run Daddy Gerry!* Jo wished Louise and Cillian were among the smattering of spectators; they could witness her sprint-finish as she dredged up the last of her energy and overtook Gerry inches from the line, the clock showing a full eleven seconds under the hour.

She floated elatedly towards the rack of medals dangling on silky blue ribbons. 'Thank a million,' she said, smiling uncontrollably at the girl who put one around her neck. She felt she should kiss her on both cheeks like they did at the Olympics, but instead she added, 'I never actually thought I'd get this.' The girl gave a brisk nod but was already turning to adorn the next medallist. Jo held up the medal and smiled at it. While the metallic carving of runners inside the tunnel was indeed beautiful, the most important prize of all still awaited her, at a stall marked LADIES MEDIUM.

'Move along the chute,' called the stewards. 'No stopping.'

The sweat of her efforts anointed the gorgeous grey t-shirt as she pulled it on. She beamed down at her chest, now officially branded with *Dublin Port 10K Finisher*. But there was no time to reflect because she was being ushered on again. She was handed a bottle of Club Energise by a man on her left, a banana by a woman on her right, and finally a flyer for the Clontarf 10-Miler, by a wiry teenage girl who obviously thought Jo looked quite capable of running it.

'Thank you,' she said, as each reward was lavished upon her. 'Thank you so much!'

Her celebrity was to end abruptly, however. Disgorged from the chute, she found herself among a large but loose crowd back at the starting area. She looked around, grinning generally at her athletic compatriots but soon realised that she was the only person who was there alone. High-spirited post-mortems filled the air. Despite having nobody to chat to, she still felt the need to linger. She leaned against one of the pristine toll booths, sipping on her drink, trying desperately not to nod along to 'Run to You' by Bryan Adams, which sounded far more catchy than usual as it blared from the BeatCaster. A few minutes later, she spotted Gerry emerging from a Portaloo; she must tell him that they'd finished within seconds of each other. But just as she began to approach, she heard the exultant cry of 'Daddy!' and now Gerry was putting his medal around his daughter's little neck. His wife and son followed, and soon Gerry's exhausted arms were pulling everyone into a laughing family hug.

Entranced by the happy clan, Jo hadn't noticed the girl, who was now touching her elbow. 'I'm Mairéad from *DublinBeat*,' she said. 'We're asking athletes to say a few words live on air about the race. Would you be—?'

'Absolutely,' said Jo. Who needed to chat to another runner when a whole listenership could hear her experience!

Mairéad pulled out a walkie talkie. 'Aengus, I've someone at the toll booths.'

'We'll be right over with herself and the mic,' came the reply.

Jo began to formulate the phrases she would use when addressing the city – *a unique triumph … I wholeheartedly recommend that everyone tries running … training hard pays dividends.* She was so busy rehearsing that it took a series of progressively lengthening glances before she properly noted the tangerine jacket with the twin white H's advancing through the crowd. The last time Jo had seen that jacket was on telly that hungover morning. This time, however, its owner was not accompanied by a neglected piebald, but rather by a headphoned technician wielding a microphone. With a rising nausea, Jo remembered the 'mystery reporter' mentioned on *DublinBeat* earlier.

'Over here, Tamara,' called Mairéad.

Jo began to edge backwards, angling for a gap where she could slip through the crowds behind. 'I've changed my mind,' she said. 'I don't think I—'

Mairéad gripped her arm. 'You'll be grand.'

In any case, Tamara had already spotted them: fleeing would make Jo look like a lily-livered twit. She glanced up at the erect arm of the toll barricade. Although it was brand new, still wrapped in plastic, she willed it to develop sudden metal fatigue, then crash down and kill Tamara, who had come to a standstill under it.

'So, who've we got here?' said Tamara, with a professionally brisk smile at Jo.

'I'm … I'm Clíona,' said Jo, though the pseudonym was unnecessary – it was obvious that Tamara didn't have the faintest recollection of the girl she'd been introduced to one night in The Shelbourne. The non-recognition was a relief to Jo but also a disappointing indictment of the utter lack of curiosity that Tamara had about the victim of her affair with Louise.

'Right, Clíona,' said Tamara, her sallow hand readying the microphone. 'I'll ask you how you found the race. Just answer naturally and clearly.'

'OK,' said Jo. She felt extremely self-conscious, firstly because of the secret coincidence of sharing a lover with this celebrity, but moreover because of Tamara's undeniable sexiness, especially the way her handsome jaw rested on the zipped-up funnel of the jacket.

'Ten seconds,' said Aengus.

Tamara defocused her eyes from them all, as though entering a transcendent state. Then, the moment Aengus gave her the nod, she awoke and exploded into the emphatic, polished celebrity Jo recognised from the telly: 'I'm here with Clíona, one of our finishers. So how did it go for you, Clíona?'

'Em, yeah it went ... I mean ...' For someone who'd been bursting with superlatives minutes earlier, Jo found it impossible to stump up even a single adjective. Tamara gave a coaxing look, but her unblinking brown eyes and the encouraging touch of her sallow hand only thickened Jo's tongue even more. She stared at the logo on Tamara's jacket and saw two a's flicker between the H's. *HaHa*. She wanted to impress Tamara like an athletic suitor, but she was just a big joke. *Ha-fucking-Ha*. She became suddenly conscious of the sweaty stench from her own armpits. Her makeup-less face had begun to burn. 'It was a unique experience to be tunning in the runnel ...' she said. 'Em, I mean—'

Tamara nodded and smiled to cover her exasperation as she retracted the microphone. 'I think poor Clíona's too tired to talk, eh, Clíona?'

Before Jo could cough up her next ridiculous response, Mairéad was pointing and mouthing, *firemen*.

'Annie-ways,' said Tamara, 'we'll leave Clíona here to recover because word is that the hunks from Dublin Fire Brigade are just about to finish ...'

Jo drifted invisibly through the masses. Her runner's high had vanished. She didn't know where her sore, stiffening legs were taking her, but she had to get away from here. Further along, beyond the last fringes of the crowds, a lone steward was picking up post-race detritus. He set down his black sack and began rounding up a drift of empty water bottles that had settled along the kerb.

Jo seized the moment, and before he had returned, the t-shirt she'd so long dreamed of owning had joined the other rubbish in his bag.

PART 2

January – March 2007

37

'Wow,' said Rob as they left the Gielgud after *Days of End*. 'That was the best play I have *ever* seen.' He reached for Michael's hand in the crowd and gave it a squeeze of thanks, firstly for the Christmas present of tonight's tickets (Rob had squealed upon opening the envelope Michael had brought to Leicester on Boxing Day) but also to show his wider gratitude for introducing him to the world of theatre in the first place. If he'd never met Michael, he would never have known the joys of a night like this – watching a riveting performance beside a wonderful man, whom he was now taking back to his flat for wine and conversation and sex. Without all this, how bland and bleak his life would be!

On Shaftesbury Avenue he smiled to see so many enlightened post-show punters, just like him, milling excitedly around Theatreland. The rest of the country was slumped in the January blues, but he felt as bright and buzzy as the neon signs that burned down the snaking street, their colour eternal, unlike the fickle Christmas lights, which had been switched off last week.

Days of End was the fifteenth play Michael had chosen for them, but during the show Rob had decided he was finally knowledgeable enough to select their next one. He would research options in *Time Out* (carefully avoiding musicals, of course, because Michael despised them) and surprise his boyfriend with tickets and a clever explanation for his choice. As they walked through Covent Garden, he began reliving the most moving scenes of *Days of End*: 'Oh Michael, didn't you want to punch that doctor? The offhand way he diagnosed poor Valentina with terminal cancer! … I nearly cried when her bumpkin of an uncle offered the shotgun to end her suffering …The deathbed scene was perfectly scripted, but the ominous lighting was just a *tad* overdone, didn't you think?'

He had so much to say that they were already halfway down Neal Street when he realised that Michael – usually brimming with post-play observations – had said little since they'd left their seats; in fact, his expression was distant and twitchy, and his gait was slow and dragging, nothing like his engineer's tiptoe. The only thing he seemed interested in was checking the time on his watch.

'Didn't you like the play much?' asked Rob, hoping he hadn't made a grave error of judgement in lauding it.

'Yes, but it was too short. Feels a bit early to be heading back to yours.' He looked around the street as though seeking out excitement in the closed clothes shops.

'Really?' said Rob, miffed by Michael's wish to delay being alone with him; and surprised too, because Michael wasn't a fan of bars. 'If you wanted a drink, you should have said it when we were still near Soho.'

'Anywhere will do for a quick nightcap.' He turned to Rob. 'I'm just worried the curly-headed castrato might still be up.'

'He's got his volleyball AGM tonight,' said Rob, winking. 'So, by the time he gets home we'll be serving and spiking in the bedroom if you know what I mean!' He tried to usher them along. 'Anyway you can have as many naked nightcaps as you like at mine.'

But Michael didn't move. 'I'm sorry, Rob, it's just …' He took off his glasses and pinched the bridge of his nose. His overnight bag slid down his shivering arm.

Rob grabbed him and pulled him close. 'What an insensitive fool I am, rabbiting on about the play without realising how much that storyline must have affected *you*. It's brought back memories of your dad, hasn't it?'

'Yes,' whispered Michael between shudders and sniffs.

Rob rubbed his arm. 'No wonder you needed a drink. Let's have a proper talk in the nearest pub.'

'Thank you,' said Michael, but in a sad boy's voice that Rob had never heard before. Whenever Michael talked about his dad's death it was all about its impact on Joan, so the man weeping into a tissue as they entered the pub on the corner was an absolute revelation to Rob. Although it was awful to see his boyfriend like this, it gave Rob a weird sense of satisfaction to be the one helping. Michael was always counselling him through meltdowns about Rachel Driffield and Orlando, so it was nice to be doing the comforting for a change.

After his second brandy, Michael gave a long sigh of relief. 'Thanks for looking after me there.'

Rob gave him a tender smile. 'I knew you'd feel better after a proper chat.'

And it *had* been a proper chat, the most proper chat he'd ever had with Michael, and now Rob swelled with an even bigger love for him. As he finished his own brandy, which he'd ordered in sympathy, he teemed with the intimate secrets made known to him in the past hour. He'd heard the story of how Michael had sat in the hospice night after night, gripping Norman's skeletal hands as the pain of metastatic prostate cancer punched through ever-increasing doses of morphine. In the mornings, Michael had shaved in the hospice toilets and gone straight into work (he'd been overseeing the critical stage of a bridge-build, so compassionate leave was impractical), leaving Joan or his brother, temporarily home from California, to begin the daytime vigil. After a month, the doctors said it wouldn't be much longer; everyone prayed that fate would enable Joan to be present at the very end. This was not to be, however, because even in semi-consciousness, Norman knew exactly whom he wanted by his side as he finally let go. This was because his departing wish could be answered by one person alone.

One night, minutes after Michael had begun his watch, the man whose eyes had been closed for days had sensed his elder son's presence at the bedside. He had lifted his head and asked Michael in a gasping whisper to look after Joan, because he alone could do the job properly. Michael had grabbed his dad's hand and said, 'Of course, Dad,' and then Norman had nodded, and peacefully breathed his last.

The story had moved Rob to tears, but in his new role as comforter he'd swallowed them back. Michael, on the other hand, had let go of so much emotion that Rob had made two trips to the bar to request cocktail napkins from the concerned barmaid.

Rob put the sodden balls of the napkins into the ashtray. 'Do you think you're OK to head to mine now, love?' he asked. He was gagging to get back to the privacy of the flat: he'd never felt closer to Michael, and his whole body longed to give voice to the deepened feeling between them.

'Just one thing first,' said Michael. He took his phone out. 'I need to check that Mum got home OK after her book club. You don't mind, do you?'

Rob smiled and stood up. 'I'll even give you some privacy,' he said. 'I know you get self-conscious when I'm hovering in the background.' He went off to the toilets, feeling bad for previously chastising Michael about his mum-calls. He'd been jealous of Joan, but Michael was simply fulfilling his father's dying wish, a wish that Joan, for all her supposed closeness to her son, wasn't even aware of. Knowing about Mr Wyles's last moments made Rob feel almost superior to the old dear now. If he ever did meet her (though his desire to do so was waning as the months wore on) then he'd find it hard to conceal the glint of one-upmanship in his eye.

Rob checked his watch as they stepped into the lift. 'Castrato's definitely back by now,' he said with a sigh. 'And he'll be in a filthy mood because I left a bowl in the sink earlier. Let's go straight to my room. You won't want him seeing your red eyes anyway.'

'That boy,' whispered Michael with a teary giggle, 'needs to get out and have some fun. And by fun, I don't mean slapping a *volleyball* around.'

Inside the flat, Rob stopped suddenly. The door to Orlando's bedroom was wide open. The stripped bed could be explained if he'd been washing the sheets, but then, as Rob took in the bare shelves and the coat-rack devoid of lurid jackets, his heart began to thump. He ran into the bedroom, yanking open wardrobes and drawers – all completely empty.

Michael came in. 'What's going on?'

Rob sank onto the mattress. 'The bastard castrato's up and left.'

'Surely not?' said Michael, coming around to recheck the drawers. 'Even *he* wouldn't …'

Rob pulled him onto the bed. 'Sweets, you're so honest yourself you just don't get how awful people can be. Look, he's probably been planning this for ages. I never said where I was going tonight; he just seized his moment. Now I'm left in the lurch with the rent.'

'Maybe he wanted to tell you but didn't know what to … oh look, is that a letter?'

Rob grabbed the envelope from the desk.

Robert, I am sorry to leave like this. Please use my deposit to cover next month rent. I must go back to Italy for family emergency.

'See!' said Michael. 'I knew it wasn't anything personal.'

'Wait,' snapped Rob, reading on.

But even if no emergency I could not live much longer here. I hope you will find new housemate that will accept your mess. But I think will be hard.

Rob flung the letter away. 'I'm not *that* messy.' He looked at Michael. 'Or am I?'

'A little bit of mess is healthy. If it weren't for Mum's fussiness, I'd be messy at home. But look, now's your chance to get a nicer flatmate.'

'Who's to say they won't turn psycho as well?' said Rob.

Michael rubbed his back. 'I'm a pretty good judge of character,' he said. 'I knew *you* were a good 'un the minute I met you. I'll help you do the interviews!'

Although Orlando was returning to Italy, he had cleared all his food and olive oils from the kitchen – no doubt everything had been spitefully dumped in the basement bins. Rob poured out two large glasses of wine and went out to Michael, who was tactfully changing the channel because *How Clean Is Your House?* was about to start.

It was only when Rob nestled into the open arms of his beautiful and selfless (how quickly Michael had sidelined his own upset to comfort Rob) boyfriend on the sofa that the idea first struck. It was so obvious that he was mortified not to have thought of it before. Maybe he had even subconsciously dismissed it, now he knew of Norman's dying wish. But *surely* there was some way Michael could divide his time between two homes without reneging on his promise?

As they snuggled on the sofa, Rob began to formulate his proposition. As the minutes wore on and they both distractedly laughed at Graham Norton's innuendos, he began to get a strange but strong sense that he was not alone in his thoughts. Michael's gaze was fixed slightly to the right of the television and he was picking at the strap of his watch; he seemed to be mulling over the very same thing. Within a few minutes their common idea had grown so potent that Rob could feel it pulsating in the air above, just waiting for one of them to reach up and grab it.

It was only right that he should speak first – it was his invitation to give. At the next ad break, he twisted slowly on the sofa. 'Michael,' he said, 'I've got important something to ask you. And I think you already know what it is.'

38

Even from the far end of the office, Rachel knew something odd was going on. Since lunchtime, Narelle's usually sluggish typing had taken on a suspicious cycle of furious key-bashing interleaved with periods of pure silence. Rachel would have sworn the PA was instant-messaging someone, except that the TreNetwork prevented it. She would find out what was happening once Lydia, who was on the phone in her own side-office, went out to a meeting that afternoon.

Rachel did her best to ignore Narelle's cyclical noise and continued her review of the media plan. She was still in awe of the budget allocated to promote Follestra in the medical press, where a double-page spread cost a quarter of her annual salary!

An hour later, Lydia came over and rested her Gucci laptop bag on Rachel's desk. 'How's the schedule looking?'

'Good, but there are a few coverage gaps. I'll call the media buyer this afternoon, make sure they plug them.'

'*Excellente*,' said Lydia, always pleased when Rachel identified both an issue and its remedy. 'Let's chat when I get back around six. And make sure Harrop's have the latest dosing guide ready for review then too.'

'Perfect,' chirped Rachel, though staying late meant she'd miss Tuesday-night training and incur the irritation of Sensei Kev, who despised absenteeism. It was annoying because she'd only recently managed to win back Kev's trust after last year's appalling tournament. Still, with the launch a mere month away, work had to come first. She would just have to excel at Thursday's strength and conditioning session instead.

Before leaving, Lydia stopped at Narelle's desk. 'Any sign of that spreadsheet I was expecting an hour ago?'

Narelle gave the kind of helpless half-laugh she used as a prelude to prevarication. 'Sorry, Lyd, my Excel keeps crashing so I'm miles behind.'

'Well get onto IT, for god's sake,' said Lydia. 'I need it on my desk by the time I get back.'

Once Lydia had gone, Narelle called, 'Quick, Rach, come take a look!'

'I'll be down in a few minutes,' said Rachel, who always made a point of deferring whenever Narelle asked her to do something. This time the delay was legitimate, however, because Rob had just emailed her the dosing guide. She was pleasantly surprised to find that, apart from a semicolon he'd missed in a footnote, everything looked good. Her new system of typing out the amendments for his designer to copy-and-paste into the document was already paying dividends. She wrote an email instructing Rob to insert the missing semicolon but then changed her mind. She was happy to let this minor omission slide until Harrop's were doing the next round of changes.

She went up to Narelle, who slid her tongue across her snaggletooth and said, 'Get a load of this!'

Rachel looked aghast at the profile page of NarNar1980, presided over by a photo of Narelle pouting drunkenly. 'Myspace? But how?'

'We've got everything we want now,' said Narelle. 'Google, Bebo, Gmail, even that new Facebook site everyone's going on about. I've been instant-messaging Stevo all morning. It was him who gave me the link.'

'Link?'

'This IT nerd he works with figured out how to bypass company firewalls by using this proxy server thing. And it works here too.'

'Just because it works doesn't mean you should be doing it.'

'Chill, no one's gonna know.' She looked archly at Rachel. 'Unless some goodie two-shoes lags, of course. Anyway, having a quick chat or checking Myspace is hardly going to bring down the TreNetwork!'

'I wouldn't know about that,' said Rachel, who thought she should probably text Lydia about this straight away, like any responsible employee who cared about Trenpharm's security would.

'Now we've got Google, let's see this mystery Stuart of yours,' Narelle was saying. 'What's his last name?'

Rachel clamped her mouth and shook her head. Nearly three months on, things with Stuart were still going strong (though the launch and judo meant only hooking up on Saturday nights right nowadays), but she certainly didn't want Narelle stalking him online. She had enough of that with Alysha, who only yesterday had discovered a picture of Stuart's old college football team. Rachel had come home to find a printout on the fridge, with a pink highlighter-heart drawn around Stuart's face.

Narelle sighed. 'Isn't there *anything* you wanna look up?'

Though Rachel didn't want to be implicated in this crazy scheme, she figured there was no risk to herself. She had no intention of ever using the hack on her own computer, so any transgressions would be traceable to Narelle alone. She'd already decided it would be better not to tell Lydia right now because, with the launch imminent, even the help of a wayward PA was better than having no PA at all.

'Look up my old club then, Hayside Judo.' Rachel had no particular interest in seeing it – she hadn't looked it up once since moving, but her current club didn't have a website, and she couldn't think of anything else. She directed Narelle to the Gallery tab, where the photos of the annual *Hayside on Ice* Christmas outing had been posted.

'Who's the dude with the gold teeth?' asked Narelle.

'That's Tiny,' Rachel said, leaning in to beam at the picture of him waving from the middle of the rink. 'Looks tough but a total sweetheart.'

As they scrolled through the other photos, Narelle wanted to know what each person was like. They saw Faith, makeup immaculate as always, and Sensei Graeme performing an ungainly pirouette. They saw Arjun, Wendy, Jamal and Lauren chained together in a precarious-looking conga.

Despite the extensive photo gallery, one person seemed to be missing. Rachel hoped Kim's absence wasn't due to her moping under the mistaken belief that she was still heartbroken. As Narelle clicked into the last grid of pictures, Rachel felt a slow pang rising inside her. She knew it was not homesickness – London was her home now, and she didn't miss the Hayside crowd, lovely as they were. She looked wistfully out the window, at the bare branches of the maples on Vancouver Avenue, and realised what she was feeling was not a yearning but rather the sadness of finality – the knowledge that she would never, ever go back.

'Last pic,' announced Narelle. 'Aw, she's bloody gorgeous-looking, who's she?'

'Which one?' Rachel tried to compose herself. Sitting tightly beside Kim in the deserted back row of the viewing area was someone that Rachel had never seen before. The girl had wavy brown hair pulled up loosely at the back, and the couple of falling-down strands accentuated the curve of her high cheekbones. Everyone else looked blotchy under the rink's lights, but not this slim and pretty twenty-something, with her flawless milky skin.

'Her, you drongo,' said Narelle, zooming in to where Rachel was already staring. 'Bet all the guys wanna roll round on the mats with that beaut!'

Rachel gave a nonplussed shrug. 'She must be new or something …' She looked again: Narelle was entirely correct – the boys in the club *would* certainly be interested in this girl, but something told Rachel that the boys' interest was unlikely to be reciprocated. Yes, she was almost certain: this girl and Kim were more than just clubmates. They were posing as platonic pals, leaning innocently close for a photo, but Rachel had seen that same gratified grin on Kim's face when they'd gone down for dinner in The Crimson after a full day of …

Narelle read out the caption:

Thanks to Kim (injured) and newest member Olivia (skate-a-phobic) for being our audience – Kim, hope your ankle gets better soon!

Rachel almost snorted at their excuses to sequester themselves in the back row. Well, it was only a matter of time before people copped what Kim was up to. She would be accused of making lesbian moves on new members.

Narelle had twisted around and was staring at her. 'You OK, Rach? You look like you've seen a ghost.'

'I've just remembered something I have to do for Lydia.' She strode down the aisle. 'And you better get a move on with your database.'

Back in her seat, her chin fell heavily to her chest. What the hell was she doing, poking into the past? She must forget what she had seen. Kim's ridiculous decisions were of no consequence to her now.

She sat shaking her head at her own idiocy for a minute, then reached for the phone and dialled Rob's number.

She had decided not to let him away with that semicolon after all.

▼39▼▼

'The bed's decent anyway,' she said, bouncing lightly on the edge as she continued to look around the room.

'They're good mattresses,' said Rob. 'And that particular one hasn't seen much, well *any*, action.'

'Oh?'

'Yeah, me and my boyfriend called the last guy the *curly-headed castrato*! He was totally asexual.'

Jo, who was Irish and had only recently moved to London, seemed to find this funny. It was yet another positive sign (in addition to the fact she was pinging Rob's gaydar) that they could get along. She was a far more desirable prospect to Rob than the previous interviewees too: the pushy Bournemouth girl who'd worryingly enquired if the sofa turned into a guest bed, and the Norwegian queen who'd tried to haggle over the bills before Rob had even offered the room.

'Does your boyfriend not want to move in, now the castrato's gone?' Jo asked, as he led her into the kitchen and living area.

'I thought the same thing. How wrong I was, though ... but that's a story for another day.'

'Well, I'd be happy to hear it sometime,' said Jo, but then she quickly reeled back her smile. 'But only if you're interested in having me here, of course?'

'Absolutely!' Rob rushed to shake her hand, which was slightly damp despite her apparent ease. 'So, when suits you want to move in?'

'Saturday's ideal, but I'll get the first month's rent and the deposit to you tomorrow.'

'Solvent *and* sane?' said Rob with a laugh. 'I have found a good 'un this time!'

She laughed. 'Solvent only thanks to this savings scheme we had in Ireland called the SSIA. That's probably the only *sane* decision I made in the last few years.' She shivered and gave a self-deprecating shake of the head. 'But that's a story for another day too ...'

231

40

'Back to standing,' said Sensei Kev, 'and straight into fifty star-jumps.'

Rachel clambered to her feet, gasping for breath. Despite her vow to excel tonight, she just didn't have it in her. She'd managed to conceal her pathetic press-ups, but now there was nowhere to hide.

'Hands fully extended,' shouted Kev as he wandered between the jumping bodies. 'We don't have any gays here so I shouldn't be seeing *limp wrists*!'

The joke, coupled with the group's asphyxiated titter, almost caused Rachel's knees to buckle and give way. But here came Kev, who'd already made a dry comment about her job hardly being more important than last Tuesday's training, so she had no choice but to force a body that hadn't slept in two nights to keep going. Every jump sent a shock into the craters she'd been chewing into her cheeks all day.

She knew it was ridiculous to drive herself mad over that photo of Kim and Olivia. She'd been so sure they were 'together' at the time, but she'd only looked at the picture for a minute, *and* over Narelle's shoulder, *and* while distracted at work – hardly conditions for a proper evaluation. Of course, what Kim did in her spare time was immaterial, but that wasn't the issue. Rachel wanted closure about the photo itself. Nothing more.

'Twenty perfect burpees!'

She'd hoped to revisit the photo on Narelle's computer, but after a further database fiasco, Lydia had despatched the PA on a two-day Excel course, saying they were better off without her while they prepared for the launch. And there was no way of checking the photo at home either because she and Alysha had no computer in the flat.

By the time Sensei ordered them to break off into pairs, Rachel was ready to collapse. 'You OK, girl?' asked Alysha, as they grabbed onto each other's shoulders for quad stretches. 'You're not your usual self.'

'Oh, I just can't wait until this launch is over.'

Alysha gave her a probing look. 'You've not had a row with sexy Stu, have you?'

'His name is *Stuart*, Alysha,' hissed Rachel. She disengaged roughly from the stretch. 'And not everything in my fucking life revolves around my boyfriend. Maybe if you had one yourself, you'd understand.' She felt besieged from all sides now; only last night, Stuart had wondered if she'd had a row with Alysha because she didn't sound 'like herself' on the phone. Who were they to determine what her usual self was like? She just couldn't win. Alysha pulled away with reddening eyes; they completed the remaining stretches in a shaky silence.

'I'm sorry about earlier,' Rachel ventured to Alysha's pissed-off profile, set off by the bright lights of WWWheldon as they walked past. 'I'm just a ratty mare at the moment.'

Alysha said nothing for a minute, then stopped and turned to Rachel. 'What you said was pretty low.'

'I'll make it up to you, I promise. As soon as the launch is over, we can go shopping on Saturdays, have brunch, lunch, whatever you like!'

'Maybe,' said Alysha with a shrug. 'But in the meantime, there's something that *might* help me forgive you.' She nodded at the kebab shop up ahead. 'A big bag of greasy chips. And don't dare tell Sensei, OK?'

They waited at the counter. Alysha cheered up further when the kebab guy started flirting with her. Rachel, however, was dreading the long hours ahead. She'd been hopeful that the exercise would end her rumination, but she already knew that sleep would evade her again tonight. Overhead, a fly who'd survived the winter was playing Russian roulette with the UV insect-light. He would hover incredibly close, then fly off to relative safety, only to incorrigibly return a few seconds later.

'Now, one bagga Wheldon best chips for Wheldon prettiest lady!' Just as the guy passed the bag to a giggling Alysha, the fly made his final sortie, meeting his end in a split-second electrocuting sizzle. At least *he* was free of his repetitive obsession. Rachel blinked into the UV bars and realised she absolutely must get closure before bed tonight.

She waited until they were much further up the high street before finally accepting Alysha's offer of a chip. She forced it down, trying not to wince as the vinegar stung her cheek-craters. 'By god, they're delicious. Think I'll nip back and get my own bag.'

Alysha offered the chips again. 'No, take more of mine. We can split them onto plates at home.'

Rachel shook her head. 'You go on ahead and brew a nice pot of our night-time tea. I won't be long.' She walked away normally, but once Alysha had turned the corner, she made the most of her tracksuit and trainers and sprinted back down the street. She shouted her order to the kebab man and said she'd be back in five. At the door of WWWheldon, she paused to check that nobody she knew was passing. Then, with her heart fluttering, she went inside.

41

Jo was standing on the balcony, her jacket over her pyjamas, when Rob came out to join her. 'I've brought you some pomegranate juice,' he said.

'Aw, thanks,' said Jo, accepting the glass. 'I just needed some air. Michael's Châteauneuf-du-Pape was lovely, but I'm obviously not used to such heady wine!'

'He splashed out especially because he's delighted I'm finally living with somebody decent,' said Rob. 'He loves you – he said you were ... *erudent?*'

'Erudite?' Jo laughed. 'I don't know about that.' Although Michael had come across as a bit conceited at times, she'd got on quite well with him. And now this compliment, especially from someone so discerning, endeared him to her that little bit more.

'Did you see his face when you were talking about Trinity College?' said Rob. 'He adored all your stories.'

'I thought it best not to mention that, unlike his beloved Oscar, I never actually graduated!' Jo sipped the juice. 'Anyway, don't let me delay you getting back to himself. You shouldn't be loitering with me when you haven't seen him all week.'

Rob plunged his hands into his hoodie pockets. 'He's already gone, Jo. He had to leave at nine.'

'You're joking. Was he scared of being here when our visitor arrives?'

'Nope. The battleaxe is having the bridge ladies round and needed him to pick up eight mini quiches from some posh deli in Mayfair. I only found this out as we were falling asleep.'

'That's a bit mean,' said Jo. 'He gave every impression last night that you'd be spending the day together.'

Rob stared across the courtyard for a moment, then turned to her. 'I know this is awful, Jo, but sometimes I'm furious with Michael's dad for burdening him with that deathbed-promise. It's just not fair on him.'

'And even less fair on you,' said Jo, giving him a sad smile. She gestured to the flat opposite, where the balcony door had just slid open. 'Anyway, good see Moobster's up early too,' she said, using the nickname she'd given to their busty male neighbour the previous week when they'd jokingly concluded – by virtue of the headset and the fact he could afford the permanently curtained flat by himself – that he must be a small-time criminal.

'And looking divine as always,' said Rob, cheering up.

Moobster always sucked his cigarettes right down to the last millimetre so they were surprised to see him jettison his half-finished fag over the balcony. 'Has his mammy popped over?' Jo wondered, as he furiously swatted away the smoke. 'He's a bit old to be getting grounded.'

'If she's anything like him, she must be well scary though!'

The figure who came onto the balcony a moment later, its head twitching suspiciously, couldn't have been further from the Moobster-matriarch, however. Jo and Rob regarded the new arrival in stunned silence. It didn't take long for the athletic, twenty-something guy in the tight V-neck and jeans to work out that his friend had been smoking. They caught Slavic snippets of chastisement as Moobster was given a lecture and had his belly and breasts prodded by someone whose flat abdomen and square pecs were a beauty to behold.

Moobster eventually threw up his arms, as though in surrender to the sermon. But the movement was just a ruse: he moved in and grabbed his fit friend in a headlock.

'Let him go, you bastard!' Rob muttered, as they watched the good-humoured struggle of muscle against flab. When the Moobster eventually emancipated his prisoner, the two men went back into the flat, smiling and patting each other on the back.

Rob fanned his face with his hand. 'Please tell me he's the new flatmate.'

'Even I've got a man-crush,' said Jo. 'That *body*.'

'And the cute face. I nearly lost my life when he smiled there.'

'Now, now,' Jo tilted her head. 'You've got a boyfriend.'

'One who'd rather be quiche-shopping than here with me.'

Jo gave his shoulder a rub. 'Right, we better make our game-plan for later. I'm starting to get nervous. What if we can't keep a straight face?'

'This was all your idea, don't forget,' said Rob as they went back inside.

Jo picked up *Diva* from the coffee table. The monotone classified looked so benign amid the ads for Pride-striped boyshorts, silicone dildos and sexy lesbian escorts. She read aloud:

Noeleen. Reliable and experienced cleaning lady (cross dresser). Will clean your home for free, in return for safe space to be myself. Period properties especially welcome.

'See, nothing to worry about,' she said. 'And his texts were so polite. Today will be cringey, but we'll soon get over it.'

'Creepy more like,' said Rob with a shudder. 'And he, I mean *she*, will be sorely disappointed with this place. You can't get much more un-period than here.'

'Where else would we get a free cleaner in London who'll tidy up after someone as messy as you? I'm not becoming your housework-bitch like the last guy.'

'And he *was* a bitch, let me tell you.' Rob walked to the living-room door. 'Right, I'm off to get ready before the French maid arrives. I certainly don't want him-slash-her sneaking a glimpse of my arse in the shower. And you better lock away your underwear – you don't want all your knickers mysteriously disappearing, do you!'

42

'Heard that!' shouted Narelle.

Rachel rolled her eyes. Her efforts to noiselessly extract the Nurofen had been no match for Narelle's selective hearing. As she necked back the pills and stowed the pack in her bag, she heard footsteps approaching.

Narelle eyed a minuscule half-moon of foil on the desk. 'I'm seriously impressed, Rach.'

'What?'

'Coming into work with a hangover!' She crossed her arms in a parody of Lydia. 'I am *ruddy* disappointed, Rachel. I always believed you were an *excellente* worker.'

'I'm not hungover,' said Rachel, looking up drily. 'I've not been sleeping great and I've got a pounding headache this morning, that's all.'

Narelle tipped her on the shoulder. 'Stu the stud keeping you awake, was he?'

'No.'

'Ah come on.' Narelle was laughing. 'Nothing wrong with a Sunday-night root!'

Rachel felt a vicious kind of electricity rising inside her. Before she knew it, she was shoving back her chair. She was standing up. She was opening her mouth. She was roaring into Narelle's face. 'Shut it, for god's sake, would you? Go and do some fucking work for once in your life. We've got the launch in two weeks in case you're too stupid to notice.'

Narelle tongue quivered on the snaggletooth. 'Jeez, I was only having a laugh.'

'Leave me alone, OK?' Rachel collapsed onto her seat and put her head in her hands. A minute later, she heard the swish of the double-doors and Narelle was gone. She couldn't believe she'd yelled like that. Her cheeks were burning on the outside, bleeding on the inside (if she kept up this gnawing, she'd soon bite a hole right through). She hadn't been lying about the headache, but a throbbing skull wasn't the only thing she'd woken up with that morning.

Even her protracted shower earlier had failed to wash away the immediacy of the dream. Alysha had noticed her odd mood at breakfast and, yet again, Rachel had blamed escalating pre-launch nerves. She'd used the same excuse to leave The Mill early on Saturday night too (infuriatingly, Stuart had insisted on walking her home and she'd had to secretly double-back to WWWheldon after he'd gone).

The office clock showed nearly ten; she must get down to work before Lydia arrived. Dr Moss had queried efficacy data they'd taken from a clinical paper. The study was eighteen pages long; with a highlighter in her still trembling hand, she began skimming through the text.

In real life, she'd never been on a scooter. Nor had she ever actually met Olivia. But last night she'd had both experiences – careering through the streets of Newcastle as the inexplicable pillion passenger on Olivia's damson and anthracite Vespa.

They didn't speak a word, but as the scooter zoomed through the deserted city, Rachel felt a gorgeous closeness growing between them. The feeling deepened further when, taking a sharp corner, she had to grasp the waist of Olivia's sawn-off shorts. It was only then Rachel realised that, as well as wearing no helmets, they were both topless. She was mortified at her own exposure, but soon her eyes fixed on the slim, milky vision in front. The temptation was too much. She inched forward on the seat, until their bodies were pressed together, and allowed her hands to venture up Olivia's bare chest. She worried her new friend might recoil, but Olivia had loved it, responding to each touch with a series of encouraging little shudders, which made Rachel press in closer, until her boobs were smashed right into Olivia's back.

By the time she'd progressed to caressing the denim of Olivia's shorts and running her nails along the sleek thighs beneath, the limitations of being on the scooter were screamingly apparent. As though aware of their desires, the Vespa sped up by itself; soon they were whizzing past the city limits, Rachel laughing every time Olivia's blown-back hair tickled her nose and lips. Out in the Northumberland countryside, the fields were a fizz of surreal green. Red flowers in the hedgerows pumped out druggy perfume. The trees whispered that it wouldn't be much longer.

At the end of a mossy laneway the scooter chugged to a halt. Olivia dismounted and turned around with a sweet, sexy slowness that made Rachel's body throb. In anticipation, Rachel moistened her own wind-dried mouth and realised that the craters in her cheeks had miraculously healed during the trip. They looked at each other for the first time, Rachel tumbling over and over into the blue pools of Olivia's gaze. With a little sigh, she closed her own eyes and moved in for the kiss.

'Here's some tea for your headache, mate.'

'Christ, Narelle!' Rachel looked up gasping, terrified the reverie was somehow visible in the air. Unlike the Nurofen, however, there were no telltale traces. Bizarrely, Narelle's arrival had cut short the absurd storyline in exactly the same place as this morning's alarm.

'I know you hate sugar, but I put in three,' said Narelle. 'Sugar's always good when you're crook.'

Rachel humbly accepted the cup. 'Sorry about earlier. Look, let's go out for a few drinks when all this stress is over, eh? My shout.'

Narelle smiled. 'As long as *la ginge* isn't invited. By the way, she's just texted to say her meeting's run over and she won't be back until lunchtime. AKA she's going for another wedding dress fitting.'

'Lunchtime?' said Rachel, as a terrible thought occurred to her. She got back to work on the clinical paper, but it was no good. After a few minutes she stood up. 'Narelle, you wouldn't happen to have details for that server bypass thingy, would you? I need to look something up for judo. Nothing exciting, in fact I could even do it here on my own computer so I'm not bothering you …'

43

Noeleen's second visit was on a Thursday morning. Jo, who was alone in the flat, was determined to be less awkward and more welcoming than she had been previously. That first visit, after a brief introductory chat about cleaning products, she and Rob – both more self-conscious than the man in the dress obviously was – had pathetically fled to Jo's bedroom, emerging just minutes before Noeleen was leaving. It was only after she'd gone that they saw how brilliantly she had cleaned – which made them feel terrible for being so distant.

And so today, while the transformation was happening in the bathroom, Jo installed her laptop at the kitchen table, meaning she would *have* to interact with Noeleen this time. A few minutes later there came the shuffle of slippers down the hall. Jo steeled herself as the door opened. Although Noeleen's outfit and persona couldn't be further from the sexualised French maid of Rob's advance scaremongering, it was still jarring to seeing a grown man wearing clothes incongruous with gender, body shape, and era – even on this second viewing.

'Hi, Noeleen,' she said, smiling at the floor-length gingham dress, the elasticated mop-cap, and white Victorian maid's apron.

'Would you be able to do me favour before I start?' asked Noeleen, who used exactly the same voice as her male iteration. She presented two clip-on pearl earrings. 'My fingers can't deal with such dainty things.'

'Of course,' said Jo, who'd always felt uncomfortable about performing girly tasks on another female. (Even now she hated fixing her own makeup or hair when someone was sharing the mirror.) She got a whiff of rose water merged with the masculine tang of shaving foam as she stood on tiptoes and fiddled with the clips, feeling like a poor substitute for the competent female companion this lady deserved. Having anchored the clasps onto Noeleen's fleshy earlobes, she gestured to the counter: 'So we bought all your stuff.'

'Marvellous,' said Noeleen, who went over and picked up one of the new microfibre cloths. 'I used to swear by retired underpants, but these are far more effective.' She nodded at the glass bottle with the antiquated, almost medicinal-looking label. 'And you managed to find the Mrs Bristleworth's!'

'It nearly came to blows in Sainsbury's,' said Jo. 'Rob didn't want to spend nine quid on floor cleaner.'

Noeleen smiled. 'The Bristleworth's range is expensive all right, but their products are completely worth the money. In fact you can't buy a better floor cleaner for the kind of maple boards you have here. I work in flooring myself and always recommend it to our hardwood clients: I say I have a *close female relative* who swears by it!' Noeleen dampened her cloth then, and started tackling the aftermath of the complicated Valentine's dinner Rob had cooked last night for Michael. Jo opened her CV on the laptop. She'd been in London over a month now, and while her SSIA could sustain her city-explorations a while longer, she wanted to start working soon. She began to type, but it was hard to focus on her own curriculum vitae when there was a far more fascinating character in the room.

'Noeleen,' she said, 'I hope you don't mind me asking, but how on earth does a man who works in the flooring business end up doing … well, all this?'

'Oh, I can trace it back to childhood,' said Noeleen over the squeaks of her cloth on the hob. 'My father was a raging alcoholic, a raging man all round. When he got locked up for glassing a man in the pub, my mother took up the bottle herself. I was eight, no siblings, always left at home while she propped up the bar. She'd already alienated her own family when she'd married my father, so I was surprised one day to answer the door to a well-dressed lady with a hat and shiny black hair. She said she was my aunt Eileen, a woman my mother had always referred to as *that stuck-up bitch*. Well, I tried to get rid of the stuck-up bitch, but she insisted on coming in. When she saw I was alone with nothing to eat in a cold, filthy house, not even a pencil to do my homework, she announced she was taking me home with her.'

Jo discreetly closed her laptop. 'But you must have been terrified!'

'I was at first. Eileen was scarily direct. On the bus I sat up straight with my hands folded, just like she told me to. I felt her fine wool coat against my shivering arm and wondered what would happen to me. During the journey, she quizzed me about my mother and things at home, warning me sternly not to lie. I told her everything. The strange thing was, by the end of that long bus journey, I'd actually begun to derive a sense of comfort from that formidable, commanding way of hers. For the first time in my life I was under the control of a competent adult rather than having to think and act by myself. I felt free to be a child for the first time. We arrived at Eileen's, where I met my uncle George and my cousin Hazel. Little did I know as I got into the spare bed that night and sank into the soundest sleep of my life that I wouldn't leave there until I was a man of twenty-four.'

'No way! But didn't your own mum want you back?'

'Oh, she said she did all right. Called around the next day and read Eileen the riot act while George wrestled her out of the house. She made a ruckus out on the street then, calling Eileen a thieving bitch. I remember the feel of Eileen's pristine velvet sofa against my knees as I watched my mother being bundled into a police car outside. I had a strange feeling I'd never see her again. Maybe it was wishful thinking ...' Noeleen stopped and looked into the fridge with dismay. 'So, who's fond of the pomegranate juice but not so fond of throwing out these old cartons?'

'A girl Rob idolises at work thinks it's going to ward off cancer because of some study she read somewhere.'

Noeleen laughed and drained the juice-dregs down the sink. 'So, three days later my mother was found dead by a social worker who'd come to inform her that I'd be staying with Eileen for the foreseeable. I was told that she'd fallen down the stairs and hit her head. I found out years later that she'd choked on her own vomit halfway *up* the stairs.'

'God, I'm so sorry.'

'Don't be,' said Noeleen with a wave of the hand. 'Anyway, you must wonder how all this relates to me being here in a dress. You see, my eyes were opened when I moved into Eileen's. She was everything that my mother hadn't been. Her house was just a regular semi-D, but to me it was an immaculate palace. My cousin Hazel, also an only child, was understandably jealous and suspicious of me, and my uncle George was a shy, hardworking man who stayed out of my way except when we'd watch rugby on telly together. But I took to Eileen like I've never taken to anyone. She wasn't able to have any more children after Hazel, so she called me her "surprise present". When I first arrived, she kept me home for a bit to settle in before starting my new school. After George and Hazel left each morning, we'd go around doing the housework together. Eileen never stopped in that house. I didn't have a clue that cleaning even existed, but Eileen taught and encouraged me to do everything: hoovering, dusting, mopping the floor. I adored helping her. I'd never had so much one-to-one attention save for when my father was kicking me round the house after he'd been in the pub. Anyway, one day we were polishing the companion set and I spilled Brasso on my jumper. Eileen said that I best cover up and put me in a little floral pinny, part of a girl's Victorian dressing-up set that Hazel, a total tomboy, always detested wearing.

'At first we giggled that I was wearing a girl's thing. But inside I was proud as punch to have my important role in my new home recognised by a uniform. I had to take the pinny off before Hazel came in from school, but Eileen had sensed how it made me feel. As she hung it back up, she winked and said, "This'll be our little secret from now on." I was thrilled beyond belief.

'When I started the local school, there was no more midweek housework. But every weekend, whenever George and Hazel would go out, I'd ask Eileen, "Can I?" and she'd say, "Of course, my love!" I'd rush to get the pinny, and around the house we'd go with our buckets and brushes, cloths and polishes, tutting about the mess that George and Hazel had left behind them, but happy to be getting everything back to shipshape.

'Once I grew too big for the pinny, I graduated into one of Eileen's old aprons – an even bigger thrill, because it wasn't a child's play costume, but an authentic woman's garment. I inherited a pair of pink carpet slippers, too. Hazel discovered discos and boys and teased me for never wanting to go out. But by then I was a cumbersome lump of a lad, always anxious I'd put my size 11s in it, so I shied away from anything to do with girls.

'Sequestering myself away from the opposite sex could only last so long, though: in sixth form I fell head over heels with this absolute beauty in my French class, Diane Somerton. I used to write *Je t'aime, D.S.* on the back of my jotter and dream about her day and night. There was a social in the youth club and I plucked up the courage to ask Diane as my date. Looking back, I don't know what I was thinking, *mais ce sont les folies d'amour.* Well, Diane threw her head back with a nasty laugh and rushed to tell her pals that Noel Moody thought he'd half a chance with her. I ran home to Eileen in tears, saying I wanted to kill myself. Within half an hour, Eileen had despatched Hazel on some imaginary errand, I had my apron on and we were chatting and laughing and scrubbing the bathroom as though nothing had happened!'

'Wow,' said Jo, now so involved with the story that Noeleen had to nudge her legs with the sweeping brush to remind her to lift them.

'I was still dressing up and cleaning with Eileen when I started working at Goodstep Flooring. She was so proud of me for getting that job. I'd just celebrated my five-year anniversary there when Eileen began to lose weight. My world fell apart to discover she had aggressive liver cancer. It was so unfair that a woman who only drank one sherry at Christmas, was being given just months to live. I practically moved into the hospital. During those visits I thought we might discuss what would become of our special arrangement after she had gone. But the moment never arose. We were both too sad to admit that our precious time together was over.

'One freezing night in mid-January, I woke with a start at four in the morning. There was an overpowering chemical smell in my bedroom: Brasso. I knew then that Eileen had gone.'

Jo blinked, trying not to cry. She lifted up her laptop so Noeleen, who had already finished the sweeping and several other tasks, could wipe under it.

'I couldn't stay in a house full of memories. Anyway Hazel and George were cross with me for grieving so much. They'd lost a mother and a wife, but to me Eileen was more than that. She was the only person on earth who knew the real me. I moved into a rented flat near work. At night the grief would hit and I would pace furiously around my three little rooms. One evening a few months later, I snuck back to the house when was no one was home. I took an old suitcase of Eileen's and filled it with aprons and cleaning cloths. I began a routine of dressing up and cleaning my flat every night after work. I felt alive again – my anguish abated, I felt so close to Eileen. But I reached a point where I was just cleaning over my own cleaning. I wanted to make *an impact*, like we had back in the house. I'd let my own mess build up for a few days, but it still wasn't enough – I was terminally unsatisfied.

'One day at work, I was asked to measure up a building in Stoke Newington. I didn't usually do measurements, so I was a bit puzzled. Richard my boss said he was only asking me as a favour because none of the other lads would go – they were too scared because it was a community resource centre for *gay and lesbian people*! As I set off that afternoon, there were all the usual jokes: don't drop your measuring tape, don't speak to any women in case they're actually men. But I was curious and excited. I'm not gay and had never met anyone gay, but I felt an affinity with people who lived outside society's norms.

'When I got to Stoke Newington, I met the centre director, a kind, soft-spoken woman called Philippa. When I'd finished measuring, she offered me a cuppa and, just to spite the lads back at work, who expected me to rush back in arse-to-the-wall terror, I accepted. Philippa told me about the difficulties in running the centre on such meagre funding. Apart from the help of a few volunteers, she was doing everything herself, even – I noted with great interest – the cleaning. I left the centre that day with a bizarre idea spinning in my head. But it was an idea that wouldn't go away, and a few weeks later Noeleen, which is a combination of Noel and Eileen, became the official cleaning lady of the centre. I would arrive five nights a week after everyone had left, change into my gear and get cracking. Philippa put me in touch with Irene, an open-minded dressmaker beloved by the transvestites at the centre. I spent half my Goodstep wages getting outfits made, even though Philippa was the only person who ever saw me! She would say I was beautiful, the most diligent volunteer she'd ever met. I spent two wonderful years cleaning that centre. Then disaster struck when it lost its funding and closed down.'

'You must have been gutted,' said Jo, standing up to pass Noeleen a tea towel to dry the freshly washed pots and pans.

'Well, before Philippa left to run an Aids charity in Manchester, she put me in touch with a couple who were open to having Noeleen clean their actual home. Libby and DeeDee were so impressed they referred me on to their friends, who in turn referred me to other women again. For many years, I was happily inundated with lesbians who needed Noeleen. But more recently things started to wane – relationships split up, clients moved on, people could no longer facilitate me. I feared having to hang up my apron, when I suddenly remembered something I'd seen hundreds of times on clients' coffee tables.'

'*Diva!*' said Jo.

'I knew it was risky, and yes I got some odd responses, but some fascinating ones too, including a percussionist with the Royal Philharmonic who's invited me to her Georgian pile in Camberwell next Sunday. And tomorrow I'm in with a couple of *goth* girls. Not forgetting, of course, yourself and Rob. Yes, I owe that little advert a lot of gratitude!'

Jo couldn't stop smiling at the adorable bizarreness of it all. 'Well, you're always welcome here,' she said. 'And thanks for sharing such a personal story with me.'

Noeleen dried the final saucepan and put it into the cupboard. 'That's the kitchen done,' she said. 'Bathroom next, and then I'll treat your floors to their first taste of Mrs Bristleworth's!'

The bearded cashier who worked evenings in WWWheldon looked up from his vampire novel. 'Usual?' he said.

Rachel nodded but was taken aback. Hundreds of people must use this place – surely she hadn't visited *that* often over the last few weeks? Then again, he looked the nerdy type who'd have a photographic memory, or maybe he just fancied her.

'Twenty-seven it is, then,' he said, accepting her money with an almost accusatory amusement. Rachel walked past the rows of customers, realising that it was simply her insistence on booth 27 that must make her memorable to him. Maybe he wondered why a girl who mostly came in wearing a sharp suit and heels (like she was tonight, having worked too late to attend judo yet again) always wanted the most clandestine computer in the café.

She sat down behind the comforting hulk of the drinks machine and went straight to the Hayfield website. Even if other users couldn't see what she was viewing, the bearded guy might be able to, via the master computer. If that were the case, he must think her an oddball, staring night after night at the same photograph of two girls, then googling the same three words: Olivia, Judo, Newcastle.

At least tonight she wasn't in a rush, or having to pretend she'd taken one of her 'head-clearing' walks around the block. Alysha had just left on a four-day adventure camp with the Sunray House kids, affording Rachel full freedom until Sunday night.

Having stared for a few minutes at the photograph of Olivia (Kim was there too, of course, but Rachel hardly noticed her anymore), she began the usual Google search, which yielded the same irrelevant results as all the previous times. To get over the impasse, she needed Olivia's surname. She'd been formulating a plan. There was a risk it would backfire and Kim would find out she'd been digging, but she had to try. She took out her phone and began to type.

Hey Tiny, how are you? Promised I'd keep in touch! Working hard as the drug launch this day next week – eeek! How's club going – busy there these days?

She re-read it twice, hoping the final question wouldn't arouse suspicion. A couple of minutes later, her phone vibrated.

Good to hear from ya! Club v busy. New folk started and we're going for drinks Friday, wish u were coming!

The plan was working. Her fingers couldn't type back quickly enough.

Hope new members are female, need to balance out all those male egos!

The question was disguised as a statement, but she prayed for a response. No reply was forthcoming, however. She drummed her fingers on the sticky mousepad, cross with herself for not just asking outright. But a minute later the phone lit up.

It was only bloody Stuart though, asking if she was free on Saturday, even for a couple of hours, to have their postponed Valentine's dinner in Nagano. As she sighed and closed his message, Tiny replied.

Couple older lads like me. And a nice lass that Kim brung along. Folk say she's your repplacement as Kim always with her!

So, she'd been right! Kim and Olivia *were* together, but they'd hoodwinked people into thinking they were just friends. She looked around for inspiration and found it on a poster taped to the side of the drinks machine: *Jedd Fletcher & The Fletchlings play hits of the 70s at The Wheldon Arms.*

She began typing again. *I know an Olivia Fletcher who does judo. I bet it's her?*

Nah this lass is a total newbie, came the reply. *Hasn't a clue but Kim's helping her learn.*

Why wouldn't the little idiot just say the fucking surname? She squeezed the phone viciously in her fist as though to extract the answer from inside. Tiny might find it weird to be splitting hairs over different Olivias, but she'd come too far to stop. She wrote:

Defo not my Olivia Fletcher then! She was a black belt.

Rachel's eyes widened as she read Tiny's response. *Nah, think this one is Olivia Whittworth or something.*

Rachel kissed the phone. She googled the name, minus the second T – that gorgeous little gem Tiny could never spell to save his life! Halfway down the results there was a Bebo page that looked promising. She clenched her jaw as it loaded, but this Olivia was a thirteen-year-old schoolgirl. She continued to trawl through more unwanted incarnations, including an international hand-model, a landscape gardener and a mum who blogged about her twin boys. Finally, she found a Myspace profile of an Olivia 'Worthy' Whitworth. Even though the profile picture showed a girl in an evening dress, with hair curled and wearing full makeup, Rachel recognised her immediately.

She sat back in the plastic seat, nodding with delight at her own wiliness. The search itself was over, but now the really interesting bit was beginning.

Name: Olivia Whitworth ('Worthy')

Age: 26

Location: Newcastle

Last login: Yesterday at 17.45

Hobbies: Kayaking, reading, and believe it or not, have just taken up judo!

Interested in: Women

Relationship status: In a relationship

But in a relationship with *whom*? Rachel clicked into 'My photos' and cursed to find that they were only viewable by Olivia's friends. Her friends list was public, however; many of them looked gay or had gay-sounding usernames. Although Kim was listed, there was no correspondence between herself and Olivia in the comments section. The most recent entry was from a pouty guy called TwinkTank.

See you Friday sexxy. U bringing the new missus?

The new missus! Is that what Kim was? She clicked into TwinkTank's profile, but Olivia hadn't responded yet – this incomplete information was worse than knowing nothing at all.

Back on Olivia's profile, she speed-read through several illuminating pages of comments: Olivia had a large circle of friends and an active social life. She'd recently taken a kayaking trip to the Scottish Highlands (might Kim have gone with her?) and had a sister called Yvonne, who lived in Madrid and felt homesick. But most telling of all was a comment from a girl with spiked hair called dyKATIE.

Yo Worthy, thanks for the add. Load of us GaydarGirls on here!

Rachel sat back and stared at the screen. This was turning out to be an interesting night, a *very* interesting night indeed. Breathing rapidly, she leaned in again and clicked on to the next stage in her investigations.

45

The girls were hoisting on their black coats. 'You're sure you don't mind staying until we get back, Noeleen?' asked Isobel.

'Yeah, it could be fairly late,' said Millie, as her waifish hands knotted the heavy leather belt. 'These role-playing nights often go on until around ten.'

'Ten would be *wonderful*,' said Noeleen, delighted at the chance to do her own kind of role-playing on a Friday night. 'Anyway, my cousin Hazel and her husband are out celebrating their twenty-fifth wedding anniversary so I can stay as late as I like, and without having to concoct a cover story!' It was just as well Hazel and Martin had gone out too, because excuses were running thin – the local library that Noel supposedly frequented was now of limited use because after Christmas it had started closing at seven. And there were only so many times he could pretend he was joining the Goodstep lads for a post-work beer, especially when Hazel kept reminding him that he shouldn't be drinking at all. He was terrified that someday she'd smell his breath and, in a bizarre reversal of *man-gets-caught-out*, find no alcohol smell there whatsoever.

'Twenty-five years? That's adorable,' said Millie with a black-bordered smile that exposed the silver ring sitting sideways across her teeth. (Noeleen was bewildered by the girls' appetite for pain – two insulin needles a day was more than enough body-piercing)

'I hope *we're* still together after a quarter of a century, eh?' said Isobel.

'Course we will, hobgoblin!' Millie winked at Noeleen and turned to the mirror to arrange the netting on her antique fascinator into an asymmetric web over her eyes. 'Right, let's go or the others will be at the fifth portal of hell by the time we arrive.' Into the night they went, like a couple of vampire sweethearts being seen off by their Victorian-maid mother, who trembled with delight at the three hours of freedom stretching out before her.

Aunt Eileen's favourite cleaning maxim had been, 'The kitchen's the worst, that's why we do it first', and it was there that Noeleen got started. The home was far from the kind of gargoyled gothic fortress the two girls should be inhabiting. The ex-council one-bed in Hackney was low-ceilinged and poky, with a tiny galley kitchen. Noeleen had learned over the years, however, that the smaller the kitchen the *longer* it took to clean: it was the same level of mess compressed into a smaller area. Just like one of those sliding-tile picture-puzzles, you needed an advance strategy to avoid undoing your good work as you went. She smiled to see that the kitchen had recently been victim to a spag-bol explosion and was desperately in need of a scrub; she put on the kettle for hot water and began devising her action plan.

It was half past eight before she finally folded the damp tea towel over the shining oven rail. She stood back, as far as space would permit, to admire her impact. Hazel and Martin would be sitting down to their dinner at the restaurant around now. Noel would feel quite the gooseberry back at theirs later – what if they wanted to mark the occasion amorously? Then again, Martin was recording the rugby and would probably be more interested in retrospectively condemning the efforts of Scotland and Italy when he got home.

There was still an hour left after Noeleen had polished, hoovered, and dusted her way through the rest of the flat (though cobwebs were gothic, she presumed the girls didn't actually want them). She decided to tackle the shower as her final task tonight. The grimy tray looked like it hadn't been cleaned in years; ridges of mildew stood out against the white tiles above, like eyeliner on a pale face. She rubbed bleach into the grout with an old toothbrush and left it to absorb. The girls had an extensive collection of dark-bottled perfumes, and before she hunkered down to scrub the shower tray, she sampled a nice musky one called *Blood Kiss* on the back of her wrist.

Her shower-tray scrubbing was interrupted by the sound of a text coming in. Sadly, it wasn't the high-pitched ping of her pink phone (currently sitting in full view on the coffee table; the poor thing needed a break from the secret sock). She went to retrieve Noel's phone from the flannel trousers folded up on the girls' bed. Annoyingly, the text was from Hazel: was the woman incapable of enjoying her anniversary dinner without sending him diabetes reminders?

Amazing news. Chloe just arrived in from airport to celebrate our anniversary! Where are you? Come home for fizz (restaurant cancelled).

He was stuck to the floor. For the very first time since living with the Sutherlands, he'd taken the risk of leaving the suitcase unlocked and not fully hidden, assuming they'd be out all night. As if nosy Chloe would need any more of an invitation to snoop than seeing an ancient case bearing her grandmother's name protruding from under her bed! She could be up in her room rummaging through his most sensitive possessions at this very moment, shaking out the clothes and holding them up, poring over the photo albums, her jaw dropping further with every page-turn. *Mum, Dad … You better come upstairs quickly!* This was an absolute nightmare. He wanted to go into the bathroom and knock back the full bottle of bleach.

He paced up and down the hall in a sweat, in a daze, trying to think. There was a chance that Chloe hadn't gone to her room yet – she might still be downstairs, milking her surprise arrival for all it was worth. He could sneak up, lock and hide the suitcase, then fake his arrival a moment later. It might already be too late, but while there was still hope of averting disaster, he must be brave and make haste.

As he changed, his hands fumbled over every button. He decided to leave his outfit here rather than arrive back holding a further bag of evidence. He would text Millie to explain. But if he *had* been found out, Noeleen would never visit here, nor anywhere else again. He would have to leave London, leave Goodstep, distance himself from everything, everyone.

He glanced into the bathroom on his way out the door. It killed him to leave the shower like that – Noeleen's last ever cleaning task would be the only one she hadn't done properly. The bleach, now blackened with mildew, was sliding down the white tiles, like the tears of a disconsolate goth.

46

Rachel dropped her suit for the launch into Dry-Klean King, then navigated through streams of revellers who had very different Friday evening destinations to herself.

'Perfect timing,' said the cashier with a wry little laugh. He nodded to the back, where the seedy man Rachel had seen a few times before was leaving booth 27, his little bag of groceries hiding his crotch. Rachel felt queasy at the thought of touching the computer directly after him, but there was no way around it – in less than thirty-six hours Alysha would be back from her trip with the kids. There was a lot to do before then.

The mouse was clammy, and the air stank of his unwashed combover. She logged into the GaydarGirls profile she'd created last night. She'd completed the bare minimum of fields with sham, bland details.

Her previous search through the members from Newcastle had been infuriatingly cut short due to a limit on the number of profiles that free account holders could view per day. Tonight, however, she'd brought her credit card, making a mental note to hide the bill later, lest Alysha saw it. She input the digits.

Hi RozBrighton! Thanks for upgrading. You can now access our premium features.

Unlike the busy 'Who's online' London chatrooms, there were only eight girls currently logged into the Newcastle room. She scanned the list of usernames and ages. There was no sign of Olivia, but that didn't matter because this new premium account allowed for advanced searches. She looked up Newcastle members in their twenties with usernames containing Olivia and its diminutives, but none of the resulting Olivias was right. She tried Whitworth, and Worthy, which was Olivia's nickname on Myspace. She put kayaking and judo in the 'interests' fields. All to no avail.

There was nothing for it but peruse every Geordie girl from A to Z. She began whizzing through profiles: curvy girls, slim girls, girls into sports and wild socialising, quieter souls who enjoyed walks and reading. Girls who were comfortable specifying sexual predilections like breath-control, wrestling and water-sports. Girls who listed fetishes such as tattoos, sneakers or stilettos, or bizarrely, 'hands'.

Under 'Types I like', users cited everything from busty girls to baby dykes to hockey players. Others preferred 'femme' girls. And some didn't want a girl at all because they fancied 'older women'. Certain others left all the descriptive fields blank, not wanting to divulge anything about their personalities, but then in a strange paradox of privacy, were happy to expose their bodily selves via lewd photos, which Rachel quickly closed, feeling more relieved than ever that her screen was shielded by the drinks machine.

Misspellings and poor grammar were rife, as was posting results to an online quiz called 'Which *L Word* Character are you?' Many claimed similarity to someone called Shane, a girl with mussed up raven hair and a penchant for see-through vests. Overall, it was simply incredible what kind of information was being shared on a site that anyone – even someone like Rachel, who wasn't actually gay herself – could access with just an email address and a credit card.

She'd just started on the profiles beginning with N when someone tapped her on the shoulder. She spun round on the chair.

It was Alysha's friend Mel. 'Just spotted you hidden away here!'

'Oh, hi,' said Rachel, who now broadened her shoulders to block the screen behind her. She couldn't remember how big the GaydarGirls logo was, or whether she'd already scrolled past it. She butted her arm up against the drinks machine, at what must appear to be a ludicrously uncomfortable angle.

Luckily, Mel was far more interested in Rachel than her screen. 'Alysha says it's going great with you and Stuart,' she said with a wide smile.

Rachel gave an eager nod. 'I'm actually just chatting to a friend back home about it all.'

'Cool. I'm only in here because Ollie's gone and buggered up our broadband by trying to do an upgrade. Men, I swear!'

'I know,' said Rachel, who cringed as her computer beeped loudly. She felt ill at the thought of what might have popped up on the screen.

'Sounds like you got another message there,' said Mel, half-glancing behind

Rachel but not appearing to register anything untoward. 'I best get back home to my disaster of a boyfriend. But do come down to The Mill for a boozy night out when your big work thing's over. We all miss seeing you.'

'Definitely,' said Rachel. She turned back to her computer, grateful that the logo had indeed been off-screen. What worried her now, however, was that the beep had signalled an instant message from a girl called Professionelle. She'd been so focused on other people's profiles that she'd forgotten her own one was visible in the online list of the South East England room.

Hello, sparse-profile girl! How's your evening going? You heading out in Brighton tonight? Lovely town I believe :-)

Rachel squirmed at this intrusion. Of all the girls logged in, why on earth had this person chosen to contact *her*? She wanted to explain that she was only here for research, she wasn't even gay, that her whole account was fake. She clicked into to Professionelle's profile – just out of curiosity – and saw blonde scrunch-dried curls framing a happy, heart-shaped face. She looked like a regular girl, no Shane-style vests or crazy hair – just nice skirts and tops and dresses, which all suited her hourglass figure. Professionelle was five foot four and worked in healthcare. True to her username, she'd chosen not to divulge details of bust size, body hair and whether she was active, passive or versatile (whatever that meant). All her description said was *Professional, recently moved to London. Looking for others in similar situations for networking, friendship, etc.*

Before Rachel could decide what to do, the message window beeped again.

Sorry, Roz, didn't mean to disturb you then :-(Saw you're in healthcare and new to South East – same as me, that was all! Anyway, perhaps chat some other time, Gwen.

Rachel drummed her fingers on the desk. This Gwen did seem genuine and nice. It would be rude not to send *some* acknowledgement, especially as Gwen could tell that Rachel was online and had opened the messages. However, she must head off any protracted chat where Gwen might ask Roz about her job as a pharmacist or her recent move to Brighton. She wrote:

A bit slow on this as new to it all! Thanks for your messages, Gwen, hope you have a good evening.

She re-read the message before sending it and realised that her lack of engagement seemed ruder than no response at all. She changed the last line to: *How are you this evening?*

She pressed send and then found herself staring impatiently at the screen.

It didn't take long for the reply to arrive.

47

Noel pressed his face against the dimpled glass of the porch window, trying to discern any signs of life from inside. The front of the house was silent and dark. Everyone must be upstairs: agog, aghast, outraged, as they picked through the evidence of his perversion.

But wasn't it just as likely that they were behind the closed kitchen door, meaning he could safely slip upstairs? He must brave and take the chance. But what if … ?

After another minute of dithering on the doorstep, he closed his eyes. *Eileen, if you're up there* … He felt a sudden surge of strength, the strength to deal with whatever was to come. He was going in.

As he raised his key, the door was pulled open. Hazel's red-rimmed eyes blinked back. He understood her upset: the poor woman had just discovered her adoptive little brother had been deceiving her all these years. 'Noel,' she cried, through a blubbering sob that made his heart stop. She threw her arms hard around him. How was she already in a position to forgive? Chloe and Martin wouldn't be won over so easily, though. But now she was pulling him into the hall, saying, 'Come have some bubbly with this emotional wreck!'

In the kitchen was a brown, slim version of Chloe, with highlights grown halfway down her head. She gave him a hug but then pulled away suddenly, pressing his cheek with the back of her hand. 'Noely-Poly, you're boiling. You OK?'

'Just from rushing back to see you!' Noel forced a smile. There'd been nothing in her hugging that suggested any detection, but he was very concerned that her luggage was nowhere to be seen downstairs.

Martin didn't show any sign of knowing either; he was bopping around idiotically to his new *Drums of Burundi* CD, holding two spoons in his hands. Every so often he would ding out his own embarrassing approximation of the tribal rhythms on the champagne glasses. He winked at Noel. 'Couldn't believe it when this little minx turned up on the doorstep just as we were getting into a cab outside. I said to our driver, "this is an uncontested scrum mate. Our daughter's just back from deepest Africa, so no fare for you I'm afraid!"'

'And I'm not going back,' said Chloe, snaking her arms around her father's waist.

Martin tapped her forehead lovingly with a spoon. 'Absolutely not, my precious!'

'Didn't you like it, then?' said Noel, resisting the urge to knock back his champagne in a single glug.

'It was grim,' said Chloe with a shudder. 'Anyway, Haiti's where it's at nowadays, so I'm applying to go next month. You get put up in actual *hotels* by the charity there, plus you get a daily cash allowance. And then everyone goes partying in Cuba on the way home.'

'I see,' said Noel. He was desperate to get upstairs, but to avoid arousing suspicion, he sat with them, feigning interest in Chloe's asinine chatter for the next half hour. Eventually he stood up. 'I must move my things, Chloe, so they're not in your way.'

Chloe laughed. 'You deffo kept my room neater than it's ever been in its life. Looks ready for an army inspection.' She made little dividing gestures on the table. 'Comb here, toothbrush there, pens all in a row.'

Noel's blood ran cold. Thank god he'd got back before she'd conducted her own inspection.

'Martin will set you up with the camp-bed in the box room for the time being, Noel,' said Hazel. 'And if my darling daughter sees sense and decides not to hightail it to Haiti, then we'll buy you a proper bed for in there.'

'I'll be completely fine on the camp-bed,' said Noel, who'd already vowed that if Chloe wasn't gone from the house in a month, then he would be. He'd steal away in the night if it came to it.

Upstairs, he found Chloe's rucksack chucked on the bed, its contents strewn on the duvet. This included a bashed box of tampons, a nearly empty pack of Imodium tablets, and an array of skimpy synthetic knickers, none of which looked suitable for grafting in the tropics, especially when one had succumbed to traveller's diarrhoea. Eileen's suitcase was exactly where he'd left it, jutting out from under the bed. He gasped when he saw a fallen pair of Chloe's pants had snagged on the metal corner. She'd come unnervingly close. His only saving grace was that, just like her mother, Chloe never bothered to pick anything up. He put the knickers back on the bed, took the key from his wallet, and had only just locked the case when Martin stuck his head around the door.

'Camp-bed's done, Moody. But I'm afraid there's damn-all storage in the box room. Hazel says IKEA have some open-plan thingies we can get you.'

'Perfect,' said Noel, though nothing could be less appropriate for his needs. 'I'll move everything now.'

When Martin had gone, he took up the suitcase and held its ancient brown weight in his hand. It was so precious, its contents so private, that the rucksack on the bed seemed a trite travesty of a bag in comparison. It infuriated him how Chloe could be so legitimately carefree with her intimate possessions, while he must now drape the suitcase with his biggest coat just to sneak it along the landing.

The second he saw the skinny camp-bed he knew there'd be a problem. And he was right: no matter which way he wedged the case between the legs, one-third of it remained visible. It reminded him of dismal games of hide-and-seek when Hazel would spy his big bum sticking out of a wardrobe or his shoulder poking through a hedge. He tried putting the case into the corner of the room instead, with the open coat thrown over it, but the effect was so odd it would catch the eye of anyone who entered. And no doubt Chloe would be snooping in here while he was out at work.

He was still racking his brain for ideas when Hazel called up. 'We're ordering Chinese before Chloe dies of starvation here, Noel. Come look at the menu. And you can have anything you want tonight, even *chips*!'

48

'You see this beer?' said Patrik, who was handing them two more bottles, 'it is made seven kilometre from my home town in Slovenia.'

'We were only just saying how nice it was, weren't we, Jo?' said Rob, raising his voice over the noise of the party. 'Of course, if we'd known we were coming we'd have brought some drinks ourselves.'

Jo nodded. 'And a birthday present!'

Patrik, who worked as a 'pizza technician' and turned twenty-three today, furrowed his beautiful brow. 'Oh no, not necessary!'

Rob couldn't believe he was over here, and with Patrik perched on the arm of the sofa beside him too! It had all happened quite bizarrely. He'd been sitting at home with Jo (Michael had to postpone tonight's meeting to urgently evaluate lorry-damage to one of Stedman Sheppard's bridges), when they'd heard loud music across the courtyard. A group, including the gorgeously fit guy they'd seen previously, had gathered on the Moobster's balcony. Jo – who was in high spirits, having secured an interview for a really good job – had shouted over, asking if the party had room for two more. The beautiful boy had peered across, given them a devastating smile, and told them to come to Flat 334. Rob was apprehensive, but with the cable TV on the blink, and he and Jo unable to agree on a DVD, the party was a more promising option than moping around at home.

'Are you not having a birthday drink, Patrik?' Jo was asking.

Patrik laughed and patted his flat stomach. 'Unfortunately, my abs do not care that it is my birthday. Beer is big disaster for muscle definition.'

'Your sacrifice is clearly worth it,' said Jo. 'I saw you a few times from our balcony and I was like, *wow*!'

Rob nudged her leg with his own. He didn't want Patrik to know they'd been spying on him. Yesterday, Rob had gone a step further than looking too; he'd wanked in his bedroom whilst watching Patrik's pert tracksuited arse moving up and down as its owner did press-ups on the balcony.

Jo was undeterred, however. She pointed at Patrik's midriff. 'Can I see?'

Patrik jumped up and retracted his t-shirt. 'You can even touch, if you like.' He winked fraternally at Rob as he flexed the muscles. 'The ladies always like to touch!'

Jo pressed her fingers into the pale brown grid, like a baker testing a traybake. 'Rob check this out!'

'Looks great,' said Rob, using the cool dampness of the Laško bottle to hide his excitement.

'You must train hard?' asked Jo.

'Six days a week. But training don't matter if you have bad diet. Look at my friend over there. He is big … but no definition.'

'Oh yes, Oleg,' said Rob. They'd already tried making small talk with Patrik's Russian pal, but the towering skinhead with volatile eyes and a tortuous nose either had little English or was just too drunk to use it. As well as Oleg, they'd also been introduced to Moobster, who was Patrik's cousin Stanko, and who was now immersed in a serious poker game in the corner.

Patrik leaned in. 'A few month ago, Oleg start to take *juice* to get even bigger.'

'Fruit juice is high in calories and fructose,' said Jo. 'So it would lead to weight gain.'

'No,' corrected Patrik. 'The other juice, anabolic steroid. Me, I would never touch those things.'

Rob nodded to the poker table. 'Your cousin doesn't seem to be very healthy either,' he said.

'Stanko is the most unhealthy guy on planet. Eat, smoke, poker all he do. At night he snores like wild pig and keep me awake.'

As they laughed Rob saw something bold flicker in Jo's eyes. 'Maybe you should sleep in the other bedroom?' she said.

Patrik looked away. 'That room is for … something else.' He was saved from further questioning because Oleg, who'd been left high and dry by the mini-skirted girl he'd been trying to chat up, had come over. He hinged one of his tree-trunk arms around Patrik's neck.

'You know this Patrik,' he said, looking drunkenly from Rob to Jo. 'He is little faggot-pussy what don't drink alcohol.' His swaying gaze settled eventually on Rob, as though he, as a fellow heterosexual, should be aware of the risks of being around Patrik. 'You know this, yes?'

'I know he doesn't drink for fitness reasons, yes,' said Rob, caught between offence at the use of *faggot*, and wishing it were actually true of Patrik. It was already clear from their earlier conversations that although Patrik could pass as a model for a gay sex-line advert, he was completely straight. Rob prayed that Jo, now bristling beside him, wouldn't be crazy enough to reveal their own gayness, something they'd avoided mentioning to anyone here, including Patrik.

Patrik wrangled free from Oleg's grip. 'You're drunk, you asshole!' he said. He gave Oleg a shove. 'Piss off and make sure Stanko don't lose all his money.' He turned back to Jo as the hulking form retreated to the table. 'Sorry about him. Big body, tiny brain.'

'And I've heard that steroids can shrink your testicles too!' said Jo, making a pinching gesture with her fingers.

'No, no,' said Patrik, shaking his head. 'Not true with Oleg.'

'Oh?'

Patrik started laughing. 'No, Oleg already have teeny weeny mini-balls before he even start the juice!'

49

After the Chinese, Noel sat with the Sutherlands, pretending to watch television. What he was actually watching was their trips back and forth to the loo – he was waiting until they'd all relieved themselves before he would risk his own trip: from the bedroom to the shed at the end of the garden. While picking at his chips, he'd had the brainwave to hide the suitcase out there until he could offload it to a client. Martin, dozy after too much Peking duck and champagne, had stumbled to the toilet ten minutes ago. Hazel had gone in next. Now, with the yawn of an overfed toddler, Chloe disentangled herself from her mother's arms and stumbled out of the room.

When she returned, and everyone seemed settled again, it was Noel's turn to excuse himself. He tried to close the sitting room door as casually as he could, though it had been left ajar all night. He sprang silently up the stairs and came back down, holding the case in a sweaty death-grip. He tiptoed past the sitting room; the TV sounded ferociously close. If someone were to pop to the kitchen right now it would be game-over. The back door groaned when he opened it – if only that arsehole Martin would bloody well oil it, like Hazel was always nagging him to. He listened out, but nobody came to investigate the sound.

He skinned his knuckles as he quickly retracted the rusty bolt on the shed door. A stripe of moonlight filtering through the cobwebbed window illuminated the terrible mess inside, but for once in his life he was comforted by chaos. He clambered between boxes, sacks and tools, and wedged the case behind Chloe's childhood bike. 'Until we meet again,' he said, touching Eileen's stencilled name. Then he covered the case with a crumbly remnant of carpet underlay.

He breathed a sigh of relief into the musty air. All he needed was to get back into the house undetected and he had done it! But then he froze. The door was being slowly drawn open. He began quivering so hard that the shed shook on its brick foundations.

Hand on hip, in the moonlit doorway, stood Chloe. 'Thought you'd gone to the loo?' she said.

'Chloe!' he gasped. 'What are you doing here?' She must have looked through the suitcase earlier and then stalked him to the shed. The snagged knickers had been a clever decoy to lull and entrap him. The sweat of surrender sprang out all over his body. It was already too late. Far too late.

'What am I doing here? Well, I could ask you the same thing,' she said, a wry smile growing on her lips. 'Except I already know the answer. Let me in and let's talk about it.' She pulled the door behind her and stared at him in the darkness. 'You're shaking.'

'I'm not.'

'I can feel it through the floor.' She sat down on the grass-box of the lawnmower and looked up at him. 'Listen Noel, I don't blame you for what you're doing. I'm just pleased my hunch was right. The second I hugged you I smelled perfume and I was like, *hmm …*'

'Perfume?' In his haste he'd completely forgotten to wash off the *Blood Kiss.*

'But it's not just that,' she continued. 'You've been fidgety as hell all evening, you never told Mum where you were earlier, and then I come down to the shed and hear *until we meet again.* It doesn't take a genius …'

He began to shake more violently now. Tears choked his throat as he spoke. 'Chloe, I'm so sorry. What must you think of me? A man of my age doing this. I suppose you're going to have to tell your parents aren't you?' His head hung down heavily; the tears began to spring.

Chloe burst out laughing. 'Tell Mum and Dad? Are you joking? Could you imagine what they'd be like.' She pretended to explosively pull on the starting cord of the lawnmower. 'Whoosh!'

'Really?' he said, looking up tentatively.

'If they find out you've got a lady-friend they'll never stop pestering you – *what is she like, when do we get to meet her, hope you're treating her properly, hope she knows you're diabetic?* It's bad enough you have to sneak down to the shed just to ring the poor woman.'

He clenched every muscle in his body in gratitude to Eileen, then took his black phone from his pocket to use as a validating prop. 'Exactly,' he said. 'I knew your mum and dad would get carried away. And the relationship's still early days …'

Chloe pulled a box of cigarettes and a lighter from the cuff of her sock. He stared at her agog. 'Chloe … ?'

She lit up and fired smoke from her nostrils with practised nonchalance. 'Took it up out of boredom in Burundi and now I'm hooked. Cigs were cheap as chips there. But they'll be even cheaper in Haiti!'

'Well, I have to say it suits you,' he said, as though describing a beautiful dress or a hairstyle, rather than a habit he'd deplored ever since his father had stubbed a Players out on his thigh because he'd wet the bed again. Still, it was impossible not to be to be generous at a moment like this.

She took a few deep drags and then stamped out the fag on the floor. 'So, you'll keep my little trips to the shed a secret and I'll do the same for yours?'

'It's a deal,' said Noel. 'But promise you'll be careful down here.' He nodded at the petrol tank of the lawnmower. 'I don't want you going up in flames.'

'I will. Now, any chance you could distract Mum and Dad while I pop upstairs to get some Impulse and chewing gum?'

He nodded. 'In fact I'll tell Hazel I forgot to do one of my injections earlier. That always causes a stir!'

As they went up the path, Chloe whispered, 'So what's she like anyway?'

'She's lovely,' he said. 'Gentle, kind.'

'Name?'

He thought quickly. 'Jo.'

She gave him a scandalised smack on the arm. 'A younger model? Look at you *go*, Noely!'

'No, no. As in Josephine.'

'Josephine! So not tonight then, eh?'

He looked at her wryly. 'Certainly not, seeing as I was summoned home urgently to celebrate your arrival.'

'Sorry about that,' she said. 'You can make it up to her next time?'

'I certainly will!'

They continued their quiet giggling until they reached the back door. Then Chloe slipped upstairs, and he went to the living room, ready to honour his part of their pact.

50

I never thought I had a particularly Welsh accent until I moved here. Now people keep telling me how 'sweet' I sound! One of my speech therapy clients even said I'd given him a Welsh accent! What about you, Roz, do you sound like a true Geordie?

Rachel smiled to herself, and replied:

I think my accent's pretty neutral but some people here in Brighton say I sound a tiny bit like Cheryl Cole. The worst is when they do Geordie impersonations – totally cringe. What part of Wales are you from anyway?

While Rachel waited for Gwen's response, she stretched out her hunched-up back. She hadn't even noticed the clientele thinning down to just three, nor her friend at the desk being replaced by another cashier. The last hour had been an enjoyable way to pass an evening, but she must soon terminate the chat. Gwen was awfully nice, and it was interesting to share stories of moving to a new town, but it wasn't fair to lead someone on, even in friendship terms, when you weren't that way inclined and might never be on GaydarGirls again.

Gwen was taking longer to respond this time. Rachel checked back to ensure that she hadn't said anything to offend. Still, apart from general netiquette, there was no guarantee or promise that Gwen *would* respond. Maybe it would be better if Gwen *didn't* write back: then Roz, who'd recently started a job as a pharmacist in Brighton, could just slip into the ether, never to be seen again.

I'm from Wrexham. (Sorry for delay, another girl just messaged me there.)

Rachel felt a bit jealous – why weren't other girls messaging her too? Then again, her bland, photo-less profile wasn't exactly enticing.

No worries, Gwen. Anyone of interest?

She's certainly attractive, wrote Gwen. *But her profile said: 'Looking for someone to have intellagent discussions with'. Hmmm, best of luck with that!*

Rachel wanted to tell her about how Rob's misspellings got under her skin too, but why would Roz the pharmacist need an ad agency? Instead,

269

she wrote something that wasn't so much as lie, as a transposition of the truth:

Too funny. But you can't expect much from the public, when even DOCTORS can't spell. We see misspelled prescriptions in the pharmacy all the time. Some drugs even have similar names, terrifying!

Gwen wrote:

That worries me, Roz! Sorry, I have to go. Corner-shop closing soon and I need maple syrup for the morning. Maybe talk to you again sometime though?

Rachel was disappointed that their conversation ranked below maple syrup, but to avoid sounding needy she said: *I'm actually doing a project for work so may still be online when you get back.*

Sorry Roz, Gwen wrote. *I'll be heading straight to bed. Definitely chat again soon.*

'No, you won't,' Rachel muttered as she frowned at the smiley. There was no point going home to the empty flat – she was far too alert to sleep. She bought a Red Bull from the machine and resumed her search through the Newcastle members for Olivia's profile.

She hadn't even copped the kayaking reference when she eventually clicked into the page of a twenty-six-year-old called Paddlequeen. But there she incontrovertibly was – a wet-suited, helmeted Olivia – grinning from a grassy riverbank, her oar standing tall beside her.

Rachel's eyes roamed greedily through the feast of information on the page. Olivia liked Asian fusion food, listening to jazz and pop, and reading Toni Morrison and Sarah Waters. She drank socially, never took drugs, had 'some' body hair and an 'average' bust. In the status area, Olivia had declared herself *In a Relationship.* Underneath this it said, *Link to my Partner's Page.*

Rachel sighed with relief. Although Olivia was gay, she wasn't with Kim, because she already had a girlfriend! But when she clicked through to check out Olivia's partner, her arm slid off the desk, almost taking the Red Bull with it. KimGeordie's profile photo was the picture of her and Olivia at the ice rink. And it was captioned: *Me & my babe.*

'Kim, Kim, Kim,' she whispered, 'I've caught you red-handed now.' She navigated back and forth between the two profiles, trying to take in the triple revelation that Olivia was seeing Kim, that Kim had a GaydarGirls profile, and that they'd probably met on this very site. But then her own message window re-opened.

Bangladeshi shopkeeper just told me I had a 'beautiful valleys accent'. What next!

At first Rachel didn't respond – she had far bigger things going on. But as she stared at the familiar ice rink photo within its weird new context, she began to toy with an idea. You could never have too many acquaintances in a huge impersonal city like London. And despite the odd way they had 'met', Gwen did seem really nice. Luckily it wasn't too late by the time she decided to act: Gwen was still online. Rachel typed:

What next indeed! Actually Gwen, I'm heading to London on Sunday to go shopping etc. Don't suppose you fancy meeting up, just to say hi in real life?

She took one last look at the picture of Olivia and Kim. Then, holding her breath, she sent the message off to Gwen.

51

'A closeted TV star!' Rob twisted to look at her. 'Why've you never told me all this before, Jo?'

'Wait until you hear the rest.' Jo took a glug of her fifth Laško and rested the bottle on her knee, which was thrumming to the tech-house that also had Patrik and his pals dancing out on the balcony. Jo and Rob were currently sharing the couch with a black-bobbed girl called Vesna. (After taking great pains to explain in minimal English that she was due at work in two hours' time, Vesna had fallen into a paralysed sleep with her head on Rob's shoulder.) Over in the corner, Stanko's gang were still in the midst of a poker session that seemed to be outlasting the litre of scotch sitting among the banknotes. Jo continued, 'So, everyone in Ireland presumes Tamara's this darling girl-next-door. She was all about wholesome kids' telly at first, but now she's got a finger in every pie going. Oh, and a couple in my ex too.'

'How did you uncover the affair?'

'It all started when Louise started going out after work. The Celtic Smoothie crowd had never been particularly sociable, but suddenly every Friday night it was someone's birthday or some sales-target celebration. Then there were the leaving dos. So many leaving dos. I'd sit alone on a Friday night wondering why everyone was leaving a company that was doing so well.'

'Couldn't you have invited yourself along?' asked Rob. 'Like, if Michael was constantly going out with his Stedman Sheppard crowd, I'd do that. Luckily serious engineer types don't go out boozing though!'

'Louise hadn't come out at work, so me tagging along would've been weird. Anyway, after a couple of months of this, she told me about yet another leaving do that Friday. I was pissed off and made a jibe about her spending time with people she saw all week rather than her own girlfriend. I joked that if any more people left, Celtic Smoothies would have to close down.'

'Nice jibe.'

'Not quite. She got all defensive. Said I didn't have a clue about the business world, that you needed to socialise to get ahead. I backed down, but I didn't mind because, after that outburst, when she *was* at home she was in brilliant form and was extra nice to me. I put her mood down to this new intensive gym programme she'd started. It had her looking fantastic and full of energy. A while later, she went to her colleague's overnight hen party in this country hotel called the Edgeworthstown Lodge. When she got home the following day, instead of acting as frazzled as she looked, she was on a total high. But when I started asking her details about the night and the hotel, she was suddenly too hungover to talk. I got annoyed, but she said that I was only prying because I was jealous she had more friends than me.'

'But where does this presenter come in?' asked Rob, gently repositioning Vesna's head on his shoulder.

'Louise had become friendly with Tamara through a work event. Sometimes she'd mention that Tamara had driven them out to lunch in Donnybrook in her Mini, which had this bespoke fox-head decal. I *was* jealous of those little excursions because I totally lusted after Tamara on TV. Louise said that Tamara wasn't her type, but that she was a lovely person beneath the looks and the fame. Anyway, like the rest of Ireland, I presumed Tamara was straight.

'Then last year, my boss asked me and my colleague to write a feature about GPS technology. As part of the research, I made some screengrabs of Google Maps. Like everyone else, I'd looked up our street when the technology first came out, but now when I went back again, there was a more recent satellite picture, with the trees in full leaf. There was a small car with a fox-head roof parked right outside our house. And butted up right behind it was Louise's car – I could even see the cushions she kept on the back shelf. The absence of shadows meant it was around midday. The thing that made my heart stop, though, was that Louise had never mentioned bringing Tamara to our house for lunch.

'Somehow I managed to act normally until that Friday afternoon. I parked at Louise's office and when she came out, her face fell in horror. I said I'd booked a surprise romantic night in a secret destination. I'd packed her overnight bag because we were going straight there. Well, she fussed and demurred, said she'd already committed to birthday drinks for a colleague, and anyway she had a gym class the next morning. But I held firm and ushered her into the car, saying it was time the *two of us* did something nice.

'She needed to tell her colleagues she wasn't meeting them after all, but I knew by her agitation and the frenzy of texts as we drove, that my little surprise had scuppered something far more exciting than birthday drinks. Her phone was on silent, but every time a text came through, it made the car-radio crackle just slightly. When I asked why she seemed antsy, she said she was just excited to find out where we were going.

'As we eventually took the turn with the signpost for Edgeworthstown Lodge, I sensed her whole body stiffen. I said she'd had such good fun at the hen that I wanted to see this place for myself. I took a deliberate wrong turn, into the services-only carpark, but she didn't correct me. She lagged behind as we went into the lobby, because she didn't have a clue where she was going. Whenever I asked where something was that evening – the spa, the bar, the restaurant – the stock answer was that she'd been too drunk at the hen to remember.

'The romantic package included a dinner, which she just picked at, saying she had heartburn. She was far more interested in ordering bottles of wine. Back in the room she actually initiated sex. I was shocked because we hadn't done it in over a month but pleased too: I thought it signalled a fresh start for us, that she had decided to give up Tamara. And ironically, it was all thanks to this trip, my supposed romantic overture! The sex was voracious but completely uncoordinated – it was like she was driving a new car for the first time, all revs and jerky gear changes. By the end we were both sweating profusely, but she refused to let me open the window or turn down the heating. I went into the bathroom and cried silently into the sleeve of my robe. I'd copped her plan: the hot room and exertion would make me want a shower, and she'd be free of me for a few minutes. I turned on the water and made some splashing sounds, even sang a bit. But then I pushed my ear against the bathroom door. It was her first moment alone since leaving work and I knew she'd seize it. As soon as I heard her talking, I burst back into the room. I knew from the way her voice trailed off just who she'd been talking to. I fucked a Gideon bible at her head, said that I knew what was going on and who it was with. She laughed and said I was paranoid, and that I should keep my sexual fantasies about my celebrity crush being gay to myself, because Tamara was straight as a die.'

'Straight as a *dyke* more like!' said Rob with a laugh.

'Exactly. So, when I told her about Google Maps, she said Tamara had come over for lunch to our house just the once and, sod's law, it must have been the day the satellite was passing. Louise had never told me because the house was in a state that day, plus I'd be upset to know my TV crush had seen my period underwear drying on the clothes horse and my Immac in the bathroom. I began to wonder if maybe I *was* just insanely paranoid? As final closure I demanded to see the last dialled number. She handed me the phone with a malicious glint in her eye. Jesus, did I feel stupid when I saw her brother Trevor was the last call. I could sense a panic attack coming on. I had ruined everything. But while the phone was still in my hand, a text came in from Trevor. She lunged for the phone, but I jumped away. She winced and crumpled as I read it aloud. *Your call dropped sexy. Anyways ring as soon as she's asleep. I'll be thinking of you in your black thong until then, Tams x.'*

'Oh, the sly bitch!'

'I roared at her to pack her stuff, we were going back to Dublin straight away. It was nearly midnight and I was completely over the alcohol limit, but I didn't give a fuck. I drove like a woman possessed down those twisty, unlit roads. I didn't care if I killed us both. She sat staring silently ahead. We'd gone about five miles when there was a bump at the front of the car like we'd knocked something down. Despite her cruelty to humans, Louise was an animal lover. She begged me to pull in and then she walked back to check. But she'd left her phone on the passenger seat and the next thing the screen lit up.

'Trevor, by any chance?'

Jo nodded. 'The text said. *Why is she not asleep yet? Way past her usual bedtime by now!* Rob, I just lost it. The next thing I knew I was driving back to Dublin alone at eighty miles an hour playing industrial techno that was *almost* loud enough to drown out my roars of rage as I read through every Trevor text before flinging the phone into a ditch.'

'I don't blame you, Jo. So how did the lying cow get home in the end?'

'To this day, I have no idea. All I know is that she turned up the following evening fit to skin me. Two days later she moved out. And we haven't spoken a word since.'

There was shouting and slow applause from the corner of the room. The poker session had been won by the small man in the pinstriped blazer. Stanko drizzled the last drops of whiskey into his glass and rested his miserable head on his chest.

'Wonder how much he lost?' said Rob.

Jo grimaced. 'The question still remains – where is he getting the cash from in the first pla— … Oh my lord, who is that *vision* in G-Star?'

Jo watched the girl, who was wearing a marl grey t-shirt and boyfit jeans, move fluidly across the room. She took the seat beside Stanko and, after a quick consolatory hug, began what appeared to be an anti-gambling lecture in Slovenian. Jo watched, taking in the sallow, angular face and the perky brown ponytail. Her lean body and the way she held it, even in sitting, suggested athleticism, and Jo shivered to think there was someone other than Patrik here tonight with fabulous abs. Unlike the other girls at the party, dolled up in dresses and glitzy leggings, this girl moved to a different, boyish beat. Even her belt, a maroon skater-esque stripe that held the jeans tight to her slim hips – oozed an androgynous cool that made Jo hot under the collar.

'Her?' said Rob, making a face. 'Really?'

'Really,' said Jo, gulping at the swell of the girl's deltoid as she reached across the table to grab a bottle of water for Stanko.

'I was talking to her in the kitchen earlier,' Rob said. 'Or rather trying to. I asked her politely for the bottle opener and she just handed it to me like I was a piece of poo on her trendy trainers.'

'She mustn't have great English,' said Jo, jumping to defend the perfect vision. In a bolt of drunken imagination, she saw them writhing topless in bed, where English – or Slovenian – would be unnecessary.

Rob shook his head. 'I heard her telling one of Patrik's friends that he wouldn't make any *hypertrophic gains* unless he *increased his protein intake*.'

Jo gave a little groan. 'Hypertrophic gains? Stop, now you're only making me worse.'

'But those icy eyes. Don't you think she's very severe?'

'More symmetrical than severe,' said Jo, stealing another glance. 'Oh look!' Stanko was discreetly handing over something small from the palm of his hand, which the girl took and quickly popped into her back pocket. Then she left the room, leaving Jo to blink at the afterimage.

'Bet you a fiver she's off to do coke in the loo,' said Rob.

'Well, if that's the case,' said Jo, pushing herself off the couch in a rush of lustful courage, 'I might ask her for just a teeny little line!'

A couple of minutes later, Jo was loitering at a polite distance from the bathroom door and praying the Slovene beer had given her enough Dutch courage not to fluff her opening gambit. She would have to pounce swiftly but casually. She couldn't help thinking of the last time she'd tried to chat up a girl – the evil Clíona, all those months ago at *Miss*.

The toilet flushed. As the door opened, Jo put on a smile and sprang forward, only to pull back as Oleg stumbled out (it was a miracle the big boor had even flushed the loo); he barely noticed Jo as he staggered back to the kitchen. Jo contemplated following because the girl must be in the kitchen too, but suddenly the door of the permanently curtained bedroom was pulled open, and out she came. The moment she saw Jo, she yanked the door behind her. Jo reignited her smile and got ready to finally engage, but the girl had already turned to fiddle with the lock.

Jo's heart sank when she saw the handbag that had suddenly appeared over the fit shoulder. A fringed mustard monstrosity, a suede aberration so big and deliberately girly, that it singlehandedly negated all previous evidence of gayness. Jo leaned against the wall, her lust fatally punctured, wondering how someone so beautiful could adorn their body with something so ugly. Of course, it hardly mattered that the girl wasn't gay now – in fact her unavailability was a blessing because there was no way Jo could fancy someone who accessorised like that.

The girl stowed the key in her pocket and came down the hall with the atrocity on her shoulder, exercising the straight woman's prerogative to carry a handbag without a second thought. She raised an eyebrow at Jo as she went past, but it wasn't the peppery gesture of one dyke clocking another, but rather the withering look of a good-looking straight girl who wondered why this lemon was standing in an empty hallway at a party, especially when the bathroom was obviously vacant.

This time Jo didn't honour the departing G-Starred arse with so much as a glance. It was of little interest now anyway, given that its owner was a rude, cold-eyed (Rob had been right!) straight girl. A straight girl with terrible taste in handbags.

52

The door opened downstairs. 'Hi Rach, I'm back!'

Mascara-wand suspended in mid-air, Rachel mouthed *fuck* to her horrified reflection in the bathroom mirror. It was Sunday afternoon, and her whole plan had hinged upon Alysha arriving back late that night, by which time Rachel would be safely home herself, ready to pretend she hadn't left the flat all day.

This was going to be tricky. Very, very tricky. Before she had time to think, here was Alysha, dumping her rucksack on the landing and coming in to sit on the edge of the bath.

'Thought you weren't due in until tonight?' said Rachel, turning only briefly from the mirror so Alysha wouldn't see her tremulous expression.

'I've just been in A&E with one of our little girls. Turns out she's got a severe horse allergy. Her throat swelled up during the pony trek and she couldn't breathe. It was horrible.'

'Oh god,' said Rachel, barely able to breathe herself. There was nowhere to hide in the bright immediacy of the bathroom, and she still hadn't devised an excuse for this afternoon. 'And how is she now?'

'She's on an antihistamine drip, she's going to be fine.' Alysha paused and looked Rachel up and down. 'Anyway, *you* look hot. Stuey whisking you off somewhere nice while I mope round on my lonesome for the afternoon?'

'I'm actually heading into London with a friend from work; you know Narelle?'

'The Aussie you're always complaining about?' said Alysha, looking at her with an incredulity that didn't quite mask her jealousy. 'Didn't think you'd want to hang out with her. Anyway, isn't she supposed to be your minion?'

'I know I moan about Narelle, but underneath the sloppiness she's a decent person. And she seems quite lonely over here in London. A lot of her *mates* have moved *overseas* recently.'

'Fair enough,' said Alysha, her crossness softening. She picked at the edge of the shower curtain. 'Wouldn't mind a few drinks myself after being cooped up with all those kids.'

'We're not actually going for drinks,' Rachel said quickly.

'Thought you said Narelle's a real boozehound?'

'Not when we have the launch on Thursday! No, we're going to see *Hannibal Rising*.' Rachel was thankful that Narelle, who *had* seen the movie last week, had told her all about it.

'Ooh, I really want to see that,' said Alysha. 'That Gaspard guy is fit!'

Rachel gave a casual laugh. 'Narelle's so hellbent on seeing him, she's already bought the tickets,' she said. 'It keeps selling out!' She hoped the idea of having to sit separately, or not being able to get a ticket at all, would dissuade Alysha from tagging along.

Alysha frowned and pushed herself up off the bath. 'Think I might just give Mel a call instead,' she said. 'See if her and Ollie fancy heading to The Mill.'

Rachel nodded heartily, but even this plan was not without risk. It was better to mention it now in case Alysha heard it later. 'Oh, I bumped into Mel the other night,' she said. 'I was up in that internet café on the high street because I needed to check an urgent email about the launch. I ended up chatting to a friend back home for ages.'

Alysha stared at her with a cold suspicion, making Rachel wonder if Mel *had* seen something incriminating on her screen and had texted Alysha to tell her. What if Alysha already knew she wasn't going to meet Narelle today and was just playing along, pretending to believe Rachel's lies just to catch her out?

Alysha blinked at her. 'So, let me get this straight, you're saying you were up in the internet café?'

'Yes'

'Alone? At night? Checking your work email?'

Rachel nodded. She was going to vomit. She stared at the toilet. The lid was down. Would she get it open in time – in the sickening, life-changing moments after Alysha levelled the gay accusation?

But Alysha just gave a long sigh and said, 'What are you like with that job of yours?' She left the bathroom shaking her head. 'The sooner this crazy-ass launch is over, the better!'

53

'OK, Gok Wan,' called Jo. 'I'm ready to rock.'

Rob came into the hall. 'Don't get too excited now. I might be gay, but as you can probably tell, I don't have any flair.'

Jo laughed; she was touched that Rob was giving up his Sunday afternoon to come clothes shopping, but in truth they'd been getting on so well they were already more like friends than flatmates. As they put on their coats there was a knock which, despite its politeness, startled them – any callers always used the intercom downstairs. Rob squinted through the spyhole. 'It's Patrik,' he whispered. 'And your friend, but without … *a handbag!*'

'What the hell is she doing here?' They'd been joking about Jo's faulty gaydar since the party, but suddenly she wasn't in the mood for Lady Bracknell.

'Who knows … I better let them in though.'

Patrik beamed at them as the door opened and said, 'Hey, recovered from the party, I see?'

'Well, we were cursing that Laško yesterday morning,' said Rob, 'but it was a great night, wasn't it, Jo?'

'Oh yeah … yes it was,' said Jo, stumbling over small words as though they were boulders. Since Friday she'd convinced herself that she'd grossly and drunkenly exaggerated the attractiveness of the G-Star girl in the first place, and was therefore wholly unprepared for what now stood in the hall before her. As the boys chatted about the party, she took in the still-anonymous hottie in a series of visual gulps: the indigo jeans, whose slightly scraggy hems rested on green Diesel runners; the thick neckstrings of the red hoodie straggling down the front of the black Superdry anorak. There was so much to like and to lust after – and that was just the clothes! Jo glanced up at her face: which wore a more approachable expression than on Friday, and was radiant in its symmetrical sallowness. As the girl turned her head to nod at something Rob was saying, the tendons stood out sexily in her athletic neck.

There was no sign of the handbag, and Jo couldn't believe she'd been prepared to deem this girl both straight and unappealing, all because of an accessory.

'So, we wondered,' Patrik was saying, 'if you'd like to see *Hannibal Rising* this afternoon?'

The girl cleared her throat conspicuously, the first sound she'd made since arriving. 'Shouldn't you introduce me first, Patrik?'

Patrik slapped himself on the head, then nudged her forward. 'Rob, Jo, this is Lucija, a friend from the gym. And from Slovenia also!'

Rob offered his hand with a nonplussed look. 'Nice to meet you. *Again.*'

Lucija gave him a fit-person's cheek-furrowing smile. 'Sorry I did not talk to you much in the kitchen on Friday,' she said. 'I was extremely tired and not in a particularly good mood.' She shook her head, sending a shiver down her ponytail, and in turn, Jo's spine.

'Don't worry about it,' Rob said, more friendly now. 'I love your name by the way. Loo-*chi*-ah, is that how you say it?'

'Precisely,' she said, speaking again in that exacting way of hers (Jo could see that, just like her body, Lucija's speech was free of unnecessary fat).

Lucija turned to Jo, who, far too self-conscious to try out her own approximation of the name, especially the wistful little *ah* at the end, simply said, 'Hi, I'm Jo,' before moving in to return the strong handshake. As they stepped back again, she got a flash of Lucija pumping iron in a backstreet gym frequented by Eastern Europeans.

'We'd love to come to the cinema but we're going clothes shopping,' Rob was saying. 'Jo has a big interview with a *newspaper* on Thursday!'

'Wow,' said Patrik, smiling at Jo in wild admiration. Lucija, however, was far less impressed – in fact, she seemed irritated to learn they wouldn't be coming. Suddenly Jo could see the afternoon's chance draining away, the strange, spontaneous invitation never to be repeated. 'Well, my clothes shopping doesn't have to be *today*,' she said. 'I can just as easily go tomorrow. The shops will be quieter too.'

Rob shot her a wry look. 'Thought you said you needed my keen eye for fashion?'

Jo blinked slowly at the sly bastard. 'Why don't I just text you pictures of me in various outfits?'

'Well I suppose you could,' said Rob, 'but it might be hard to judge from just a pho—'

'*I* can come with you tomorrow.'

The conversation froze as though a cast iron dumbbell had been dropped from a height. Everyone turned to Lucija. For someone whose English was perfect and far less accented than Patrik's, she certainly knew how to invoke a hard, Slavic gravity when required. The utter deadpan of the delivery made Jo wonder if it were just a big joke – who on earth offered to go clothes shopping with someone they'd only just met? She cringed to think of herself twirling awkwardly outside a changing room while Lucija scrutinised.

It was clear from Lucija's steadfast expression that the offer was serious, however. 'Well?' she said.

Jo gave a nervous laugh. 'Are you sure you want to? I'm the world's worst shopper. When I was eleven my sister deserted me in a department store. She threw my bus fare under the curtain of the cubicle and stormed off because I was being so difficult.'

Lucija cut through the boys' laughter. 'I finish work at four, so tomorrow suits me fine,' she said with a sternness that prohibited further demurral. She raised her eyebrows and fixed Jo with a stare as unwavering as tomorrow's new arrangement.

'Cool, thanks.' Jo nodded gratefully.

Lucija retracted the cuff of her hoodie to check a G-Shock watch substantial enough to withstand a plummeting dumbbell. 'Let's go or we'll be late,' she said. Jo and the boys nodded and followed her obediently to the door: it seemed that, like tomorrow's shopping date, today's trip to the cinema was now also under Lucija's control.

54

Rachel wished Gwen had picked somewhere quieter for their rendezvous. The cinema was teeming with people seeking escapism from the wintry afternoon. Poised on the balls of her feet just inside the entrance, she was dizzy from scanning so many faces (the downside of not sharing her own photo was that the onus for finding each other lay solely with her). She still felt bad about lying to Alysha earlier – what a deceptive web she'd had to weave to conceal an innocent meeting with a potential new friend!

Anxiously, she scanned the next wave of incoming faces. Of course, it wasn't the moment of meeting she was most apprehensive about, but rather what she must do directly after that. There was a thirty-minute window before the film started, ample time to say: *I'm sorry, but my name isn't Roz, it's Rachel. I don't live in Brighton but in Wheldon Green. My job's a marketing assistant, not a pharmacist, and I'm into judo, not aikido.* It would be incredibly embarrassing, but she absolutely must say everything up front, especially if they were going to become friends. Hopefully Gwen would see the funny side and think Rachel had just been playing it safe online. She might even take Rachel's burst of honesty as a compliment and their friendship would be off to a flying start. Perhaps Rachel hadn't been the only one to transpose the truth either: Gwen the speech therapist might actually be Jennifer the dentist or Gillian the nurse – one of these personae could be outside the cinema right now, rehearsing a revelation of their own.

Well, whatever Gwen or her alter ego was up to, she was ten minutes late. Worried that she might have somehow missed Gwen's arrival, Rachel set off on a circuit. She checked the seating areas outside the screens, the cinema café, and even took a trip upstairs to the pick 'n' mix kiosk where, on their second date and despite her protestations, Stuart had bought her an obscenely big bag of sweets. She'd been annoyed at the waste, but the proxy gift of the still-bulging bag had later delighted Alysha back at home.

She returned to her waiting place by the door. The minutes trundled on

– the film would be starting soon. She wished she could text Gwen, but they'd never exchanged numbers. Rachel couldn't have divulged hers, especially when her voicemail said *Hello, it's Rachel* … Maybe Gwen had sent her a Gaydar message about cancelling – she could be ill or have cold feet about meeting a faceless stranger. Still, it was only polite to wait for a while longer, at least until the film was starting. And so she stood patiently, continuing to scan the faces of the people streaming in.

55

'I'm serious, Jo, please stop looking over.'

Jo turned back to their foursome in the queue. 'Hard *not* to be curious after everything you've told me.' She wanted to see the infamous Fussbudget, who was responsible for Rob's increasingly stressed-out mood lately, but so far had only glimpsed the back of her homophobic head as she'd passed them by.

'I don't want her knowing I'm here,' Rob said. 'I doubt she'd condescend to say hello, but I won't give her the pleasure of ignoring me either.'

Jo gave a sighing eyeroll at Patrik and Lucija as if to say Rob was being stupidly uptight, but really, she knew that *she* was the one acting out of line, if not slightly out of control. Her nervous, lustful energy around Lucija had manifested in a kind of silly hyperactivity ever since they'd left the flat.

The ticket queue shortened and as they shuffled up, Jo was careful to keep her arm from brushing off Lucija's. Her ability to touch off someone she fancied was always inversely proportional to how much she wanted to be tactile. Standing this close, she was able to observe lots of new things – the small pitted blemish on Lucija's temple (a chicken pox scar?), her double-pierced but bare earlobes, the green aglets capping her brown shoelaces. Most gorgeous of all was the white pixel on her incisor; the dentist had filled a little chip with more luminous material than the surrounding enamel. As Lucija spoke certain words the dot would flash out like a pop-art *Ding!*

As the chat turned to how scary (or 'marvellously unnerving' as Lucija put it) Anthony Hopkins had been in *The Silence of the Lambs*, Jo wondered what had motivated the pair to invite them out. Could she dare hope it was more than a neighbourly gesture? She and Rob still hadn't come out to them, but maybe Jo *had* piqued Lucija's interest at the party, and this had led to the invitation. Patrik's 'forgetting' to introduce Lucija earlier could have been a decoy, so that their motive wasn't as baldly obvious either. If this were true, then the shopping trip tomorrow would be their first date! Jo stifled a shiver as she imagined yanking on those hoodie cords and planting a long, hot, kiss …

Suddenly Rob was pulling everyone around, hissing, 'Hide me!' As they corralled, Jo got a whiff of Lucija's sporty-fresh perfume. Rob's eyes flicked through the gaps. 'She seems to be looking for someone,' he whispered. 'Wouldn't surprise me if the witch has been stood up … Oh, phew she's gone.'

'So, who exactly is this person you must hide from?' asked Patrik, as they ungrouped.

'Only *the* worst client I've ever had in my life,' said Rob. 'As well as being really hard to work for, she seems to have taken a personal hatred of me lately.'

'This is at the advertising agency?' asked Lucija.

Rob frowned. 'How'd you know where I work?'

'I was asking Patrik about it yesterday.' Lucija gave him a beaming smile. 'It must be a fascinating area!'

Jo crumpled inside to realise that Lucija's target today was not her, but Rob. It all made miserable sense now. Lucija had been standoffish to Rob at the party because she *fancied* him. Tomorrow's shopping expedition was not a date with Jo, but a means to befriend *Rob's* friend. Jo was a mere dispensable extra in Lucija's heterosexual quest! She should have trusted her hunch that Lucija was straight; she'd let lust overrule logic. Even though Lucija hadn't led her on – in fact, she'd seemed rather uninterested in most things Jo had said today – Jo couldn't help but feel wronged.

'So, what do you do for a living yourself?' Rob was asking Lucija.

'Oh, I'm a barrister.'

'A *barrister*?' Rob sounded only half as shocked as Jo – who'd assumed Lucija worked in the service industry like Patrik – suddenly felt. Lucija gave a little nod, as though inured to such double-takes about her job. Jo couldn't cope with this revelation. She glanced at Patrik for signs of misunderstanding or lying, but all she saw was a big confirmatory grin at his friend's professional success. Jo cringed to think of their talk of her own 'big interview with a newspaper' back in the flat. No wonder the hotshot barrister hadn't looked especially impressed.

'Wow, that's amazing,' said Rob, and as the queue moved up, Jo felt his knuckle dig into her hip – either a sign of incredulity, or encouragement to *get in there*. 'So, do you enjoy life at the bar?' he asked.

'Mostly, yes,' Lucija said, regarding them both in turn as though they were members of a jury that needed convincing. 'It can be challenging too, early mornings, late evenings.' She folded back the cuffs of her hoodie and Jo realised that all this relaxed urban gear must be worn in free-time defiance of the restrictive dark tailoring of the bar. 'A lot depends on the client,' continued Lucija. 'They are standing in the dock and you must do your utmost for them. Usually they're so grateful, but some others barely thank you, even when they're happy with the service.'

'I know *that* feeling,' said Rob, looking around comically for where Rachel had last been seen.

'But I must always remember,' Lucija continued, 'that my clients are often beleaguered people, dreadfully worn down by the system.'

Jo nodded along but found it all a bit sickening. If Lucija were gay, then this barrister-talk would be a further turn-on. But with Lucija hitting on Rob, it brought out a competitive kind of inter-female resentment. For the first time in her life Jo felt territorial over a man. She couldn't wait to see Lucija's flirtatious face when she discovered that Rob was – as Oleg would say – a *faggot-pussy*. No doubt tomorrow's shopping trip would be called off once Lucija discovered that befriending Rob's female friend would yield no benefits. Jo didn't want to go anyway! As the tiresome barrister-chat continued, Jo resolved to drop the gay bombshell before they went into the film.

56

After an hour, Noeleen needed to ask an important question. She shuffled back along the Persian runner that lined the hall, pausing halfway to admire the trio of gilt-framed paintings. Her favourite one depicted a satin-gloved lady with ringlets and a serene smile. But beautiful artwork was just one of a multitude of delights in this magnificent Georgian home: every time Noeleen turned her head she was finding something else to see and to savour. She hoped that over time she'd become intimately acquainted with this house and its many treasures – it truly was a privilege to be working in a place like this!

At the bottom of the back stairs, she peered through the leaded glass of the door. The kitchen beyond was dim, the only light emanating from an oil lamp on the long wooden table. The slim, androgynous figure of Sheelagh Pendlebury sat at the far end. Bent over a piece of sheet music, she was silently nodding out a complicated rhythm, stopping now and then to tut loudly and make a pencil-annotation on the page.

Noeleen watched for a while, both out of fascination and the desire not to disturb. Earlier, she'd seen a photograph in the bathroom of a tuxedoed Sheelagh performing at a concert in the Barbican. It was a most arresting image – moppish grey hair sticking out chaotically, face fixed in an almost hostile concentration, drumsticks moving so quickly they were blurred arcs in the air. The photo had given Noeleen a shiver of orchestral excitement, but if anything, the scene before her now was even *more* evocative – the ancient table, the oil lamp, the crumpled tail of Sheelagh's grandfather shirt hanging over the bench – this could be a middle-aged Beethoven composing a symphony by candlelight!

Poor Sheelagh seemed to be growing increasingly frustrated with her sheet music. As she reviewed the next page she cried, 'What codswallop', then flung her pencil away and banged her head on the table, causing the shadows to dance. Noeleen thought she should make her presence known.

She rapped on the glass with the handle of the duster – very tentatively, because both duster and glass were antiques in themselves.

'Sorry, didn't see you there,' said Sheelagh, getting up from the table. 'And no wonder when this place is so ridiculously dim.'

Noeleen stepped forward, stifling the desire to curtsey to the lady in residence. 'So sorry to bother while you're composing.'

Sheelagh gave a snort as she pushed a curl away from her equally wiry eyebrows. 'It's nothing so grand as *composing*. Just some notes for tonight's recital.' She rolled the jettisoned pencil back and forth under the toe of her tasselled loafer. 'The score those imbeciles have provided is vexing to say the least.' She squinted around crossly. 'And it would greatly help if my wife would allow proper lighting in here so I could see what I was reading!'

Noeleen risked a nervous giggle. 'I wanted to ask if you'd like me to clean the xylophone in the drawing room?' she asked. 'Or maybe you shouldn't like me to approach it whatsoever?' She loved that the house was even antiquating her language.

'Oh, the *marimba*?' said Sheelagh. 'Approach her with ferocity, my dear, she's horribly dusty.'

'Are you certain?' said Noeleen. 'I should hate to damage her.'

'Oh, don't worry, you should see the abuse she takes from my mallets.'

'She certainly looks the part up there, sitting between the two sash windows.'

Sheelagh snorted. 'Try telling that to Aurelie. She complains that the Georgians wouldn't have percussive instruments lying about the way we do. Last week she relegated my kettledrum to the bedroom. I buggered up my back hauling it up four and half flights.'

'Oh dear. Sounds like your wife is quite the stickler for authenticity!'

Sheelagh gestured to the duster in Noeleen's hand. 'An authenticity that stretches to cleaning materials too, I'm afraid. I wouldn't be surprised if those are actual *dodo* feathers that thing's so old.'

Noeleen ran her thumb lovingly over the ornate ceramic handle. 'This is actually far better than those awful plastic dusters. And those Mrs Bristleworth's products Aurelie has in the cleaning basket are second to none. However, there *are* some modern items that might be useful …'

'Write a list and I'll procure same,' said Sheelagh. 'Though we'll have to conspire to hide them from you-know-who. You'll get to meet her next time, of course. She said you sound like *une femme merveilleuse*.'

'That would be … *merveilleuse*,' said Noeleen, feeling the double thrill of being asked back already, as well as getting to meet *La Française*. She saw her relationship with this historic house stretching far into the future: years after Noel had retired from Goodstep, Noeleen would still be working these feathers through the slats of the marimba.

'She had hoped to be here today,' continued Sheelagh, 'but a brass bedwarmer she's had her eye on suddenly came up for auction in York. She darted off in the Triumph at cockcrow and won't be back until midnight.'

'Such dedication!' said Noeleen. It had been intriguing to hear Aurelie's interesting life story from Sheelagh over their Earl Grey earlier. Five years ago, the wealthy French heiress had sold off her famous antiques dealership in Bordeaux to fulfil a lifelong dream of restoring a Georgian house. The ensuing labour of love had lasted over three years. One night, seeking respite from the travails of what had become an onerous project, Aurelie had attended a classical concert. There, she had first set eyes on Sheelagh; they'd hit it off famously at the after-party, and eighteen months later they were preparing to move into the finished house as newly wed civil partners.

Sheelagh sighed. 'All that way for a bloody bedwarmer …' She bent down to retrieve her pencil, then stood up and blinked frankly at Noeleen. 'I can't see what's wrong with an electric blanket. Or even a bit of *how's your father*. Even her darling Georgians did that too, surely!'

57

'Please, *please* tell me you're Roz?'

Rachel spun round to look at the owner of the breathless, Welsh-accented voice. Despite her resolution to come clean about her real name immediately, she instead gave a dumb nod of confirmation.

'Oh Roz, thanks so much for waiting!' Gwen pointed at the green beret pulled over flustered blonde curls. 'I accidentally left this at the station and had to turn back. It was a pressie from my late nan and I'd die if I lost it. I kept thinking, *if only I'd asked Roz for her number – she'll think I'm a right so-and-so when she's travelled all the way from Brighton.*'

'So glad you found it,' said Rachel. 'And I'm glad you're here too. See that scruffy guy standing over there?'

Gwen looked across. 'Double-denim, yeah?'

'I was wondering if *he* was the one I was meeting, the way he's been staring at me for the past ten minutes. One of those creeps who set up fake online profiles to lure in women.'

Gwen's laughter filled the foyer. 'Oh, Roz, you're cracking me up already!'

Rachel gave a quick smile but was growing more uneasy with every passing mention of Roz. Gwen had a loud, clear, speech therapist's voice so it sounded like a massive Welsh choir was belting out *ROZZZ* whenever she said it. It was time to confess before this went any further.

Gwen took out her wallet. 'Let this be my treat for keeping you waiting, Roz.'

'But won't the film have started?' Rachel hoped they'd go to a nearby pub instead, where, with privacy and a stiff drink, her disclosure would be easier.

'I insist,' said Gwen, already heading to the ticket window. 'They always play a shedload of trailers anyway.' While Gwen paid, Rachel glimpsed the NHS ID in her purse, abruptly ending any hope that Gwen might be lying – Gwen Elizabeth Peters really *was* a speech and Language Therapist at

Charing Cross Hospital. The discovery made Rachel feel even worse.

Gwen handed her a ticket. 'Screen number one, Roz. Let's be having this Hannibal!' Rachel vowed that she would say something by the time they got to the door of the screen: she would turn to Gwen on the stairs and put an end to this awful charade. But as they ascended, Gwen started gushing about how much she'd liked Jodie Foster in *The Silence of the Lambs,* leaving no gap for Rachel to interject, let alone make a serious revelation. Nor would it be possible to say anything inside the auditorium: by the time they opened the door the film had already started. Rachel sank uneasily into her seat. A minute later she was staring blankly at the face of the child Hannibal – if that's who he even was; she wasn't able to focus. Still, at least while the movie was playing, there wouldn't be any more mention of *Roz.*

Her hopes were unfounded, however. A few minutes later, during a scene with little dialogue, Rachel felt something crinkle against her elbow. 'Jelly beans, Roz? ... Ah go on Roz, I've got tonnes of them here!'

58

Just before six, Sheelagh came into the dining room, a paisley cravat tucked into the neck of her overcoat, and announced that she was heading to her recital. 'You're an absolute marvel,' she said, blinking in admiration at the freshly polished mahogany table. 'If you don't mind just pulling the front door hard when you've finished everything?'

'But of course!' Noeleen was both shocked and flattered to be left alone on her first day. She'd expected to be leaving when Sheelagh did. 'I'll be finishing up soon anyway.'

'And we'll see you same time next Sunday,' said Sheelagh, as though it had already been firmly agreed.

Noeleen paused. She'd arranged to return to Millie and Isobel's that day, but as lovely as her gothic friends were, and as badly as their half-cleaned shower needed to be finished off, there was no competition between their flat and this dream gig. 'Perfect,' she said, making a mental note to reschedule the goths to a later date.

'Smashing,' said Sheelagh. 'I'll text that morning to confirm we're still on. Just in case anything crops up last minute.'

Noeleen crossed her hands and stepped forward. 'Since I'll be returning so soon, might I ask the favour of leaving this outfit here? My home situation is a little … *sensitive* at the moment, so I'm keeping whatever I can in clients' homes.'

Strangely, Sheelagh didn't appear terribly happy to oblige, however. In fact, her mouth twisted to one side as though she were about to refuse. How odd that the owner of a four-storey pile wasn't keen to accommodate one little bag when Noeleen's clients in cramped bedsits were always happy to help! But still, better not to impose lest it ruin the good feeling. 'If it should be a problem, Sheelagh, I can just—'

'Oh, *I* know where!' cried Sheelagh, snapping out of her negative trance. 'The *cubby hole* under the stairs. But do stash it right at the very back, behind all of the coats etcetera.' She gave a quick, colourless smile, then turned towards the door. 'Your outfit's so pretty, Aurelie and I would hate anything untoward to happen to it.'

59

'That didn't even hold a candle to *Silence of the Lambs*,' said Gwen, as the crowd filed slowly towards the foyer.

'Not half as gripping,' said Rachel, who'd been gripped by nothing but her own predicament throughout the film. As the credits rolled, she'd resolved to make her admission the second they got free of this crowd.

'Then again *Silence of the Lambs* does have one ingredient that *Hannibal* doesn't.'

Rachel laughed. 'A thrilling plot?'

Gwen threw her head back. 'Come *on*, Roz, I mean Jodie Foster!'

'She's a fantastic actress all right.'

'And the rest! How lush was she in that basement scene?'

'Yeah, s'pose,' said Rachel in a choked kind of whisper. She was acutely aware that people around could hear them (impossible *not* to, given Gwen's elocution). She'd allowed herself to forget that Gwen was a full-on lesbian, and so this conversation was a jarring and unwelcome reminder of how they'd met. An older woman glanced over at them dubiously. Rachel wished she could exonerate herself by explaining the situation.

'Jodie not do it for you, then?' Gwen said as they finally reached the foyer and the crowd dispersed.

Rachel gave a grim little smile. 'No.'

'So, let's go for a drink so I can find out who really does ring Roz's bell!' She thrust her beret into Rachel's hand. 'But first, hold this while I pop to the ladies.'

Rachel stood by the wall biting her cheek. She was sorely tempted to leave before Gwen returned. It would solve both the Roz-problem – now at farcical proportions – *and* the impending inquisition about who she fancied. Disappearing without trace would be easy. The Roz-persona had been the cause of this predicament, but now it could be the cure too: Rachel had left no trail to her actual life. She could delete her profile, making Roz vaporise into London's ether, and leaving Rachel to get back to the normal safe world of Alysha and judo and work. And, of course, Stuart – the poor guy hadn't seen her in a week; surely she should be affording her boyfriend more attention instead of meeting up with gay strangers? And on her last free day before launch-week too – she needed her head examined!

Sick of her own hesitation, she acted definitively for the first time that day. She strode across the foyer. Gwen would think her cruel, but it would be even crueller to waste any more of her time. But as she clenched her fists in dogged resolution, she felt Gwen's beret in her grasp. She looked around – if she left it on top of the bin beside the stairs, it would surely be safe enough for the next few minutes. If it really were as precious as Gwen claimed, how had she let it out of her sight twice today? The story had probably been fabricated to excuse her lateness.

At the bin, she checked that no one was watching, lest they think she was a terrorist leaving a suspicious device. As she looked around, her eyes snagged on a familiar face – a face that happened to be angled in her direction at that moment. He was standing as part of a small group. To her horror, he had seen her, and even worse, knew that she'd seen him too – his eyebrows were raised in salutation. Before she could give him a passing wave to absolve him of further obligation, he'd already left his friends, and was quickly approaching.

'Rachel, what a coincidence … *again*. How are you?'

'Fine thanks, Robert,' she said. She did not return the question. She recalled the awkwardness of meeting Rob's boyfriend that time. Even more reason to get this over with before Gwen returned.

'All set for your big week?' he asked.

'All set, yes,' she said.

'The backdrop should be arriving in the hotel tomorrow. The printers rang on Friday evening to say they were printing over the weekend. Your stage will be so impactful!'

'Great.' She gave an ostentatious glance at her watch. 'I'm actually in a bit of a hurry, Robert. I have to meet someone outs—' She squirmed as she felt the hand on her elbow.

'*There* you are,' said Gwen. 'I figured you must've bumped into someone you knew!' She nodded at Rob, waiting for an introduction.

Rachel felt she was standing on the sharp central-ridge of a terrifying, double-sided precipice: at any moment Gwen could say something gay, or Rob could mention her job. Or call her Rachel. Or everything could happen at once.

Gwen didn't let the lack of introduction temper her friendliness. 'Were you at *Hannibal* too?' she asked, smiling at Rob as she took her hat from Rachel's sweating hand.

'Bit disappointing, wasn't it?' he said. 'Certainly no *Silence of the Lambs*, anyway.'

Gwen doffed him delightedly with her beret. 'I was only just saying it was missing one key ingredient, wasn't I, Roz?'

'Yes,' said Rachel, afraid to look at Rob now lest he'd copped the 'Roz'. Before Gwen could launch into her Jodie Foster speech Rachel put a hand against her back and began to turn her towards the door. 'Nice seeing you, Robert,' she said. 'No doubt I'll talk to you tomorrow.'

'Talk to you then,' he said.

Rachel steered Gwen away, hyperventilating with relief. It was only then that the call came from behind. 'Bye, Rachel!'

It was loud and it was incontrovertibly clear, and Rachel could tell by Gwen's mystified expression, and then her slow, suspicious turn of the head, that she had certainly heard it too.

60

An hour after Sheelagh's departure, Noeleen found herself back in the master bedroom, placing books and magazines into tidy, systematic piles on the floorboards. It was getting quite late. She'd only planned to stay a short while after Sheelagh had gone; back in Croydon, Hazel was probably fretting about Noel's whereabouts and injections. But being left at large in this house had energised Noeleen so much that, rather than leaving, she'd returned upstairs to tackle a massive mahogany bookcase she'd seen earlier. Despite the tightly closed glass doors, the unit had a fantastically dusty interior. With the shelves finally emptied, Noeleen now set about giving it the clean of the century (which was actually quite possible, given its age).

Beside the fireplace sat Sheelagh's contentious kettledrum, and as Noeleen worked, she kept catching sight of herself in the curved copper bowl. The sepia reflection of a bonneted maid with her duster was a vignette straight from a history book! She thought about her predecessors, the girls and women who'd tended this house over the ages. Sheelagh hadn't mentioned the place being haunted, but Noeleen wondered if there might be someone – a servant girl or a scullery maid – spying from behind the heavy velvet curtains, or even stifling a giggle as they dangled from the chandelier that hung over the bed.

When the bookcase was so resplendent that even the ghosts would approve, it was time to refill it. Many of the books were about antiques, and others were so old they were antiques themselves. Among the leather-bound tomes and glossy modern volumes depicting vases and ornate fireplaces, Noeleen smiled to see some old favourites she knew from years of cleaning lesbians' shelves. She didn't even need to read the scarlet spine to recognise *Tipping the Velvet*. As she lifted it up, along with its shelf-fellows *Affinity* and *Fingersmith*, a folded-up article torn from a French newspaper fluttered down from between the books.

Noeleen had been longing for a glimpse of the infamous Aurelie but hadn't managed to find a single photograph on display. However, the image accompanying an article entitled *Mon Rêve georgien – Aurelie Le Floc'h* made Noeleen wonder why Aurelie didn't have pictures of herself all over the place! She had a handsome, angular face, confidently flared nostrils and dark eyebrows that meant business. Her hair, while as short as Sheelagh's, was quite unlike her wife's wiry mop; rather it was coiffed up in superb brown waves that elegantly framed her face. In a crisp pink shirt and slender fawn slacks, Aurelie stood beside a scaffold in a chaotic building site that Noeleen eventually recognised as the hall downstairs. Although the article referred to *le stress intensif, les pratiques exaspérantes des constructeurs anglais,* and worse again, *une infestation de rats au sous-sol,* Aurelie appeared serene and unruffled, her high-heels rising shinily from the fragments of plaster and broken brick that littered the floor.

Noeleen knew that she would blush when she met this supreme creature next week. She smiled shyly at the picture, and then secreted the sheet exactly as she had found it.

This truly was the gig that kept on giving!

'And now, ladies and gentlemen, what about this pair of pretty young ladies who are deep, *deeeep* in conversation …' A thick signet-ringed hand plunged a microphone between their faces. 'Pray tell me your names, my lovelies?'

Rachel bit her lip and looked at Gwen, who looked back at her. Then they both burst out laughing over the PA system.

Karaoke Dan pulled back his mic and appealed to the handful of other early evening punters in the bar – a soulless dive with smeared chrome fittings, whose only recommendation had been its proximity to the cinema. 'Glad these two find me so funny anyway,' said Dan, pouting his rubbery mouth. Gwen downed the last of her second vodka and coke, then called Dan back and grabbed his microphone.

'It's not you …' she announced between hysterical giggles. A shabby man hunched over the bar turned and stared. 'We're just laughing because you asked us our names, and I've just found out this girl here's got *two*!'

'Two names?' said Dan. 'Ooh, I do like a nice double-barrelled name like Anne-Marie or Emma-Louise.' He patted the straining brass buttons on his waistcoat. 'In fact, I've always had a soft spot for a nice Mar-*Eclair*!'

Gwen pulled back the mic. 'No, I mean like two totally separate names,' she said. 'Her real name's Rachel, but she's got this alter ego called Roz, who's much more … how shall I put it … ?'

'Adventurous!' Rachel shouted into the microphone. She felt high on two kinds of new relief – firstly, that she'd got the secret off her chest; and secondly, that the revelation itself had gone down so well with Gwen. She couldn't believe she was making a public joke out of something that had been causing her such private anxiety just hours earlier. She'd wanted to murder Robert for saying her real name, but at least it had forced an end to her torture. Outside the cinema, head hung low, she'd come clean to Gwen about her name, her job and where she lived, adding that she completely understood if Gwen wanted to terminate their afternoon right there. But Gwen, whose eyes had welled up with tears, had hugged Rachel and said it was only natural that someone with such an important job in a big corporation should be cautious online. Rather than end the rendezvous, Gwen declared they must start it afresh, and more importantly, with a drink in hand!

Since arriving in the bar, they'd been having such a good chat (about working in the healthcare sector) and a good laugh (mostly at the expense of poor Dan) that Rachel couldn't believe she'd been prepared to dump Gwen's precious beret on top of a bin.

Dan jutted out his blubbery lower lip. 'So would Roz-Rachel and her lovely Welsh friend care to sing some Girls Aloud, perhaps?'

'No,' cried Rachel. 'We want to do … Tina Turner!'

'Yeah, "Steamy Windows"!' Gwen said, trying to control her laughter. 'Just give us a minute to wet our whistles.'

'Five minutes to Tina, ladies and gentlemen,' said Dan, who went off to his little stage and began a retching rendition of 'It's Not Unusual'.

'We better get out of here,' Rachel said out of the corner of her mouth, as she clapped along.

Gwen nodded. 'Actually, there's this fun bar I've been to with some nurses from work, just for a girly bop. You've got your big week ahead, so it'd just be for one drink, obviously.'

Rachel checked her watch. It was only half eight. If she deferred getting home Alysha would be in bed, exhausted after the adventure camp and the pub. There would be no tricky inquisition about the movie or Narelle. She polished off her vodka. 'Sounds like fun.'

They waited until Dan had turned round to adjust the karaoke machine; then, with coats and bags in hand, and their bodies racked by the suppressed laughter of two schoolgirls bunking off behind teacher's back, they made their escape.

62

With all the books back in the case, and the dust they'd left on the rug vacuumed up, Noeleen was finally ready to go downstairs and change. She gathered up the Dyson (thankfully, a decent vacuum cleaner was among Aurelie's few concessions to modernity), and switching off lights as she went, began to carefully descend the four and a half flights. Turning off the switch on the final landing, the only illumination that remained came from a streetlamp filtering atmospherically through the fanlight above the front door.

She heard a rattling noise below on the ground floor. She paused on the landing and listened – those basement rats must have worked their way up to beneath the hall floorboards. She must give the ladies the name of the pest control company Goodstep used in the warehouse. She started on the final flight, only to freeze two steps down: she thought she heard female laughter. Had the spectral maids come to tease the big man in a dress trying to better them at their job? But no, it was not ghosts, but real people – two dimly lit figures – coming in through the front door, which slammed hard in the shadows behind them.

'Sheelagh? Aurelie?' she called politely, trying not to startle them. They would turn on the light in a moment and see her standing at the top of the steps, realise that she was still here. Their respective events for the evening must have finished up early and they'd never have expected her to stay on this late. There was no response, however – only a sudden thump as the coiffed figure of Aurelie was pushed, rather roughly, against the door by Sheelagh, who now seemed to be wearing some kind of cap. There were gasps and then the slippery sounds of passionate, if not slightly vicious, kisses. Noeleen gulped; this behaviour seemed a bit odd for a couple who'd lived together for so long. But as she'd learned from her years of cleaning, it took all sorts. And were not the French the world's most passionate lovers?

All the same, she hoped the embrace would be quick so she could make her presence known and spare both sides any embarrassment. She looked down at her slippers and half-listened, but after another minute it was clear from the gasps, the muffled bangs against the door, and the metallic whizz of a zip opening, that the situation was in fact escalating into quite the sexual frenzy. When she dared to peep again, she saw clothes on the floor and a writhing eight-limbed spider. It was far too late to announce herself. No, she must sneak back upstairs, wait until they'd finished and then come down, pretending she'd been working on that bookcase all along.

Depositing the Dyson silently on the landing, she stalked to the top floor, where she slipped behind the door of the spare bedroom. Her heart was pounding; she felt her blood sugar dipping. She'd been so engrossed in her work she'd forgotten to eat the banana sandwich she'd left in the kitchen. She willed and warned her body to stay strong – a hypo right now would be unthinkable. She put her ear to the gap between the hinges for any signs of the liaison abating. After a few minutes, everything went quiet. She wiped her sweaty hands on her apron and then stepped out, ready to turn on lights and make a slow, noisy descent, affording them ample time to dress.

'Hurry up, Aurs, we ain't got all night.' The sound of stomping on the stairs sent Noeleen haring back to her hiding place. She stood panting behind the door and wondered what in god's name a south Londoner was doing in the house.

'Is difficult to run with the trouser open, you know!'

The footsteps were arrested by a massive crash of plastic. 'Ow, me ankle!' shrieked the Londoner, who only sounded about twenty.

'Mandy, what happen?'

'Tripped over the shitting hoover, innit!'

'The 'oover? No. I don't believe!'

'Don't believe me all you want, but watch your arse coz it's right here on the landing.'

'No, I just can't believe Sheelagh finally do some housework,' said Aurelie. 'She promise me to vacuum every day for the last three month.'

'Well the bitch has crippled me in the process. I can barely walk.'

'I will kiss better. *Viens* ...'

A moment later their tangled shadows passed by the crack in the door. Then Noeleen heard the light in the master bedroom next door being clicked on.

'No, Mandy,' said Aurelie. 'Turn off.'

'But you know I like doin' it with the lights on.'

Then came a silence. Noeleen sensed them coming together to kiss. She wondered what to do. She was at a double disadvantage because of her outfit – unlike a regular intruder, she couldn't just sneak out onto the street. And Aurelie clearly knew nothing about Noeleen, given her comment about the hoover. Aurelie would call the police. There was nothing for it now but to wait until they were *in flagrante delicto*, then sneak down, change and get the hell out. A hypoglycaemic wave crashed through her thigh muscles. As she fell back against the wall to steady herself, her foot touched something on the floor. Something that then rolled with a loud, hollow sound, over and over, across the moonlit floorboards.

'*C'est quoi, ça?*' said Aurelie sharply. Noeleen held her breath as one of Sheelagh's maracas eventually settled against the leg of the spare bed. She saw herself spending the night in a police cell, all the officers taking turns to look in and laugh at her outfit. It was so bizarre it would make the papers: *Pervert man-maid caught peeping in Camberwell mansion.* She waited for the footsteps to approach, but all she heard was Mandy saying, 'Oh my days, you're right. I ain't never seen your bed made like that. What's going on with all the 'ousework?'

There was the squeak of springs. 'No don't touch the bed,' said Aurelie. 'It could be a trap.'

'Thought you said your missus don't suspect nothing?'

'I think we should go next door,' said Aurelie. 'Just in case.'

Noeleen's heart began to hammer.

'Nah, that spare bed's tiny,' replied Mandy. 'Anyway, I'll make this one up perfect when we're finished. I'm great at doing beds – my one was always the neatest on the wing. *Sheets tighter than a nun's cunt*, the girls used to say.'

There was a muffled laugh and then Aurelie said, 'You know I like when you tell me about 'Olloway. You and all your girls there. Remind me again what you used to do …'

'I might,' said Mandy. 'Or … I might not. Now, c'mere and shut up, you French whore!'

Noeleen needn't have worried about being heard on the stairs – the ensuing laughter, spring squeaking and skin smacking would have drowned out the descent of a trumpeting elephant. It was clear that while Aurelie wanted everything in the house to be old and elegant, when it came to the bedroom, she preferred things young and rough.

Having changed back to Noel, he shoved the outfit into his bag: that glory-stealing Sheelagh had only told him to use the back of the cubby hole so Aurelie wouldn't spot anything on her return. Well, this *femme merveilleuse* of a cleaning lady wasn't half as *naïve* as Sheelagh herself, considering she didn't even know what her own wife was doing behind her back!

He walked up through the hall, where the air echoed with low grunts and high-pitched shrieks that would have evaded the staves of Sheelagh's sheet music. The gilt-framed Georgian lady remained serene despite the carnal soundscape, but it was only now that Noel noticed how pathetic and ineffectual she looked. And it wasn't just the painting – no, the whole house had lost its magnificence for him. He would rather be knee-deep in grease in the goths' minuscule kitchen, or scrubbing food off Rob and Jo's hob, than have to deal with the sordid pretence of a place like this.

'*Comme c'est bon… Je jouis … I come, I come!*'

Aurelie was finally reaching her climax. Noel rolled his eyes and let himself out the front door, pulling it as hard as he could behind him.

63

'Oh, I recognise this street,' said Rachel, looking out the window of the black cab. 'Yeah, this is the route Lydia takes to our events company!'

'She's the redhead with the Saab, right?'

'Oh, Gwen, you should see how she powers it through every little gap in the traffic.'

'Sounds incredibly sexy.'

'It is. Cream leather seats, walnut dashboard, even a sat-nav.'

'Doh, I didn't mean the car,' said Gwen. 'No, this Lydia chick sounds foxy, like Scully from *The X-Files!*'

'She's actually nothing like her,' Rachel said sharply. She stared out the window as though it revealed something far more fascinating than closed shops and a council worker tipping a bin into a rubbish cart. There hadn't been any lesbian talk since the cinema (Gwen's promise to discover Rachel's ideal woman had been sidelined by the Roz-revelation and then Karaoke Dan), but it appeared that the convenient moratorium had just expired.

Gwen unclicked her seatbelt so she could turn to Rachel. 'Be honest, haven't you ever wanted to give her one while working late?'

'Of course not,' Rachel muttered into the window, whose glass was cool against her burning cheeks. She was sobering up as quickly as she'd become tipsy, and prayed that the taxi driver, a Black man with greying neck hair, wasn't hearing all this through his perforated partition.

'Fair enough,' said Gwen. 'It's just that every lesbian I know has a fantasy of topping a hotshot businesswoman. Slamming her onto the desk, ripping off her power-suit, tearing through her tights—'

'Oh, please!' said Rachel. She nodded towards the driver, trying to make a scapegoat of his sensibilities in place of her own.

'I'm sure he's heard a lot worse,' said Gwen.

The driver's head remained inscrutably still until they eventually pulled up under a flamingo-pink neon sign that said *Tearaways.*

At the door, the bouncer regarded them suspiciously. 'Been here before, ladies?' Rachel thought his power-trip pathetic – a bar with such a trashy facade should surely be glad to have such well-presented patrons.

'Course we have,' said Gwen. The bouncer chewed his gum slowly and looked at them again. It wouldn't be the end of the world if they got turned away. As well as being annoyed about the Lydia thing in the cab, Rachel was having flashes of concern about the week ahead. She was about to suggest they just call it a night when Gwen grabbed her arm and said, 'We're always in here, aren't we, sweetie? We even know the girl behind the bar. The one with the pink hair, yeah ... *Jules!*'

'Don't they all ...' sighed the bouncer, wearily pushing open the door.

'What was that all about?' said Rachel, as they went inside. 'We not good enough?'

'He was making sure we aren't unwitting young ladies who'd be shocked out of our minds.'

Rachel couldn't imagine anybody being upset by this place, however. It was just a regular bar, yucca trees in the corners, a pine-plank floor and a few disco lights tinting the punters, of which there were a reasonable number, considering it was Sunday. Gwen ordered them the special-offer cocktails that everyone was drinking. Pink-haired Jules gave them a wide ultraviolet smile as she finessed their drinks by squeezing limes from a theatrical height.

'Whoa, these are seriously strong!' said Rachel, sipping the liquid though the slim black straw.

Gwen giggled and took a mega-sip that drained her own glass by an inch. 'There's a quieter area upstairs,' she said. 'Too many boys down here anyway.' Only then, as they made their way towards the stairs, did Rachel notice that the place was eighty per cent male. It was no wonder the girls from Gwen's work liked coming here! She must tell Alysha about this place – for both the men and the music, which was upbeat pop: Girls Aloud and Kylie.

'Much nicer here, eh?' said Gwen as they found a little table upstairs. She cupped her hands around the red candle-holder. 'Romantic. Well, almost!'

'Yes, lovely,' said Rachel with a vague laugh. She hoped that Gwen, who'd drunk most of her cocktail on their way up, hadn't started to get any strange ideas about the two of them. She excused herself to the loos. The deserted cubicles were covered in crazy graffiti. The message in the middle of the door caused her pee to stop mid-stream.

Jules and Emily 4eva

She blinked at the statement, which someone else had overruled in red marker with: *As if! Jules = London's biggest lesb-ho.* Her eye scanned the rest of the door, but wherever she looked, she only found more evidence: *Steph loves Thea … Mandy & Michelle … Kara-Jane Landers thinks she's SHANE but she's really just a SHIT.*

'Oh Driffield, what the fuck have you got yourself into?' she said aloud, then stood beside the loo, infuriated at her naïveté. Her instinct was to leave straight away, but surely being in a gay bar, especially by accident, wasn't a big deal? It didn't even necessarily incriminate these days; a couple of party-girls in college had often accompanied a gay male classmate to Foxie's without drawing any suspicion about their own sexualities. If Rachel bumped into anyone she knew, which was highly unlikely anyway, she'd say she was here with a friend who happened to be gay. Tonight would be both her first and last time upon this infamous gay 'scene': her challenge was to seize this unique opportunity to observe this other world. Anyway, it would be unfair on Gwen to scarper, especially when it was Rachel's round next; no, she must go to the bar and get two more LimeLights.

Emerging from the cubicle, she discovered she was no longer alone in the toilets. Even from behind, she could tell that the slim figure at the sinks was one of those arty types who frequented The Mill, the kind who thought any girl less trendy than themselves was worthy of a glazed look of contempt. She was wearing ripped grey drainpipe jeans, a scruffy navy military jacket with red epaulettes, and a battered trilby hat, which sat lopsided on her brown hair. Spotting Rachel, she cocked her head in the mirror and said drily, 'Don't worry, babe, I don't bite.'

Rachel gave a quick grin, which was not returned, and then squeezed in alongside to self-consciously wash her hands. The girl's handbag sat open inside the other sink. She was rummaging with increasing impatience through the contents, which included a notepad with dog-eared corners, a plastic pink carnation and an *A-Team* purse with a bullet chained to the zip. Rachel stole a glance at her downturned face in the mirror. She was more striking than pretty, with her wide cat-like bone-structure and pouty mouth. Despite her general dishevelment, her tricolour eyeshadow (blue, yellow and gold) had been applied under her unplucked eyebrows with geometric precision. Whatever she was looking for was obviously very important – the search came to a histrionic head with the handbag gathered up and shaken as though she were trying to throttle a turkey. With an anguished 'Fuck!' she flung the bag against the mirror, then pushed up her sleeves so the epaulettes stood to attention. Hyperventilating, she leaned heavily on the sink, as though trying to prise it off the wall.

'Have you lost something?' Rachel dared to ask.

'Top marks for observation.' She took off her hat and ran her hands crazily through her hair. 'Sorry. I'm just so pissed off. My mobile ... must have dropped it on the way here.'

'Have you tried ringing it?' said Rachel. She dried her hands on her jeans and held out her own mobile.

'Fuck all point, probably in the window of some dodgy unblocking shop by now.'

'It's worth a try, surely?' said Rachel, thinking about the time her dad had actually *bought* a charger to switch on a phone they'd found on the street so they could contact its rightful owner. 'There *are* some honest people out there.'

'Right, I'll try, but I'm not holding my breath.' Using Rachel's phone, she rang the number and listened. 'See, Pollyanna, no ring tone. They've already ditched my SIM.' She slammed her hand against the tiles. 'I had loads of personal shit and ideas saved on that thing.'

Rachel took back her phone and checked the screen. 'Hang on, the signal's terrible in here.' She stood beneath the skylight and redialled. A moment later there was a strange metallic purr near the mirror.

The girl cried, 'You little fucking beauty!' She pulled a tin geometry set from her bag. Inside was the phone. Rachel smiled on humbly, but it soon became clear that the 'little fucking beauty' had been addressed to the phone rather than Rachel: the girl had already turned her back and was making a call of her own.

'Where are you?' she asked, as she re-feathered her fringe beneath the brim of the trilby. 'Well, I'm not waiting round like a lemon in this hellhole … Oh, come *on*, being stoned isn't a proper excuse …'

Though Rachel felt like a lemon herself, she decided she best hang on because the girl would be annoyed if she never got to say thanks.

'Well, if you don't get here soon,' said the girl, now moving towards the door, 'then you're brains on toast … hah what's that?' Still laughingly absorbed in her call, she pushed past Rachel and left, without so much as a glance of gratitude, nor even a doff of that ridiculous trilby hat.

Despite agreeing to have only one drink, Gwen was delighted when Rachel returned with more LimeLights.

'Sorry I took so long,' she said, deciding not to mention what had happened in the toilets. 'Queue at the bar was mental. But I got talking to a really sweet psychiatric nurse called Rodney while I was waiting.'

'See,' said Gwen, pushing the straws in her glass aside so she could take a full-on glug. 'Told you the ward sisters loved this place!'

The funny thing was, Rachel wasn't exactly hating Tearaways now herself. She was pleased at how well she was coping – the chat with Rodney and the sneaky tequila he'd bought her had done wonders to quell her uncertainty. And even trendy Jules had given her a friendly frown and said, 'First time here, darling?' The upstairs lounge had filled up a bit, and mostly with girls too, but she wouldn't be fazed; she continued to sip and chat, as though she'd been in the presence of this many gay people a hundred times before.

'So,' Gwen said, 'back to that conversation you were too embarrassed to have in the taxi.'

'Which … ?'

'The kind of girls you like. You haven't said a word about your love life all evening. I think our Rachel's a bit of a dark horse. Some passionate ex still lurking in the shadows?'

Rachel stared into her glass and punted the ice around with the straw. The animated chatter of the people around seemed to surge up and highlight her silence. She was annoyed with herself for thinking she could handle this place – she should have known that Gwen would press her again.

'Well?' asked Gwen, her gaze unwavering.

'So, my love life …' Rachel paused to slowly suck back the last three inches of her LimeLight, wishing there were another six still in the glass. She could hardly tell Gwen that she was going out with a man. Or that she'd been on Gaydar just to pry on Olivia. Or that Olivia was the new girlfriend of someone Rachel had been, well … *with*, over the summer. 'Um …'

I can tell there's something on your mind,' said Gwen softly. 'Look, it's better to get stuff out in the open before it devours you from inside. It's not healthy.'

Rachel bent the straw in her glass back on itself, so hard that the black plastic blanched at the bend. Her molars locked onto her inner cheeks – a reminder that she must keep her mouth clamped, reveal nothing. But the strong cocktails, Gwen's openness, the exciting, friendly vibe in this gay bar were all conspiring into a single propelling force against which she could not fight. She had downplayed what had happened over the summer, the way she'd felt about certain girls at school, the fact that Stuart and his predecessors had never excited her the way Kim had. But denying things didn't mean they didn't exist. It was no wonder she'd taken such joy in punishing Rob for every little mistake lately. She'd convinced herself she didn't like him, that he was shoddy, no good at his job; in reality she was deeply jealous and resentful of his life, of his bravery in embracing his true self, when she was running so scared from hers.

She released the bent straw from her pincer grip, but it remained at half-mast, the damage permanent. She looked up, dizzy with disbelief at what she might be about to say. As she pushed her glass to one side, she felt both derealised and strikingly alive, miles away and yet viscerally present. Her jaw magically relaxed, releasing her poor ruined cheeks.

'So ... before I came to London, I was kind of seeing this girl back home.' She waited for the music and chatter to shut down, for every face in the room to turn and stare.

But nothing happened, except that Gwen's eyes flashed. 'OK,' she said. 'Name?'

'Kim.' The three letters uttered in this odd new context sounded so alien that Rachel had to say it again, just to be sure it was true. 'Yeah, *Kim*. We weren't together long or anything, but it was quite ... intense.' She had to search for the appropriate word because this was a story she'd never told, even to herself.

'I knew it!' said Gwen. 'Did you meet online?'

'No. She joined my judo club.'

Gwen gave a wistful sigh. 'Sounds like of one of those erotica novels – *Black Belt Babes or* something. So, lust at first sight in the changing rooms then, was it?'

Rachel shook her head. 'The girls in the club are quite wary of new members, but I liked Kim the minute I met her. She was sweet and deep, sensitive.'

'She sounds adorable. So, when did you start having feelings for each other?'

'The club went out every Saturday night, and after a few weeks I realised how much of an effort I was making to always sit beside Kim. I thought my attentiveness was just the novelty of having a new friend, but in hindsight it was because I properly, y'know ... *liked* her.'

'Oh, come on, you must have known.'

'No, honestly, Gwen, I didn't.' Rachel swirled the meltwater in her glass and blinked at Gwen. 'Until then I'd never been with a girl. I'm not just new to London, I'm new to all this. I've never even been in a gay bar until tonight.'

Gwen grabbed Rachel's wrist. 'Oh lord! I was right about you being a dark horse.'

'Not dark enough, that's my problem. Always followed the main crowd, and now look at me, confused as fuck, five years behind where I should be. I'm sure you don't want to hear any more, Gwen. You've wasted your whole evening with a pathetic weirdo you met online when there are plenty of normal girls you could've met up with!'

Gwen gestured around the room. 'Do you honestly think none of these girls have any skeletons in their closets?'

'Well, at least they're not still *in* the closet with their skeletons. Gwen, I've never told another soul about this.'

Gwen's face fell in humility. She rubbed Rachel's arm. 'Oh you poor lonely little lamb. Look, every coming-out starts with painful baby steps out of the closet. You're doing amazing. Now keep going with the story!'

'A while later, Kim opened up to me about losing her mam to MS when she was young. We connected deeply over this because my own mother was never in my life. We texted all week, did brunch every Sunday, even though we'd already talked to each other for five hours in the pub the night before! People in the club started calling us *The Inseparables*. When we weren't together, I'd be thinking about her, excited for our next meeting. I'd never had a best friend, the way other girls did, so I put my excitement down to finally having one. We talked about everything: boys we liked, judo, work, but no matter how much we talked it was never enough.

'One night, a clubmate brought her brother along to the pub. I could tell immediately this lad fancied Kim; he kept trying to get her attention, and when I went to the loo, he nicked my seat. I got back to find them deep in conversation. I stood at the bar chatting to other people, but I couldn't stop looking over. When Kim laughed flirtatiously at his jokes, this horrible feeling rose up inside me. Later, when he slid his arm around the back of her seat, I had this clear vision of smashing my beer bottle on the counter and glassing him.

'I eventually managed to catch Kim's eye and nodded towards the toilets, but she shook her head and continued chatting to him. I tramped off to the loos and caught sight of my boiling face in the mirror. I wondered if I subconsciously fancied the lad myself. Then Kim came in. She could see my expression, but she didn't ask what was wrong; if anything, she looked rattled too. We just stood there, staring at each other, saying nothing, while the words took shape in my head: Oh my god, it's *her* that I fancy.

'The next thing we were in one of the cubicles. She was hugging me, I was crying. Then I was hugging her and she was crying. Then, in all that mess, we were somehow kissing. Full on. For ages. When we pulled apart, I was so weak at the knees I slid down the tiles onto the floor ...'

Gwen broke her solid stare with a couple of quick blinks. 'That is one cracking-hot story, Rachel. I'm honoured to be the first to hear it.'

'You think?' said Rachel, to whom the whole saga seemed far less glamorous – seedy even – now it had been put into words. 'How it ended wasn't so hot. We were both living in different house-shares and neither of us would stay over in case it aroused suspicion. But it came to the stage that sneaky snogs in the judo changing room and pub toilets weren't enough. We checked into a fancy hotel on the far side of town. The weekend was so intense that I could barely cope afterwards. I was terrified of how hard I was falling. I made a concerted effort to look for a job away from there. That's how I ended up in London. Away from Kim, away from everyone, everything.'

With Gwen gone to the bar to fetch much-needed drinks, Rachel oscillated between horror and relief at everything she'd just said. Her phone buzzed with a text. She couldn't cope with Stuart or Alysha right now. But it wasn't them. She didn't know who it was, yet the number was nigglingly familiar. And even odder again, it was not a text but a picture message. She gasped when she saw it. The rough pencil sketch was the undeniable likeness of herself and Gwen, their heads tilted forward in confidential conversation over a candle with a heart-shaped flame. Emanating from Gwen's head was a thought-bubble that read, *I'm sooo hot for this chick!*

'That Jules,' said Gwen, suddenly and swayingly arriving back with the drinks, one of which was already half finished. 'She made me take my fiver change out of her cleavage. With *my teeth*. Not that I minded though.'

Rachel laughed and plunged her phone into her pocket. A quick glance around revealed no trilby hat up here. There wasn't much opportunity to keep looking anyway because, in a reciprocation of intimacies, Gwen was gushing forth with her own *'coming out shhtory'* – a tortuous tale involving a series of unrequited crushes in ballet class, sea scouts and tennis camps. Rachel nodded along, but as the intricate tale wore on, her thoughts were increasingly absorbed by the picture and by the artist herself. She was fascinated to see both again.

'When I went to my all-girls secondary school the whole thing only got worse …' said Gwen, leaning in so close that Rachel wondered if the artist's thought-bubble might be in fact accurate. 'People used to joke that me and my friend Geth were the only two gays in the village. And it was actually true. We would get the bus to Cardiff and Geth would scare everyone on it by reading the *Gay Times* sex tips out loud.'

Rachel laughed, but she was conscious of something far less amusing happening beneath the table – Gwen's thigh had slid up against her own, and due to the positioning of the table, there was little room to move away. When Gwen next touched her hand to emphasise a point, Rachel could no longer bear the physical infringements or her growing suspense over the artist. She excused herself to the loo.

In the cubicle, she pored over the picture on her phone. It was such an excellent resemblance – what a shame she wouldn't be able to show it to anyone else! It seemed only polite to acknowledge it anyway. While she tried to compose a text that didn't make her sound like a tit or an idiot, someone ran into the other cubicle and slammed the door. Retching was soon followed by the splash of vomit hitting the water. When the puking stopped, there was a knock on the wall and a weak voice called out her name.

She went into the other cubicle to find Gwen lolling on the toilet seat, her face as green as a LimeLight. 'Sorry, Rachel,' she said, wiping her mouth with her sleeve, 'it's those bloody cocktails.'

Holding her breath against the acidic stink of bile and LimeLight, Rachel reached over and flushed the loo. She pulled Gwen back up. 'Let's get you into a taxi.'

Gwen grabbed Rachel's arms and stared at her. 'I've ruined everything. I'm so sorry, Rachel.' Then she closed her eyes and moved in.

Rachel pulled back so hard from the dry, bilious kiss that her head hit the tiles behind. 'Christ, Gwen, what are you doing?'

'That story … you and your ex in the toilet,' said Gwen, slurring but undeterred. 'I thought *we* could …'

Rachel needed to tear away from Tearaways. A minute later, she was using her coat and bag to scythe through the swathes of gay men downstairs. She collided with a man's drink, spilling it onto his t-shirt. As she rushed on without apologising, she heard his tall friend say something about 'dyke drama'.

Out on the street, she was distraught to discover her handbag hanging wide open. A rummaging check confirmed her purse and keys, but her phone was missing – it must have fallen out as she'd fled. She stared at the door, panicking about going back in. But then there was a waft of music and out came the artist girl, waggling something in her hand.

'Oh my god,' said Rachel, rushing over to accept her phone.

An eyebrow disappeared under the rim of the trilby. 'A second later and it would've been mashed into the floor by a lanky queen's Pradas.'

Rachel laughed. In the pink glow of the entrance, the girl looked even more striking than before. 'Thank you so much,' she said.

'Least I could do, seeing as you found my one earlier. Sorry I never said thanks, by the way, I'm a thoughtless little troll at times. Hope the sketch didn't freak you out? It was only meant as a belated thank you.'

'No, it's amazing actually,' said Rachel. 'And the thought-bubble was spot on too.' She gave a little shudder. 'Hence me pegging it out the door.'

'Figured that might be the case. Oh, I'm Xenna by the way.' A hand was extended but then temporarily withheld as she added, 'spelled with an X but *always* pronounced with a zed.'

'Got it!' said Rachel, gripping the chilly, ink-stained fingers and wondering if she'd ever need to refer to this spelling directive beyond this footpath. She was beginning to hope, if not feel, that she might. 'I'm Rachel.'

'So, Rachel Driffield …' As Xenna weighed up the name on her epaulettes, Rachel realised that her soliloquy in the toilet hadn't been a soliloquy at all. 'Got a nice English ring to it,' said Xenna. 'Like something from a *Bunty* comic.'

'Not half as exotic as Xenna, though.' Rachel shrugged and smiled and blinked away a ridiculous vision of lunging forward to kiss the lips beneath the trilby. She hoped the ambient pink neon was enough to mask the blush rising in her cheeks.

'Everyone thinks Xenna's something to do with that closeted warrior princess or eastern philosophy. They think I must have cool hippy-dippy parents.'

'And do you?' asked Rachel.

'A couple of chemistry professors!' She looked into the distance. 'Yes, my parents' eyes met across a Bunsen burner in university. Xenon has always been my mum's favourite element. It's a gas or something.'

'Yes, it's a noble gas,' said Rachel. 'Quite an unreactive one too, if I remember my chemistry lessons correctly!' She realised that she was doing more smiling now, out here on the street, than she had done all day; she only wished the past six hours could have been spent with Xenna.

'Noble and unreactive?' Xenna laughed. 'Huh, they certainly got *that* one wrong.'

'But imagine if your mum had had a thing for *boron*?' said Rachel. Even jokes, which she was usually rubbish at, were flowing effortlessly out of her mouth.

Xenna's highly reactive laugh was interrupted by the bouncer. 'Move away from the exit ladies.'

'Now *there's* a boron!' said Xenna as she led them along. 'You look like you need a stiff cup of chamomile after your fright in there,' she said. 'My flat's nearby if you fancy one?'

'But what about the friend you were meeting?' Rachel heard herself ask quickly, but only because she was terrified to give voice to the big YES that was bouncing around inside her stomach.

'Little bitch never turned up in the end,' said Xenna.

'I see,' said Rachel, who now dismally realised what was going on – she was merely a fallback because Xenna's real date had been a no-show. She followed Xenna towards the main street, where she would take a cab straight back to Wheldon. She was due at her desk in only eight hours' time for god's sake.

'And I bet you a tenner,' said Xenna with a sigh, as they reached the corner, 'that he's holed up with some hot Gaydar cock.' She gave a nodding, malevolent smile. 'But he'll pay for it dearly when I see him next.'

'You mean he's *brains on toast*, then?' Rachel was regaining her playfulness tenfold with the relief that it had been a man Xenna had been meeting, and a gay one too, gay like Xenna was and … maybe Rachel herself … Her thoughts lurched on again, to an unknown flat and the things that might happen there.

Xenna looked at her and gave an impressed little nod, then raised her arm to catch them a passing cab.

64

Jo hadn't been up this early since the morning she'd landed in Stansted with her life in two suitcases. It was only seven, and she was pacing around the kitchen table in her pyjamas. 'Part of me wishes I'd bloody well asked her,' she said.

Rob set down his pomegranate juice and grabbed his tie. 'But what would you have said: Pardon me, Lucija, but how come you've got *a handbag* coming out of the cinema, when you didn't bring one in?'

'I thought I was hallucinating when the lights came on,' said Jo. 'When did she go out to the toilet, anyway?'

'Around twenty minutes from the end, I think. I was so excited about my arm touching off Patrik's muscly bicep that I wasn't paying much attention.'

'Well, at least we know they're not homophobic, anyway,' said Jo.

Rob eyed her sourly over the points of his upturned collar. 'Thanks so much for your *Rob's boyfriend Michael is a theatre-buff*. I love how you didn't say anything about being gay yourself.'

'I just wanted to stop her from flirting with you before it went any further. Anyway, I don't see what the big deal is about whether I am or not – neither of them seemed to bat an eyelid about *you*.'

'I think they'd already worked it out about both of us.' He bit his lip in guilt. 'And I think I know how.'

Jo ground her toes into the floor tiles. 'What are you about to tell me?'

'Remember when that girl at the party fell asleep on my shoulder?'

'Vesna, yeah.'

'So, after you'd gone off in pursuit of Lucija, I saw that her eyes were half-open. She closed them when she saw me looking, and then did this big fake snore.'

Jo felt her stomach lurch. 'Please, *please* do not tell me she was listening to all that stuff I was saying about Lucija?'

'It would explain it, though,' said Rob. 'Vesna tells Lucija that you like her, and Lucija comes over to let you know the feeling's mutual.'

'But I still don't know if Lucija really *is* even gay. She barely gave me the time of day yesterday but was all chat and charm with you. The clothes are dykey, yes, but then there's that handbag.'

'That bag is nothing but a *mustard* herring,' said Rob. 'I'm starting to think Stanko's a dealer and that she's his mule.'

'She's certainly not a barrister, anyway,' said Jo with a laugh. 'I'm still wondering if that was just an innocent miscommunication …'

'She knew what she was up to,' said Rob, as he began flicking through the messages on his Blackberry. 'She must have loved how impressed we looked when she spoke about her *clients* and *the dock*!'

'Technically, it was all true though.'

'It was a deliberate intention to mislead the jury, your honour! Your face was priceless when she finally handed over her … *business* card.'

'Oh, stop!' Jo whacked the cuff of her pyjama top at him. (She'd discovered the same top on the floor of the bedroom at three that morning, having woken from a dream in which she and Lucija had been rolling naked around on the floor of a Slovenian cinema.) 'And there was me expecting parchment card with copperplate calligraphy.'

'She *will* need a barrister if she gets caught carrying around handbags full of drugs,' Rob said. 'It was practically bursting at the seams.'

'I sincerely doubt it was full of coke or heroin,' said Jo.

'Then explain how Stanko has hundreds to lose in poker. It's all to do with that secret bedroom. Could be a massive stash or even a chemical lab in there, for all we know. In any case, I don't want to get tied up any further with them. Patrik's lovely and easy on the eye, but if he's hanging around with wrong 'uns like Stanko …'

'Well, I'm still going to meet her today,' said Jo, shrugging to hide her mounting excitement.

'Even though she deliberately tricked us with the barrister thing?'

'*Because* she deliberately tricked us,' said Jo. 'It takes a certain kind of intelligence to do what she did without so much as a tiny lie. I'm actually more impressed by her now than when I thought she *was* a barrister.'

'Impressed?' he said. 'Turned on, more like. I can tell you still want to bang her.'

Jo sank into a chair and huffed out her cheeks. 'Rob, what if she *is* gay and today *is* an actual date?' Before he had even looked up from his Blackberry, she was crossly correcting herself: 'No, I need to accept that she's just a straight girl who enjoys misleading people. She probably had a right laugh when Vesna told her what she'd overheard. Oh, I'm morto now. Maybe I *will* bail out of later. Clothes shopping is cringeworthy enough as it is ...'

But Rob was more concerned with a message that had just buzzed in on his Blackberry. 'Sorry, I've got to rush off,' he said. 'The backdrop artwork for the launch doesn't match the metal framework, apparently. The height's been mixed up with the fucking width.' He stood up, gritting his teeth. 'Shit, this is all I need, especially after Fussbudget's mood in the cinema yesterday!'

He fled the flat, forgetting in his distress to wish her good luck. Suddenly Jo found herself alone, with seven hours in which to continue her rumination about Lucija, and to begin her meticulous preparation for their meeting.

65

A strange scratching noise preceded Rachel's awareness of the thin, unfamiliar pillow. The noise would come on bursts, stop dead, and then resume. It reminded her of something, but she couldn't think what ... Oh yes, it was like Narelle on her instant messenger! But Rachel was not at work. She turned over on her side. The mattress felt weirdly compacted, as though all the springs had been removed. She caught a whiff of stale patchouli overlaid with a sharp woody smell reminiscent of primary school. *Pencil shavings.*

When she opened her eyes, the first thing she saw was Xenna's lamplit profile, tucked behind the easel in the far corner of the dim basement bedsit. Xenna was wearing exactly two things – a string vest with nothing underneath, and a pair of tiger-striped boxer shorts. The afterimage of the trilby was still visible as a kink halfway down her hair. She must have heard Rachel's unintentional little gasp – without looking up from her scratchy pencil strokes, she muttered, 'It lives.'

'Morning,' said Rachel, rubbing her eyes, more out of sheepish disbelief than actual tiredness (in fact she felt surprisingly well despite all the alcohol and the meagre amount of sleep). As she propped herself up on the futon, Xenna's seasoned sheets rubbed against her bum, and she remembered that she was naked from the waist down. She'd put her bra and top back on during the night, after she'd set her alarm for work, but hadn't been able to find her knickers in the dark. Now it was slightly brighter, she saw that they were hanging off the cover of the crackly Pat Benatar record Xenna had put on last night, while the chamomile tea was brewing. Two songs later, the same Ms Benatar was spurring Rachel on to lean across the sofa and hit Xenna with her *own* best shot. And it hadn't ended there: the sweet, tentative kisses had quickly evolved into rampant snogging, and soon they were standing in a topless tangle in the middle of the room. By the time Pat had started to sing about battlefields, they were falling onto the futon as a single writhing unit.

Xenna was working under the illumination of a gooseneck lamp that was taped to the top of her easel. Behind her, a worrying amount of daylight was seeping through the batiked indigo sheet that served as a curtain. 'What time is it?' Rachel asked.

Xenna made another few strokes and then stood back, pencil clamped in her mouth like a horse's bit, to regard her own work. 'Nineish.'

'Please tell me you're joking?'

Xenna licked her thumb and rubbed at the paper. 'I know. Way too early, isn't it?'

Rachel grabbed her phone from the rusty-edged tea chest that was the bedside table. 'But I set my alarm for half six!' she said, almost in a wail. 'I even got up in the middle of the night to set it.' The early start would have given her enough time to get home in a cab (she had planned to tell Alysha she'd paid Stuart a booty call after the cinema and ended up staying the night), grab a shower, then rush into work on time.

'You looked so tranquil that I reached over and switched it off,' said Xenna. She took a scalpel to her pencil, letting the parings fall straight onto the carpet. 'But it woke me from an amazing dream that's given me the inspiration for this CD cover I've been struggling with for weeks. Apparently we only remember dreams we've had directly before waking up. So, if your alarm hadn't rung, I would've missed that muse!'

'That's great,' said Rachel, 'but you've no idea how much trouble I'm going to be in at work.' Holding the duvet across her middle, she grabbed her still-damp knickers and struggled into them.

'So, what's the worst that can happen?' Xenna gave her the same narrow look as last night when she'd learned where Rachel worked. 'Some asshole loses a couple more hairs because you didn't market him your baldy drug?'

'I better ring in,' said Rachel, trying not to let the sting of Xenna's comments show in her face. 'What will I say?' She'd never played truant in her life, not even in school, where it would have been easy with her dad working double shifts at the garage.

'Say you were up until all hours having red-hot lesbian sex,' said Xenna, who then rolled her eyes and added, 'duh, tell them you're not feeling well.'

'Right,' said Rachel, colouring a little but also cheering up at the *red-hot*. She hoped it wasn't yet another example of Xenna's general sarcasm. 'What illness should I say?'

'I found a twenty-four-hour stomach bug always worked a treat when I used to work in ... well, in a few different places.'

'Perfect,' Rachel said, though she doubted that Xenna's *places* had the exacting standards of Trenpharm or the combined penetrating eyes of Lydia and Narelle. She pulled on her jeans and went out to the privacy of the bathroom.

The toilet cistern was covered in an array of paintbrushes stuffed into grimy jam jars. Rachel stared at the bristled heads – all different heights, sizes and angles – for inspiration. She took a deep breath and called Lydia's direct line. Rush-hour traffic droned on the street above, and higher up again she could make out the whirr of a helicopter. In the little anxious gaps between the ringtones, she could hear the helicopter coming to hover directly above this Acton flat. She pictured a surveillance team feeding back information on her movements to Anthony P. Watson's office, and his disgusted face when he discovered that the bright young thing he'd met at the webcast had turned out to be a sexual truant.

It didn't help her paranoia that Lydia wasn't answering. She would have to leave a voice message. But a message could be listened to over and over, especially if it sounded unconvincing. Her toes clawed at the paint-crusted bathmat in preparation, but even after about fifty rings the voicemail still hadn't activated. She remembered that Narelle was supposed to switch it on when Lydia hadn't made it back from a meeting on Friday afternoon – the idiot must have forgotten. Now Rachel would have to ring Narelle instead.

This time the phone was picked up immediately. 'Ooh, Rachel,' said Narelle archly. 'I can't believe you're late!'

'I've been sick during the night with a stomach thing. I'm sure it'll pass soon. Where's Lydia?'

'My money's on another dress fitting because she's been starving herself so much. No wonder she's been such a moody cow ...'

Rachel clenched her fist. 'Look, when she arrives, please tell her I'll be in once my stomach settles down. Not great timing for the week that's in it, but I best wait it out.'

'Shitty timing for the shits all right!' said Narelle with a laugh. 'Actually … now I think of it, that dude Rob's been on twice already. Throwing a hissy fit because he couldn't reach you.'

'But what does he want? Everything should be in production by now.'

'He said the printers can't print the backdrop. Someone got the measurements arseways. Artwork was meant to be fourteen foot high by twenty foot wide, not the other way around.'

In the mirror, Rachel saw the colour drain from beneath yesterday's makeup; her guts lurched as though she was actually going to have the runs. She must have mixed up the measurements when they'd met Corinne in that ghastly little Italian café. Or during that weird meeting in Rob's office. The big day would be nothing without that backdrop: she imagined Professor Geddes giving his address from a bland, unbranded stage to an audience who felt they were at a college lecture, not the launch of an exciting new product they were expected to sell to doctors. She pushed herself off the sink with a panicked shake, thinking this must be punishment for her crazy behaviour last night. 'Right, Narelle, I'm on my way in to sort this out.'

'Whoa, hold your ring of fire,' said Narelle. 'I don't want you coming in infecting me. Anyway, you'd be too late – they need the artwork in the next half an hour or it won't be printed in time. That's why Rob urgently needs the wording.'

'But the wording isn't going to change just because he has to change the shape!'

'He said they're not allowed to insert text on any job unless it's been copied and pasted from an email from us. And that this is technically a new job because it's a new size. What drongo came up with such an anal rule?'

'OK, Narelle, listen very carefully,' said Rachel, speaking as loudly and clearly as she could without Xenna hearing. 'I need you to email Rob urgently with the same line that we have on everything else: *At 24, Rob deserves more.* Then ask him to get the resized artwork straight to the printers.

Tell him there's no way that this deadline can be missed, Narelle. Absolutely no fucking way.'

With work taken care of, and a text sent to Alysha saying Stuart was driving her to work, Rachel turned to the bathroom mirror to address the next crisis – her appearance. With her pillow-frictioned frizz, streaked mascara and scuzzy tongue, it was no wonder Xenna seemed uninterested. She ran a toothpasted finger around her mouth, tied up her hair and scrubbed her face with Xenna's Vegan Skin facewash.

Looking and smelling a lot better, she went back in. But Xenna barely looked up from her easel. Nor did she ask how the phone call had gone. Feeling awkward, Rachel went to examine the table dividing the messy kitchenette from the rest of the room. The table was covered in a varnished collage of sensationalist headlines cut from newspapers: PERV LANDLORD SPIED ON TENANTS … MURDERED BY BISEXUAL EX-LOVER … TWELVE-YEAR-OLD PORN ADDICTS. Right in the centre was a pink sticker that said EAT PUSSY NOT ANIMALS.

'That's my *Sex on Legs* table,' came the voice from behind the easel.

'It's really cool!' Rachel said, with a smile and a laugh.

'It's really filthy too – in more ways than one. Had to sack my cleaning lady, hence the inch of dust on everything around here.'

Rachel picked up a sea urchin shell that had been spray-painted silver and took a sly peek through the centre at Xenna's bum in the boxer shorts. 'Did she do something wrong?' she asked.

'Oh, it wasn't her fault.' Xenna stood back from the easel, tilting her head to one side. 'See, I'd mixed up this gorgeous purple paint colour on a saucer – it had taken two full days to get it just right. But when my back was turned, Noeleen put the whole thing in the washing-up. Obviously thought it was another one of my herbal tea spillages. I didn't say anything, just went into the bathroom and silently screamed. And now I can't face having her back.'

Rachel's shoulders sank in sympathy. She called upon the little bit of knowledge she had about art and design. 'It's a pity you didn't know the exact colour-value so you could recreate it, you know, the—'

'Ugh stop!' Xenna shivered, causing her erect nipples to catch on the mesh of her string vest. 'Please don't utter the P-word in my company. I absolutely despise all that.'

'But how can you hate colours?' said Rachel, focusing back on Xenna's face and forcing herself to remain still, despite the lust rushing up inside her. 'You're an artist!'

Xenna rolled the pencil along the pale skin of her inner thigh. 'I can't stand the thought of something so emotive as colour being reduced to an ugly little number. What right has some big corporation to claim that a particular shade is to be known forever more as 23017?'

'Never thought of it like that,' said Rachel. She nodded towards the easel's mystery contents. 'Do you mind if I ... ?'

Despite Xenna's half-hearted shrug, Rachel came and stood behind her. She gave a little gasp when she saw the sketch. Shown from the waist up, the girl and boy stood shoulder to shoulder. Each was as beautiful as the other. The girl's cheek was tickled by a shaggy side fringe, her slim arms exposed by sawn-off t-shirt sleeves. The boy, topless and tattooed, had a gravity-defying fauxhawk and a ring through his pouting lip. There was something hypnotic about their gaze; Rachel leaned in over Xenna's shoulder, and realised that their irises were also tiny clock-faces, each eye displaying a different time. The most striking thing about it all, however, was how weirdly familiar the picture felt to Rachel – even though it had only been conceived that morning, it was reminiscent of something she'd seen before. She couldn't think how or when, but the memory was somehow soaked in negative emotion. She put it down to a strong case of déjà vu – it wasn't surprising her mind was playing tricks, given the barrage of unprecedented events the last twenty-four hours had brought. 'It's fantastic,' she said, finally remembering her manners.

Xenna tapped her pencil on the girl. 'It'd be a lot cooler if Lynette could be topless too, but the record company wouldn't dream of allowing the singer's nips on the front of her own CD.' She glanced coyly over her shoulder at Rachel. 'But then I'm biased because I adore drawing tits.'

'Really?' laughed Rachel, recalling how Xenna had paid *her* boobs plenty of attention last night – thankfully the hickey on her left one was well below the neckline of her work blouses.

'I like to get a nice pair of hooters, sometimes even *two* pairs, into every painting I can,' said Xenna.

Rachel smiled to cover the shuddering realisation that the X in the tribute message on *Hooters on a Scooter* had not been a sign-off kiss from the artist to her bare-breasted subjects, but rather the first initial of the name of the artist standing two inches in front of her now. She brimmed over, ready to spill the coincidence, but there was no way to explain how she'd ended up in Xenna's friends' apartment on that November night, let alone with a man, one who was now her boyfriend. She knew now that her sexual rabidity that night had been a desperate attempt to prove to Stuart, and moreover to *herself*, that she was in fact nothing like the painting's subjects.

But if she really was nothing like those girls, then why – even as Stuart came inside her that night – had she been thinking about what usually went on between those same sheets? If she were nothing like those Vespa-riders, then why had she been thrilled to go home last night with a girl who'd picked her up at a gay bar? And why, right now, was she allowing her own hands to slide from behind around that same girl's waist, while simultaneously resting her chin upon on the milky skin above the back of the girl's string vest. She had no clue about morning-after etiquette when it came to lesbians. She prayed she wasn't making a fool of herself: in uni, the unwritten rule had been to never loiter in a man's digs after a one-night stand (and nor had Rachel ever wanted to). But this felt completely different. And although Xenna seemed more focussed on her sketch than what Rachel was doing, she wasn't exactly shrinking away either; within a minute, and remembering that it had been *Xenna* who had switched off the alarm that prevented an early departure, Rachel felt suddenly licensed to move in and begin to dot tentative little kisses on the wispy hairs on Xenna's sweet neckline.

'Theo's not bad, but Lynette needs a lot more work,' Xenna muttered, but mostly to herself. 'Yeah her eyebrows are way more obtuse, and her philtrum's too short. At least Theo's a good likeness though ...'

The self-critique turned Rachel on even more. 'So this ...' she whispered between kisses, while her hands moved from Xenna's waist, one up to feel her boobs through the rough synthetic netting, the other down to the boxers which, being men's, had an open flyhole, 'so this is going to be ... an actual CD cover?' Rachel bypassed the fly for now and began a slow grope, crumpling the cotton up between Xenna's legs.

'Only if it passes muster with the corporate cocks at Versality,' said Xenna. She gave a long, deep sigh that Rachel prayed was the result of her busy hands, rather than exasperation with the record company. 'It's already a miracle they agreed to let an unknown female watercolourist from Acton submit something in the first place. Lynette had to beg them to even consider me. Now if I was some trendy male artist from Hoxton ...'

'You know the singer personally, then?' Rachel asked, as she pulled Xenna tight into her own excited body.

'Erm ... yeah,' said Xenna, suddenly stiffening. 'Lynette's my girlfriend. She's in Sweden at the moment recording the rest of the album. Thought I told you about her last night?'

Rachel's fingers froze in the fly of the shorts. Her other hand fell away. Xenna turned around and looked at her. 'The picture's confused you,' she said. 'But Versality are hardly going to show two lesbos snogging now, are they? Heterosex sells. The suits have even briefed Lynette to say she's single and straight during interviews.' She frowned at Rachel. 'Are you OK?'

Rachel felt like she'd been dumped on her back by an Olympic judoka. She could barely breathe, but she couldn't show how insanely jealous she felt about someone she'd only met last night. 'I just didn't know you were seeing someone,' she said, trying to sound casual. 'It doesn't seem fair on your girlfriend.' She realised that the same thing could be said about her and Stuart, but somehow that didn't count.

'Don't worry about that,' said Xenna with a bemused shake of the head. 'Myself and Lynette have an understanding. The lucky slut rang from the

330

studio yesterday to tell me that a blonde snowboarding chick with laser-cut abs was waiting for her back in the hotel room.'

'OK, right' said Rachel, dreading to think how she herself might be later described to Lynette … *a gagging-for it corporate sellout, whose Geordie accent sprang out as she came* … or maybe *an ingénue who was pretty decent at licking clit but who hung round the next day like a bad smell.* She thought she was going to cry – all morning she had been stupid enough to harbour hopes that this was the start of something, but last night had merely been Xenna's random, tit-for-tat response to Lynette's Swedish conquest. Rachel had made an even worse fool of herself in the last few minutes too – pawing at a girl who, now that she thought about it, hadn't paid her the slightest interest this morning, a girl who'd got what she wanted last night and now wanted rid so she could focus on a picture that was far more sexy and important and out-there than Rachel could ever be. 'I actually better get going,' she said, cross at the incontrovertible catch in her voice. She began gathering her things. 'My boss was a bit off with me on the phone earlier. About being late and all.'

'Cool,' said Xenna, now retrieving an eraser from the bottom of a chaotic fishbowl of bric-a-brac.

By the time Rachel was leaving, Lynette had been relieved of her nose and eyebrows. 'Station's straight up Horn Lane,' Xenna mumbled, as she leaned forward to draw a new, obtuse angle. 'You can't miss it.'

'Thanks,' said Rachel, who had no clue where Horn Lane was. She put her bag over her shoulder and pulled the warped front door behind her. By the time she was halfway up the basement steps, the tears were already streaming down her cheeks.

66

Jo stalled in the mouth of Goodge Street station and squinted anxiously across the road. It didn't take long to spot the place – its signage depicted a coffee cup with a big D-shaped handle. She had looked at the little card bearing the same insignia ten times already that morning and now, inside her pocket, her fingers felt for its rectangular reassurance.

She contemplated a calming walk round the block, but Lucija might already have clocked her through the tinted glass of The Dock's facade – she would think Jo ridiculous for missing the place when it was practically in front of her. Instead, Jo gave an exaggerated nod of recognition – as though she'd just located the café at that very second – and crossed the street. She went inside, trying not to think about everything Vesna might have relayed to Lucija after that party.

A scattering of afternoon customers were dotted around The Dock. The place was surprisingly nice inside; between the gentle lighting, comfy tub chairs and the just-audible jazz, Jo could tell that this chain was positioning itself as an antidote to those new seat-less, industrial-style outlets, where the intense lighting was just as jolting as the coffee itself.

A girl was clearing off tables, and though she couldn't have looked less like Lucija (she was Hispanic and heavy, her waist and hips straining against the regulation white blouse and café-au-lait chinos), Jo in her confused nervousness approached her, only to divert at the last second when she realised her ridiculous error. The girl looked up, her eyes dopey and hopeless, then gave the nearest table three big blasts of her cleaning spray. The chemical spritz caught in Jo's throat; she had to hack it out with a couple of hard coughs. She was grateful that Lucija, whom she'd just spotted operating the barista machine, had been facing the other way. Despite all Jo's self-talk about playing it cool, it had already been a most inauspicious entrance.

Though not here as a customer, Jo still had to join the queue, which in the post-lunch lull consisted only of a baggy-eyed woman in smart business attire, who was leaning exhaustedly against the pastry display. The strap of her heavy briefcase cut deep into her shoulder pad. The woman was perusing a never-ending list of unread emails on her Blackberry, her expression growing more pinched with every click. So this was one of those *beleaguered clients worn down by the system* that Lucija had mentioned at the cinema!

In contrast to her exhausted client, Lucija couldn't have been more alert as she went about preparing the woman's coffee. Jo seized upon the unfair advantage of observing someone at work and stole a long look at Lucija from behind. Her back looked gorgeous in the white shirt – a perfect inverted triangle tapering down to her waist, around which a barista's apron was lashed. Her ponytail sprayed out through the aperture of the beige baseball cap, and there was something adorable about her nerdy black work-shoes, so at odds in colour and comfort to her usual footwear. She tamped the coffee down into the filter, and then, like a master mechanic tightening a nut, locked the unit into its shiny silver mothership. As the coffee began to dribble through, she prepared the milk. Her sleeves were rolled up sexily beyond the elbow, and the tendons pinging in her forearms as she worked the steam-knob and pulsed the jug soon had Jo in a hot froth of her own. The involuntary little sigh she emitted was luckily covered by the machine's hiss.

Jo could not conceal her presence indefinitely, however, and her spying came to a necessary end when Lucija – having poured the milk from a decreasing height into the precisely tilted cup of espresso – presented her client with the result, along with a panini that had been grilling in the interim.

'Oh, that's awfully pretty!' said the woman, suddenly springing to life. She went off with her tray, smiling at the multi-lobed heart atop her latte – perhaps the only nice thing anyone had done for her all day.

Meanwhile, Jo felt her own heart begin to throb. 'Hi,' she said, stepping up to the till and grinning into Lucija's face, which, to borrow the businesswoman's phrase, seemed even more *awfully pretty* today, its features darkened and defined by the shadows of the cap.

Lucija nodded but showed no sign of surprise. If anything, she even looked a bit annoyed.

'Sorry, I didn't mean to startle you by sneaking up like a customer, I mean a *client*,' Jo rushed to say. 'I kept trying to catch your eye but …'

'Don't worry,' said Lucija, her face thawing slightly. 'I could see you the whole time in the reflection of the machine.'

'Aha,' said Jo, cursing the chrome that had facilitated secret observation of the not-so-secret observer, and praying that her expression hadn't been too lustful, nor her eyes too roving, as she'd waited. 'That reminds me of a teacher who used to have a kirror in the morner, sorry … a *mirror* in the *corner* of the blackboard so she could see who was messing in class.' Jo couldn't believe she'd managed to ruin a single-sentence story with a spoonerism.

Lucija didn't seem impressed by either the story or its delivery. 'It's just how baristas check how many people are waiting,' she said with a shrug.

'Useful trick!' Jo's mouth was becoming more desiccated by the second. All these vocal problems were in stark contrast to earlier, when she'd elatedly sang along to 'Good Fortune' – on repeat on the CD player – while ironing her shortlist of four t-shirts. There was an awkward silence then, in which Jo dawdled at the counter, sure she'd blown things before they'd even begun. She could see Lucija calling off their shopping trip – she certainly gave no indication of finishing work any time soon. Jo wouldn't blame her if she suddenly pretended she had to stay late.

Before the inauspicious start had a chance to deteriorate any further, a door behind the counter opened. 'What the actual … ?' The acne-riddled man striding out had over-gelled hair and a badge that said *Marcus – Manager*. Lucija kept her eyes fixed on the cash register. Nostrils flared, Marcus raced through the tables, almost upsetting the latte in the hand of the businesswoman. He grabbed the bottle from Lucija's colleague and slammed it down on the nearest table. 'How many fucking times do I need to tell you, Yésica? Clients want to smell *coffee*, not cleaning spray. Wipe that away now!'

Yésica nodded and extended her quaking hand to take back the cloth.

'With a clean cloth, you moron,' he said, waving it out of reach. 'If head office had a secret sipper in here right now, we'd all be out on our arses.'

He stomped back behind the counter but wasn't pleased at what he saw there either. 'You blind or something, *Loo-see-ya*?' he spat. 'There's a client in front of you, in case you hadn't noticed. Whenever you're *quite* ready, you might like to serve them.'

'Yes, Marcus,' she muttered. Jo wanted to press his cystic cheeks onto the hot-plate of the panini maker.

'And remember to up-sell,' he continued. 'You didn't offer any of our confection-selection to that last client.'

'Sorry for the delay, madam,' said Lucija, looking up at Jo as though for the first time. 'What can I get for you?'

Jo knew she must play along, especially now that Marcus, suddenly finding the need to measure the levels in the syrup bottles, was hovering close by. 'Ehh ... a coffee please.' She cringed at her own vagueness – it was like to going into a travel agent and asking for 'a holiday'.

'Americano?' asked Lucija.

Jo, who'd barely eaten all day, thought of her butterfly-filled stomach being attacked by black acid. 'Maybe a ... latte?' Her pronunciation sounded so embarrassingly drab: with her flat Irish accent, it was no wonder she still feared saying *Lucija*.

'And which size *latte* would you like?' asked Lucija, the word so sexy and authentic even through her deadpan expression.

'Small is perfect,' said Jo.

Lucija frowned at her meaningfully, like a wartime spy receiving an unexpected instruction. 'Are you sure?' Jo was at a loss, but as soon as Marcus turned away to count tea bags, Lucija drew a little rectangle in the air.

It was ironic that Jo had forgotten the card at the critical moment, given all the attention she'd paid it this morning. 'Sorry, I have this,' she announced. 'I think I'm due a free one?' Marcus looked up sharply from his inventory, but he could have no issue with the loyalty card, whose little inkings Lucija must have painstakingly faked, all at varying angles, degrees of intensity, and smudge.

Lucija counted the stamps aloud, then looked at Jo with her tongue in her cheek and said, 'Yes, you're due a free *large* latte.'

'Why, that's wonderful,' said Jo, their little in-joke helping her relax at last.

Marcus continued to glower over, as though waiting, if not actually hoping, for Lucija to fail on the last aspect of the transaction. But she waved her hand over the glass cabinet like a magician's assistant. 'And would madam care for one of our delicious pastries to accompany said large latte?'

'Oh, let me peruse …' said Jo, bending over the display so Marcus wouldn't see her laughing. 'My my, they look delectable.' She stood up and patted her concave abdomen as though it were distended. 'But I just couldn't manage one right now.'

'No problem whatsoever,' said Lucija, her eyes narrowing under the shadow of the hat. 'Now let me get you your *free, large* latte. It will take a couple of minutes if I may trouble you to wait.'

'That was too funny,' said Jo, when they were finally out in the sunshine and heading towards Oxford Street. 'Such a patronising little prick!' She turned to smile at Lucija, drinking in the snapshot of her urban clothing against the blurred city background. Rush hour was underway and, for the first time since moving here, Jo felt she was beating in tandem with London's pulse, that the opportunities proffered by this metropolis, with its intoxicating blend of ancientness and up-to-the-minuteness, might now start belonging to her too.

'I call him *Marcus Interruptus*,' said Lucija, 'because he's always butting in when you're serving someone.' Her incisor pixel flashed. 'Now you see why it gives me so much pleasure to falsify loyalty cards for my friends!'

'The coffee was lovely anyway,' said Jo, concerned that 'friend' had been used to delineate the boundary of their relationship. Slightly disappointing too had been the design on the top of Jo's latte. She'd been looking forward to her own love-heart and worried that the benign fern had been a tactful way of communicating that Lucija wasn't gay, or worse still, *was* gay but not interested in Jo beyond the platonic. Whatever the case, it had been into the fronds of the same fern that Jo had whispered 'sweet fuck' when Lucija had emerged from the staffroom in her civvies. The sight of her in a grey

Fenchurch anorak, zipped up to the chin, had only amplified the jitters that the coffee – strong, beneath all the froth – had already evoked in Jo. Lucija seemed to have a never-ending stream of gorgeous urban gear, all of it suiting her so perfectly that it would have been a travesty if she'd lived in an era where ripstop nylon jackets, boyfriend jeans and slim-fit t-shirts had not yet been conceived.

In Fitzrovia, they passed an outdoor pub-table full of punters enjoying the afternoon. Their lager glinted in the spring sunshine. Jo wished she were bringing Lucija for a few drinks rather than to a fashion show with Jo as the sole, mortified model. They could have talked freely in the pub; there were so many things Jo wanted to find out, especially the (probably quite sad) story of how someone so naturally intelligent had wound up as a barista under a horrid little jobsworth like Marcus. Maybe Lucija's family didn't have enough money to send her to uni; or maybe Lucija, if she were indeed gay, was enticed away from a homophobic hometown by the anonymous pink liberty of London. Jo's mind raced ahead to a future where she could encourage and enable Lucija to do some kind of course – even a basic qualification in something might save her from a lifelong rut of jobs like the one she had now.

Lucija suggested they try H&M first – but a comprehensive flick through their smart-casual rails revealed, to Jo's relief, nothing worth trying on. Seemingly determined to make good an initial failure, Lucija then led them up the street, into a gigantic Topshop playing squelchy electro. 'There's some potential candidates over there,' she said, nodding at the furthest wall. 'Come on!'

Jo diligently followed through the aisles. She was so fixated on Lucija's handsome back that her own elbow caught on a protruding hanger, which fell to the floor with a loud plastic *clack*. Cursing her own clumsiness, she bent down to pick up the fallen item – but so had Lucija. Suddenly they were hunkered together between the rails, each holding the opposite end of a raunchy G-string. Lucija looked matter-of-factly at the tiny garment, then cocked an accusatory eyebrow at Jo, who quickly surrendered her side of the hanger and stood up with folded arms. She remained there, blushing as red as the lace trim on the pants, until Lucija, who was thoughtfully thumbing the diaphanous black fabric on the pubic triangle, eventually deigned to ascend. As she put the hanger back on the rack, she whispered into Jo's sizzling ear, 'Well, at least that's your interview underwear sorted then!'

67

Rob waited outside the lift, fantasising about his baggiest tracksuit bottoms, a stiff drink and a nice long phone catch-up with Michael. Not that he'd be telling his boyfriend, or Vicky or anyone else, what had happened at work that morning. He could scarcely believe it himself. Now, as he recalled what he'd done, or rather *not* done, he was overcome with a pang, not of guilt (Fussbudget had driven him to it and deserved whatever might be coming), but of fear that he'd be blamed and get into terrible trouble at work. *Not like you, Rob. Not like you at all.* He imagined Edmond escorting him out of HarropAds, never to return.

Inside the lift, he blinked at the dead man's reflection in the mirrored wall. But as it ascended, he reminded himself how watertight his story was: all he'd done was follow Trenpharm's own orders to the letter, or in this case, *to the number.* It felt as though karma, through a series of coincidental events, had gifted him this once-off opportunity to wreak revenge for the way Fussbudget had been treating him. It would have been wrong to break the fateful chain the universe had created for him! Probably nobody would even notice on Thursday anyway – they'd be too busy blowing smoke up each other's arses in poncey Gravenden. As for his own arse, it was completely covered. He'd be just fine.

When the lift opened, he found a stressed-looking Patrik flanked by two huge suitcases. 'Rob,' he gasped, as he held the lift-door open. 'Please, please can you help me with something?'

'Umm …' Rob eyed the suitcases, both large enough to conceal a dead body, or enough drugs to invoke multiple life sentences. He was about to say no, that he needed to get home, but then he saw how unbelievably hot Patrik looked today, with his muscles puffing out the sleeves of his pizza-maker's polo shirt and the thighs of his work trousers dusted with flour. The thought of accompanying him anywhere, even on some dubious task, was too good to resist; anyway a little adventure would be fitting on this

339

day of living dangerously. 'OK then,' he said with a flirtatious wink at Patrik as he got into the lift. 'I'm all yours.'

'Oh, my gay lifesaver!' cried Patrik who, for a wonderful moment, looked like he might kiss Rob but then leaned across and pressed the button for the basement carpark instead. 'Stanko's phone is off, I cannot find him,' he said, 'and I have to be back at work before the evening rush. Time's already really tight.'

Rob's prior knowledge of the basement had been limited to the bins area beside the lifts, but now he was getting to see the full concrete expanse. He carried his suitcase between the cars, avoiding the drips falling from the foil-covered pipes above. The case felt empty, and he still didn't have a clue what he was doing. But there was no time to ask Patrik, who hurried ahead with the other suitcase, like someone about to miss a flight.

Beyond the furthest grid of car spaces was a dimly lit area where a wall of water pumps hissed and clicked behind metal grilles. Checking that no one was watching, Patrik led them behind this wall, into a concealed alcove.

'You take your time,' said the huge man. He was leaning against the back doors of a white van, which had been precision-parked with only inches to spare in the narrow oblong space. He looked at Patrik and then glowered at Rob – annoyed at not being able to place him, or perhaps just hating him on what *he* believed was first sight. Rob did recognise him, however; it was Oleg, the gay-hating Russian from the party. He seemed even bigger and more menacing today, his neck starting at his earlobes, his arse as wide as the van door. He caught Rob looking at his number-plate. Rob smiled quickly and said, 'Hi Oleg,' to prove he was cool and could be trusted – though with what, he still didn't know.

Oleg stared at him, flicking at the ridged button of the Stanley knife in his hand. Rob had a flash of being blindfolded, spun around, bundled into the van. *Robert Rippin found in ribbons*, the papers would say. He must get back upstairs immediately, leave them to their sordid deeds. But suddenly

Oleg was spinning around, like a massive magician, and yanking open the van doors. The suspension bounced as he leapt in between the stacks of unmarked brown boxes. 'Why that cunt no answer his phone anyway?' he said as he knifed through a strip of sealing tape.

'He has to meet someone,' said Patrik. 'He told me to come instead.'

'And bring your boyfriend, because you little gay pussy!'

'Shut up,' said Patrik, rolling his eyes at Rob in apology.

'But you two still better than Stanko,' Oleg conceded. 'Last time he make *me* bring them upstairs because he too lazy to move.' He gazed into the freshly opened box. 'So how much he want today?'

Patrik pulled an envelope of banknotes from his pocket and read out the handwritten list on the back. 'Twenty-thousand Businessman and ten thousand Benson.'

So, this was about cigarettes! Not as shocking as drugs or dead bodies, but even still, Rob couldn't believe the quantities involved.

Oleg was also incredulous at the figures, but for a different reason. He slammed down his knife and came to the door of the van. 'I drive all the way from Dover for pissy little order?'

'Sorry,' Patrik said. 'Stanko doesn't have enough money this week.'

'That asshole lose too much at poker,' said Oleg. 'And he can't make any new money if he don't take his usual order. I won't supply him if this shit continue.' Shaking his head, he began to toss large duty-free style cartons of Benson & Hedges out onto the ground. Patrik showed Rob how to fit them into the suitcases, breaking open the last carton to pack every little gap with individual cigarette boxes, like a game of Tetris. When they were finished it looked as though the cases were stuffed with a kind of carcinogenic gold bullion.

Back in the lift with their tightly packed luggage, Patrik said, 'I'm sorry Oleg is so homophobic. He doesn't even know you are gay.'

'Don't worry about it,' said Rob. 'Actually, Oleg was the reason I never came out to you at the party. I hope you didn't think we were dishonest for not telling you up front?'

'Not at all,' said Patrik. 'I already knew that you and Jo were both gay.

You didn't need to tell me.'

Rob smiled. 'You heard from your friend Vesna, didn't you? She was listening to me and Jo talking on the sofa.'

Patrik frowned. 'I wasn't talking to Vesna since the party. Anyway, she hardly understands English. No, I thought it because the guy who used to live with you before Jo was *really* gay, so I always presume it's a flat of gay friends.'

'I'm not surprised you worked *him* out,' said Rob with a laugh as the lift doors opened. 'You could see Orlando was gay from the moon, never mind across the courtyard.' He dragged his case out of the lift with a limp-wristed mince.

Patrik laughed but then added, 'Well, I didn't notice that so much. But when he kiss and also … how you say … ?' He made a grasping movement that stopped an infuriating centimetre from Rob's crotch.

'Grope?' said Rob.

'Yes. Anyone who *grope* and kiss another man on the balcony must be gay!'

'Hang on,' said Rob, unable to move. 'We're definitely not talking about the same person here. Are you sure you were looking at *my* flat?'

'Dark curled hair. Always wear tracksuit.'

'Christ,' said Rob. 'We thought Orlando was never with any men at all. My boyfriend Michael and I used to say he had, you know … no balls!'

'Well this Orlando have plenty balls when I see him with the other guy. One time Stanko shouted, *dirty faggots*. I was so embarrassed.'

'I don't actually blame Stanko,' said Rob, as they bumped the cases over the threshold of Patrik's flat. 'If I saw Orlando kissing someone it'd make me feel homophobic too. Anyway, what was he like, the other guy?' asked Rob. 'I'm sure he wasn't good-looking, was he?'

Patrik began unlocking the door to the mystery bedroom, though right now Rob was far more concerned – perturbed even – by Orlando's mystery love affair. Rob and Michael had never even held hands on the balcony in all their time together – in fact, Michael loathed even going out there, thanks to the same fear of heights that made him dizzy during engineering inspections of bridges and high-rise buildings. 'No, he didn't look too good,' said Patrik as he revealed an empty room whose floor was messy with cellophane and discarded cartons. He turned and shrugged at Rob. 'He look a bit ugly. Also ... boring.'

Rob gave a relieved laugh as they hunkered down to unpack the two suitcases. 'Now why doesn't that surprise me!'

68

The trendy teenage assistant pulled aside the curtain. 'My name's Tilly,' she said. 'If you need other sizes, just hit the call-button beside the mirror, OK?'

Jo nodded and sank onto the cubicle seat, glad to be alone. She felt slightly out of control; the mirror revealed eyes pinned with coffee-jitters and lust. Her mouth was dry; she scraped her teeth across her tongue and tried to swallow the dried foam. She didn't know what to make of the incident with the G-string – had it been lesbian flirting or just a humorous girly interlude, indemnified against deeper meaning by Lucija's straightness? There was no time to analyse it, though: Lucija was waiting out beside the entrance to the changing rooms, and after Jo's earlier maladroitness, she didn't want to seem incapable of dressing herself too.

Mercifully, the first outfit Jo tried on didn't actually look too bad. The horizontal stripes on the black shirt broadened her skinny shoulders, while the trousers sat exactly on her hips, meaning no camel toe or overlong crotch! She couldn't believe that the dreaded ordeal was already over. Within a few minutes she'd be inviting Lucija to that lovely little pub for a thank-you drink.

But Lucija was less enamoured with the outfit. 'Hmm,' she said, regarding Jo's comedic twirling with a series of angled frowns. 'It's not quite right.'

'It's all a bit … *dull*, innit?' agreed Tilly, coming out from behind her little counter to inspect.

Lucija said, 'What about the burgundy shirt, Jo? The whole thing needs a lift.'

'OK,' muttered Jo, now feeling outnumbered as well as overexposed. She sensed their conspiring eyes on her back during the lonely catwalk back to the cubicle, and heard their continuing critique beneath the electro music. Just as she went to retract the curtain however, there was a wolf whistle, followed by Lucija calling, 'Nice ass in the trousers, though. You should definitely get those!'

Jo hurried blushingly into the booth, delighted but also confounded by the compliment – like so many other signs today, it proved nothing concrete about Lucija's real predilection or motives. Jo yanked off the shirt, with apologies to Topshop for having sweated into the armpits, then put on the burgundy one, only to discover it had about thirty little pearly buttons down the front. On top of this infuriating design feature, the holes were slightly too tight. Pushing the buttons through, especially with trembling hands, was proving almost impossible. She'd only managed to close the bottom two when there was a swish, and Lucija's head appeared halfway up the curtain.

Jo pulled the shirt across her bra and crossed her arms. 'What's up?' she asked, trying to sound casual but feeling like Sister Brigid, who'd always drawn across her blazer when speaking to the school caretaker.

'Whoops, sorry,' said Lucija. She averted her eyes to the floor, but this only made Jo feel worse – in concealing her body, she'd exposed her own stupid prudishness. But she couldn't blame herself either – female nakedness might mean nothing to a straight girl like Lucija, but to Jo it was a precious currency exchanged only by lovers. Lucija said, 'You were taking so long I wanted to check you're all right?'

'It's all these stupid buttons. Give me a couple of minutes and I'll be out.'

But instead of leaving Jo to her struggle, Lucija slipped in around the curtain. She bent down as though about to propose, and grabbed the end of the shirt. 'Right I'll do the bottom ones and you do the top. And in the middle we shall meet.'

'Cool,' said Jo, though she felt anything but. With her forearms still protecting her breasts, she started to work.

After a moment Lucija gave a little grunt. 'You're right. These buttonholes need an episiotomy!'

Jo loved the medical reference but was desperately trying to manage two opposing physical impulses right now – her belly kept flinching every time Lucija's fingers brushed against it, while her arms were almost twitching in their desire to grab Lucija and yank her up into a kiss. 'Episiotomy ...' she said eventually, to cover the awkward silence as they worked. 'That's a really clever way of putting it!'

Lucija looked up from her task and shrugged as though it were nothing special, but then her eyes narrowed when she saw Jo's trembling hands, which had only managed to close a single button. 'Are you OK, Jo?' she asked, rising to touch her on the forearm. 'You're shaking.'

'It's the coffee,' said Jo with a quick laugh into Lucija's face, now level with her own. Lucija was *so* easy to look at that, paradoxically, Jo found it extremely difficult to do so. 'It always makes me a bit jittery, to be honest. Just how much espresso did you put in that thing anyway?'

'Two shots,' said Lucija. 'As is completely regulation for such a beverage, I might add.'

'Well, they must have been pretty potent shots, so!' said Jo, with a nervous laugh and a shake of the head that freed her momentarily from Lucija's piercing gaze.

'It was actually a *decaffeinated* bean, Jo,' Lucija said with a guilty wince.

'Decaf?'

'Yeah. You seemed antsy when you came in,' Lucija said. 'So I took the liberty ...' She looked down at the floor, almost shyly. As she glanced back up, their eyes clicked, and Jo was sure she felt a two-way charge in the air between them, but still, not *quite* sure enough: this could be absolutely everything or absolutely nothing. They remained silent for a moment. The song that had been playing segued into the next, a minimal track with a filthy rhythm and a robotic vocal that kept repeating the line 'I know you want it'.

And then suddenly it seemed Lucija, perhaps spurred on by the song, was raising her hands to Jo's chest and moving in. And everything was being revealed in a kind of dream-motion to Jo, who half-closed her eyes and allowed her body to fall the few inches so that her back was against the wall; she was steadying herself to accept and reciprocate what must surely now be, after all the confusion and mixed messages, their very first kiss.

There was a swish. Tilly's head appeared. 'Another size in the burgundy, is it?'

'No … this one fits her fine, thanks,' said Lucija, looking up calmly from Jo's bust where she was suddenly back working on the buttons. Jo was too startled to speak; it was impossible to tell whether Lucija's hands had coolly diverted within a millisecond of Tilly's appearance, or whether Jo had misinterpreted everything, and a kiss had never been imminent.

'No worries,' said Tilly. 'Just thought you needed something because you pressed the bell.' It was only then that Jo felt the metal knob compressed by her scapula: she didn't know whether to curse it for ruining the moment or thank it for averting an unthinkable misunderstanding. Tilly regarded Jo in the half-buttoned shirt and nodded to Lucija. 'Anyway that burgundy looks bangin' on her doesn't it? She should totally get it.'

'Perhaps,' said Lucija. 'However the buttonholes are incredibly tight …'

'Ah don't worry about those,' said Tilly. 'They'll loosen once she's worn it for a few hours, I swear!'

'I wonder how the girls are getting on with the clothes shopping,' Rob asked, as they came up in the lift with the second round of filled suitcases.

'The date!' said Patrik. 'I had forgotten all about it.'

'Ooh, so today *is* a date, then?'

'But of course.' Patrik looked at Rob disappointedly. 'Wait, did Jo not know this?'

'Not quite. We weren't sure if Lucija was a lesbian or not. There were some … mixed signs.'

'Well, Lucija is definitely lesbian. After the party she asked me if I knew who the *interesting pale girl in the sneakers* was. When I said she was from the gay flat opposite, Lucija was really pleased. The cinema yesterday was her idea actually.'

'Right,' Rob said, slightly jealous that no one had ever made private enquiries after him or boldly turned up on his doorstep the next day. He must text Jo with this enlightening information as soon as he'd finished helping Patrik. Hopefully Jo had already worked it out for herself.

'And what about Jo?' Patrik asked. 'Does she like Lucija?'

'I honestly don't know,' said Rob, pulling his vaguest face. 'She's never mentioned Lucija to me.' Jo would be furious if he revealed too much, especially now their Vesna-fears had been unfounded. It was safest to say nothing.

Patrik frowned. 'Oh, that's a pity. I hope Lucija doesn't make a fool of herself today if Jo is not interested.'

With the second batch of fags now deposited in the bedroom, they raced back down (Patrik was already dead late for work) to pick up the last lot from an increasingly irritated Oleg. Rob was grateful they'd managed to avoid detection by any other residents during the suspicious-looking trips. As the lift ascended for the last time, he smiled at Patrik, happy he'd been brave enough to help out a friend.

The suitcases had been full for the first two trips, but this time they were practically bursting. Taking pity on Stanko's financial predicament, Oleg had thrown in an extra three thousand Businessman on credit, along with a warning that if Stanko didn't pay him back next week, his dick would have a date with the Stanley knife. Rob and Patrik were laughing about how hard it would be to even *find* Stanko's dick when the lift stopped at the second floor.

It was a smiling late-forties couple, whom Rob had never seen in the complex before. They were holding hands. Instead of seeming annoyed at the lack of room caused by the suitcases, they both smiled.

'You go on up, boys,' said the man, standing back. 'We'll pick it up on the way down.' There was something strange about the way he spoke, however – to Rob it sounded like he was reciting a script rather than speaking spontaneously. The woman seemed odd too: she was beaming at the bulging suitcases, and her outfit comprised a belted trench coat, patent high-heels, and a laptop bag so flat and floppy that it couldn't possibly have a computer, or anything else, inside. It was as though she were wearing a 'businesswoman' costume, complete with props. Also, she was a lot better looking than her companion. They didn't seem like a real couple.

Patrik, not being English, was completely oblivious to all this, however. To Rob's horror, he backed into the corner and pulled his case close to his legs. 'Please,' he said. 'We will all fit!'

'Thanks so much,' said the woman, her eyes narrowing in false gratitude. The pair made a joke of squashing in. As the door sealed them all inside, and the now-heavy lift began its agonisingly slow ascent, Rob stared at the YKK printed on the zip of his suitcase and felt the sweat gathering on his lower back. He wondered if the undercover officers would bust them right there in the lift, or hold off and shadow them back to the apartment in the hope of capturing the stash.

He wondered how the couple had timed their arrival to coincide exactly with this delivery, and it was then he remembered the domed security camera above the bins in the basement. It was there to deter unlawful dumping but must have been seconded by HM Customs to monitor the movements of Stanko's cartel. It was no wonder Stanko had suddenly gone AWOL – he'd been tipped-off that a long-overdue bust was finally on. And as a result, the silent black and white footage that the jury would watch in a courtroom (a courtroom that included Rob's sobbing family and a horrified Michael), would depict not Stanko but a silly young Englishman – incontrovertibly Robert Rippin – wheeling masses of contraband around while laughing, chatting and being blasé, as though he'd done it a hundred times before.

'You two been on holiday?' The woman's sudden voice made Rob jump. He looked up to see her nodding enthusiastically at his suitcase.

The man looked into Rob's eyes with a piercing pretence of friendliness and said, 'Yes, boys, been anywhere nice?'

Rob fiddled with the zip on his case. 'Em, well …'

'We're just back from *Mykonos* actually,' said Patrik, flashing a smile at them.

The woman gave a jealous groan. 'Lovely to get some sun on your skin at this time of year, isn't it?'

'Um yes,' said Rob, the colour draining from a face that obviously hadn't seen any sun in months. He was conscious of other giveaway signs – his own wool coat and suit trousers, Patrik's flour-dusted work clothes, and the two suitcases being devoid of any airline stickers. These officers probably heard all sorts of pathetic cover stories, but this would surely take the biscuit.

'You're lucky to have missed the dreary weather here recently,' said the man.

'Well, it was not one bit dreary over in Mykonos,' said Patrik, ostentatiously grabbing Rob's arm. 'In fact,' he said, winding out the words from inside a grin. 'We got *engaged* over there, didn't we, baby?'

Before Rob could answer, the excited congratulations had exploded. 'I knew you were a couple the second I saw you,' said the woman, as they all piled out of the lift together. She poked her boyfriend's belly with her ringless hand. 'What a lovely idea eh, Dennis? To come back from holidays engaged!'

'Lovely all right, Helen.' Dennis rolled his eyes in fraternal fright at the two boys and whispered, 'We only moved in together last week!'

They chatted briefly to the couple until Patrik said he was due back at work after his holiday, and had to get ready.

Helen said, 'Now we're neighbours, hopefully we'll bump into you again and hear how the wedding plans are going.'

'Absolutely,' said Patrik. He slapped Rob on the back. 'In the meantime, let us hope that my boyfriend – sorry, my *fiancé*, don't become a bridezilla!'

Still overcome with relief that they hadn't been arrested, and feeling turned on by the thought of being Patrik's bride, Rob finally found his voice. 'I'm sorry,' he said, with a kind of theatricality that would have befitted Lady Bracknell. 'But if anyone's likely to get their knickers in a twist over flowers and party favours it's *this* one!' Then he gave his husband-to-be a playful shove, and off they went with their suitcases, leaving Dennis and Helen almost crying with delighted laughter behind them.

70

'So here it begins,' said Lydia, as the Saab swung onto the long, undulating driveway of Gravenden Estate. 'We certainly picked a ruddy nice day for it anyway.'

Rachel turned down the Amy Winehouse CD and gazed out the windscreen. She'd been to Gravenden twice before – once with Lydia and later with Corinne from Ascendant Events – but nothing could have prepared her for how breath-taking the estate looked today. It was as though the house and gardens understood the importance of the occasion and had chosen *this* morning, out of all the mornings in their three-hundred-year history, to look their absolute best. Rachel gave a quick gulp at the dashboard faces – always willing to share in her excitement – and gazed out the windscreen with privileged disbelief. The rolling Buckinghamshire parkland was so alive she could almost taste the springtime zing: the trees bristled with the first leaves of the season, the luxuriant grass had been set ablaze by swathes of gold and mauve crocuses and, away in the distance, the boating pond reflected back an inspiringly perfect sky.

Presiding over all this was the magnificent mansion itself. As they drove along, the sunlight caught the granite facade. The random millisecond glints reminded Rachel of the camera-flashes on TV the day she and her dad had sat watching the Olympic closing ceremony in Seoul like nothing had happened, as if her mum hadn't deserted them that same morning. But there was no time to dwell on the past. No, today Rachel must sparkle as bright as that mica, because everyone who mattered was coming: Trenpharm senior management, Professor Geddes, and not forgetting the entire sales force, some of whom she'd beaten to win the marketing assistant job. The absolute perfection demanded by the occasion had even caused Lydia to exclude Narelle – originally promised the role of steward – from attending at all. As Lydia had said on the drive down, neither of them needed Narelle's 'sloppy incompetence' on the most important day of their careers.

As they got close to the house, they saw two huge bouquets of damson and anthracite balloons being unloaded from a van – there were so many that Rachel imagined the man holding them might take off, Mary Poppins-style, and fly up past the tall windows and the stately chimney stacks.

'Now that,' said Lydia, pursing her lips in admiration as he weighted them down safely on either side of the portico, 'is the cherry on the cake.'

'Or rather the *damson*!' said Rachel. 'We are talking about our corporate colours after all.'

'Hilarious!'

The carpark was beside the new accommodation wing, a modern building tucked behind the main house so as not to spoil the view. Although there was loads to do before everyone arrived, Lydia paused after switching off the engine. She propped her Gucci sunglasses up on her perfectly blow-dried hair and turned to face Rachel, whose own hair had been curled by a half-asleep Alysha at six that morning. 'Rachel, I want to say that I'm seriously impressed at how brilliantly you've pulled everything together. And it takes a lot to impress me, in case you hadn't noticed.'

'Oh, please don't jinx things, Lydia!' Rachel said, with a flattered laugh. But in truth, she'd planned everything so well, and managed Ascendant so closely, that the spectrum for mistakes was negligible. Even the little indiscretion with Xenna had caused no negative effect on the final preparations – if anything, she'd been *overcompensating* at work since her lateness on Monday, checking every last detail ten times over.

'Which is why,' continued Lydia, 'I've upgraded your bedroom to a *deluxe*.'

Rachel gasped. 'The ones in the main house … with the four-poster beds?' Only Professor Geddes and Trenpharm's top brass had been allocated such rooms – everyone else was out in the new wing.

Lydia nodded. 'Nothing less than you deserve, Rachel.' She opened the door of the car. 'Right,' she said, blowing out her cheeks, 'let's do this!'

An impressive stage and lighting scaffold had been erected at the top of the ballroom, and the roadies were bent over, duct-taping streams of cables onto the carpet. Hanging at the back of the stage was the custom-made silk curtain. Commissioning it in the Follestra aquamarine had cost a fortune, but seeing it now, Rachel and Lydia deemed it completely worth the expense. After lunch, at the event's climax, Anthony P. Watson would release that curtain to reveal the massive rendition of the Follestra advertisement currently hiding behind it.

The room was filled by sixteen round tables, onto which white-gloved banqueting staff were laying three rows of cutlery and gleaming glassware. The manager, a camp older man whom Rachel had met on a previous visit, swooped in now and then, like a meticulous hawk, to finesse a flower arrangement or primp a bow on a seat cover. Corinne emerged from a side door, clipboard in hand and saying, 'Get a bloody move on' into her mobile phone.

'Over here, Corinne!' called Rachel, keen to show that, as well as everything else, she had Corinne (who was forty and even more stylishly dressed than Lydia) under control.

Corinne hung up and rushed over as quickly as her tight skirt permitted. 'Sorry, ladies, didn't see you come in,' she said, offering them a slightly sweaty hand.

'How's everything shaping up?' asked Rachel.

Corinne pegged her chewed biro into her clipboard. 'Everything's coming along *perfectly*.' She beckoned for them to follow her through the tables. 'Let's go into the conservatory,' she said, over the shoulder of her bolero, 'so you can see how we've set up the registration area.'

Rachel stopped dead. 'No, Corinne,' she said. 'We need a proper look at the stage first. Seeing as that's where all eyes will be focussed.'

'Of course,' said Corinne, turning back a bit uneasily.

'Good call,' whispered Lydia. 'First things first.'

The stage was reached by three metal steps. Rachel went up and paced around, ensuring the platform was both level and sturdy. She looked down and imagined the tables encircled by important people. Lydia would be making the main speech and taking the sales reps through the printed materials that they'd be using to sell Follestra to doctors. Rachel's role was to introduce not only herself (as the person from whom the reps must order their marketing materials), but also Professor Geddes. She had memorised his long biography and now inspected the lectern from which she would apprise the audience of his impressive list of clinical credentials. 'What way will the lights and sound be set during the presentations, Corinne?' she called down.

'Oh, that's all been sorted, hasn't it, Vince?' said Corinne, deferring to the nearest roadie, a sour-lipped, mutton-chopped man of fifty who was winding a lead around the length of his forearm.

'Yup', he said, barely looking up. 'We done a check of everything earlier so it should be fine.'

But 'should' meant nothing to Rachel today. 'If everything's fine,' she said, catching his eye from the stage, 'then you won't mind me having a quick try now. Can you switch on the lights and microphone, please?'

Vince shot her a look more menacing than the hatchet-wielding skeleton on his Iron Maiden t-shirt; then trudged to the mixing desk at the back, where he reluctantly knuckled some switches. An array of coloured beams bathed the stage. Rachel cleared her throat and spoke into the microphone. 'Testing one-two.' Just like in that tacky karaoke place with Gwen, she hated hearing her own voice amplified. It didn't help that Vince was staring at her with derision, as though at an idiot-girl in a suit who thought she knew how to test a microphone. But Rachel didn't care a jot what he thought. 'Testing, testing, *one*-two, one-*two*.' She looked at Lydia, who gave her a nod to show she was impressed yet again by Rachel's tenacity.

'See,' said Vince with a sigh. 'All completely kosher. Can I knock everything off now?'

'Wait a moment,' Rachel said clearly through the microphone. Now she pretended to *be* Professor Geddes, and looked towards the pull-down screen where his slides would be shown. It was lucky she did, too. 'That amber beam there,' she said, holding her hand to her forehead, 'it's catching my eyes whenever I turn to the screen.'

Shaking his head, Vince dimmed the light's intensity, but still Rachel squinted. 'Vince, you're going to have to *move* the light, I'm afraid,' she said. 'We can't have our keynote speaker blinded, thank you very much.'

Vince harrumphed into his sideburns and went off to fetch a ladder. While the light was being repositioned, Rachel went to the back of the stage to check the *pièce de résistance*. Feeling like Prince Charles at the opening of a new hospital wing, she pulled on the tasselled rope. The silk gave way and slipped elegantly to the floor, but then she and Lydia both gasped: there was nothing behind except the bare wall of the ballroom.

Corinne lunged forward. 'No need to panic, ladies! My chap simply forgot a small but essential section of the metal framework. He's belting it back down the motorway as we speak. We'll have tonnes of time to erect it before guests arrive.'

'Well, we better have,' said Rachel, realising why Corinne had been so keen to divert them to the conservatory earlier. She walked to the front of the stage and sternly folded her arms. 'Corinne, there was already confusion about the backdrop because you never sent me the measurements in writing. And now this? Ring that imbecile and tell him to step on it!' She turned to Vince who was descending a ladder. 'Is there some way we can look at the actual artwork in the meantime?'

'Course we can,' he said, weirdly chirpy and compliant. 'Yeah … the guys could roll the panels out flat on the stage.'

'Great,' said Rachel. She was keen to see their advert blown up to such a huge size.

'But …' Vince fixed her with a sinister stare. 'If the vinyl gets kinked or ripped in the process, it'll be on *your* head, OK?'

'Um …' Rachel looked down at Lydia. 'What do you think?'

'We can't risk it being damaged, Rachel. It has to be immaculate.'

'Agreed,' said Rachel. Descending from the stage, she shot Vince a look of contempt. If the misogynistic asshole thought he was going to spoil her show with a damaged backdrop he was surely mistaken. 'Right, Corinne,' she said, 'let's take a look at that registration area!'

Although Rachel had laid out her pyjamas, her dry-cleaned suit, and her dress for tonight's gala dinner on the brocade counterpane, there was still space to get into the four-poster bed for a quick rest before getting ready. Lying on the massive mattress, with her head propped up on the bolster to protect her curls, she wondered what Xenna would make of this place. She saw them driving down here in Rachel's company car some day. As an artist, Xenna would be agog at Gravenden's architectural aesthetic, especially the oak-panelled reception with its statues and oil paintings. But she might just as easily hate the place too – for its long association with wealthy people (the original aristocratic dynasty had sold Gravenden to an even richer hotel corporation in the nineties). Rachel smiled to imagine Xenna proclaiming that the back of the house had been 'bastardised by the cynical addition of the new wing' or that the beautiful artefacts were mere 'props in a soulless show for the stinking rich'. She half-closed her eyes and pictured the battered trilby scandalising the antique hat-stand in the corner of the bedroom, while the pair of them were trapped together, happy and hot, under these leaden bedclothes. After their lovemaking, Xenna would take her pencil and sketch pad to the winged chair by the window, where she would sit cross-legged and capture the landscape in her own inimitable artistic style.

But there was no point Rachel imagining any of this because it was clear Xenna wanted nothing more to do with her. Xenna's standoffishness on Monday morning was one thing, but it had been quite another to discover later that she'd been tampering with Rachel's phone while she slept, deleting the picture message as well as her own number from the redial list. If it weren't for the yellowing hickey on Rachel's boob, she'd be convinced she had dreamed up the whole thing.

She got up and looked out the window. The carpark was beginning to fill up with Saabs and BMWs. Leaning on the open door of his Mercedes was Anthony P. Watson, talking to a couple of attractive female reps. Their combined eyes, as well as the eyes of all the others, would be trained on Rachel in less than an hour. Her stomach lurched, but she remembered her dad's mantra. *Nerves means that it matters.* She smiled to think of him seeing

357

her in such a place, at an occasion she'd been central in creating. This was simply another chance to prove her aptitude for managing challenges. She'd been doing brilliantly so far – she just needed to keep that brilliance going until she was back in that four-poster, tired and satisfied at a job well done. And now, gleaming as it travelled slowly up the avenue, was the limousine that she'd booked to collect Professor Geddes from the airport. With a shiver of excitement she stepped into the cool marble of the bathroom, and began to get ready.

71

The coffee table in the foyer bore testament to *commUte*'s newly extended metropolitan reach. As Jo waited, she pulled last Monday's Dublin edition out of the pile. Perching nervously on the seat, she began to leaf through a paper she'd once regarded as a nemesis but now represented a flare of fresh hope.

It turned out that Jo wasn't the only traitor either. On the centre spread, she discovered her old colleague CeeBee pouting back from a double-page header. It was hardly surprising that the social columnist had jumped ship back home – her new offering, *DubliNights with Ciara Behan*, was so much fancier than the few photo-less inches she'd had in *Dublin AM*. It seemed only appropriate, given Ciara's elevated realm, that she'd ditched her puerile pen-name too. Her main article was surrounded by a montage of glitzy photos. Jo began to read:

L ast Saturday a cabal of biz-moguls and socialites assembled at a mysterious event in The Shelbourne, at which the host, Louis 'The Tycoon' Muldoon revealed in his after-dinner speech just what he's been hiding up the sleeve of his Armani suits these past few months.

El Magnate lived up to his name, unveiling plans to transform a derelict Georgian terrace on the south-city quays into Dublin's first Italian Quarter. Inspired by Tuscan summers at Villa Muldoon, the mosaicked micro-village will feature two trattorias, a prosecco bar, designer boutiques, and an artisan deli-bakery.

The revelation caused intense excitement in the crowd, especially Tamara Nic an tSionnaigh who, in a size-zero LBD, was the first to congratulate Louis on his news. *CommUters* will remember how I recently touted this ever-ascending televisual talent with the ever-decreasing waistline as being the girl most likely to tame Ireland's most eligible bachelor before he hits the big four-oh next year. Louis has always kept his love life extremely close to his well-defined pecs, but even through the haze of too-much complimentary Cristal, this columnist could again detect *Tamouis'* burgeoning attraction for one another. Check out the piccie below-left should you need any proof!

'Joanna Kavan-augh?'

Jo tore her eyes from the three smug smiles, suddenly remembering where she was. The receptionist gestured to the lift. 'Angela's ready for you now,' she said. 'Fifth floor, second door on the left.'

As she read, Angela Tallett's nicotined fingernail picked distractedly at the staple binding the sheaf of *SciFacts* columns. Jo sat opposite, hands sitting neatly on elegantly crossed legs, wondering if the low sounds emanating from the throat of the London managing editor – maybe late-forties, most definitely smoke-damaged – signified approval or its opposite. Perhaps Angela was merely trying to clear the phlegm brought on by her latest fag (smoked while Jo waited downstairs, if the metallic tang in the room was anything to go by). Whatever the case, Jo hoped Angela wouldn't make it to the last page, a piece about the new electronic cigarettes and how, in Jo's opinion, they offered a somewhat healthier option for 'helpless addicts who can't live without their nico-fix'.

'These aren't too bad, you know,' Angela said, looking up just before she reached the offending page.

'Thank you,' said Jo, hoping it was meant as a compliment. 'I used to love putting *SciFacts* together every week.'

'Why in heaven's name did you give it up, then?' said Angela, dropping the sheets in favour of her pen and notepad.

Jo leaned forward like an innocent witness in court. 'Oh, I didn't,' she said. 'The sponsor, Emerald Pharmacies, changed their marketing focus to cosmetics so *SciFacts* got the axe in favour of a beauty column.'

'Charming, eh?' said Angela, who with her straw-like hair and kippered skin, didn't look like she had much time for beauty reviews. 'And after all your work building it up …'

'I was still employed to write general news and feature articles,' said Jo. 'But without my column I lost the passion for the job.'

Angela gave a nod that woke a small flake of dandruff, then reached for Jo's CV. 'I see you studied medicine … ?'

Jo nodded. 'Trinity College only takes the top exam scorers in the country, so it was a huge achievement to even get in.'

'And it would've been an even huger one to graduate surely?' said Angela, raising an eyebrow. 'Then you wouldn't be sitting here desperately trying to cadge a newspaper job off me!'

Jo shrank back and stared at the fine stripes in the trousers Lucija had chosen for her. Lucija. Yet another fuck-up to add to her life's ever-growing list. The shopping trip had petered to a rather pathetic end – without any arrangement to meet again, nor even the exchanging of numbers. While Jo had been paying for the burgundy shirt and the trousers, Lucija had pretended to receive a text from Yésica saying she'd scalded her hand. Marcus wouldn't let her go to A&E until she got someone to cover her shift. And so, on the pavement outside Topshop, Lucija had uttered a rushed goodbye and then bounded off a *tiny* bit too ostentatiously, Jo thought, in the direction of The Dock.

But it was hardly surprising that Lucija had excused herself away after Jo's jittery performance. On the bus home from shopping, Jo had kicked herself when the text came through from Rob saying, firstly, that Vesna hadn't relayed anything back from the party and, secondly, that Lucija *was* gay and the meeting *had* been intended as a date.

Angela's steely gaze told Jo there was no point in prevaricating. 'During college I had some personal issues I needed to deal with,' she said, looking at Angela bravely. 'I sublimated them into my studies. But during my second-year exams they finally surfaced and … well, they needed my immediate attention.' For a second, she could taste the puke she'd spewed over the Botany department's sweet peas as the city sky fell down around her. Despite all the fascinated eyes watching as she'd fled her exam desk, not one person one had come out to help. She'd stood up after her first-ever panic attack, brushing off soil, sick and sweet pea leaves. It was in that moment she had realised that she would never be a doctor. Because it was *gay* she needed to be instead.

Angela flicked imaginary ash from the end of her pen. 'The psyche always overrules ...'

'Exactly,' Jo said, with a calm smile to show that mental frailty was well behind her. 'I took a year out to get to grips with my issues, and then began studying journalism.'

'And what drew you to apply here?'

'I've always greatly admired the *commUte* model,' Jo said. 'It's been a template for so many other freesheets around the world, including my most recent job at *Dublin AM*.'

'Yet despite admiring us so much, you never thought to apply for a post in our Dublin office?'

Jo shifted in her seat. 'I fancied a change from Dublin altogether. Hence why I'm over here.'

'Funny time to emigrate, though? I would've presumed Dublin's *the* place to be, what with this Celtic Tiger we never stop hearing about.'

'But that's exactly it,' said Jo. 'Ireland's so carried away on its newfound wealth that everything's turned into a pretentious rat race.' She felt a sense of treachery, putting down her homeland, especially to an English person, but she had no choice. She'd already told Angela about the demise of *SciFacts* and her psychic crisis. She would look like a total victim if she revealed she'd left Dublin due to the double-loss of girlfriend and best friend, and the eternal fear of running into either. She'd had no contact with Cillian since the day of the race and it made her happy that he probably didn't even know she was living abroad. 'Anyway,' she added brightly, 'I believe it's good to expand one's horizons.'

'Indeed,' said Angela, who appeared to think this perspective refreshing, but then added with a wry laugh, 'I just hope you don't discover that London's more of a pretentious rat race than Dublin!'

Jo came back down in the lift, weary after the inquisition. She wasn't sure if the meaningful glance Angela had given her at the end, while saying that shortlisted candidates would be called back within a fortnight, had been one of congratulation or consolation. Jo asked the receptionist if she could take the Dublin edition from the coffee table, then ducked into a doorway further down the street to examine the photograph.

She had to admit that Louise – or 'Louisa Kealy' as they had (to Jo's delight) doubly miscaptioned her – looked well in her pink dress, diamante necklace and professionally done makeup. The last time Jo had seen that face it had been contorted with rage, but now Louise smiled demurely for the camera. On the other side of the snazzily besuited Muldoon, with her arm interlinked with his, was Tamara. Jo snorted at the idea of him being the girls' beard and their buffer. Surely it must gall Louise to be relegated to Tamara's 'close friend', to constantly feel too paranoid to publicly touch her lover – probably even platonically! And it must be quite the ordeal to have to censor every little action. Something as simple as a kiss caught on a security camera, or a double-bedded hotel booking could set off a career-ruining cascade for Tamara.

Judging by Tamara's appearance, the stress of living a lie in public must be taking its toll too. CeeBee had got Tamara's love life all wrong, but she'd certainly been right in calling her a size zero. She was a breadstick in a dress, her cheeks concave, her collarbones protruding like plough-handles. The only big things about her were her forced grin and her cocaine-dilated pupils. She must be getting through quite a bit of the stuff these days to deal with the problems of being in the closet as her celebrity ascended.

For a second Jo almost felt sorry for Tamara, but then a passing bus blew the newspaper into her face, and she realised she was surmising things to suit herself. She looked again at the picture and saw not a sad addict living in fear of being outed, but rather a rising star with a catwalk waistline who was having the time of her life in the social swirl of the Celtic Tiger. And as for Louise, well, secrecy was a tiny price to pay to shag Tamara on demand and share in the fruits of her success. Jo assumed that Muldoon was in on the joke, but now started to question if he might be gay too? She'd always believed his immaculate grooming and beautiful suits to be signs of affluence, and assumed his romantic privacy was a tactic to keep gossip-hounds at bay, but if he *were* gay then it would make perfect, symbiotic sense for himself and Tamara to actively paint themselves as a nice hetero couple. Their coupledom would dispel any whisperings that might damage their respective careers in kids' TV and red-blooded business, while simultaneously raising both of their profiles. If that was the plan, then it was certainly working. Jo imagined Tamara, Louise and Louis (the matching names would be hilarious if the whole thing weren't so vile) cackling with hilarity on his yacht in Dublin Bay as they scripted the next act in the Tamouis' pantomime, a show whose twists and turns would continually enthral the dumb masses. Louise, with her first class degree in duplicity, wouldn't be short of storyline-ideas, and Muldoon had the cash to make it all happen – a new car for the lady, romantic getaways for two (but secretly for three), even a sparkler to mark the start of a never-ending engagement to Tamara, just before he turned forty.

Jo sighed. Theirs was no difficult double-life – it was an absolute blast, a riot for all three. She slammed the paper closed, then trudged back to the station.

72

Rob left his desk and headed for the stairs. His legs were trembling and his palm trailed sweat on the banister, but by the time he reached Edmond's door, he'd managed to pull himself together. He arranged his face into the expression he'd been perfecting since Monday, a look of innocent ignorance: chin tilted up, mouth slightly ajar, a lucid look in his eyes, which were neither wide with fright nor hooded with deceit.

He took a final, steadying breath, then rapped on the door. 'You wanted to see me?' he said, smiling calmly at Edmond, who looked anything but calm, his cheeks red and his hair chaotic. He stood behind his desk, giving the back of his chair the kind of brutal massage his hunched-up shoulders looked like they needed themselves. 'I've had an email from Lydia,' he said.

Rob tilted his head. 'Lydia ... Bigham?'

'How many bloody Lydias do we deal with? She's threatening to tear us a new one.'

Rob closed the door behind him with a quick sensitivity and turned back to Edmond, his face filling with urgent concern. 'Not something wrong at the launch today, I hope?'

'Just take a look at this.'

Rob went behind the desk and looked at the photo on the screen. He made a little noise of recognition, then looked back at Edmond. 'That's the Follestra backdrop ...'

'Keep looking!' Edmond hissed.

Rob eyes scouted around the photograph, ensuring they didn't snag, even for a millisecond, on the error (noticing it immediately would make Edmond wonder why it hadn't been spotted before). But the mistake was plain as day – screaming out to be read first. Behind the photo, Lydia's email was partly visible; Rob saw the phrases *appalling ... wouldn't have happened if you'd assigned Vicky like I'd asked ... seriously reconsider the account.*

'For Christ's sake, don't you see it?' At that moment, a fleck of

Edmond's vitriolic spittle landed on the error itself, making the offending pixels twinkle in full RGB glory.

Rob quickly turned his head away from the screen. 'Um … no, sorry …' he said, shrugging at Edmond. 'Mind you, I've been looking at this Follestra stuff so long I'm probably blind to it now …'

Edmond rammed his fingertip onto the issue. 'I can't fathom how you allowed this to go to print. If it looks this shit on a small screen, imagine it three hundred times the size. It's turned Lydia's launch into a fucked-up farce!'

Rob gasped. 'Oh, gosh. Now that you say it … Oh no!' He stared silently and sombrely at the screen until enough time had passed. 'Actually, *hang* on a minute, Edmond …' He nodded slowly, as though undergoing a eureka moment. 'They can't blame us for this mistake.' He turned to the boss with a smile. 'Because this is all down to Rachel's Driffield's rule!'

'And which rule is this?'

'She gave me strict instructions that we aren't to type up or edit any text ourselves. She supplies it by email and we're not allowed make a single change.'

'But why did she create this rule in the first place?'

'Oh, she totally over-reacted one day Daryl made a couple of minor typos that I didn't have time to spot before sending it back to her. So she told us to always copy-and-paste *her* text. I never bothered to mention it to you because it was all so silly in the first place.'

Edmond looked back at the screen. 'So, you're telling me that the text on this backdrop was emailed to you by the client?'

'Copied and pasted in without any amends whatsoever,' he said, choosing his words carefully so as not to disclose that it had actually been typed up by the ditzy Australian PA. 'Usually I'd pick up on a mistake like that – you know me – but we'd already been given mixed-up measurements, so everything was redone in a rush.' He folded his arms and gave a little laugh. 'But let's face it, Edmond, even if I *did* have enough time to proof, there's sod-all point because we're not allowed touch their text anyway!'

Edmond smacked the desk so hard that the pens in his Kandinsky mug shuddered. 'If anyone's playing the pedant, it's you, Rob. You should be mortified for not spotting that error, but you only seem to care about covering your own arse, citing some rule that only arose because *you* – and I don't believe for a millisecond that it was Daryl, by the way – kept messing up in the first place. I can't help but get the impression you're actually *glad* Rachel Driffield's day has gone tits-up. You never have a good word to say about the girl, even though she's your most important client right now.' He pushed his chair violently across the room, but one of its wheels snagged on a frayed tuft of carpet, and it came to a rather pathetic halt only three feet away. 'This is all diametrically opposed to what HarropAds stands for!'

Rob quivered. He'd never seen Edmond like this. 'Oh god, no, I would never take joy in—'

'Shut up,' said Edmond. He dialled an extension on his phone. 'Marjorie, I need you to bring a P45 form up to me here. You can insert the name, *Robert Rippin*.'

Rob stared at the mouse pad, which featured a photo of Edmond and his wife at an advertising awards ceremony. He had noticed it on his very first day here, and in the intervening years the couple's smiling faces had been worn away to nothing. He was being fired. And without notice or a reference. What other agency would touch him once word got out? How would he afford his rent? He'd been insane to think he could get away with this.

Edmond started shouting down the phone. 'No, Marjorie, I *don't* know where we keep the forms. I've never had to actually fire somebody before. Download one from the revenue website ... what's that? ... well if you're unable to "work" the internet, then ask someone with at least half a brain cell to help you.'

Edmond slammed down the receiver and turned to Rob. 'I don't know what's got into you lately, but ever since that morning I caught you sneaking in late, there's been something amiss. The person in front of me – and I won't dignify you by saying *man* because you're just an insolent little schoolboy right now – well, he's nothing like the Rob I hired three years ago.'

Rob hung his head. He prayed that Marjorie would be quick. Finally, the door opened. But it was Vicky, puffing and flushed from the stairs, who came in.

'Marjorie told me,' she said with a gasp. 'Please don't fire him, Edmond. I'm not sure what's happened, but if it's anything to do with Follestra, it's not Rob's fault. That Rachel Driffield has stressed him out so much he was bound to make a—'

Edmond raised his hand. 'Vicky, this is none of your concern.'

Rob watched in trembling amazement as Vicky closed the door and laid her hands flat on the desk. 'But it *is*, Edmond,' she said. 'If Rob leaves, then who'll manage his clients? We can't just replace him tomorrow ...'

Edmond gave a sharp snort. 'Rob may not *have* any clients by tomorrow, the way things are going with Trenpharm.'

'But that's nonsense, Edmond,' said Vicky. 'Rob's other clients adore him. Hettie King calls him her "little diamond". I see how hard he works to keep them all happy.'

Edmond shook his head. 'Well, Lydia's far from *happy* at the moment.'

'You don't know this,' continued Vicky, 'but ever since Rachel Driffield accidentally discovered that Rob was gay she's treated him horribly. Clients have the right to be demanding, yes, but this was pure homophobic bullying. All utterly illegal in a work situation by the way, Edmond. It's *support* that Rob needs from Harrop's right now, not his P45.'

Rob's jaw fell open at Vicky's genius move.

Edmond turned to face him. 'Rob, if this is true then why didn't you say something?'

'You've always been very supportive of my sexuality, Edmond,' he said quickly. ' I didn't want you to see my differences as a problem for the company.'

Wiping sweat from his ashen forehead, Edmond went over and sank into his pushed-away chair. His head fell heavily into his hands. 'Oh, I don't know what to do next ...' he muttered. 'This is all too ... too much.' Although a successful businessman, Edmond was a sensitive, creative person at heart – a decent soul who cared about his employees. Rob felt awful; he worried Edmond was about to have a heart attack.

Vicky cautiously approached the chair. 'Would it help if *I* took over on Follestra with immediate effect? I mean, Lydia requested me in the first place ...'

'Lovely idea, Vicky,' said Edmond, looking up. 'But not when you've got your other clients to contend with.'

Vicky shrugged. 'I don't mind working late for the next while. It's not like I've anyone to go home to in the evenings.'

Rob caught her eye, trying to convey his monumental gratitude. He would make it his life's mission to repay Vicky. When this was all over he would bring her out on the town, find her a nice man. It was a travesty that such a beautiful human being should be lonely.

Edmond eventually sat up. 'Rob,' he said. 'I want you to go home, right now, and think about what you've done. Don't even disgrace the doorway of this building tomorrow. And then, on Monday, I want the old Rob back in here, right?'

'Of course. I'm so sorry, Edmond. Nothing like this will ever happen again.'

'It certainly won't.' Edmond rose from the chair. 'Now bugger off, both of you, and leave me to ring Lydia. Let's hope to Christ that she accepts the new arrangement as my apology, and doesn't fuck us off the account altogether.'

73

It had been a day full of newspapers and Jo wasn't sure which had exhausted her more – the interview with Angela or what she'd seen in *commUte*. She lay morosely on the couch, crumpling the clothes ironed so meticulously that morning. With the interview over, and no feedback expected for a fortnight, she suddenly had nothing to distract her from thinking about Lucija. She kept mentally replaying scenes from Monday. If she'd acted like a romantically competent adult rather than a scared little twit, then instead of lying here sickened by the story of Tamara and her two Lous, she could be having a post-interview drink with a far hotter *Lu* of her own, making her giggle at her witty descriptions of Angela Tallett, and then taking her out for a nice dinner, after which Jo would move in masterfully to kiss her.

It was awful to have been practically handed someone so gorgeous, only to ruin it from the get-go. But ruining things was Jo's specialty, it seemed. Even the tea she made after finally rolling free of the couch turned out grey and tasteless, despite being brewed with the Lyons teabags her mum had kindly posted over. Needing some fresh air to quell her headache, she trudged out to the balcony with her mug of self-punishment.

The afternoon had brightened up, and the courtyard was bathed in sunshine. Over in Patrik's, the curtains remained resolutely closed on Stanko's little warehouse. Through the living room window, she could make out a svelte shadow flitting around; Patrik must be home between split shifts at the pizzeria. Jo hoped he wouldn't come out onto his balcony. He must surely have heard what happened on Monday, because he and Lucija went to the gym together every morning. Jo imagined him almost dropping his dumbbells as Lucija told him that the journalist with the 'big interview' had turned out to be a sweating, tongue-tied wreck. They probably thought Jo was rude and ungrateful too – she had been so focused on her own anxiety that she'd neglected to thank Lucija for her help in choosing the outfit.

She sipped on her tea and watched Patrik's shadowy form. It would be impossible to continually avoid him, especially now he and Rob had bonded over Monday's cigarette expedition. She wondered if it might be easier in the long run to go to Patrik's now and ask him for Lucija's number. Jo could then close off the fiasco with a no-response-required text thanking Lucija for the clothing advice. It would show that even if Jo was a twit, at least she was a polite one; it would show that she had no hard feelings over Lucija's fabricated reason for her departure.

Five minutes later, Jo was standing back, smoothing the couch-creases from her clothes and hoping it would be Patrik rather than Stanko who would answer.

It turned out to be neither of the men. Instead, Lucija's face appeared in the gap. 'Jo … ?' she said, but she might as well have exclaimed, 'What the hell are you doing here?' because her expression was undeniably horrified.

The horror was mutual. 'H-e-*hey* … !' said Jo, managing to stammer over a single syllable. She found, yet again, that she was unable enunciate the girl's name; despite whispering it miserably into her pillow over the past three nights. Why should she bother saying it anyway? They would never see each other after today. There was an awful pause then, in which Lucija didn't open the door any further, but looked at Jo through the gap as though at a dodgy travelling salesman.

'I needed to ask Patrik something,' said Jo.

'He's at work. Do you want to come in and leave a note?' The invitation sounded less than encouraging, but suddenly Lucija was pulling the door open, and moreover, giving Jo a first look at the rather alluring post-gym vision.

'No no, you're grand.' Jo stepped backwards, trying not to stare at the damp hair loose about the shoulders of the black Nike hoodie, nor at the sleek capri pants, nor the ribs of sweat across her grey vest. 'It was just a question about … the *bins*.'

'The bins?'

'Yeah. I've forgotten the door-code for the basement and Rob's not home. But by the time Patrik gets back, Rob will be home and I'll be able to get the code from Rob, so I don't need to ask Patrik.' She turned to go before the embarrassing ramble could continue. 'Sorry to have bothered you anyway.'

Lucija looked relieved. 'OK then.' She gave a business-like flash of her eyebrows. 'Bye Jo ...'

Jo headed down the corridor. The hot bloodrush in her ears was so loud that she didn't even hear the door closing behind her. It was both telling and unsurprising that Lucija had said *bye*, rather than *see you*. Jo only hoped she could get back to her own flat before the tears started. She was about to go through the double doors near the lift when there was a shout.

'Wait! You never told me.'

She spun around. Lucija stood in the corridor, her black-clad body cutting a sexily athletic silhouette against the magnolia walls. Jo had to stop herself from racing back – she'd been a pathetic little puppy, following Lucija's every command in Topshop, but there would be no such subservience today. She held her ground and raised her voice. 'Never told you what?'

'How the interview went.' Lucija, it seemed, would also rather shout than approach.

Jo had to raise her voice too. 'I was grilled for an hour by the editor, so it was pretty tough. But she seemed impressed with my old column.' Jo was glad to make some kind of self-redemption. She was even happier still that she hadn't moved an inch: it was plain that this interchange was intended as both final and finite, born out of the polite pretence that Lucija cared about an interview she'd probably forgotten all about in the interim.

'Sounds good. I really hope you get the job, Jo.' Lucija looked away pensively for a moment, before turning back with a furrowed forehead. 'But I do hope something else, too.'

'What's that?'

'That you ironed your clothes first.' She gestured at Jo's outfit with a smiling wince. 'They look pretty terrible, you know!'

Jo looked down in mock surprise and began comically smoothing the creases with her hand. She looked up, biting her lip. 'You don't think they'd have noticed … ?'

They came together in the corridor giggling, shaking their heads in admission of how silly the long-distance shouting had been. 'I can categorically assure you,' said Jo, 'that I did look a *little* bit smarter at the actual interview. It was so tiring that I fell asleep on the couch afterwards.'

'And I'm not much better myself,' said Lucija, with an apologetic gesture that took in her unwashed hair, her sports gear and her makeup-less face. 'I popped here after the gym to collect something for my friend.'

'Oh, don't be silly,' said Jo. 'You look good. You look … well … *fit.*' She'd always fancied good-looking girls the most when they were without their 'faces'.

'Well … fit?' echoed Lucija, the white pixel flashing momentarily in her devastating smile. 'Now, would that be the same as *well-fit, innit?*'

Jo gazed evasively at a fire extinguisher on the wall behind them. She could do with its cooling foam, such was Lucija's hotness at this moment. 'Well, while I did intend the phrase to be taken in the *athletic* rather than the *Lahndan* sense.'

Lucija tipped her arm playfully. 'I'm just kidding,' she said. She nodded back towards Patrik's door. 'Anyway, I was in the middle of making a protein shake to stop my muscles from catabolising. Care to partake of one too?'

Jo smiled broadly – at both the invitation and the gym bunny's incorrigible penchant for pseudoscience. 'Why not … ?' she said with a happy shrug.

'*Whey* not indeed!' said Lucija. With a sexy wink, she turned and led the way back to the flat.

74

'Devilishly handsome edition, isn't it?' said the assistant as Rob handed over his purchase at the till. She was lesbian-looking with short grey hair, and tortoiseshell glasses dangling down a paisley waistcoat. She must be the owner of The Whel-Read Bookshop, this adorable little place with creaking floorboards and mismatched shelves, which Rob had happened upon quite by chance, after getting off the bus in Wheldon Green.

Rob nodded vigorously. 'The second I saw it, I just had to have it.'

'I can resist everything except temptation, is it?' She smiled and put on her glasses to read the price on the back.

'Exactly,' said Rob, thrilled to have got the coded joke. Only ten months ago, before he'd met Michael, conversing about literature with a well-read person would have been beyond him. But now he was holding his own. He must even *appear* more intelligent nowadays, otherwise his new bookish friend wouldn't have hazarded the reference at all.

She slowly typed the price into the ancient beige till. 'That'll be twenty-four pounds ninety-five,' she said, 'unless you'd like it gift-wrapped for another three pounds … ?' She gestured to a roll of paper behind her – like the book itself, the paper was beautifully designed, depicting book spines sitting on pleasantly distressed wooden shelves.

'Certainly!' He wasn't particularly flush right now, but this little shop was helping him forget about the trouble at work earlier; anyway the expense would be paid back tenfold as soon as Michael got his surprise. (Michael probably had most of the material in *The New Collected Works of Oscar Wilde* already, but this book, in its lime and chocolate corduroy binding, would look the part on any shelf for years to come.)

She began to crunch carefully through the gift-wrap with a massive shears. 'Somebody's birthday, is it?' she asked.

'A present for my boyfriend. My boss let me off early, so thought I'd sneak over to his office and surprise him.'

'How awfully thoughtful!' she said. Rob beamed – so now she thought he was both intelligent *and* kind!

When the book was wrapped and taped, and his new friend Fenella had carefully placed it in a ribboned bag (which cost a further three pounds ninety), and attached a hand-stamped gift tag (two pounds eighty-five) with rustic twine (sixty pence), it was time for Rob to leave. 'Well, I do hope your dear beau enjoys the book,' she said.

'It'll be impossible for him not to love such a pretty edition, Fenella,' said Rob. 'As the great Irish wit said: *A thing of beauty is a joy forever*!'

'But, wasn't that … ?' Fenella cocked her head, obviously bamboozled to find that he knew even *more* about Wilde than she'd imagined. But then she said, 'Oh never mind, you two have a wonderful evening!' and sent him off with a wave and a nod of her sweet owlish head.

75

Jo rolled the viscous pink liquid around the glass. 'This is actually quite palatable. The tubs they sell in gyms look so butch I assumed it would taste like anabolic steroids or something!' She took another sip, glad of the distraction of the glass as well as the chance to moisten her mouth, which had run dry with excited desire. 'Not that I know what steroids taste like, of course.'

'All I care about is the protein content,' said Lucija. 'Twenty-six grammes per serving in this one *and* it's whey isolate – the purest form you can get.' They were leaning against opposite counters in Patrik's kitchen. The infamous handbag lay, empty and deflated, on the table between them, like a dead, mustard-coloured reptile. The door to the living room was open, and Jo could see Stanko's cowboy boots sticking out over the end of the couch; Lucija said he was sleeping off a 'particularly catastrophic' poker game. Now and then he would let out a snore so ferocious that it made the two girls look at each other and silently snigger.

Jo finished her whey and cleared her throat. 'Listen,' she said, 'I'm sorry I never thanked you for helping with clothes shopping.'

'I didn't exactly give you a chance to say anything … what with me running off like that.'

'I don't blame you for running off either,' said Jo with a dismal, self-deprecating laugh. 'I *do* hope Yésica's hand was OK, by the way?' She gave a blunt flash of her eyebrows to show she knew it had been a cover story.

Lucija looked down and began to pick at the printed design on her glass, the first unnecessary movement Jo had ever seen her make. 'I was actually quite grateful to poor Yésica for scalding her thumb,' she said quietly. 'It gave me the chance to escape before I made an even bigger a fool of myself.'

'A fool of yourself?' Jo almost spluttered. 'It was *me* who was making a fool of myself, being all anxious like that …'

Lucija looked up from her glass, shaking her head. 'Anyone would feel anxious if they had someone they didn't fancy suddenly coming on to them, during what they thought was a *shopping trip!* I'm sorry for misreading the signs, Jo. I thought you were shaking because you were excited. I thought the reason you never say my name was because you were self-conscious around me, but for the *right* reasons. When I finally plucked up the courage in the changing rooms, I was convinced you wanted to kiss me as much as I wanted to kiss you. Anyway, when I told Patrik what happened, he wasn't surprised – Rob had told him you'd never spoken about liking me, that you didn't even know our trip was meant as a date. When I heard that, all your behaviour on Monday fell into place.' She raised her empty glass at Jo in a toast of sad congratulation. 'Pressing that bell in the changing rooms was a pretty slick move, by the way.'

Jo was beginning to wonder if she was caught in one of the Lucija-dreams she'd been having this week – the kind in which they made coy confessions to one other and then fell together, kissing. Maybe she was actually still asleep on the couch in her interview clothes? She ground her spine into the counter behind her until it physically hurt. She blinked slowly, expecting the mirage to evaporate. But Lucija was still there, leaning against the cutlery drawer, adorably anxious herself now, with her quads relaxing and contracting in a rhythm betrayed only by the sheerness of the capris, and her thumb pulsing up and down on the cord-lock on her hoodie drawstring, as though she were shooting an enemy, or maybe even herself, for saying too much.

In the oven's reflection, Jo watched her own legs step forward. 'Look,' she said, 'about all this …'

Lucija snorted. 'Oh, spare me the sympathy speech, Jo.' She pushed herself sharply off the counter, then went to the table and tried to open the buckle on the handbag. 'I can take rejection, so please don't patronise me with platitudes. The whole thing is humiliating enough as it is …' Her trembling hands eventually managed to open the pocket, from which she pulled out a handwritten list and some banknotes.

'No wait,' said Jo, coming over to the table. 'I need to explain …'

The list quivered in Lucija's fingers. 'So … three hundred Marlboro

Lights,' she read intently to herself. 'Then one hundred and sixty Businessman and eighty Benson.' She directed a doubtful laugh at the page itself. 'That's wonderful, Jelena, but who knows if Stanko even has even that much stock in there nowadays.' She slipped the money under the tattered box of playing cards on the table and put the folded list in her hoodie pocket. 'Right,' she said, laying her hands on the bag and glancing at Jo. 'I better fill this thing and get going. I'm in work in an hour and need to drop these cigs to my friend *en route*. Come on, I'll see you out first.' She put the bag over her shoulder and made for the doorway.

'Lucija!'

The sound of Jo saying the long-evaded name arrested its owner immediately. Lucija remained still for a moment, one foot in front of the other, her eyes fixed resolutely on the floor, as though playing a game of musical statues.

'I didn't mean to press that bell,' said Jo, rushing forward now, across tiles that seem to dissolve beneath her feet. She stood in front of Lucija and grabbed her hand. 'It was just a clumsy accident.'

Lucija stared incredulously at her own fingers in Jo's grip, then gradually began to raise her head, inch by torturous inch – until she revealed a brow crumpled in a hopeful kind of puzzlement. To see such open uncertainty on that gorgeous, angular face made Jo's insides capsize five times over. Lucija said, 'So you mean … ?'

Jo looked into the dilated pupils and confirmed it all with quick but resolute nod; then she stopped breathing as Lucija's fingers – drier and colder, and unimaginably sexier than they had felt in Jo's dreams – closed in to return her grip.

They stood hand in hand then, staring at each other for a long, mind-blowing moment, as powerful as the adrenaline that was now flooding Jo's body. Hyperventilation, palpitations, feeling derealised, tingling limbs – it was like an immensely pleasurable panic attack, one where the world was *beginning* rather than coming to a terrible end!

The handbag slipped to the floor. Their two noses brushed briefly and obliquely off each other. Jo's heart and crotch had fallen into hard tandem gallop – like two beat-matched techno tracks on adjacent turntables. She gazed down at Lucija's mouth, at the jagged perimeter of the white filling on her incisor, at the particles of whey on the vermilion border of her lips. She was so gorgeous and adorable and meltingly sexy that Jo could hold back no more; she closed her eyes and moved in for the kiss.

But her hungry mouth found nothing: Lucija had pulled back.

'What's wrong?' whispered Jo. She prayed this wasn't some big mistake, some cruel booby trap.

Lucija blinked at her slowly. 'Say it again.'

'Say what?'

'My name. I liked how you said it just then.'

'*Luci*—' Jo closed her eyes and whispered into the fast-closing gap between their lips, letting the final '—*ja*' melt into their first-ever kiss.

76

Fenella had wished him a wonderful evening, and as Rob meandered down Wheldon High Street towards Michael's office, he felt that it would be, despite everything that had happened with Edmond and Fussbudget's backdrop earlier. He'd already spotted Nagano, which would be perfect for an early dinner later on. It would be nice to get a sense of Michael's working life by spending this evening in Wheldon, especially with his home life so impenetrable. Rob had still only been to Reading that one time, and with Norman's two-year anniversary approaching, poor Joan was going through a bad patch, which meant meeting her wasn't yet appropriate. But meeting Joan didn't matter right now: as Rob pushed open the steel-framed door of Stedman Sheppard Structural he got a thrilling sense of how life had progressed since the night of his secret visit here.

The back wall of the foyer was covered by a massive photographic mural of a suspension bridge, all rivets and plaited cables – no doubt one of Michael's projects! As Rob waited for the receptionist to finish her phone call, he flicked his eyes beyond the mural and up to the ceiling. Suddenly he could *feel* Michael's presence just a few floors above. It felt like an invisible beam was connecting them – a beam so strong it could penetrate through the concrete and the metal and whatever other fancy load-bearing structures SSS had engineered into their own building. Rob wondered if Michael, sitting there in his chinos and one of his neat gingham shirts had noticed the feeling too – he would look up from his desk, puzzled by the sudden, inexplicable buzz of warmth and love.

Well, he wouldn't be puzzled for much longer, because the receptionist was finally off the phone. Rob stepped forward. 'I'm looking for Michael Wyles, please.'

She frowned at him and his gift bag for a second, then ran her finger down a list of names on a clipboard beside her. 'Michael *Wyles*, you said … ?'

'He's one of the engineers. A *senior* engineer, in fact!'

'O-*kay.*' She turned the page and Rob realised she must be a temp because she didn't have a clue. There was little point in telling this one that the three interlocking S's on the sign outside would soon have to make room for a W, once Michael's directorship was announced.

'I'm afraid Michael's actually working from home today,' she said eventually.

'At *home*?' Rob felt the invisible beam evaporate. Michael was out in bloody Reading! He pictured a laptop open on Joan's dining table and the old bint hovering around, disturbing her son from his work just like she disturbed him in everything else.

'He often works from home on a Thursday.'

'Oh?' The suspension bridge swung on its wires like a fairground swingboat. Michael had never mentioned working from home at all, let alone on frequent Thursdays. This news was a confusing worry, and quite hurtful too. But Rob knew there must be an innocent explanation for it all; Michael probably wouldn't consider it newsworthy enough to mention whether his backside had been on a seat in Wheldon or in Reading. He was such a great conversationalist that he didn't need to resort to gabbing about every triviality of his life.

The receptionist nodded. 'Most of the *actual* engineers are in-house on Thursdays for the team meeting, so the subcontractors tend to clear off. We're actually a bit short on workstations in here nowadays!'

'OK,' said Rob, by now completely confused, because Michael was an *actual* engineer rather than some random subcontractor. He didn't bother correcting the temp's mistake – he wanted to keep her sweet for his next request. He held up the gift bag. 'Can I please leave this for Michael to collect tomorrow morning instead then? It'll be a nice surprise for him.'

'Sorry,' she said, nodding at a camera above. 'Security's up to the max here since 7/7. We're not allowed to take in anything unofficial.'

'Well, I'm hardly a terrorist now,' Rob said with a laugh. He untied the ribbon. 'See, it's actually just a book by Oscar Wilde. I'd open it to show you, only this wrapping paper's just cost me a fortune!'

She shook her head. 'Look, if you're so desperate to get it to Michael, why not just pop round to his place and give it to him yourself?'

He gritted his teeth at her idiocy. She needed a basic geography lesson if she thought you could just 'pop round' to Reading from here – it must be fifty miles! Even more infuriating was her suggestion that Michael's was the kind of house you could just call to unannounced. She wasn't to know about the eggshell-complexity of the Joan situation, but Rob still wanted to punch her for suggesting something so preposterously impossible. 'It's fine,' he snapped. He turned on his heel, muttering, 'I'll give it to him in person on Saturday.'

Outside, he tramped down the steps, wondering what the world was coming to when you couldn't leave a beautifully wrapped Oscar Wilde book in your own boyfriend's office.

It killed Jo to stop kissing the salty skin above the neckline of Lucija's vest, but it was impossible to ignore the issue for any longer. Shifting her weight off the windowsill, she reached down and freed the ends of the dangerously tautened curtains from beneath her. 'Sorry,' she whispered, 'but it would've been ignominious to get killed by a curtain pole ...' She pulled Lucija back between her thighs, loving the silky feel of the capris as they glided against her interview trousers.

Lucija kissed her grin into Jo's mouth, and a moment later they were snogging as though making up for a year of absent yearning rather than the few seconds it had taken to free a curtain. Jo was already in love with Lucija's lean, muscular tongue; she closed her eyes and drifted into the random rhythms of their kisses, falling over and over in this deep, unbelievable dream.

It was funny that they'd wound up among the little piles of cigarette cartons in a room whose mystery had intrigued for so long. Their initial clinch earlier in the kitchen had come to a necessary halt when Lucija's hoodie – the only piece of clothing either of them had discarded so far – had, in its removal, knocked the protein shaker onto the tiles. Stanko had shifted on the couch and called out in sleepy Slovenian. With a finger pressed to Jo's mouth, Lucija had led them to this bed-less bedroom, where the closed crimson curtains had painted everything a sultry bordello-red.

Jo was glad of this forgiving tinge to proceedings, especially now Lucija was getting to work on the top buttons of the interview shirt. The dim red light would hide both her Irish pallor and her frugal application of Holiday Skin, which she'd limited to the areas that would be visible at the interview.

'That Topshop-Tilly was such a liar,' Lucija growled between kisses. 'These buttons haven't eased up at all!'

'No buttons on yours, though,' said Jo with a cheeky smile. She yanked Lucija's vest over her head in a confident movement that released a warm waft of degrading deodorant. She dropped the top onto the nearest pile of cigarette cartons.

'That's cheating!' said Lucija, but Jo was thrilled at her own boldness, because neither her earlier palpations through the vest nor her wet dreams during the week could have prepared her for Lucija's torso in a Nike sports bra. Jo almost wanted to push Lucija back to take in the magnificent vision as a whole but had to make do instead with little close-ups between kisses and Lucija's dogged unbuttoning. She loved how Lucija's pecs flared beyond the edges of the grey bra and was awestruck by the four-pack embellishing her bellybutton. There were the sleek obliques too, which ended in abrupt muscular ridges just above the leggings. And all these wonderful structures were encased in sallow skin so uniform, without freckle or imperfection! Jo could be an abstracted admirer no longer. No, she needed all this perfection pressed hard against her own bare skin.

'Your shirt!' said Lucija when she saw what was happening.

'Fuck the shirt ...' Jo tugged even harder at the placket, until the remaining buttons popped off their threads too. A second later their chests and bras (Jo was thankful she'd worn a good black one for the interview) were rammed together in a hot mess, while Lucija's newly emancipated hands clamped Jo around the waist and pulled her into a tight pelvic grind that made her nearly explode through her trousers. As they kissed again, Jo ran her fingers slowly down the slopes of Lucija's lats, tracing the amazing taper down into the wiry little waist. On their way back up, Jo's fingers found something they couldn't explain – a fascinating, callused patch on Lucija's spine, just above the Y of her bra.

'From squats,' said Lucija. 'The barbell ... abrades the skin.'

'Oh no,' said Jo, melting into protectiveness. 'Doesn't the gym have those foam pad things?'

Lucija pulled back. 'Real squatters don't use the *pussy pad*, my dear!' she said. 'Anyway, those things cause mayhem with the leverage mechanics.'

'Well, that's me told,' said Jo with a smile and snuffle. 'You gym bunnies are so into your little bits of science. A guy in the gym once lectured me about my *posterior deltoids*, you know, the muscles at the back of the shoulder.

It was hilarious!'

'You think?' Lucija asked drily, as Jo's hands slid down to check out the *real* evidence for all these squats. As she massaged the pert, self-assured ass through the Lycra, Lucija responded with a succession of deepening sighs. But even in her reverie, Lucija's dexterity hadn't deserted her: in a deft, single-handed movement she reached back and unclasped Jo's bra. Jo shivered with pleasure as the length of Lucija's gym-hardened palms ran over her boobs. She thought of reciprocating the favour, but Lucija's racerback would be harder to take off, and anyway the sight of her erect nipples flanking the bra's white swoosh was so incredibly sexy in itself. Instead, Jo got more daring elsewhere, sliding her fingers under the waist of the leggings and touching the curved, knickerless skin, something which made Lucija, despite all her squat-strength, go momentarily weak at the knees. After a moment she pulled Jo's right hand round to the front. 'Touch me,' she whispered.

Everything was suspended. Jo gulped at the thought of what she was about to do. To *Lucija!* But then came the weird sense of being watched. Yes, Louise was smirking in the shadows by the door. She was loving the show between a pent-up Jo, who pathetically hadn't been with anyone since they'd split up, and a coffee-shop girl, and it all happening in a stash-room for smuggled goods.

'Jo ... ?'

Jo blinked and found that nobody had come to judge – there was just the two of them. Alone. Here in this strange red room. And her hand was inside the gym-pants of an absolutely gorgeous girl, touching clipped pubic hair that was as soaked as Jo's own. What the fuck was she waiting for? With a little grin at the bra's *JUST DO IT* swoosh, her fingers sprang back to life. But just as they made their first, teasing stroke through the wetness, there was a sudden shout from the sitting room.

'Lucija? Luci-*jaaa!*'

They froze and waited, panting into each other's mouths. Jo prayed that Stanko would assume Lucija had already left and would fall back asleep. But then came the incontrovertible clatter of cowboy boots hitting the sitting-room floor, and just a moment later, those same boots seemed could be heard advancing quickly towards the bedroom.

'So what did you tell Stanko?' Jo asked, as they came out onto the street. She was trying to look composed, but it was impossible to contain this weird mix of hot-faced elation and blue-balled disappointment. She felt like a twit in her button-less shirt; despite her best efforts to hold it closed, the ends flapped up with every passing car.

Lucija, back in her vest and hoodie, betrayed no such traces of sexual discombobulation. She swung Jelena's cigarette-filled handbag over her shoulder. 'Oh, I just told him to give us two minutes because we were in the middle of a hot making-out session.'

'No!' gasped Jo. 'What did he say?'

'That next time we are to use *his* bed. But we have to wake him up first because he wants to watch.'

Jo laughed. In the lift down she'd nearly suggested they divert to her own bed in the opposite block. But Lucija was due at work, and anyway the momentum had been spoiled by the arrival of Stanko, whom Lucija had managed to arrest at the bedroom door, before he caught too much of an eyeful. Now, as she walked Lucija to the crossroads, Jo thought it would be better to deliciously digest what had just happened, and then start afresh the next time. Her insides tingled at the thought that, as soon as tomorrow, she and Lucija could be naked together in Jo's bed, or even Lucija's, wherever that might be. Jo still hadn't had the opportunity to find out where she lived; she didn't even know her surname! But those were things she would delightfully discover very soon.

Lucija grimaced at her watch. 'I better head off.'

'You don't want Marcus Interruptus getting annoyed!'

'I've already had enough interruptus for one day,' Lucija said, making Jo smile wildly because, after an hour of paying homage to Lucija's physicality, she'd temporarily forgotten about her mental prowess. Jo decided at that moment that she must get Lucija started on some kind of educational course without delay – if Jo got the *commUte* job, she could even contribute towards the fees! She pictured herself helping Lucija with her assignments and giving her pep talks and shoulder massages before her exams. On the day that the new student proudly received her certificate (perhaps her first-ever qualification), Jo would be showered in gratitude. Lucija could repay the tutelage in her own unique way – by teaching Jo how to lift weights properly. Jo saw her newly defined biceps wrapped around Lucija's sexy neck, their taut stomachs stuck together, their iron legs entwined.

But such things were in the far-off fun of the future. Right now, Jo needed to know something much more immediate. 'Are you working tomorrow?' she asked.

'Seven to four.'

'I could meet you at The Dock at four, then?' She would take Lucija to that pub in Fitzrovia. As they shared sweet smiles and life-stories over pints, their knuckles would drift sensually together on the bench.

Lucija shook her head. 'Not tomorrow. I have to go to college after work.'

'You go to college?' Jo said, unable to hide her surprise. She was cross at missing the chance to become Lucija's educational saviour but then realised that everything from traveller's Spanish to DIY was taught in so called 'colleges' nowadays. It might even be a 'barista college' where you learned to create ever more elaborate hearts and ferns. Well, Jo could certainly help her to achieve more than that!

Lucija seemed to sense Jo's suspicions. 'Yes, I go to college,' she said, before adding sharply, 'or *uni* as they prefer to call it here.'

Jo clung precariously to the edge of her self-made pedestal. 'Wow, uni,' she said in a small voice. 'Are you studying anything … interesting?'

'I'm doing a PhD in human bioenergetics.'

'A PhD?' Jo gagged on each letter.

'The logical continuation of a Masters, surely … ?' said Lucija, as though speaking to a clueless child at a university open day.

Jo swallowed. She didn't have a Masters, let alone a PhD, nor any scientific qualification at all. She was scared by Lucija's cold expression. 'I'm only surprised because you never mentioned uni, so I assumed you just worked at The Dock,' she said. She hated how snobby it sounded, and cringed to remember her earlier digs at gym-bunny science.

'I *just* work at The Dock,' said Lucija in acidic imitation of Jo, 'so that I can pay my way. And having a manual job gives me the headspace to plan out my thesis too ...'

'Wow, fair play to you for juggling all that,' said Jo, who'd never had a part-time job during term-time and had *still* managed to fail medicine.

Lucija raised a patronised eyebrow, then hammered hard on the button for the pedestrian crossing. 'I'm going now, Jo,' she said, her eyes fixed on the middle of the road.

'OK.' Jo was afraid to say any more lest she put her back-pedalling foot in it again. The lights changed and Lucija and the handbag crossed the street, leaving Jo alone in her gaping shirt, and with the lump that had been throbbing between her legs now firmly lodged in her throat.

78

Even Rachel's wheelie case seemed intent on punishing her. As she went down Wheldon High Street, it kept lurching forward to savage her ankles, one of which was now bleeding through the hole in her tights. But she could have no complaint – no, she deserved all the pain coming to her, and a lot more besides.

She wasn't even supposed to be walking home, but Lydia's original offer to drop her back had been silently and unsurprisingly rescinded. Since their breakfast in Gravenden, Lydia had barely spoken to her. The lavish hotel spread had turned Rachel's stomach. She'd forced down a lump of melon, aware of the looks and the dim – but not *quite* dim enough – whispers of the reps who were breakfasting, so heartily and happily, around her. Sitting opposite and avoiding all eye contact, Lydia had sipped her black coffee as though it were battery acid. This forced Rachel to focus on the conservatory behind, where, worse again, she kept catching the thunderous eyes of Anthony P. Watson each time he turned the page of his *Financial Times*.

The drive back to the office had been appalling too. Rachel had stared ahead, her molars ravaging her cheeks, wanting to smash her head off the dashboard until her skull split open like a walnut shell. *Sloppy incompetence* – a phrase previously reserved for Narelle, but which Lydia had levelled at Rachel directly after the launch – had played over and over in a sickening mental loop. When Rachel had tried to explain what had happened (it was only fair to offload *some* of the blame onto Narelle and HarropAds), it had only infuriated Lydia even more: 'Given the resize was a joint effort between that dimwit Narelle and an agency with poor attention to detail, why didn't you check the artwork when you finally arrived in on Monday? I trusted you to get everything right, Rachel. I wish I hadn't been so fucking stupid.'

She passed the Wheldon off-licence, where a youthful queue was buying Friday night supplies. She wanted to get a bottle of some particularly toxic spirit. She'd heard that absinthe knocked you right out. She could drink herself to death, or at least into a stupor where she'd temporarily forget. But she couldn't face pushing her way through a shopful of denimed trendies in her stupid suit and ripped tights. She was so tired and uncoordinated, she'd probably knock down that big vodka display anyway. She hadn't slept a wink in her four-poster prison; she'd lain rigid all night, reliving the moment when her excited pride had changed into a desire to die. The dreaded dawn had revealed bloodied drool on the silken pillowcase, and her evening dress lying unworn, like a corpse, beside her.

WWWheldon looked busy tonight too. She spotted her creepy, comb-overed counterpart through the window, his lips ajar as he savoured whatever unthinkable images were on screen 27. Rachel walked quickly past the door, realising she was no better than him: hadn't she spent night after night sequestered in that same sordid corner? And for what? A sequence of events that might now have ruined her own career, as well as Lydia's. If she'd needed a sign to stop this insane dabbling in the lesbian world, then she'd duly received it.

A van stencilled with *Jedd Fletcher & The Fletchlings* was parked up on the footpath outside The Wheldon Arms, leaving only a narrow gap. Rachel remembered borrowing that very same 'Fletcher' in order to extract Olivia's surname from Tiny – all that stupid trouble she'd gone to, and for what? A middle-aged roadie who'd just extracted a bass drum from the van saw Rachel's approach and took great trouble to get out of her way, clutching the heavy instrument tight against his chest. 'Sorry, my lovely!' he called at her through the gap, 'you come on through!' This simple act of kindness, the only nice thing that had happened to her all day, brought tears to her exhausted eyes, and by the time she reached the flat, the sleeve of her good coat was soaked in snot and tears. It was ironic that the kindness had been bestowed by a roadie, given that Vince had been the one to take *the* most pleasure out of her misfortune. She'd had to endure his jibes during the de-rig earlier, while Lydia was out in the foyer desperately trying to salvage her reputation with Anthony.

'At *forty-two* Rob deserves more!' Vince had sung it over and over as he wound up the cables and dismantled the scaffold. Rachel had sat alone at a stripped banquet table, trying not to look up at the stage, where the backdrop hung like an unending scream (taking obvious delight in her discomfort, Vince had instructed his crew to 'leave that thing up until the bitter end, boys'). She kept recalling the moment when Anthony's cuff-linked wrist had released the curtain with a flourish, and his beaming pride had faded to puzzlement as he wondered what the audience – and even Professor Geddes himself – found *quite* so amusing about the new Follestra ad campaign.

Before Vince uncoupled the microphone from the lectern, he'd switched it on one last time. 'No need to look so sad, love,' he'd boomed down over the speakers while giving a nod to the backdrop. 'If your new drug can make every forty-two-year-old look as fresh-faced as this dude, you lot'll be *rolling* in it!'

'Is that the pharma-launch queen?' Alysha called from behind the sitting-room door.

Rachel froze in the hall. 'Just give me two minutes to freshen up, OK?'

'No,' said Alysha. 'Get in here *now* and tell all.'

Rachel dried her eyes and forced a smile. Inside she found Alysha sitting barefoot and cross-legged on the sofa, her body turned towards Stuart like an attentive yogi.

Alysha waved her hands as though displaying a prize on a game show. 'Look who I found loitering beside the meals-for-one in Tesco!'

Stuart stood up hurriedly and said, '*Rachel*,' as though it was both a greeting and an apology. Rachel found she was utterly unable to approach him. Alysha took the inertia as excited surprise, however, and beamed at her own stroke of genius.

Stuart said, 'I knew you'd be tired, but Alysha practically kidnapped me!'

'Resistance was futile, eh, Stuey?' said Alysha. 'Well come on, give her the …'

He bent behind the sofa. Rachel cringed at the crinkle of cellophane.

'Sorry, they're only Tesco's,' he said. 'Just to say congratulations on your launch!'

She took the flowers, but all she could look at was the label: *Large Mixed Bouquet. Display Until 25/2/07*. Beneath that, Stuart had peeled off the price tag, but a triangle of stickiness remained on the lurid cerise wrapping. It was ridiculous that they still couldn't invent stickers that could be cleanly removed. She stood, unable to speak, the bouquet growing so heavy it took all her energy not to drop it.

Alysha got up. 'So say thanks, you daft mare.'

Stuart gave a nervous laugh. 'I should have gone to the nicer Interflora place …'

'Nonsense,' said Alysha. 'They're gorgeous.'

Their conversation seemed to fade into the background, like sounds heard directly before falling sleep.

She's just knackered, Stu … I know, Alysha, probably up late with the pharma crowd toasting her success … She'll come back to life with some TLC … That's my plan, Alysha!

'I'm sorry,' Rachel's voice was weak, woozy. 'I'm just so … *tired* after everything.'

Alysha sighed with relief and put on her trainers. 'Right, this gooseberry's off to Mel and Ollie's.'

'But it's Friday night!' Rachel's voice sprang back to life. 'They'll be in The Mill.'

Alysha gave her a strange look. 'Nope, they're at home.'

'But you told me they went every Friday?'

'I didn't mean every *single* Friday,' said Alysha. 'You're way too literal, girl.' She gave them a saucy wave as she left the room. 'You lovebirds have fun. But don't use up *all* your energy Rach, as we've got our long-awaited shopping date tomorrow!'

Stuart took the flowers gently from Rachel and laid them on the couch. 'You must need a hug after working so hard.'

Her cheek pressed against his shirt as he massaged her back. So much had happened since she'd last seen him; things she could never reveal to him or anyone else.

'So, I better tell you about my next surprise,' he said.

'What?'

'Now the launch is over, I'm booking us a weekend away in Cornwall. I've found a cute little cottage—'

Her eyes sprang open on his shoulder. 'Sounds idyllic,' she said, thinking quickly, 'but Sensei's told me I cannot miss another Saturday.'

'Which is precisely why,' he said, raising her chin to look into her eyes, 'it's happening during your annual judo break!'

She shook her face free of his hand. 'What?'

'Sensei Kev always goes to Tenerife the second week in March. Don't worry, me and Alysha have it all worked out.'

If she thought the previous day's events had broken her, she was wrong. Something inside her – some last thin little stick – snapped sharply in half. 'So Alysha's been conspiring with you to rearrange my life? Well, that's just delightful.'

He stepped back. 'God, we weren't conspiring, we just thought you needed a break from—'

'You two don't know the first thing about what I need,' she roared.

His face crumpled. 'Well, you obviously don't *need* me around here right now. Do you? ... Answer me Rachel. *Do you?*'

She shook her head. She felt awful for him, but he'd find a new girlfriend no problem. The question was: who was *she* ever going to find?

He snatched his jacket and waved it crazily at the door. 'I'll just piss off then, shall I? I should never have let Alysha drag me here, she said you'd be over the moon to see me.'

Rachel gave a sarcastic laugh. 'She only invited you here because she wants to fuck you herself!'

'Well, at least *somebody* wants to,' he said. 'I've been so patient about your stupid launch, Rachel, and *this* is my reward?' He stared at the switched-off television, his chin trembling. 'So, who is he then? Some hotshot pharma bloke with a flashy Saab? Up all last night fucking him in the posh hotel, were you?'

Xenna's anything-but-posh futon ... her intoxicating kisses ... Rachel's face between her legs, then Xenna's between hers ... writhing ... sucking ... licking ... then that gut-wrenching brush-off at the end.

She turned to him. 'Just go, Stuart.'

'With pleasure.' He grabbed the bouquet and rattled it violently in her face. 'And I'll take my poxy flowers with me.'

The door slammed in the hall. Through a blur of fresh tears she watched a pink petal flutter slowly down, coming to rest on the carpet. Then, with a visceral wail, she crumpled onto her knees beside it.

79

Rob turned the business card over in his trembling hands. 'And you're absolutely sure you found this in *Jo's* bedroom?' It was Saturday afternoon in the kitchen, and if it weren't awkward enough having a man in a dress cleaning your home, something terrible was unfolding.

'Of course Noeleen's sure!' said Jo.

'I haven't even ventured into your room yet, Rob,' said Noeleen in a matter-of-fact way that made Rob want to punch her, or him, or whatever the hell *it* was. 'My duster brought it down from the top of Jo's wardrobe, so I left it on her bed in case it was important. Hope I haven't done something wrong … ?'

Rob glowered silently at Noeleen. He felt sick – the toast he'd eaten earlier was coming back up, crust first. He slumped onto a chair.

'It could just be old,' said Jo, examining the card again. 'Maybe Michael *was* a freelance CAD technician when he first started out.'

'Then how do you explain the qualifications list on the back?' said Rob.

'Certificate in Advanced AutoCAD, 2006,' read Jo. 'Only last year?'

'And, worse still, look at his address, Jo.'

'Flat 47, Block D, Wheldon Court, Wheldon Green Road. But I thought he lived in Reading with mummy dearest?'

'Didn't we all,' said Rob, with a sad, tart laugh to fend off the tears. 'I could understand if it was the Hammersmith flat he had before his dad died, but *Wheldon Green*? It's no wonder the Stedman Sheppard receptionist told me to pop over to his place. I could've walked right past the lying bastard's flat on the way home for all I know. Maybe he looked out the window during a dull moment of his *freelance CAD* work and saw me trudging along with my Oscar Wilde book.'

Rob hadn't even noticed Noeleen putting on the kettle, but suddenly she was placing a cup of strong tea in front of him and stirring in two heaped sugars.

'Hang on,' said Jo, tapping the card off the table. 'You two met online, didn't you?'

'His profile said *An engineer who's Wilde about theatre*,' said Rob. 'Wilde about lying more like! Anyway, what's that got to do with this?' He took back the card.

'*Everyone* tells white lies online,' said Jo. 'Maybe he's been wanting to come clean about not being a high-flying engineer for ages. He could have secreted that card in my room so that I'd find it first and tell you. A kind of staggered revelation.'

'If he's so into managing his impression,' said Rob, 'then why pretend to be tied to mummy's apron strings when he actually has his own place? No, this whole thing stinks.' He got up and began pacing around. 'We're meeting later on and I'm going to have it out with him.'

Noeleen stepped forward. 'Rob, I really don't think you should confront him tonight.'

Rob shot her a look of contempt. What on earth did he-slash-she know about relationships? 'I can't wait around, Noeleen,' he said. 'I'm going more insane by the minute, in case you hadn't fucking noticed.'

Jo shoved his shoulder. 'No need to be so rude, Rob.'

But Noeleen remained composed. 'I was actually suggesting you don't wait until *tonight* to confront him,' she said with a slow nod at the card.

'You mean … ?' Rob stared down at the address, then looked back at her.

'Why suffer a second longer?' said Noeleen. 'I think you should go over to Wheldon Court right now.' She gestured to Jo to get the magnetic pen and notepad from the fridge door. 'I know the place very well, in fact. Let me write out some directions for you.'

80

WHSmith on the high street was so hot and airless that Rachel thought she would faint. Standing behind Alysha (who was unashamedly reading magazines she'd no intention of purchasing), she loosened her scarf and fanned herself with a Littlewoods insert that Alysha had let slip to the floor. She had no idea how she was going to face judo at two.

Alysha tilted a page towards Rachel. 'That dress would be fab on you.'

'You think … ?' Rachel cursed herself for promising Alysha they'd go shopping in Wheldon as soon the launch was over. Alysha still had no clue about the dual disasters of the launch and last night. That morning, she'd excitedly brought breakfast-for-two into Rachel's bedroom only to learn that Stuart had been 'called away' in the early hours to turn off an alarm at one of his properties. She'd assumed Rachel's wild hair and puffy eyes to be the consequences of crazy sex – claiming she'd even heard Rachel yelping amorously through the wall during the night. Little did she know the sound had been sobbing. Miraculously, Alysha hadn't noticed the absence of last night's bouquet, but only because she was too caught up in helping to arrange Cornwall, a trip which Rachel was pretending to be delighted about, while simultaneously racking her frazzled brain for a way to explain why she wouldn't be going there, nor anywhere else, with Stuart ever again.

Alysha picked up a thick edition of *Cosmopolitan*. As Rachel looked around for an escape, something printed beside Amy Winehouse's beehive on the cover of *NME* caused her to double-take. She went over to the music section and frantically leafed through the pages.

Even if the article hadn't been titled 'Get LOST this Summer!' she would have recognised the cheekbones and shaggy fringe in the photo as being the same ones from the pencil sketch. Since Monday she'd been dying for an opportunity to google Xenna's famous girlfriend. Now, as she stared at the photo taken in a graffitied toilet – not unlike the one where Rachel had met Xenna – she throbbed with her proxy sexual connection to a singer the magazine was touting as 'the new empress of wonky-pop'.

It seemed Rachel wasn't alone in having to hide her liaison with Xenna, either: in the accompanying interview Lynette admitted to being 'terminally single' and to having a 'megacrush' on actor-model Theo Lindahl, her Swedish co-star in the video for her debut single, 'Loved Every Minute', which was due out at the end of June.

'*She's* a scruff, whoever she is!'

Rachel jumped like a husband caught reading a top-shelf magazine. 'I wish you wouldn't sneak up on me like that,' she gasped. She threw the *NME* back on the shelf, cross at the shock and Alysha's insulting of Lynette.

'Just remembered I need to send a birthday card to Nicole in Luxembourg,' Alysha said, leading them across the store.

As Alysha perused the cards, Rachel wandered around in a daze. She picked up a card with a cartoon duck, hearts swirling in its eyes, that read, *I'm quackers about you!* She imagined sending it to Xenna. She didn't know her address, but she could surely find the flat again. She would drop the card in the letterbox, with nothing written inside except her name and phone number – Xenna would appreciate the artistically spontaneous gesture, despite the card being a mass-produced one made by a big corporation. Last night Rachel had dreamt about Xenna arriving in Gravenden, her paintbrush loaded with the exact Pantone used in the backdrop, and changing the 42 to 24 before anyone noticed. Her reputation saved, Rachel had paid thanks to Xenna in the four-poster. For all she knew, Xenna might be regretting how they'd parted on Monday; she might even be wishing they'd hook up again, before Lynette returned from Sweden.

'Someone's all gooey after last night!'

Rachel jumped again. 'No, I just liked the cartoon.'

As she went to put back the card, Alysha pinched it from her fingers. 'It's time *you* did something nice for Stuey after the flowers and Cornwall,' she said, heading to the till. 'Anyway, it's buy one get one half-price, so it's on me!'

'Of course, if you finished early on the Friday, you'd catch the sunset.'

'S'pose,' mumbled Rachel. The post-office queue moved up; in a matter of minutes, she would have to write and then post the card to the man she had screamed away last night. It was preposterous. She contemplated telling Alysha they'd had a silly row over the flowers, or that he'd dumped her and she'd been too upset to mention it, or they'd decided to take a break because things were moving too quickly. But such excuses would provoke further questions from Alysha, leading to ever-more-convoluted track-covering. Her brain spun as she wondered which lie might be least problematic.

Alysha sighed because an elderly man was holding up the queue with a dozen questions for the teller. Despite the delay Rachel still couldn't think of what to say. She thought she was going to collapse with stress and confusion. But as they waited a thought struck her. There was actually a way out of this: yes, right in the middle of the cover-story vortex of confusion and lies was a perfectly calm zone, like the eye of a storm.

It involved simply telling the truth.

She gulped as she imagined taking Alysha to some private place nearby and unleashing everything – Kim, Olivia, Gaydar, Gwen, Xenna, the launch. Using the knife of her own nerve, she would hack herself free of this strangling net of deceit. Alysha would be shocked but also sympathetic. She would take Rachel's hand and say that her only regret was not knowing sooner, that she hated to think of Rachel struggling alone. The lies would end then. She would feel weird, raw, exposed, but the deceit would be over.

'Hel-*lo*?' Alysha was waving their newly bought stamps, and in an instant, the real world, full of light and noise, a world constrained by rules, regulations and other people's expectations, flooded back in. Insomnia and stress must be warping Rachel's mind. She could never tell Alysha about her 'lesbian tendencies'. She had already left it too late anyway. The revelation would paint her as a sly liar who'd moved in under false pretences. Alysha would think back to all the times she'd been tactile with

Rachel on the sofa, or half-naked in front of Rachel on the landing, or even entangled with her on the judo mats. She would tell an equally nauseated audience at The Mill that she'd been duped into giving an undercover lezzy her daily sexual thrills, the same lezzy that had strung poor Stuart along for months, only to break his heart at the end.

While she could never tell Alysha, neither could she bring herself to write the card now lying in front of her on the post-office table. While Alysha wrote to Nicole, Rachel picked at the sticker that held the cellophane around her own card, as though it was imperative to remove it intact, unlike the label on Stuart's flowers last night. Then she pretended that the card was so tightly wrapped that she must slowly ease it from the plastic, millimetre by millimetre. When the card was finally out, she took up one of the chained post-office pens and pressed it onto the space above the inside message. Two minutes later, the nib was still sitting in the initial dimple it had made on the paper.

'Writer's block?' said Alysha, sidling up. 'What about, *Hi sexy, last night was sublime!*' Rachel's grip almost cracked the pen in half. Alysha's giggles died away. 'Oh, just write the goddamn thing or I will!' She gave Rachel's elbow a tiny nudge, which in turn caused a disproportionately huge blue swoosh, messing up the card. 'Jeez, Rach, what's got into you today?'

'I …' Rachel could feel the words lining up one by one, like a parachute squad waiting to jump out of a plane in a predefined sequence. She wasn't sure if she'd be able to hold the words inside. She was losing control. 'I … I …'

Suddenly, she was bolting towards the door.

81

'Oh dear.' Noeleen brought her mop to a standstill on the bathroom floor. 'And no contact since then?' With Rob having urgently departed for Wheldon Court, she had been listening to Jo's Lucija-woes while working her way around the flat; it certainly didn't sound like a good situation.

Jo sat down on the edge of the bath and shook her head dismally. 'And I don't blame her either. Typical me, to get with the most gorgeous girl of my life, only to fuck it up within an hour. I doubt I'll ever see her again, let alone do all the things I'd planned, including … well, y'know.'

Noeleen rested the mop against the sink and nodded to Jo to shift up so she could sit beside her. The gesture seemed to surprise and touch Jo, but such moments were by no means new to Noeleen. How many times had she lent a floral shoulder or a pearly ear to clients with lesbian love issues, or 'dyke drama' as Xenna used to inelegantly put it? Noeleen had amassed so much knowledge about the Sapphic heart that Anouska once said *Diva* should have an 'Ask Noeleen' advice column. She turned to Jo. 'Don't torture yourself my love. How could you know about the PhD when she'd never mentioned it?'

'I just wish I hadn't sounded like such a snob when I found out, though. I said to her, "But I thought you *just* worked at The Dock" like it was the worst kind of menial job.'

'Why not ring to apologise? You have nothing to lose.'

'Never got her number. And she certainly wasn't volunteering it after all that.'

'Can't you get it from her friend across the courtyard?'

'I'd say Patrik's under strict instructions not to give—'

They looked at each other and stiffened. The knock at the door of the flat was a shock, not just because of its closeness (the bathroom was just inside the front door) but also because of its insistence – three hard raps that seemed to say they *knew* someone was home.

'I'll check the spyhole,' whispered Jo. Noeleen hovered by the bath; of course, if she weren't dressed up there would be no issues with unexpected callers. In an instant she felt her role being relegated from lesbian agony aunt to giant liability.

Jo came back looking panicked. 'I completely forgot Rob rang the landlord about the cable TV. I think that's him out there with the cable guy. Which means they probably have a key.' She skidded out and returned with Noel's holdall. 'Right, lock yourself in and get dressed while I deal with them. If anyone asks, you're my uncle who emigrated to London in the eighties!'

Noeleen locked the bathroom door and began to undress. It was annoying to have to prematurely exchange the floral for the greys and browns of uncle Paddy, but it wasn't the first time this had happened. Over the years there'd been several close shaves when Noeleen had to hide while a client dealt with an unexpected visitor – a gossipy neighbour wanting to borrow a curling tongs, a plumber arriving early, even a great-aunt who'd called in without warning. In the last case the poor girl had to conceal not only the fact she was living with another woman, but also Noeleen's presence!

As he swapped outfits, Noel could hear them talking to Jo in the hall. Both the landlord and the cable man seemed to have foreign accents. He pulled on his trousers, holding his belt carefully so the buckle wouldn't clank. The voices were heating up. Fully changed, he tiptoed to the door.

'No. Call your friend *now*.'

'Yah,' said the other man. 'Where he is?'

'I already told you,' said Jo. 'This has nothing to do with Rob. Could you just go, please?'

The front door slammed and Noel thought the men had left, but then a second later there was the scuffle of shoes on the floorboards. Jo screamed, but her voice was quickly muffled, as though by a hand. A moment later, something – and Noel feared it was Jo herself – was flung against the bathroom door.

He watched his nostrils quiver in the mirror as the skirmish seemed to kick its way down the hall. There was another bang and a breakthrough yelp from Jo, but this was followed up by a slap and, 'Sit down and shut up, bitch.'

Then the sitting-room door slammed, and suddenly he heard nothing.

82

She wasn't sure how long she'd been slumped among the empty mail cages before she heard the frantic yells of 'Rach-elll?' She looked up to see Alysha racing towards her, down this lane, which must be behind the post office. 'I've been looking everywhere,' Alysha gasped, pulling away the cages and hunkering down beside her. 'What the hell's going on?'

'I ... I don't know.' Rachel had no memory of leaving the post office or coming down here. All she knew was that her coat was soaked through with sweat and that the craters in her cheeks were burning with stomach acid.

Alysha stroked Rachel's arm, rubbed her knee; she wouldn't be touching her like this if she knew the truth. 'You even took the pen!' Alysha said, and Rachel looked down and saw it clamped in her fingers, poised as though she were about to write. From the top hung the remains of the little metal chain, evidence of what must have been a violent detachment.

'I presume it was you who puked up the lane there too?' said Alysha, taking out a tissue and gesturing to Rachel's lips.

At last she had a believable cover story! Rachel wiped her mouth. 'I must have picked up the winter vomiting bug. I had to rush out before I puked all over the post office. A couple of people at the launch had it. You better not come too close ...'

'Bullshit,' said Alysha. 'You've been acting weird all day.' She stood up and offered her hand. 'It's to do with Stuart, isn't it? That's why you couldn't bring yourself to write that card.'

Rachel got to her feet. She patted down her coat and looked up and down the narrow lane but no, there was no space to roll this boulder past Alysha – all plausible excuses, evasions and diversions had been thoroughly exhausted. Even if she could muster up something, there was no point: it would only add to the pile of lies. The once-triumphal triangle of love life, job and judo had already been dropped on its head by her own stupid actions, and now she was about to lose her home, and her only friend in this huge, hard city. A friend who'd raced around the streets of Wheldon to find a random girl she'd met online because she was deeply worried about her. A friend who was looking at that same girl now with tears in her own eyes.

Rachel felt her challenge mutate from concealment to the far harder task of self-exposure. Once she spoke, she would hear whatever home truths – liar, cheat, pervert, creep – her soon-to-be ex-friend might unleash. There were so many nice, normal girls looking for flatshares that Alysha would have no trouble finding someone. Rachel would have to move out, start all over again. But this upheaval was a fair punishment for deceiving someone as lovely as Alysha.

Alysha was zigzagging her head, trying to catch Rachel's eye. 'You've *got* to tell me,' she said, tearfully.

Rachel glanced up at the Saturday sky, but its plain greyness offered no encouragement. 'There *is* something, Alysha,' she said eventually.

Alysha grabbed her hand. 'OK … OK … right.' She looked around and pointed to a low wall beside the loading bay. 'Let's get you sitting down.'

Rachel shook her head. 'No. We should go to The Mill. The back room will be empty at this time, won't it?'

83

Rob paced up and down outside the gated archway leading into Wheldon Court, wondering whether to just ring the lying bastard on his mobile. He'd already pressed the bell for Flat 47 three times, but no answer had come through on the creaky old intercom. The lack of response didn't necessarily mean Michael wasn't home, though. Perhaps he never answered for fear that someday Rob would come here, as he had now, wanting to know what the fuck was going on.

He was about to ring the bell again when a Vespa whizzed up to park on the path, passing so dangerously close that he had to jump back. He watched as the rider and her female passenger removed their helmets; they were more concerned about flirtatiously reshaping each other's trendy hairstyles than the person they'd nearly run over. They didn't notice him or his disgusted glower as they went by, joined hands swinging between them. Their carefree gayness made him feel even worse about being at a random block of brown flats, stalking the man to whom he'd given his entire body and mind over the past ten months.

But there was a silver lining to encountering the sickening lovebirds: they had keys to Wheldon Court! They were so wrapped up in each other they didn't notice him slipping behind through the closing gate, then following them into the courtyard. Their use to him ended when they let themselves into Block A, but a minute later Rob had located Block D and was peering through the glass door at its locked entrance. He pictured Michael skipping out of that old lift, checking his pigeon-hole for post, and then sending a text as he wandered through the courtyard: 'Just leaving Reading now, Robbie, see you anon!'

Rob stood back shakily and tried to work out which balcony was Michael's. He knew from the intercom bells that Flat 47 was the second-last number in the whole complex. That meant it must be among the three on the top floor. And no matter which direction the numbering went, it *had* to be the middle balcony, which had laundry drying outside on a clothes horse. The wash was white except for a little red splash: the England rose. Never in a million years would Michael wear a rugby jersey. But what if he was living with, or even *going out with*, someone who would?

Having another man would certainly explain Michael's efforts in concealing this place. It would explain so many other things too – things that now started rushing towards Rob in a horrifying ghost train of realisation. He staggered to a bench in the middle of the courtyard and realised that every sacrifice he'd made for poor bereft Joan had been instead for the benefit of a rugby-loving man who couldn't do without Michael's attention for five minutes! He had worried himself sick over a drunken one-off with Salvador while Michael had been fucking his secret hunk night after night. And so much for their 'emotional' trip to the clinic – maybe Michael was fluid-bonded with this other man too, which meant Rob must rush back to the same clinic on Monday. His family, Vicky, everybody would be devastated for him. Except Craig and the gang – they'd piss their pants that steady old Pipe and Slippers had been a filthy two-timer all along. His head sank to his chest; between this and the trouble at work, his life was a horrible mess.

He was so deep in his misery that he barely registered the person coming through the gate and walking past the bench. It was only after the grey jeans cut though his downturned gaze like a pair of scissors, that he realised who it was. He sat up and stared at the retreating figure, horrified he'd nearly missed the very person he'd come to confront. Michael, with his jaunty walk and his Sainsbury's bag swinging from his fingertips, hadn't even bothered to glance at the obviously distressed man on the bench. He was too caught up in his own blissful existence to care about anyone else at all. Anyone except the man waiting in Flat 47, of course, the man with whom this weirdly chilled, upbeat version of Michael was about to share his groceries.

Michael had obviously been too distracted by goodbye kisses from rugby-man to remember where he'd put his keys. He set down the bag on the doorstep and patted the pockets of a khaki, urban-style jacket Rob had never seen before. Even weirder was that Michael wasn't wearing his glasses – usually only removed for sex, sleep, and showering – yet he seemed able to see perfectly well.

On the doorstep, the handle of the shopping bag had slipped down to reveal the neck of a wine bottle. Rob shivered, picturing the romantic lunch about to happen upstairs, the prelude to afternoon sex, then a cheeky siesta before Michael went out to meet his unsuspecting little fool-boy.

Michael chortled to himself as he eventually found his keys. As he was about to pick up the bag Rob let out a yell of *Michael!* which echoed through the courtyard. Michael spun round, and upon seeing Rob, his unspectacled eyes gave a couple of quick blinks.

Rob stood up and gave a fast, dramatic wave. Michael came over to the bench in an accelerated version of his engineer's tiptoe, his eyes suddenly squinting as though trying to focus without his glasses. 'Christ, Rob, what are you doing here?' he said, concerned and cross, as though addressing a child who'd clambered into a power station to retrieve a frisbee.

'Never mind me,' Rob said calmly. 'What are *you* doing here?'

Michael gulped and paused. 'It's so complicated Robbie, I don't know where to start ...'

'Start by explaining this place and why the hell you've been pretending to be an engineer all this time.'

Michael's chin fell. 'So, you know about that too.'

Rob pulled out the card. 'Cleaning lady found this back at mine.'

'It must've fallen out of my pocket,' said Michael, his eyes welling up. He gestured shakily to the bench. 'Can we please sit? This will take a while.'

Rob sat down at the far end, maximising the gap between them. He stared ahead, vowing not to cry. 'OK. I'm ready to hear it.'

'I only pretended to be an engineer on MaleDate to impress random strangers during chit-chat. I never dreamed I'd meet someone like you on there. I considered coming clean about it after our first few messages, but your photo was gorgeous and you had this hot job in a sexy ad agency. I worried you'd be turned off. By the time I'd fallen for you in real life it was too late to admit I'd been lying. And that meant I could never tell you about *this* place because if you googled *Michael Wyles, Wheldon Court* you'd see me listed as a CAD freelancer on various online professional directories.' He reached over and touched Rob lightly on the knee. 'I've agonised over this every single day, Robbie. I completely understand if you want to walk away right now.'

For a moment, Rob was overcome with sympathy for a man who had so little self-confidence that his only option had been to lie. But then the rugby shirt flashed like a red-eyed ghoul in his peripheral vision, and his sympathy swung firmly back to himself. 'So, if you live here,' he said, eyeballing Michael, 'then who do you live here *with*?'

Michael looked confused for a moment, then burst out laughing. 'God, no wonder you're so angry! I don't actually *live* here. I mean I did before we met, but when Dad died, I moved back to Mum's.'

'You said your flat was in Hammersmith, though?'

'But can't you see, sweets, I *had* to say it was anywhere but Wheldon because of the stupid engineer thing.'

Rob dug his trembling thumbnail into the wood of the bench. 'Then why did your work receptionist say you lived nearby?' he said. 'I called in yesterday with a surprise present for you, by the way. What a waste of time *that* was.'

Michael groaned. 'You're so sweet! I never told Stedman's I moved back to Reading. They're such dyed-in-the-wool Wheldonites they only award work to local subcontractors.'

'I see. But if you live in Reading, why are you here right now?'

Michael gave a sighing smile. 'I told you this would take a while. My lease here had four months left when Dad died. I knew my stickler of a landlord wouldn't release me early. I know subletting's illegal, but Mum needed me home and it was ludicrous to pay for a place I wasn't living in. Anyway, Nin's so discreet there's no danger of the landlord finding out. I've actually just come from Reading now to help her with something.'

'Nin?' Rob wasn't sure if it was even a real name.

'She's repeating third-year medicine at UCL. Has to keep her head down and stay away from booze and boys, otherwise daddy, who's this Kuala

Lumpur insurance mogul, won't pay another ringgit towards her studies. She's been such a good tenant that when the lease came up for renewal, I signed it myself and continued our secret arrangement. Once the sublet was up in August, and Mum was finally back to herself, I'd planned to come clean to you about everything so we could move in here together.' He slid tentatively up the bench and pressed his leg to Rob's. 'Imagine it, Robbie. Our own little love nest!'

Rob stared ahead. Whatever about the fantasy of them living here, there was something even more fantastical about Nin. Her overly intricate backstory seemed like the work of someone who'd been preparing for months. Michael, already a proven liar, probably thought himself a regular old Oscar Wilde as he finessed his dramatic masterpiece. 'So, this Nin, she supports England rugby, does she?' Rob asked. 'Bit weird, when she's from Thailand?'

Michael chuckled. 'Kuala Lumpur's in Malaysia, Robbie!'

Rob looked at him sharply. 'What I'm asking you is whether Nin likes English rugby?'

'What has rugby got to do with this?'

Rob nodded at the balcony. 'I've worked out the numbering, Michael. Flat 47 *has* to be in the middle. I might not be as intelligent as you but ...'

Michael laughed. 'Bless you for trying to work it out. No, apparently the builders were all half-pissed when they did up the numbering on their last day. My flat's the one on the right. Keith and Janet live in the middle with their daughter. Look, there's her little bike.'

Rob blinked at the shocking pink bike that sat only an inch from the clothes horse, wondering how in god's name he'd missed it before. How utterly blinded he had been by his own paranoia: Michael wasn't a two-timer with a secret shag-pad, but a man exhausted by having to hide his actual job for so long, a man who'd never meant to deceive, a man who right now looked terrified of what might happen next. Rob grabbed his boyfriend's freezing fingers. 'I haven't been completely truthful about myself either,' he said slowly.

Michael glanced down with cautious hope. 'Really?'

'I lied about Harrop's being sexy – it's just a run-down old office with shabby carpets and an old receptionist whose boobs rest on the Garibaldis as she carries in the tea tray. And my salary's not that hot either. But what Harrop's *does* have are good graphic designers.' He looked wincingly at the lawn. 'So I actually got one of them to retouch my MaleDate profile photo, just a little bit.'

Michael retracted his hand. 'Good gracious. Not sure I'll consort with you after learning such a hideous truth.'

'I'm so dreadfully sorry!' said Rob, as they sidled up to one another. He imagined them picnicking in this courtyard in the summer; rivalling the Vespa girls as the most loved-up couple in the complex. It would be sad to leave Jo, of course, but she'd find a new flatmate, a girlfriend even – maybe the Vespa girls would have a single friend for her! He smiled at Michael. 'You look nice without your glasses, by the way.'

'I thought that glasses would make me look engineerish. The ones I wear don't even have corrective lenses. They're just plain glass.'

Rob kissed his cheek. "No wonder you never let me try them on! Well, I prefer the *real* Michael.'

'Things are going to be much better from now on, Robbie. And there's other good news too – Joan has found herself a Darby, or should I say, a Cyril!'

'Cyril?'

'Retired headmaster with a pristine white beard and a small but valuable wine collection. He's started bringing her to tastings too, which means I'll be free to spend lots more time with you.' He smiled up at the empty balcony. 'I can't wait for us to move in, but not before you've finally met Mum, of course. We could even make it a double date with her and Cyril.'

'I can't believe that such a shit day has turned so brilliantly,' said Rob.

They sat together then, silently enjoying the start of this exciting new honesty-phase in their relationship. But as Rob surveyed the place that would eventually become his home, something caught his eye. It seemed they had both forgotten about the Sainsbury's bag on the doorstep. A bottle of wine was a strange gift for a girl who was meant to be off booze? He felt bad for being suspicious after everything they'd just admitted to each other; he tried to distract himself with thoughts of them of choosing new bed linen, planting flower pots on that balcony, browsing in The Whel-Read on Saturdays, but his eyes kept snapping back to that bag. He even wondered if Michael had deliberately 'forgotten' about it so it would remain out of sight. Rugby-man had turned out to be a hetero red herring, but that didn't mean there wasn't somebody else waiting for Michael in his own flat.

'You OK?' asked Michael. 'You've gone all restless.'

'I don't want you to keep your tenant waiting.'

'Gosh, I nearly forgot! Yeah, the kitchen sink's blocked so I brought over some stuff. Or at least I thought I had.' He made a fuss of checking under the bench, then surveying the courtyard. He sighed in relief when he eventually spotted the bag on the step.

'You came all the way from Reading just to do that?' said Rob with a quick laugh. The bottle didn't look remotely like any of the black, bull-necked plastic bottles of drain cleaner that Orlando had insisted on pouring down the shower plughole once a month.

'I need to stay on Nin's good side so she keeps schtum about the sublet,' said Michael. He got up. 'I better hurry if I'm to make it back to Mum's to freshen up before our date tonight. Come on, I'll walk you to the gate.'

Rob followed obediently, though he was itching to race back to the doorstep. Confirming wine rather than drain cleaner would give him the absolute right to challenge Michael about what was really going on. But if his paranoid eyes had made yet another mistake and it *was* just drain cleaner, then he'd look like a mistrustful madman. Michael would be so insulted by the accusation that he'd call off their future living arrangement, if not the whole relationship. The chance to examine the bag was becoming more distant by the second anyway, as Michael walked them quickly along. 'We'll have to go somewhere nice for dinner to celebrate our new era of openness,' he was saying. 'Why don't we meet around here later so you get your first taste of Wheldon nightlife? Let's go to that Nagano place I was telling you about before!'

'Lovely,' said Rob, knowing he couldn't eat a grain of rice with the doubt currently contracting his insides. By the time they reached the archway, there was no hope of getting back to the bag. But what he *could* do was ask about it and watch for Michael's response. He would have to ask quickly too, before the gate closed on his opportunity to ever know the truth. Halfway out, he stopped. 'I need to ask you something,' he said, his body twitching with the simultaneous desire to both speak and shut up before he ruined everything.

Michael held the gate open. 'What is it, sweets?'

Rob opened his mouth, but the sound that followed was an elderly voice calling, 'Coo-eee!' They peered back into the courtyard, where an elderly woman leaving Block D had stooped to pull a tall green bottle out of the shopping bag. 'To whom belongs the Mrs Bristleworth's Sluicing Fluid?' she shouted.

'Apologies, Miss Proudley,' Michael called back. 'I'll be over in a moment.'

'Come *now*, please, Mr Wyles,' she said, waving her walking stick at him. 'For something that unblocks drains, it's ironically causing quite the obstruction!'

Michael winked at Rob. 'I better go before the battleaxe goes ballistic. I used to bring down her bin bags when I lived here, not that she ever thanked me, mind you. Oh wait, you wanted to ask me something?'

'Don't worry about it,' Rob said, bursting with secret gratitude for the old dear's magnificent timing. He blew a kiss to his boyfriend through the closing bars of the gate. 'It wasn't anything important at all.'

84

The glass in the coffee table rattled as Oleg patrolled the sitting room. Jo was rattling too. On the couch, she held a cushion to her pounding heart. She couldn't believe she'd got caught up in this, and all because of a tenuous connection with people across the courtyard. Her foot was throbbing – as she'd struggled against them dragging her in here, she'd managed to bash her ankle off the door frame, so hard that she worried her fibula might be fractured.

She'd never seen the smaller man – now poking around the kitchen – before. He had a pinched, sinister face and a pock-marked bomber jacket that suggested he'd recently been ground up against a pebbledash wall. His right ear had been subjected to far worse in the more distant past, however – the top arc of the pinna was missing, but in a very exact way – like someone had taken a ruler and scalpel to it. He was becoming just as edgy as Oleg. Tired of opening and closing kitchen cupboards, ear-man turned his attention to the extractor fan, which he began to switch on and off in a hellish rhythm. He came to the kitchen door and shouted an order in Russian to Oleg, who parted the curtains to peer again at Stanko's balcony.

'*Nyet*,' Oleg reported, then came over to prod Jo's sore ankle with his bovver boot. 'What time you say your friend home?'

'I've told you ten times already. I do not know when he'll be back. He is not answering his phone. Anyway, *he does not know where Patrik and Stanko are, OK?* He is not involved with cigarettes. Do you understand?'

Oleg's shark-eyes tightened. 'Then why he bring cigarettes up with Patrik last week?'

'He was just helping his friend.' Jo buried her nose in the cushion. She was going to kill Rob when she saw him, if she didn't get killed or gang-raped before then. What had the idiot been thinking? Well, she knew what he had been thinking *with* anyway. She hoped whatever cock-throb he'd got from helping his beloved Patrik last week was worth her personal safety, maybe her life.

Rob wasn't the only man who'd let her down today either. Fifteen minutes ago, while Oleg and ear-man were arguing, she'd heard a click from the hall, indicating Noel's exodus. The self-serving bastard had been so concerned about getting changed, he'd managed to miss the fact that she was being roughed up by two heavies. He was probably relaxing on the bus to Croydon now, chuckling at his near-miss with the landlord. But Jo didn't need some ineffectual man right now; no, she needed Lucija's hard sexiness. Lucija would flex her muscles, narrow her eyes and send the men scuttling like puppies with a few stern words – uttered in perfect Russian, of course, because she probably spoke that too.

Ear-man came back in, sipping cautiously on a carton of pomegranate juice he'd nicked from the fridge. Neither man seemed familiar with the drink, and there was a heated debate in Russian over what it might be. Oleg wanted to try it too. He held the first gulp disgustedly in his jowls for a moment, then let fly a huge magenta spray, causing ear-man to bray like a donkey.

Jo flung down her cushion and jumped up. 'Do you mind, you anabolic asshole?' She waved her hand at the dripping liquid. 'We don't own this place. I need to get a cloth before it stains the wallpaper.' She was shouting her head off in the hope that one of the neighbours would hear and come around to complain. Oleg stepped forward and shoved her onto the couch. 'Shut up, cunt, sit down.'

She jumped up again. 'Let me fucking past.'

This time Oleg caught her by the throat. Suddenly she was up against the wall with his fingers pressing into her neck. She thrashed about, but his furious face continued to swim in front of hers, his skin empurpled, his eyes popping as though he were the one being asphyxiated. Her feet left the ground. She was being lifted up. By her neck. She was going to die. The edges of the room started to brown out. Oleg was going to fucking kill her.

'Let her go!'

At first Jo thought it was a floral apparition brought on by hypoxia. But as she slid down the wall, filling her lungs with desperate breaths, she understood. The two men remained incredulous, however – they gaped at the bonneted figure filling the doorway, then looked at each other for validation of this reality. They gave a unified utterance, which Jo presumed was the Russian for 'What the fuck?' As Noeleen crossed the room, they started to titter. But heavily, slowly, her steps came, so different to her usual slippered shuffle. It was the sound of a man, a large, heavy man, heavier than Oleg even, a man who meant business. Jo looked down and saw the big brown Eccos beneath the dress. Mixing a little bit of Noel with a whole lot of Noeleen had been a genius move.

'What's going on here?' said Noeleen.

'Get out,' spat Oleg through a sarcastic laugh. 'You gay pussy pervert.'

'Yeah, fuck off, faggot,' said ear-man. 'We busy here.'

'I'm not going anywhere,' boomed Noeleen. 'But you two should get out. Now!'

The Russians looked at each other; then Oleg gave a battle cry, and they both lunged at Noeleen. Oleg's first punch sent Noeleen staggering back to the wall, clutching her jaw. Jo saw that, despite the brave intentions of the man in the dress, they were now *both* in danger. She wished Noeleen had snuck out and called the police instead. The clothes-tactic had backfired and now these homophobes would take special pleasure in beating Noeleen to a pulp. The men skidded over, ready to attack again. But despite her punched jaw, Noeleen was now grinning crazily; she was taking something from the pocket of her pinny.

The men's fists fell to their sides. Everyone stared at the glinting needle and the scarlet-filled barrel beneath it.

'So, who's for some blood eh?' said Noeleen. 'You know, pussy-faggot blood?' She stepped forward and waved the syringe in the men's terrified faces. 'Oh, don't be shy. I've got plenty to go around.'

85

'The barman thought you were my dad,' said Rob, as he returned to the table with the two pints.

Noel looked up. He seemed quite pleased. 'And what did you tell him?'

'I said you were actually my cross-dressing cleaning lady. And that if there's ever any trouble in here, you're able to sort out the hardest of thugs.' He set down the drinks, laughing at Noel's shocked expression. 'No, I said you're a good friend of mine.'

And it was true. Since last month's incident with the Russians, Rob had been learning that, besides being a brave and quick-thinking hero, Noel was an incredibly interesting, intuitive and wise man. He felt awful for misjudging Noel's motives back in the beginning. Over the past few cleaning sessions, they'd been having some fantastic chats. Earlier that afternoon, Noeleen had even taught Rob her secret method of cleaning the hob.

Still smiling, Noel looked around. 'Oh, I do like a nice peaceful London pub of a Saturday afternoon. Can't believe you've never been in here, seeing as it's your local.'

'I've always been intrigued by the name, The Blithe Viscount, but I never had anyone to come in with. It's not Michael's kind of place.' Rob raised his glass. 'Anyway it's high time I repaid you in beer for your bravery. Cheers!'

Noel clinked his glass and took a sip of his pint. 'Speaking of Michael,' he said, 'is it tonight you're finally meeting Joan and her gentleman-friend?'

Rob laughed. 'No offence, Noel, but if it was, I wouldn't be here relaxing with you. I'd be at home steam-pressing my best shirt and slacks.'

'Not another postponement, surely?'

'Remember Cyril couldn't meet last week because of a head cold? Well, now it's gone south and he's on strong antibiotics. He feels OK, but being a wine-buff, he can't bear going out to dinner without a tipple, so we've had to defer again.'

Noel grunted. 'Suits himself this Cyril, doesn't he?'

'I can't complain. Since he's come along, Michael has had a lot more free time. And I can look forward to some fancy wine when we finally do meet. I'll probably need a lot of it to cope with Joan anyway. Now that Michael's told her all about us, she's *dying* to meet me, apparently. Michael says that, once we move in to Wheldon Court – which is now probably going to be September, by the way, because Nin has to re-sit some exam – Joan will be dropping by every five minutes!'

Noel picked up a shamrock-shaped coaster left over from St. Patrick's Day and turned it slowly in his hand. 'Rob, you won't like what I'm about to say. And obviously I've never met Michael so I can't offer an *actual* impression of the man. But aren't you a bit suspicious about all these delays? I know you said that Michael had a watertight cover story for Wheldon Court but …'

Rob felt his chirpiness dissipate. Noel had touched a nerve. A nerve that Rob had been studiously stepping around in himself for the past few weeks. 'I suppose I *have* sometimes felt suspicious,' he said. 'But I've told myself to stop worrying and to just accept what Michael says at face value. Anyway, even if I *did* want to investigate Wheldon Court further, there's no way to do it without looking like an insecure stalker. It'd ruin everything if Michael found out I don't trust him. And just when things are on the up again.'

Noel stared at the coaster for a minute, then tapped it on the edge of the table. 'There might be a way around all this,' he said. 'You drink your beer and I'll explain.'

Doleful brown eyes flicked up from beneath the baseball cap. 'Can I help you, madam?'

Jo, the last person in what had been a long, slow-moving queue, stepped forward. 'Hi,' she said in her most sensitive voice. 'It's Yésica, isn't it?'

The bill of the cap bobbed warily.

'I'm looking for Lucija. Is she working today?' Jo felt like a stalker. She hadn't seen Lucija since the post-clinch *faux pas* last month, but there was no other way of contacting her now that Patrik and Stanko had disappeared. (The morning after her ordeal with the Russians, she'd woken to find the cigarette-room's curtains wide open and the bathroom window devoid of the blurred line-up of Patrik's grooming products. Two days later, Rob had seen a letting agent showing a straight couple around.)

Yésica looked confused until she deciphered Jo's flat pronunciation. 'Ah, you mean Lu-*ci*- ja?'

'Exactly! We have a mutual friend and I just wanted to ask her if he's OK?' Concern for Patrik was the perfect cover story for coming here, but of course Jo's real motive was to show Lucija she wasn't a condescending bitch and to try to win her back. Lucija would surely be impressed by Jo's good news in the interim too; she was starting in *commUte* next week!

'Lucija is no more working here,' said Yésica. 'She left few days ago.'

'Oh?' Jo stared hatefully at a cinnamon plait under the glass. 'Do you know where she went?'

'Ehh, she went to Ireland,' said Yésica, picking at what appeared to be a healing scald-scab on her thumb knuckle. 'To Dubleen.'

'Dublin? But that's where I'm from!'

Yésica shrugged. 'She say she wanted something new.'

'But what about her PhD, her university?'

'University?' Yésica's lips puckered doubtfully. 'Lucija does not go to university. She only work here.' She cocked her head and laughed. 'You sure we talk about the same Lucija?'

Jo gripped the counter. 'Do you have her phone number?'

'She gonna send me her Ireland number some time,' said Yésica, who now leapt to get a cloth because Marcus had just appeared and was regarding them with thin-lipped suspicion. She moved down and began polishing the pastry display.

Jo followed in parallel. 'What's Lucija's last name?' she asked over the glass. 'So I can find her online.'

'Ehh, I don't remember,' said Yésica from the corner of her mouth. 'I think it start with Z ...'

'Yésica,' Marcus shouted, 'why aren't you serving that client?'

'You must go,' Yésica whispered, polishing more furiously as Marcus began his approach.

'Just one more question—'

'No,' hissed Yésica. 'Please go *now.*'

87

'You ready?'

Noel nodded and exhaled through his nostrils.

Rob pressed the bell for Flat 47 and stood back. It was eight o'clock on Friday night and they were standing at the gate to Wheldon Court.

They cocked their heads towards the speaker, but no response came. Rob pressed again, for longer this time. Eventually there was a clunking sound on the line; someone was picking up. Rob crossed his fingers, praying to hear the chirpy voice of a female Malaysian medical student, the '*hey-llo?*' of skittish Nin who was mad for the boys and the booze. But no voice came. He nudged Noel to speak first, part of the plan they'd made in the pub last Saturday.

'Anyone about?' said Noel, leaning in to the speaker. 'Only I've got a package 'ere for a … Michael Wines. Delivery from D-*aitch*-L.' Rob smiled; Noel was playing such a cockney blinder that poor Nin probably wouldn't even understand him!

'Michael *Wyles?*' came the reply, deep and English and male. 'Yes, that's me.' Rob's heart began to pound. He reminded himself that this much proved nothing. Michael might be over to collect the rent from Nin. Or maybe her sink was blocked again. 'But wait,' added Michael, 'I don't remember ordering anything … ?'

Noel shot Rob a wide-eyed look and then leaned back to the intercom. 'Looks like it might be a present. Maybe somebody loves ya! In any case, you better get down quick, mate. Me van's blocking the frog and toad.'

'Well, just give me a minute to turn off the hob.' Michael said with a cocky little laugh. 'I'm in the middle of cooking a rather complicated dinner!' Then he hung up.

Rob and Noel looked at each other. They both knew what this meant. 'Sure you'll be all right?' said Noel.

Rob nodded. 'I have to do this on my own.'

As Noel went off, Rob heard footsteps inside the courtyard. He stood back behind the wall and, as Michael opened the gate, sprang out to reveal himself. He took in Michael's sauce-spattered apron, from which emanated the aroma of herbs and hot tomatoes.

Michael's face drained. 'Robbie ... ?'

Rob pushed his way in through the gate and closed it behind him. He opened his dry, quivering mouth. 'Michael, I don't want you to say anything. No more of your nonsense. Or should I say *Nin*-sense. I was stupid enough to fall for your story last time, but let's face it, the only reason you're here in an apron is because you've got another guy on the go. Someone you choose to *live* with over me. Someone who rings to disrupt, distract and make demands whenever we're together. Someone you pretend is your mum. Someone who, thanks to your disgusting behaviour, has put me at risk of an STD, for fuck's sake!'

Michael reached out and took hold of Rob's arms. 'Robbie, please calm down. I do *not* have someone else. I just needed my own space for a little while. To be completely honest, I'm finding it hard to cope with Dad's death at the moment. I only moved in here last month anyway, so it's not like I've been lying for long. I was going to let you move in after the summer when I was in better shape mentally.'

Rob shook himself free. '*Let* me move in? Oh you're so kind, Michael. But I don't want to live with a liar, thanks very much. I don't want—'

There was the sound of a throat being cleared. The two Vespa lesbians Rob had seen before were coming through the gate with a six-pack and a takeaway pizza. 'Excuse us please,' said the blonde one, barely able to contain her amusement as she and her girlfriend passed through the epicentre of the temporarily muted storm. As they went past, Rob heard the girlfriend mutter, 'Looks like someone's been caught two-timing again.'

'Hope the dude upstairs doesn't get wind of this,' said the blonde one. She paused and half-turned, catching Rob's eye, before calling, 'I'd run for the hills if I were you, love!'

Rob shot a look at Michael's sickened face, then shoved him hard in the chest with the heel of his hands. It felt wonderful to let the trembling stress out. A thought he'd been too sickened to even *entertain* lately now rushed up into his throat. 'I bet your dad isn't even dead, is he?' He grabbed the straps of Michael's apron and yanked them back and forth, wanting to inflict whiplash. '*Is* he?'

Michael looked shakily down at the ground. 'No,' he whispered.

Rob roughly released the apron-straps and turned to the gate. 'Well, I wish *you* were dead, Michael. Don't you ever contact me again. This …us … whatever the fuck this has been – it's over.'

PART 3

June – July 2007

88

The harassed staff at the gate had no idea what was happening. Just like the overhead screens, all they could report was that the 15.15 to Glasgow was 'delayed'. Rachel, who'd forfeited her seat in the waiting area far too early, stood in the static boarding queue, gazing out the window at the sun-baked Stansted apron. The ground crew appeared even more puzzled about the delay; they sauntered around in the heat, looking at their watches, plucking off their earmuffs to chat with one another. Even from here, Rachel could see the sweat-sheen on their faces. June had been exceptionally hot and dry, and now, on the last day of the month, the sun showed no signs of abating. The Met Office were touting July to be even more blistering, with Europe bracing itself for the most intense heatwave in years. After another ten minutes with still no news, Rachel watched the ground crew give up their pacing and take refuge in the cruciform shadow of the plane.

Despite the best efforts of the air conditioning, the temperature continued to rise in the giant glasshouse of the terminal. The woman in front fanned herself with her boarding pass, and sat down on her suitcase, which looked way too big for the cabin. She turned to Rachel, revealing smoker's teeth and sweaty, sunburnt cleavage. 'This is a fuckin' joke, in't it?' she said in raspy Glaswegian. 'Are they gonnae tell us whit's goin' on?'

'I just hope it's nothing sinister,' said Rachel.

'I wouldnae be surprised, the way the world's going nowadays. That poor wee lassie abducted in Portugal last month, then those bombs down here yesterday. Though I doubt terrorists would bother wi' Glesga.'

Rachel nodded. The terrorist threat had already come far too close: the previous evening, Alysha had arrived home from a work day-trip extremely upset. She'd been queuing outside the National Gallery with a group of Sunray kids, when a massive team of police with megaphones had swarmed in to evacuate the whole area. Last night Alysha had woken up screaming after a nightmare where one of her little boys had been bombed to pieces. Rachel had rushed in to comfort her with hugs and soft words until she finally settled back to sleep.

'I wouldn't be too sure that Al-Qaeda have no beef with Scotland,' said a well-spoken middle-aged man in the queue behind Rachel. 'Our new PM's from there, after all.'

'Gordon Brown!' said the woman. 'Maybe ya have a point there.' She folded her arms across her sun-ruined boobs. 'I cannae stand that walloper, he's a pure fanny.'

Fifteen minutes later, the Glasgow-bound travellers watched jealously as the gate opposite opened for the flight to Palma de Mallorca. Rachel smiled to see two teenage girls being dragged away from the internet booths by their dad, the web obviously a more exciting place to spend time than the Balearics! She was growing irritated by the Glaswegian's chit-chat, and her hot feet were swelling up, so she went over to the screen just vacated by the teenagers. She put a pound in the slot and logged into her GaydarGirls profile. She was delighted with her new profile picture. Alysha had taken it during their picnic on Wheldon Common last Sunday, and Rachel loved the cool, retro photo-effect they'd applied afterwards, using the new laptop they'd bought for the flat. It seemed Rachel wasn't alone in liking the pic either – a message had come in overnight: *I see you do judo too. Msg if you fancy a chat sometime.* It was from Kitkin76, a cute judoka who worked in the legal field. Aged thirty-one, this Kitkin seemed a lot more interesting than the twenty-somethings who'd been in touch lately, none of whom, Rachel and Alysha had agreed, were particularly great date-material, let alone potential girlfriends.

Not wanting to appear over-eager, Rachel decided she'd reply tomorrow using the hotel's internet. She'd have lots of free time before the dermatology conference started on Monday anyway. Lydia, who'd been in high spirits since her wedding, had actually suggested Rachel travel to

Glasgow in advance: *You've been working so ruddy hard to make up for what happened, Rachel, I think Trenpharm can stump up for a couple of extra hotel nights.* Rachel had never been to Scotland before, and was looking forward to sightseeing and shopping on the Style Mile. She might even brave a quick visit to a gay bar, just to see how they did things up there.

Of course, all this depended on the plane taking off. For now, she logged into Hotmail and smiled to re-read Narelle's latest update.

Ah Rach, you'd love it here in Sydney. So many lezzes. Heaps of them come in to the travel agent (yes I got that job!) because we sell those Olivia Cruises. You should visit next year during Mardi Gras. We'll have a blast & I'll find you some hot aussie chicks. Miss you loads, NarNar xx (ps. Tell the ginge witch I say hi hahaha!)

Narelle's contract had been up for renewal in May, and she'd taken great pleasure in telling Lydia (who'd been busy laying down a strict set of provisos and performance indicators for her continued tenure), that she and Stevo were moving back to Australia. Rachel and Lydia were currently interviewing for a replacement, and while they had shortlisted some really competent candidates, Rachel suspected none would be as much fun as Narelle.

Just as her internet minutes were running out, there was a ripple of shushing anticipation; it seemed they were about to make another announcement.

'We regret that this afternoon's flight to Glasgow will be delayed due to … *a terrorist attack on the airport.*'

As the initial gasps turned to anxious chatter, Rachel quickly shoved another pound into the machine. Details were already coming through on the BBC news site. A jeep packed with explosives had tried to ram into the Glasgow arrivals hall! One of the terrorists had been stumbling around with his clothes on fire. Witnesses reported the smell of petrol and burning flesh.

'Argh,' muttered a female voice from behind the divider with the adjacent computer. 'Stupid thieving fecker!'

Rachel leaned back and saw a neat bum in dark jeans, and the hem of a fitted grey t-shirt. She took note of these pleasing artefacts, then returned to the unfolding news. She was reading about how the terrorists had been brought under control by brave bystanders, when a head peeped around the divider.

'Sorry to disturb you, but is your computer working OK? This one took my money and now it's just hanging.'

'Oh no,' said Rachel, her insides lurching at how attractive her neighbour was. She took in the pale skin, the blue eyes beneath the brown side-fringe. 'Mine's working fine,' she said. 'Actually, I'm nearly finished if you want to use it?'

'Thanks a million. I might, yeah, but please don't rush on my account.' Rachel had initially wondered if the girl was Irish, but hearing how she slushed out the T's in the *might* and *account* now left no doubt. 'I only wanted to see what's happening in Glasgow,' continued the girl. 'My friend just rang to say Sky News has reported a fella walking around in flames … ?'

'It's true!' said Rachel, with a big upbeat smile, despite the appalling subject matter. She nodded at the screen. 'I'm looking at the photos if you want a peep.'

The girl pulled her chair around. As Rachel scrolled through the pictures, she noticed the perfume – sporty-fresh citrus with a hint of floral – and the cute summer freckles dotted about her knuckles. The fingernails were short, unvarnished. There'd been an *is-she-or-isn't-she* scene in *The L Word* (Alysha's new favourite show) where clipped nails were deemed auspicious, but still, it was no guarantee. Neither was the girl's tomboy look conclusive, because lots of people chose casual comfort when flying. Rachel reined in her hopeful theories. Even if, and it was a *huge* if, the girl was gay, it made no difference; the flight to Dublin would probably be called in a minute, and Rachel would never see her again. She clicked on through the gallery, keeping her mouse-hand at a respectful distance from the freckled fingers leaning on the desk.

As they reached the last photo, the girl shook her head. 'Not sure I even want to go to Glasgow now!'

'Glasgow?' said Rachel, wishing she hadn't sounded so thrilled. 'I'm going there myself – well, hoping to.'

'Yeah, I know you are,' said the girl, who was quick to add, 'only because

I was behind you in that interminable queue earlier.' Rachel was flattered but also unnerved at being noticed. She wished she'd sounded more intelligent and less impatient while chatting to the Glaswegian. There was an awkward silence then, which Rachel ended by standing up and grabbing her case. 'I've read enough for the moment,' she said. 'You go ahead.'

The girl's hand went to her trendy messenger bag. 'Here, let me give you some money for the minutes left.'

'No,' said Rachel. 'You've already wasted a pound!' She walked away with the girl's final smile still shining in her mind, feeling a mix of frisson and disappointment. Whether the flight took off or got cancelled, it was unlikely they'd naturally cross paths again. She wandered round the duty-free shops, spraying little cards with perfumes that looked like they might be sporty-floral. As she browsed, she kept stealing glimpses of the girl at the internet booth in the distance, but on no occasion was the girl ever looking around to see where Rachel herself had got to.

Unable to find the scent, Rachel went into FlySounds. Beside the Top 10 CDs, she stopped and shuddered. If the girl were to click on 'History' she'd see GaydarGirls listed as the very first thing in the session. Rachel had been so distracted by the attack that she hadn't even logged out of her profile! No wonder the girl looked so enrapt by the screen right now – she was probably laughing at Rachel's inane chats with random lesbians. She wandered around the music shop in a daze, trying to convince herself that a stranger would hardly click into the history. But what if the girl just kept clicking 'back' whilst looking at the news stories and arrived upon the page? She thought about pretending she suddenly needed the computer again, but that would just look weird, especially as the girl might already know by now that Rachel was gay. She desperately wanted to ring Alysha for advice but knew she would say, 'So what, Rachel?' This had become Alysha's stock phrase whenever Rachel got spooked about some other aspect of her coming out. In any case, 'Alysha's lesbian helpline', as they'd named it, was temporarily unavailable, because its host was currently on an all-important second date with a lovely paramedic called Evan, whom she'd met online (their new laptop was already paying for itself!) No, there was nothing for it but to stay well out of the girl's way while they were stuck together in Stansted.

She was clacking distractedly through a random rack of CDs, still feeling uneasy and embarrassed, when her ears pricked up at the song that had started to play in the store. The female vocalist, the lovelorn lyrics, the sombre electronic beat; it wasn't her usual kind of music, yet she somehow felt heavily drawn to it. This strange feeling of resonance remained inexplicable to her until the arrival of the chorus: as it played, she froze on the spot, then frantically began searching for the nearest staff member. A blue-haired guy, whose forearms were half-covered by tattered festival wristbands, was bopping his head to the beat as he slotted CDs into racks. 'Excuse me,' Rachel said, pointing at the speaker. 'Is that singer called Lynette Lost, by any chance?'

'Yeah, actually,' he said, looking impressed. 'Called "Loved Every Minute". Just came out yesterday. Well-dreamy tune, innit?'

'Totally!'

He checked there was no one around and added, 'Much better than the mainstream muck we're usually allowed play in here. Anyway, the CD's over there by the tills if you want one. Some pretty sick remixes on there too.'

Outside the shop, Rachel took the CD from its bag and gazed at Xenna's masterpiece on the cover. The artist had certainly been busy since the initial sketch – Lynette's likeness was fantastically accurate now, and everything had been carefully painted in with zingy watercolours. The background, however, had been spattered with flecks of watery grey paint that added a devil-may-care feel to proceedings. Rachel was so entranced by all these little details that she hardly noticed someone approaching from her left.

'Hi again,' said the Irish girl. 'Great news, isn't it?'

'What is?' said Rachel. She scanned the cute face for any traces that GaydarGirls had been detected but found none.

'We're boarding in an hour.'

'Wonderful!' said Rachel, trying to stop the signs of attraction from showing on her face. 'I must have missed the announcement while I was in the music shop.'

The girl grimaced. 'If you could even call it a *music* shop. I went in earlier – so, so bland.'

'Mainstream muck, if you ask me,' said Rachel, screaming silent thanks that she hadn't just purchased the latest cheesy pop offering. 'Think I bought the only decent tune in the whole shop.' As they walked towards the gate, she handed the CD to the girl for a look.

'Cool cover, anyway! Is this … ? Oh my god!' The girl stopped dead. She looked as though she'd been handed a long-lost and very personal belonging.

'You know it?'

She turned the CD carefully over in her hand. 'I heard this as an early demo a long time ago. On this completely crazy night when my best friend, now my ex-best friend, was DJing.' She blinked into the distance. 'Though I didn't know it at the time, that same night marked the beginning of my decision to leave Dublin.'

Rachel was amazed. 'Bizarrely, I have a story about this song too,' she said, 'also involving a completely crazy night.'

'No way!' The girl nudged her almost flirtatiously. 'OK, you go first.'

Rachel looked around, her stomach fluttering. Telling the story about Xenna meant she'd have to out herself. This might well inspire a reciprocal coming out from the girl. But if not, then Rachel would have exposed her private life to a straight stranger who might feel creeped out. 'It's a bit of a long story,' she said. She took a breath. Despite being in an airport, she had a sense of pushing herself far out into an expanse of deep open water. 'You don't fancy going over to The Dock there for a coffee, do you?' Her voice quivered a little as she asked it; if nerves meant that it mattered, then this really must matter.

'The *Dock*?' The girl shook her head. 'Nah, I'll pass, thanks.'

The verbal punch stunned every butterfly in Rachel's stomach. She had overstepped the mark. Her intentions had been found out. 'No worries,' she said quickly. 'Think I'll head back to the ga—'

'No, no,' said the girl with a laugh. 'It's just that caffeine gives me palpitations.' She nodded towards the bar. 'But a nice cold beer wouldn't go amiss in this heat.'

'I wouldn't mind one myself, actually!' said Rachel, the butterflies revivifying and furiously multiplying.

'Grand so, beers it is!' As they began walking towards the Sky Bar, the girl stretched out a hand. 'Oh, and I'm Jo, by the way.'

Rob paid Fred and brought the next round over to their favourite little table in the alcove. 'Anything more on Glasgow?' asked Noel, as he accepted his pint.

'Fred's got BBC News on up at the bar. They're saying that an off-duty baggage-handler wrestled that burning terrorist to the ground!'

Noel shook his head slowly. 'I'm so glad Jo's plane wasn't landing just as this was kicking off.'

'I know,' said Rob. 'Fred says they've raised the terror alert to imminent.'

'Imminent? Oh lord.'

They both shivered despite the heat. The windows in the Viscount had been wedged fully open on the last few Saturdays; today was so particularly stifling that Fred the landlord had gone out earlier to buy a fan, which was now rotating on the bar. Noel clinked his glass off Rob's. 'Anyway, here's to us all staying alive … and to your big night out later, of course.'

Rob leaned forward and pinched the edge of the table. 'I'm so anxious, Noel. What if Cath doesn't like me?'

'I sincerely doubt that will happen. She gave birth to Rodney, who worships the ground you walk on. And you say Rodney's really close to her. Hence she'll click with you too. What's the plan for later, anyway?'

'So me and Rodney are meeting her off the train from Ipswich at five. We've got brilliant seats for *Hairspray*, followed by dinner and drinks in Soho. Then, if Cath's still standing, she wants to go to Tearaways for a bop! Tomorrow we're all having brunch with Vicky and Glen because Cath's dying to see where myself and Rodney first met. Vicky's even promised to do a re-enactment!'

It terrified Rob that he might never have met Rodney, but he liked to believe the universe had intervened after all his bad luck with Michael. One bright Sunday morning in May, he'd arranged to meet Vicky and her adorable new teddy-bear of a boyfriend, Glen (whom Vicky had met at a speed dating event that, despite her protestations, Rob had enrolled her in). Glen loved brunch and had brought Rob and Vicky to his favourite Sunday spot in Clapham. Just as they finished eating and were merrily ordering more mimosas, a pale man with entrancing pink lips had sat down alone at the next table. Even before the man took a psychiatry textbook from his bag to peruse over his cup of green tea, Rob was smitten. Clever Vicky, sensing Rob's attraction, had struck up a conversation with the sexy-lipped stranger. A conversation that had, for Rob, ultimately turned into a phone number, a first date, a kiss, and now all this!

'I must say Cath sounds wonderful,' said Noel, 'and you're actually getting to *meet* this woman, unlike that elusive Joan.'

'And her even more elusive, and very alive, husband. Ugh, when I think of all the lies I fell for.' Rob sat back and shook his head. 'Michael despised musicals, said they were like squatters preventing theatres from showing *proper productions*. Well, this will be the third musical I've been to with Rodney, and I'm loving every minute. I finally told him the whole sorry break-up story last Sunday as we were lazing in bed. He reckons that Michael has narcissistic personality disorder!'

'Well, he'd know the symptoms, being a psychiatric nurse. And speaking of hospitals, I got some good news on Thursday. Dr Ling says she might let me move back to my flat soon. My diabetes management is exemplary, apparently.'

'Get you, doctor's pet!'

Noel winced at the glasses. 'Just don't tell her about our cheeky beers on Saturdays. Anyway, I think Hazel and Martin will actually be glad to be rid of me. Chloe's already hating Haiti, *quelle surprise*, and wants to come home. She'll need her bedroom back.'

They both looked up then, because something was happening at the door. A cackling gang of young men, all carrying sports bags, was coming into the pub. They were certainly not the Viscount's usual kind of clientele, and their loud chatter and dramatic high-fives to each other caused the Saturday regulars – mostly solo drinkers of around Noel's age – to look over with irritation.

'There goes our quiet drink,' said Rob. The men, who had damp hair and flushed faces, flung their sports bags down beside the bar and began to shout overlapping orders at a confused Fred.

'Seems to be some kind of sports team,' said Noel. 'Definitely a victorious one anyway.'

'Definitely a gay one,' said Rob sourly. 'That tall one in the spray-on jeans is giving me the creeps, the way he's poncing about. And look, now they've got poor Fred making cocktails. This isn't Balans, you twats!'

When their cocktails were finally ready, the tight-trousered man schoolmarmishly silenced his friends, then raised a glass in his limp wrist. 'To the *championes*.'

'*Championes, championes … olé, olé, olé!*' screeched the others. Fred shuddered and returned to watching the news, while Noel and Rob resumed their chat about terrorism. Fifteen minutes later, they were interrupted again, however – this time by laughter and wolf-whistles. A newly arrived figure in a purple tracksuit had paused dramatically in the doorway, his back turned to the pub. He was holding aloft a trophy crowned by a big golden ball, and shaking out an immaculately blow-dried bob – as straight and shiny as a woman's. His knee and hip pulsed, like a camp pop star about to reveal himself to a packed stadium.

'What time d'you call this?' shouted the man's tight-trousered teammate.

'Obviously having a nice long blow … *dry*!' said another, to riotous laughter.

It was only when the man in the doorway finally spun around that Rob realised who it was.

'So, the couple having the shag party, are they from Dublin too?'

'Elaine and Carl are actually my old next-door neighbours,' said Jo, who was still in a hot spin over Rachel's story of Xenna, the artist who'd done the CD cover. 'Elaine kept in touch after I left Dublin,' she continued. 'I used to help her daughter with her homework. Despite the daughter's boyfriend egging my house when he discovered I was gay, mind you.' She took a swig of beer and watched the revelation register in Rachel's eyes. Since the Xenna story, Jo had been waiting for the opportunity to reciprocally come out. And now she had finally done it. She couldn't believe that this infuriating flight-delay was turning out so well, nor that she'd had the nerve in the first place to pretend her internet booth wasn't working so she could get talking to the fit stranger she'd been watching in the queue! She prayed the plane wouldn't be taking off any time soon.

Rachel was frowning with concern. 'God, that's terrible,' she said. This was quickly followed up by, 'Gosh, I mean about the eggs. Not about you being gay. Obviously.'

'Obviously!' Jo laughed. 'Anyway, it's pure coincidence that I was heading to Glasgow for a work thing at the same time as the shag party.'

'Quite progressive, isn't it, having a mixed hen and stag?'

'This seems more about Elaine not trusting her wayward fiancé to go abroad without supervision,' Jo said. 'The party itself wouldn't be my kind of thing, and I don't know any of their friends, but sure I'll pop in for a drink or two anyway.'

'Did you ever confront the brat who egged your window?' said Rachel.

'Nah. He's probably off annoying some other poor neighbour now.'

Rachel shook her head. 'I'd have put him in an armlock he wouldn't have forgotten too soon!'

'An armlock?'

'Yeah, I do judo.'

Jo willed her pupils not to dilate. 'I figured you looked pretty athletic …'

'Did you now?' said Rachel, with a bashful but flattered kind of laugh.

Jo felt her face redden around her grin. 'I tend to notice stuff like that, especially, well, when—'

'Passengers for Glasgow, please return to the gate as your flight will be boarding shortly.'

'At last,' said Jo, relieved to end her dreadful attempt at flirting. 'Actually, I better run to the loo lest we end up sitting on the tarmac because of some further act of self-immolation!'

'Go on,' said Rachel laughing. 'I'll mind your stuff.'

Jo's hands trembled under the dryer. She fixed her hair, applied tinted lip balm, and read the reply Rob had just sent:

Cute judo girl? Well go get her number!

She pulled her shoulders back and returned to the bar. No matter what happened, she would get that phone number before they boarded.

She found the table empty. Her suitcase, as well as the plastic folder with her passport, boarding card and hotel confirmation were gone. What had she been thinking, leaving everything with a total stranger? A stranger who'd pretended to be gay in order to steal her stuff. That story about the cover artist was as convenient as it was outrageous. EU passports were worth thousands on the black market nowadays. Hers was probably halfway down the M11 by now, or about to be flown to somewhere else. After waiting for hours, she would be stranded in Stansted, unable to board and, worse still, unable to *leave* the airport because she had no passport. She would have some job explaining herself to airport police on a day when the terror-threat was spiking into the red. She stood by the table in a hyperventilating disarray.

'Jo, over here!' She spun round to see a wave halfway down the boarding queue. She jogged over, feeling quite the eejit.

'Thought I'd keep us a place.'

'Cheers,' said Jo, accepting her case and plastic folder. The staff, presumably wanting rid of the passengers before something else happened in Glasgow, were pulling the queue through at high speed. Jo still needed to ask for Rachel's telephone number, but there were too many people within earshot. She would wait until they were in the tunnel to the plane.

A commotion ahead brought Jo's side of the line to an abrupt halt.

'Naw, you listen ta me.' It was the loud sunburned woman with the huge suitcase Jo had seen talking to Rachel earlier. 'The lassie at check-in never said it was too big, so you can get tae fuck if you think I'm payin' mair …'

Passengers around sighed and groaned, but Jo was too happy and excited to be annoyed. She stood on her tiptoes to observe the scene. As the dispute grew louder, she turned to ask Rachel why there weren't also surcharges for having an oversized gob, only to find that the other side of the queue had already advanced. Her amusement turned to dismay as she saw Rachel handing over her ticket and being ushered quickly through the doorway behind.

'So, what's he saying up there?' Rob asked, as Noel returned with more drinks.

'Oh, he's full of self-congratulation about winning the final.' Noel sat down. 'Look, stop worrying about him. Let's just relax and enjoy our beers. God knows they might be our last, the way the world's going.'

But Rob could not relax. It was bad enough seeing that liar Orlando again (so much for him moving back to Italy), let alone on a day when he was brandishing a trophy and surrounded by fawning friends. And if Rob had hated Orlando's curls, it was nothing compared to his disgust at the new hairdo, which wouldn't look out of place at Crufts. 'He used to say I kept the flat like a *peeg*-sty, Noel. Well, I'd love him to see how clean it is right now. I'd pretend I'd done it all myself too.'

'Maybe you should go over and tell him you didn't appreciate him walking out on you like that. Get it off your chest.'

'There's no point. Anyway, if it hadn't been for him leaving, then I'd never have met Jo.'

'And I,' said Noel, looking at him frankly, 'would never have met the two of you.'

Rob laughed. 'Maybe I should be toasting Orlando instead of hiding in the corner seething.'

'To Orlando,' Noel whispered.

They tilted their glasses towards the tracksuited back and took giggling sips of their drinks. But Rob's laughter didn't last long. He stared in disbelief at the doorway, where a newly arrived leather-jacketed man was surveying the room as though looking for a free table.

'What's wrong now?' said Noel.

'Noel, that's *Michael*,' Rob hissed. 'What the fuck is he doing here?'

Rob grabbed Noel's newspaper and used it to shield his face. He didn't want that asshole seizing upon the weird coincidence of them both being here to try to make amends. But it seemed Michael had already found his intended target somewhere else. The newspaper fell limply to the table.

It was not the way Michael rubbed Orlando's back and kissed him on the lips that bothered Rob the most. Nor was it the way Michael shouted to Fred for a bottle of his best champagne. Nor the way he took up the trophy and smilingly admired it. No, the most galling thing of all was that Orlando's teammates all seemed to know Michael very well indeed. They rushed to share their joy with him and to explain just how instrumental Orlando had been in securing today's victory.

Rob was in danger of crushing his suddenly empty pint glass. 'I'm going over.'

'Rob, might it not be better ... ?'

Noel's voice trailed off behind him. As he walked, Patrik's words filled his head: *Orlando had a guy who look a bit ugly and also boring ... Groping and kissing on the balcony.*

As Rob made his way across the pub, all noise and voices seemed to disappear, as though glugging down a distant plughole. One that had just been sluiced free of Orlando's curls by Mrs. Bristleworth's. He was anxious at what he was about to do; he nearly turned back halfway – he couldn't do this. But suddenly he was fortified by a mental flash of Rodney – his compact, sexy body in his boxer shorts, his luscious pink-lipped kisses, his dulcet voice singing 'On The Street Where You Live' as he whipped up pancake batter on a Sunday morning. Rodney was what he had needed all along, not that conceited, two-timer, Michael.

Finally reaching the bar, he laid a hand on each of his targets' backs, feeling the hot polyester of Orlando's tracksuit and the cool, familiar leather of his ex-boyfriend's jacket. He forced his own head into the intimate gap between theirs.

'Well, well, well,' he said as the two horrified faces turned to look at him. 'Michael Wyles, the wily liar, and his curly-headed, sorry *straight*-headed, castrato.' He grinned crazily at one and then the other, feeling a strange new power rise within him. 'Well, at least you won't have *curls* blocking up the shower in Wheldon Court now, I suppose!'

'Jo, come have a bop, would ya?' Dappled in disco lights, Elaine reached over the table and swung Jo's arm in time with the first few bars of 'Put 'Em High'.

Damo waved his big sister away. 'We're actually having an important chat, if ya don't mind,' he said.

'Yeah,' said Carl's best-man Squishy, sitting on Jo's other side. 'She's grand with us here.'

Elaine regarded the two men with tipsy suspicion. 'Well, no funny business, right? Yiz haven't a snowball's of Jo turning straight. Specially not you two mingers!'

She winked at Jo and shimmied back to her gang, who were now raising their arms in a dancefloor circle around a very drunk Carl, who was attempting to breakdance in the middle.

Jo clapped her hands. 'Right, where were we?'

Squishy pointed at his wallet on the table. 'You were showing what to do with the, eh …'

'Oh yes, the G-spot!' The two men watched in awe as Jo put the slightly sweaty, Celtic-crested wallet onto its side and flared open the edges to act as the female anatomy. 'Right,' she said, inserting a finger past Squishy's bank cards and up into the folds. 'You're going up, but towards the front.'

'The front?' said Squishy. 'Jaysis, I never knew that!'

Jo pulsed her finger. 'Then you apply pressure.'

Damo was equally agog. 'But how'd you know if you've got the right place?'

'Oh, you'll know alright.'

Squishy stood up and blew out his cheeks. 'I think this calls for more Jägerbombs, lads!'

'Maybe even some *Screaming Orgasms* this time?' said Jo, to their uproarious laughter.

'Ah, Jo, it's a fuckin' shocker that we never hung out with ya before tonight!' Squishy elbowed his friend. 'Damo, you better come help carry. Multiple orgasms it is! And bring me G-spot wallet so we can pay for them.'

Smiling, Jo reclined on the sticky leatherette. After six months in London it was lovely to be around Dubliners. Her reservations about being seen as a 'posh' anomaly tonight couldn't have been more wrong. Instead, she was the novelty addition that everyone wanted to chat to, especially after Elaine had introduced her as 'a famous journalist'. She'd been having such a laugh that her plan to stay for an hour had dissolved with every drink she'd been handed. (Despite several attempts to pay for a round, no one would let her.) Now, several hours later here she was – a happy, foot-tapping drunk among the shirts and skirts in a bustling Glasgow nightclub whose name she couldn't even remember.

Later on, after several more drinks, Jo found herself in the toilets with Elaine and her 'disco-auntie' Paulette, a fifty-year-old whose synthetic appearance – hair, nails, clothes, skin-tone – was offset by the most natural laugh Jo had ever heard. As Paulette emerged from the cubicle, she smacked her niece's cheek with a kiss. 'Ah, I cannot wait to see yiz married, Elaine!'

'It's not gonna be any different than it is now, Paulette,' said Elaine. 'Same old me, same old Carl. Same old shite.'

'No, it's going to be *bew-riful*,' cried Paulette. 'Pledgin' your lives to each other ... imagine!'

'Shut up with the sop and give us the stuff, for fuck's sake.'

Paulette's neon nails plucked a wrap of coke from her bra.

'Jo, don't listen to anything outta that one's mouth,' Elaine warned as she locked herself into the cubicle. 'Complete head-the-ball, so she is.'

Paulette took a massive brush from her zebra-skin bag and re-bronzed her mahogany face in the mirror. 'Any marriage on the cards for yourself, Jo?' she asked. 'Are you seeing some nice young one?'

Jo leaned against the sink. 'Not at the moment. Though I did chat up an extremely hot girl in Stansted earlier.'

'And?'

'I thought I was in there, but then we got separated. I waited by the baggage carousel for so long that the Glasgow police nearly dragged me into an interview room.'

'Ah, that's a pisser.'

'I know,' said Jo, wishing Rachel were here now so she could drag her into one of the toilets and kiss her. 'Anyway, I'm afraid gay people can't even get married back home in Ireland.'

'Ah shite, yeah,' said Paulette. 'We don't even have that civilian partnership thing yet, sure we don't?'

Elaine emerged from the cubicle, sniffing. 'It's *civil* partnership, you muppet. Anyway, leave poor Jo alone. If you're so into getting married, then why haven't you ever done it yourself?'

'Eh … hello?' said Paulette, circling her face and cleavage with her bronzing brush. 'Sure, what man could handle all this?' She popped her hip and gave a Marilynesque pout into the mirror. As they all fell together in hysterics, Jo felt Elaine press the wrap into her hand.

Chopping up on the cistern, a few little rocks ricocheted from Jo's hotel key-card. But the boys had bought so much of the stuff – from a Celtic fan they'd met in a pub earlier – that wastage hardly mattered.

Elaine rapped on the door. 'Go easy, Jo. That stuff is wicked strong.'

Smiling to herself, Jo bent down to inhale a sensible line. As she swapped nostrils, Paulette called, 'Yeah, we don't want another Tamara Nic-Nac Charlie-Whack on our hands!'

Jo strode out of the cubicle buzzing with the drug and laughing at Paulette's hilarious moniker. She'd never told Elaine about her connection to Tamara, so it was coincidental that the name had come up at all. 'I'm glad somebody else thinks that Tamara Nic an tSionnaigh looks like a total cokehead,' she said. 'The social pages keep saying that she's on some wonder diet. Yeah, she is, it's called the diet *coke* plan!'

'Well, everyone'll know the truth soon enough,' said Paulette, now reapplying mascara.

'Why's that?'

'Me brother's a taxi-man, and on Thursday night he saw this snazzy Mini with two girls in it break the lights on Leeson Street and plough into the side of a people carrier. When he went over to help, he saw it was yer woman Tamara. Coked off her box so she was, sniffing away and her eyes like dinner-plates. She didn't even apologise to the family whose car she'd wrecked. All she cared about was making out that her friend had been driving, not her. But the friend was having none of it; she started letting rip at Tamara, then legged it before the guards arrived. Tamara was meant to be presenting the music awards last night, but this bullshit statement went out saying she had food poisoning. The truth'll be out tomorrow, though, mind you.'

'Tomorrow?' asked Jo, watching her own eyes expand to dinner-plates in the mirror.

'The *Sunday Star* is doing an exposé on her massive coke habit. A photographer turned up that night and caught her being led away from the crash in handcuffs. Me brother put him in touch with another taxi driver who actually *seen* Tamara doing lines in his cab last month. Yer man done an interview with the *Star* and sold them the footage he'd kept from his taxi security camera – Tamara and the same friend from the crash snorting away like goodo in the back seat. Anyway she's in deep shit now; there's feck all her millionaire Muldoon fella can do to keep this one quiet!'

The zebra stripes on Paulette's bag had started oscillating like a barber pole. 'Are you alright, Jo?' Elaine's voice sounded soupy, distant. 'You look like you're about to pass out.'

Jo felt Paulette's long nails lifting up her chin. 'You'll be OK in a second, love. That charlie's just a bit strong.'

Jo took a few breaths to compose herself, then threw her arms around her concerned companions. 'Let's go have that bop, will we?' she said, looking from Elaine to Paulette.

Then, as the three of them fell laughingly out of the toilets and headed to the dance floor, Jo shook her head in disbelief to hear what song had just started to play.

Despite declining Squishy's offer to accompany some of the lads to a lap-dancing club, it was still after four when Jo bounced back to the hotel, the hi-NRG remix of 'Loved Every Minute' still eddying in her head.

The elderly night-porter left the reception desk to let her in. 'Had a good night, hen?'

'Great, thanks, but a bit strange too!' She patted down her pockets. 'Sorry, I seem to have lost my card somewhere along the way. Room 304. Jo Kavanagh.'

Back behind his desk, he issued her with a fresh card, untainted by cocaine. 'The system here says you've got a message,' he said. 'I'll just print it out for you.'

'A message?' Jo pulled her mobile from her pocket, but there were no missed calls. It was weird – apart from Rob, no one even knew which hotel she was staying in. 'There's no need for an envelope, really,' she told him.

'It's nae problem, pal!' His shiny old hands tucked the flap closed. He handed it to her with a slow wink. 'You have yourself a good wee rest now.'

Inside the lift she stared at her slightly dishevelled reflection. She wondered where Louise and Tamara were right now and whether they had any inkling what was coming. She thought about Cillian finding out tomorrow, his mouth agape as he bought his Sunday papers. Maybe she should give him a ring about it all; it was probably time to forgive and forget. She shuddered and opened the envelope.

Inside, was the hotel's letterhead with 'While You Were Out' printed on top. This was followed by a short but arresting message. At the end was a mobile phone number. And the name *Rachel*.

Thank you ... and a little request

Thank you so much for reading *Inverted Triangles*! If you enjoyed it, I'd be very grateful if you could leave me a review online (eg. Amazon or Goodreads), even just a couple of quick lines. Reviews really help both authors and readers alike.

(f) www.facebook.com/KarenFaganAuthor

(twitter) karen_de_facto

(instagram) karen.defacto

(mail) karenfaganwriting@gmail.com

(home) www.karenfaganbooks.com

Acknowledgements

I would like to convey massive thanks to:

My wonderful editor, Brian Langan, whose eagle eye and finely tuned ear have been integral to the completion of this novel, and whose input and support on every level have helped me immeasurably.

My parents, Anne and John, and my sister Emma, for their unswerving care and kindness throughout the writing process, and during my life in general. And to my late grandparents, whose love will never be forgotten.

My lovely in-laws, Vinny, Rose and Mick for all your support.

Rachel Wolahan Lyons for her invaluable feedback on the early draft.

Kim Fogarty, Pauliina Kauppila, Jana Lyons, Eimear McBride, Barbara Morrissey and Alison Moore for reviewing the almost-final manuscript and providing excellent suggestions for improvement.

Those who provided brilliant insights into languages, accents and dialects: Aislinn Delmotte, Daniel Molinuevo, Jennifer Reynolds, Kylie Jarrett, and Stephen Henderson.

Paula Quigley, who so patiently and creatively designed and illustrated the cover.

David Prendergast for the expert interior design of both the print and ebook.

Pete Britton for his awesome wizardry on my website.

Paul Scannell for taking my lovely headshots.

My friends and extended family, who have endured me banging on about this novel for many years, and never stopped supporting me, especially Catherine, Dee, Dolores, Eibhlín, Fiona, Geraldine, John, Mairéad, and Rebecca.

My friends and book-club mates at Dublin North West Repeal. Your friendship is a constant source of joy and support to me.

Tracey – my wife and ideal reader – for the unending wealth of information and inspiration that helped me shape this novel. For feeding and minding all six foot two of me. And for making me laugh daily with her self-penned kitty-ditties.

And finally to my beautiful cats, past and present, for not deleting *too* much text as they sat on the keyboard as I was typing. And for all the furry fun throughout the years.

About the Author

Karen Fagan was born in Dublin in 1975. She studied Psychology at Trinity College and went on to work in a creative agency. She lives in Dublin 7 with her wife Tracey and a reasonably manageable clowder of cats. *Inverted Triangles* is her first novel.

CPSIA information can be obtained
at www.ICGtesting.com
Printed in the USA
LVHW100823121222
735007LV00004B/82